The Ambitious Lives of Evan Sanderson
Copyright 2023 by Shawn Inmon
All Right Reserved

Chapter One

Evan Sanderson sat on his balcony, watching a series of glaciers as the cruise ship slowly turned in a full circle. Beside him, Becky set her cup of split pea soup down and made an *ooh* sound, as though she was watching the grand finale of a Fourth of July fireworks display.

Evan supposed that to her, this was like the grand finale of their cruise. She had talked about seeing Glacier Bay since she had first booked the cruise six months earlier. To Evan, the glaciers were nothing special. Just ice in a large formation. They were in Alaska, so of course there would be glaciers.

Even though he wasn't impressed by the natural beauty of Glacier Bay, he was pleased to see it because it meant that the cruise was almost over. In a few days, he would be able to get back to work—to the hospital—and settle back into the deluge of cases he was sure had piled up while he was away.

Left to his own devices, Evan would rarely have taken a day off, let alone gone on a nine-day cruise up the Inside Passage.

There were compromises in every aspect of life, and that was certainly true of a marriage. It was true even in a good marriage, and he couldn't claim that about his marriage with Becky. It wasn't that it was a *bad* marriage. After thirty years, it was just that they had long since settled any questions and come to agree on how problems would be dealt with.

One of those compromises was Evan agreeing to let Becky pick a vacation destination once a year. Normally, she was about sun, sand, and surf, but this year, she had opted for an Alaskan cruise.

If he had been capable of being honest with himself, Evan would have admitted that his marriage had always been a little bloodless. Marrying Becky—the daughter of the Chief of Surgery at the hospital where he worked—was as much a merger as it was a passionate endeavor.

Evan appreciated Becky for her good qualities. Being the daughter of his boss was maybe foremost among those, but there were others. She was attractive, intelligent, made a nice home for them, and was an excellent hostess at parties they needed to have. He had just never felt any warm, overriding sense of love for her. He assumed that feeling of romantic love was something manufactured to sell romance books and movies.

Instead of calling her his *wife*, he often referred to her as his *partne*r long before that became a popular phrase. Everyone, even people as self-contained and buttoned up as Evan, let their true thoughts and feelings leak out in one way or another.

Becky looked at the small ceramic bowl that sat on the table between them. "It's all gone," she said, as though there was some mystery as to how the split pea soup inside had disappeared.

"If you call, they'll bring you a whole tureen of it," Evan said. "Or, you can just have mine." He pushed his own still-full cup of soup toward her.

She accepted it and spooned a bite of the thick green soup. "Even cooled off, it's so delicious. I don't see how you can pass it up." She nibbled at the soup, then set it back on the table. "I better contain myself, though, or I won't be able to eat dinner."

Food was never a problem on a cruise. Managing to get hungry enough to eat sometimes was. Beyond the formal dining room, there were ten other restaurants onboard, at least a few of which were open twenty-four hours a day. You couldn't starve on a cruise, but you could easily gain ten pounds.

Becky had been walking complete laps around the ship, determined to continue to get her ten thousand steps every day. She had vowed not to gain any weight on the cruise, though Evan wondered why she worried about it. She still weighed what she had when he first met her.

If she was going to get fat, he thought, *she would have done it by now.*

That thought might have sounded cruel to someone who didn't know Evan, but it revealed much about who he was. He didn't worry about social niceties, often to his detriment. He had the habit of saying exactly what was on his mind. His mind was generally too preoccupied with important thoughts to spend much time worrying about how his words might impact others.

Nurses often warned patients that Dr. Sanderson wasn't known for his bedside manner, but that he was a wonderful surgeon, nonetheless.

The captain's voice came over a speaker above their heads. "That's it, folks, hope you enjoyed the show."

What show would that be? Evan wanted to ask. *A collection of frozen water that moves inches per day.*

He managed to keep that thought to himself and instead turned to Becky with a forced smile. He had no interest in showing her how bored he was by the whole vacation. He knew that would only lead to a discussion he didn't want to have.

Becky stood and stretched happily, leaning over the deck a little and turning her face to the warm sunshine. "It feels strange to be so close to the glaciers, but it's seventy degrees outside."

Evan contemplated explaining the science of the situation, but realized that Becky didn't want to know. This was another of her patented non-observations that passed for conversation between them.

"Kind of odd, hmm?" he said instead.

"I'm going to go walk a few laps around the ship." She glanced at the slim gold watch on her wrist. "Then there's a film about grizzlies being shown in the theater. Want to meet me there?"

"I think I'll stay here and take a nap," Evan answered.

That was a lie. He knew it, and she knew it. Evan virtually never slept during the day, even on vacation.

"Okay, honey," Becky said. She leaned down and brushed her lips against his cheek. "By the time the movie's over, it'll be time for dinner. It's formal night tonight. Don't forget to put on your suit."

"Of course." That brought a genuine grin to Evan's face for a moment. They had seen older couples who went all out for *formal night* during the cruise. Men dressed in black tie and tails, women in glittering evening gowns that had been in fashion decades earlier. That wasn't Evan's style. He would wear the same muted dark suit and blue tie that he wore any time he was forced to dress up.

Becky waggled her fingers and walked out into the narrow hall. The door closed with a *clunk* behind her.

Evan took a deep breath, rolled his neck, and sat on the bed. He pulled his iPad out of his briefcase and tapped in his password.

They had of course paid for a Wi-Fi package, but it was intermittent at best. This wasn't their first cruise, though, so Evan had prepared. He had downloaded all the reading material he might need onto his iPad before they left home.

He brought up *Warren Buffett, The Complete Biography* and found his place. He had read the book three times, but he tried to read it again each time he was on vacation. There were always new lessons to be learned from the great man's life.

By almost anyone's standards, Evan had lived a very successful life. Almost anyone except for Evan himself, unfortunately. He didn't weigh himself against the average person. Instead, when he compared his life to someone like Warren Buffett, he found himself severely lacking. He was comfortable. Wealthy, even. He owned his own practice and a beautiful showplace home in Seattle. He had enough money in the bank that he never needed to worry about it again.

And still, by his own standards, he felt he didn't measure up.

When he had told Becky he was going to take a nap, he'd had absolutely no intention of actually doing so. But, as he tried to focus on the book, he suddenly felt tired. Exhausted, even.

That was an odd feeling for Evan, who was normally in constant motion, in his mind if not in body.

He fluffed his pillow to give his neck proper support, tested it, and found it wanting. So, he grabbed Becky's pillow and doubled up. That felt better.

He lay back and closed his eyes. He decided to use the downtime to review the last few surgeries he had performed before being forced on vacation. He judged that his own performance was optimal, but there were a few slipups by his team members, which he wanted to discuss with them when he returned home.

The feeling of exhaustion really settled in. He felt too tired to even lift his head off the pillow.

Minutes later, he fell into a deep slumber.

Inside his chest, a biological time bomb that had been waiting to go off his entire life finally did so.

Chapter Two

Evan Sanderson opened his eyes.

He was in the break room in Middle Falls General.

Evan knew that was impossible, of course. For one thing, he had left the Middle Falls hospital decades earlier. He had grown tired of being the big fish in the tiny puddle and had decamped for a hospital in Seattle. More importantly, he knew he was actually on a cruise ship in Alaska. Becky was watching a movie about grizzlies, then they were going to have a nice dinner.

Still, this felt different from a normal dream. It perfectly matched his memory of what this room had been.

"This is the most realistic dream I've ever had," Evan said.

"You had a realistic dream?" a man beside him asked. "You must have really conked out. I get it, though. The hours they put us through are not realistic. No human can work this much and not fall into a coma now and then."

Evan turned his head. He hadn't realized he had spoken out loud. When he looked to his left, he recognized the man who had spoken as Neil Cartwright. Which was another impossibility. Neil had been dead for almost ten years. In this dream, he was young again. There were bags under his eyes, and he looked like he hadn't shaved in a few days, but he was young.

Evan shook his head but didn't bother to answer. Why should he? He knew whatever he was seeing wasn't real. He looked around and saw that the room was truly a remarkable facsimile of the dingy break room for staff at Middle Falls General.

There was a Mr. Coffee next to the sink. It looked like it had several cups left in the pot, but judging by how dark the coffee was, someone would have to be fairly desperate to drink it.

There was a scarred kitchen table with plastic chairs around it. A small television sat in the corner, turned on, but with the volume down low. Walter Cronkite sat at a desk, reading the news.

Overhead, a voice came through the small speaker. "Dr. Cartwright, please call 223. Dr. Cartwright, 223."

Neil stood up, dumped the dregs of his cup into the sink, stretched, and said, "Back at it, I guess, whether I want to or not." He walked out the door into a long hallway, leaving Evan alone.

Evan sat patiently for a few minutes, waiting for whatever was going to happen next. He couldn't remember ever having a dream this vivid, or one that lasted so long without lapsing into some funhouse mirror version of reality.

The reality of the break room refused to budge. It sat there in its green-walled, ugly tiled-floor sort of way.

Evan frowned. He really didn't want to still be asleep when Becky got back. It was hard for him to tell how long he'd been sleeping, but he was certain time was slipping away.

He focused all his willpower on waking up.

I know I'm dreaming. WAKE UP! he shouted inside his head. He tried to send a bolt of energy along his synapses to startle himself awake.

The room remained unchanged.

He slapped himself. First on his right cheek, then on his left. He did it hard enough that it left a red mark, but that did nothing to change his circumstances.

He nodded, willing to accept that these first experiments had not succeeded. Initial forays rarely did.

He stood, shook his arms, rolled his neck, then jumped up and down vigorously.

As he was doing this mild calisthenic, two women walked in. They were both dressed in nurse's uniforms. One was a slender Black woman of perhaps thirty, the other an older Hispanic woman with dark hair streaked with gray.

They both stopped and looked at Evan. The older woman said, "It always gets to them eventually. Someday he'll be making the big bucks, but we'll always remember when we saw him hopping up and down like a kangaroo in the break room."

The two women giggled a little, shook their heads, and walked to the sink. One picked up the coffee pot, smelled it, and shook her head again. She poured the last of the coffee down the drain and refilled the pot. They seemed to have forgotten all about Evan.

He had stopped jumping when they walked in, embarrassed. He sat back down and tried to think what the next natural experiment would be. He was certain there was a way to get back to the cruise ship. He just had to find it.

He studied the two women. They looked vaguely familiar, but he couldn't come close to putting a name to either of them.

He frowned and tried to focus.

There's got to be a way back. There has to be.

Overhead, the speaker crackled again, then the same woman's voice said, "Dr. Sanderson to the emergency room. Dr. Sanderson, please report to the emergency room."

Evan heard it. He knew it was directed at him. He ignored it. He didn't plan to give any legitimacy to anything in this dream world.

The older woman arched her eyebrows and leaned toward Evan. "I think they're playing your song."

Evan nodded and stood up. Until that moment, he hadn't noticed what he was wearing. He had slightly stained blue scrubs on. He shrugged. The exact type of scrubs he had worn from the time he had started his residency. Another detail this dream world got right.

He crossed the room and pushed out into the empty hallway. He had worked at Middle Falls General long enough that he remembered the layout perfectly. The emergency room was to the right, down another long hall, then another right.

Evan had always had an excellent memory.

He turned in the opposite direction. He had no intention of reporting to the emergency room.

He made a few turns from memory and saw the door that hospital staff used to come and go. He pushed through and stepped outside.

It was a beautiful day. The sun was low in the sky and the remainder of its warmth reminded him of what he had felt so recently standing on the balcony of the cruise ship. He took a deep breath and the aroma of an unidentified flower came from somewhere nearby.

As if he was in a dream—because he was convinced he *was* in a dream—he stepped out into the parking lot. He was surprised to see that all the cars were of a mid-seventies vintage or older. The lot was filled mostly with sedans, with a couple of VW Bugs and sports cars mixed in. There wasn't an SUV or oversized pickup anywhere in sight.

"Damn," he said out loud, impressed by the details that must have been dredged up from his own mind.

He was even more surprised when his eye fell on a car he recognized as his own—a 1966 Ford Galaxie.

He had always hated that car. It represented being a poor, overworked resident in his mind. It hadn't been the most reliable car in the world, but it had been even worse when he had to park it alongside the sports cars that so many of the other doctors drove. He hated coming in second in anything, but when it came to something as obvious as the car he drove, it really rankled him.

He was drawn to his old car like it was a magnet. He instantly recognized a long scratch down the back quarter panel, the result of trying to wedge it into a too-tight parking spot. He reached down and tried to pat his pockets, but the scrubs he was wearing didn't have pockets. No pockets meant no keys.

He caught a glimpse of his reflection in the window. He instinctively reached up and patted his hair. He had gone gray a decade earlier, but now his hair was dark again. And longer. He never would have worn it that long as a respected surgeon.

It wasn't just his hair that was different. His face had no worry lines. He had never been heavy, but there was still just a hint of the fullness of youth. He let his hand touch his cheek and watched his reflection do the same.

He tried the door, and it was open. Of course it was. Who would want to steal this car? He sat in the driver's seat and checked the ignition for the keys. No luck. He pulled down the visor, but there was nothing there.

In a flash, he knew where his keys would be—in his jacket pocket in the dressing room, where he changed into his scrubs at the start of his shift.

He climbed out of the Galaxie and shut the door. He had no interest in going back into the hospital, keys or no keys. Since they had paged him a few minutes before, they would be sending a nurse looking for him if that aspect of this dream was as accurate as everything else had been. He didn't want to get buttonholed and dragged back to the ER.

He still had experiments to conduct. One way or another, he was going to find his way back to the cruise ship.

For just a moment, he felt a little nostalgic about his life. He had his dream job, a perfectly acceptable marriage to Becky. They had a gorgeous house in one of the nicest neighborhoods in Seattle, with a view of Lake Washington. They had never wanted kids, but that had been mostly Evan's doing. Becky never complained, but he sometimes thought he saw a touch of wistfulness in her eyes when she looked at other people's children or grandchildren.

Not Evan. Once he decided something, he couldn't see what good regret would do him.

As a resident, he had struggled. He had worked like a dog for no immediate reward. He'd had faith that good things would eventually come, but they weren't evident yet. He had no interest in going back to that earlier, more difficult part of his life.

"Okay, think, Evan," he mumbled to himself. "You can come up with something. What could cause this? A glitch in the matrix? Did I eat something that is disagreeing with me?"

Whenever Evan felt stymied in his life, he had always just pushed harder, until whatever obstacle in his way was overcome. That was what he did here. Not worrying that he was still wearing his scrubs, he walked out of the parking lot and turned right on the side street. He walked four blocks until he came to Main Street, where most of the businesses were in Middle Falls.

He hadn't been back to his hometown in decades, but he was pretty sure that *something* should have changed. In this dream, everything looked exactly the same as it had.

He knew that if he turned left, he would walk through the business district, eventually arriving at Artie's Drive-In. That thought made his stomach turn over. He actually thought about walking to Artie's and getting a burger basket. Maybe even a shake.

He shook his head.

Nope, he thought, *not going to buy into this whole thing. Eating an Artie's burger would be like admitting that this place is real. I know it can't be, so why pretend?*

Instead of turning left, he went right.

He walked along the sidewalk until it ended, then stepped onto the shoulder. He had come up with the next experiment to get back to the cruise ship. At the edge of town, he passed a sign that read, *Just ahead! The Silvery Moon Drive-in Theater.*

He remembered going there with his parents when he was younger.

Having a specific goal in mind made him feel better. He swung his arms a little as he walked. Evan was not a whistler, but if he had been, he would have whistled a tune.

He walked out of town until he came to a road that turned off at an angle. There was a green sign that read, *Middle Falls Falls ¼ Mile*.

He took that road and walked until he came up to the viewing area of the town's namesake. There was a series of benches where people could sit and look at the water as it tumbled over the rocks and fell to the pool below. In front of that was a low chain link fence.

Evan climbed over it and, with no hesitation, threw himself off the small cliff.

He had hoped that the shock of falling would wake him up and he would be safely back on the cruise ship.

Instead, he fell awkwardly. His right shoulder hit a round rock, breaking it. That sent him spinning. A bolt of pain jumped into his brain, but Evan had enough time to think, *Well, that didn't seem to work.*

Then his head slammed into another rock.

Chapter Three

Evan Sanderson opened his eyes.

He was in the break room at Middle Falls General. He frowned, then closed his eyes for a few seconds.

This was a critical piece of information, and he needed to process it.

After a few seconds of trying to do so, he realized this new piece of the puzzle was too big. It was too much to be instantly processed. He would need time to work his way through it.

He was sure about one thing, though. All of his experiments to get back to his old life had failed. It would do him no good to leave the hospital and jump from the observatory at Middle Falls Falls again.

A weird, watery feeling in his stomach made him shift uncomfortably.

For the first time, a new thought arrived in his brain.

What if this isn't a dream at all? What if this new situation is, in its own twisted and impossible way, the new reality?

He rolled that around in his brain for a time, looking for explanations. He remembered being stretched out on the comfortable bed in their cabin, reading the biography of Warren Buffett. Then he had felt tired, which wasn't like him at all.

He recalled not feeling well and drifting off. Not into sleep, really. It had felt more like he had gone unconscious.

Finally, he remembered the weight on his chest and a sharp pain. He had been nearly completely under, but he had enough consciousness left to remember that feeling.

Did I die?

Evan was not a heart surgeon, but he knew enough about it to recognize that he had likely had a myocardial infarction or other severe crisis.

Holding onto that thought—realizing that he had probably died—took some getting used to. Not least of all because here he was, blood pumping, brainwaves functioning, all systems go.

It was just that *here* was a place he never expected to see again.

"You okay, man?" It was Neil Cartwright, leaning toward him. "You feel all right?"

"Yeah, I'm fine," Evan answered, though he was anything but fine. He swallowed hard, then said, "Really, I'm not sure I am okay. I'm not feeling quite right."

"Too many twenty-four shifts and subsisting on frozen burritos," Neil diagnosed. "It's a good thing we go through this when we're young or we'd never survive it. How many hours do you have left on your shift?"

"I don't know," Evan answered honestly.

"You must be feeling rummy if you don't know what time you get off." Neil walked over to a clipboard hanging on the wall and ran his finger down a piece of paper. "Lucky you. You're almost done. Just two more hours."

"Two more hours," Neil repeated dumbly.

Overhead, the speaker said, "Dr. Cartwright, please call 223. Dr. Cartwright, 223."

"Guess I'm back at it whether I want to or not. I'm not as lucky as you. I won't get out of here until the sun comes up." He glanced at Evan. "Maybe grab a little something to put a pep in your step." Then Neil was gone.

"Right. Pep in my step." Evan hadn't thought about the things they had done to keep themselves up and awake for those twenty-four sessions in many years. For some doctors, it became a problem.

THE AMBITIOUS LIVES OF EVAN SANDERSON   15

For those unlucky ones, the solution to tiredness became worse than the problem. Evan had been lucky, though. He had never become too reliant on the pharmaceutical pick-me-ups and had left them behind completely once he started working more normal hours.

At that moment, his problem wasn't exhaustion, it was confusion. He didn't think there was anything he could take that might clear that up for him.

The two nurses came in again, but this time, Evan wasn't jumping up and down like a kangaroo, so they ignored him. The older of the nurses went to the coffee pot, poured it down the sink and set about making a new pot.

The voice came from above summoning him. "Dr. Sanderson to the emergency room. Dr. Sanderson, please report to the emergency room."

Evan nodded at this new piece of information.

Some things change. Others stay the same. The nurses didn't make fun of me, and this time my conversation with Neil was different. But the hospital operator called us both in just the same way. So I can impact and change what happens.

He knew he had a decision to make. He could go and retrieve his keys from the changing room, get into his street clothes, hop in the Galaxie, and disappear into the sunset. Into what uncertain future, he could not determine.

Or he could answer that call. That would mean he was capitulating to this new reality. Giving it power and admitting it was real.

He noticed that the two nurses were giving him the side eye, wondering why he wasn't heading off to the ER.

He decided that the path that gave him the widest array of future options was to go to the ER, finish his shift, then get away so he could think and plan what he wanted to do next.

He put this plan into action immediately. Ignoring the nurses, he walked out of the break room door, then turned through the maze of hallways until he came to the emergency room.

It was almost always a little chaotic in the ER. There was a mixture of people who had waited too long to seek care, terrible accidents, and those who had not known a visit to the hospital was in their future when they had woken up that day.

A pretty nurse who looked to be in her late thirties approached him. For some reason, her name popped into his head. She was Ann Weaver and had been one of his favorite nurses to work with.

"What have we got?"

"Multiple choice," Ann said. "You're probably going to end up with both of them, because Dr. Darnell is going to be tied up for a while."

That was fine with Evan. If he was going to be in the hospital for the next few hours, he would rather be busy than sitting around doing nothing.

"Number three is a boy who fell off his bike. He hasn't been to X-ray yet, but to my eye it looks like a non-displaced radius fracture."

Evan nodded. "Okay. And the other?"

"Number six is a woman in her twenties who woke up feeling fine, but now can't stop vomiting."

"Good." It was likely that only an ambitious young ER doctor would reply *good* when presented with these problems, but at that moment, Evan felt better than he had since he had woken up in these strange circumstances. He had tasks in front of him. His skills were needed. "Let's get the boy off to X-ray to confirm your hunch." He leaned close. "I would never bet against your instincts, but that will give us something to show his parents. Meanwhile, I'll see about the vomiting woman."

"Thanks, Doctor," Ann said. She hurried off to ER room three, and Evan knocked on room six.

The next two hours flew by in what felt like minutes to Evan. It had been many years since he had practiced this sort of on-the-fly doctoring. For decades, his life had been ruled by appointments and surgeries that were scheduled months in advance. That had satisfied his sense of order and had been much more profitable than working in the ER, but he realized he had missed the chaos.

Ann Weaver had been right about the boy's broken radius. A simple, non-displaced break that wasn't near the growth plate and would heal nicely. He hadn't really had a clue what was causing the woman to throw up. Even forty years later, that would probably still have been the case. There were no quick tests for symptoms like that. Fast onset symptoms normally meant either food poisoning or a stomach virus. He treated the symptoms with prochlorperazine, the best anti-vomiting suppository that was available at the time, then advised bed rest and lots of fluids.

He saw three other cases. Simple things, like a baby with a fever and a soccer player with a badly sprained ankle. Simple, but satisfying.

After that, Ann passed him in the hall and under her breath said, "One of us should not be here anymore, and it's not me."

That brought a smile to Evan's face. He had gotten so caught up in the challenges in front of him that he had lost track of time.

"Of course," Ann said, "you're free to work a quadruple shift instead of a triple if you want."

Evan waved, nodded, and said, "I'm getting out of here while I can."

"Good choice," Ann said, returning the wave.

Five minutes later, he had found the changing area, slipped on his jeans and shirt, and was headed for the parking lot. As he had suspected, he found the keys to the Galaxie in his jacket pocket.

It was dark outside, but he was able to walk straight to his car. In his memory, he had seen where it was parked very recently, not in another lifetime. He still didn't feel much love for it, but he was starting to feel very tired and was glad he didn't have to walk to...to where?

He stopped cold and realized he had no idea where to go next.

Evan had lived in two different places during his residency. The first was at the River Crest Apartments. After a few years there, his mother, Camille, had gifted him the down payment on a condo in the Covington Arms. He had lived there until he had moved away from Middle Falls.

The problem of the moment was that Evan wasn't sure which of those two places would be his home, because he wasn't sure *when* he was. Everyone he had seen so far—from Neil to Ann Weaver—could have been at any point in his residency.

He decided that he needed to solve that problem first. He pulled into an angled parking spot in front of Smith and Sons Grocery, went inside, and grabbed a copy of *The Oregonian*. The date on the paper was April 4, 1973.

Evan had known it would be something like that, but even so, seeing it in print caused a little jolt to his system.

Halfway down the front page, there was a story about the World Trade Center opening in New York. That was another shock. In Evan's mind, the Twin Towers had fallen more than twenty years earlier. Seeing the picture of the buildings glistening in the sun made his heart ache a little.

He dropped the paper back down in the rack. He couldn't think of a reason to actually buy it. He looked around the store, which was obviously preparing to close. A young boy was sweeping the aisle in front of him and glancing his way as if to say, *Please don't stay long. I want to go home.*

Evan walked back to the Galaxie and got in. He didn't turn the key. He needed to think.

April 1973. Second year of my residency. Damn. That means I've still got a long way to go. He thrummed his fingers against the steering wheel. *But that means that I'd be in that crappy little apartment.*

He sighed, started the car, and drove toward the River Crest Apartments.

He took one wrong turn, but soon enough pulled into the apartment complex parking lot. He had to cruise up and down the lot to find a spot. Late in the evening, it was obvious most people were already home and there weren't many vacancies. He found one eventually and pulled in, then looked up at the building.

I have no idea which apartment is mine.

He pulled his keys out of the ignition and studied them. Sure enough, there was a key that looked like it would fit one of the doors, but which one? He could remember that he lived on the third floor, but beyond that, he was lost.

He couldn't imagine walking up and down the entire third floor, sticking his key in the lock to see if it opened or not.

He focused his brain, trying to remember anything about when he had lived there—what his view had been, how close to the stairs his unit was, anything. He came up blank.

He was just beginning to think that he might have to spend the night sleeping in the Galaxie when a soft knock on the driver's side window startled him. He jumped as if he had been doing something wrong.

As he looked through the window, his jaw fell open slightly. There was a beautiful young woman smiling at him. He didn't have to search his memory this time. He knew instantly who it was.

He rolled the window down and choked out, "Mel?"

"Who else, Evan? You got girls lined up to see you tonight?"

Chapter Four

"Uhh...no. No other girls."

Marilyn French, who he had always called *Mel*, raised her eyebrows, leaned toward Evan, and said, "You better not, or I'll make you pay."

That was the kind of thing that could be playful banter between a couple if they were both on the same page. In this case, the words were threatening, and her expression was intense, but only for a few seconds. Then the clouds parted, her smile reappeared, and she said, "Come on, let's go in."

Marilyn was one of the most beautiful girls Evan had ever known. Long, strawberry blonde hair fell carelessly down her back, her brown eyes sparkled and her smile was radiant. On this warm spring evening, she was wearing a white halter top and even though it was dark, she had a pair of oversized sunglasses perched on top of her head. She was lovely.

She was, as it turned out, also volatile, unstable, and prone to violence, though it had taken a bit of time for Evan to realize that.

He thought back to the way their relationship had ended in his first life—which he was now thinking of as his *alpha* life—and swallowed hard. He knew just how much of a wallop her threats could pack.

"Sure, let's go in," he said, trying to keep the sudden nervousness out of his voice. He realized that he had the same problem he had before Mel arrived. He didn't know which apartment was his, but now he would have someone with him to witness how lost he was. How could he possibly explain that he had forgotten his apartment number from the time he had left for his shift to now?

He thought quickly, then opened the door of the Galaxie. Mel stepped back, and Evan couldn't stop his eyes from wandering down to her long legs, set off nicely by a pair of cutoff jeans so short the pockets dangled down.

He tore his eyes away, then went around to the trunk, inserted the proper key and opened it up. He tossed the keys to Mel and said, "I've got to grab something. Would you go ahead and open the door for me?"

Mel shrugged and said, "You're acting really strange tonight, Evan Michael Sanderson. Are you on something? If you are, why didn't you wait and share with me?"

Mel had been the only person other than his mother to call him by his full name. "I'm straight as a board, I promise. I'll be right behind you." Evan could tell by her expression that she wasn't completely buying what he was saying, but she did turn and walk toward the stairs. He searched desperately through the trunk, looking for anything he could find to carry with him. Aside from a jack and a spare tire, the trunk was empty. His heart fell. He was a terrible liar.

He peered into the backseat, hoping to find something there, but he had always been persnickety about keeping his vehicles clean, even this Galaxie that he kind of hated. He looked up and saw Mel open an apartment door. He quickly counted how far she was from the stairs—six units—and walked up the stairs behind her, empty-handed.

Mel had turned the lights on in the apartment. It was as Evan had remembered it. A narrow porter's kitchen to the left, a small living room filled with second-hand furniture, then a short hall with a bathroom and bedroom. It was in every way a basic 1970s apartment.

She looked at him. "That's what you had to bring up, huh? What is it, your invisible friend?" Her tone was joking, but there was an underlying sense of slight menace. Mel had a temper, and it wasn't unusual for something small to set her off.

Evan looked down at his hands as if he was surprised to find he wasn't carrying something. "I thought I had put my duffel with my scrubs in the trunk, but I guess I left them in my locker at the hospital. I was going to wash them, but I'll have to grab them tomorrow."

That seemed to satisfy Mel, who walked into his living room, spread her arms, and twirled around. "I love what you've done with the place," she said enthusiastically.

Evan looked around. There was a small couch, an uncomfortable chair covered in ugly green fabric, an old coffee table and a floor lamp. In one corner, there was a 19" television sitting on a low table. A single painting hung on the wall, courtesy of his mother. It showed an orange and red sunset over a harbor filled with sailboats. Evan had disliked it but remembered that he'd always kept it up in case she dropped by.

"Really?" Evan asked.

Mel stopped twirling. "No. You haven't done anything. We need to go somewhere and get you some things to spruce this place up. It's drab, man, drab. You don't even have an ashtray, or a statue of Buddha, or even an incense burner. We should go down to Bluebird Music and get you some good stuff."

"I don't want people to smoke in here," Evan said automatically. He had forgotten that was not a common house rule in the early seventies.

Mel had a purse slung over her shoulder. She methodically opened it, took out a pack of Pall Mall cigarettes, and tapped one out. Maintaining eye contact with Evan, she pulled out a silver lighter, flicked it, and put the flame to the cigarette, taking a deep drag. She held it in her lungs for a moment, eyes closed, savoring either the smoke or the show she was putting on. Tipping her head back, she exhaled a blueish cloud toward the ceiling.

Evan glanced up at the popcorn-textured ceiling and saw how yellow it was from thousands of previous cigarettes.

Mel walked into the small kitchen, hips swaying in an exaggerated motion. She pulled a saucer down from the cupboard and sat back down on the couch. After expertly flicking her ash onto the small plate, she leaned back, crossing her long bare legs. She smiled a little, knowing what effect she had on him with so little effort. What effect she seemed to have on almost all men.

"I swear, you're being so odd tonight." She took another puff, narrowing her eyes at him as if she was trying to piece together a puzzle.

Evan said, "Excuse me, I'll be right back."

He hurried into the bathroom, which was painted an awful shade of burnt orange. He sat down on the toilet and tried to think.

She's the first person I've had a real conversation with and she has already noticed that I'm different. Is that okay, or should I try to make more of an effort to fit in? What would happen if everyone thought I was different? Not much, probably.

A series of jumbled and out of order images ran through Evan's mind. They all centered on Mel, and though a few of them were good memories, they all ran toward that bad, awful, horrific ending.

He felt his stomach tighten and his mind turned toward the most critical question: *How could he get away from Mel without that happening again?*

In his alpha life, Evan had met Mel on New Year's Day, 1973. It might be more accurate to say that *Mel met him*, as her actions seemed to have a specific purposefulness that night. Evan had been twenty-seven, and though he was still poor at the time, he was already a doctor with a bright future ahead of him. Mel was twenty-three and working part-time as a carhop at Artie's while also taking a few classes at Middle Falls Community College.

She was plenty smart—Evan had always thought that she was likely smarter than he was—but she had never focused much in high school, so it was community college for her.

Smart, savvy, and gorgeous young women often had a plan, and that was true of Mel. She had locked in on Evan at a small get-together with friends and for a time, that had been that. Initially, he was flattered to have the attention of such a lovely girl. Over time, though, he recognized the signs of someone who might not have all oars in the water, and he tried to get away.

There had been small steps in that direction, but Mel had never been willing to take the hint. The more he drifted, the more she followed.

When Evan finally became more abrupt with her, it had not gone well. Each time his memory came to that scene, it stopped, unwilling to give it a full play in his mind.

And now Mel was here, in his apartment. Evan knew exactly when things had gone bad with her. The date of the denouement of their relationship was July fifth. He already knew that things could go differently in this life, that he could impact the future and change its path. He figured he had three months to find a way to change what had happened.

He reached back and flushed the toilet, then ran the water in the sink for a full minute, still gathering his thoughts. He stepped out into the hall and saw that the lights had been turned out.

"Mel?"

There was no answer. He stepped into the kitchen, where the clock on the stove said it was 10:18. He looked around the corner and into the living room. The blinds were open on the window and enough light came in that he could see the room was empty. The saucer with the cigarette and ashes still sat on the coffee table.

"Huh," Evan said quietly to himself. He had been wondering how he was going to get rid of Mel, and she seemed to have done the job herself. She must have gotten tired of waiting for him. That felt like a weight off his shoulders. It would give him time to think about this unlikely situation he found himself in and make a few plans to handle it.

A new thought arrived. *Maybe there's an opportunity here. If things play out essentially the same way, I can use that to my advantage. I can choose better paths, avoid disasters. Specifically, disasters like Mel French.*

At that moment, he realized how exhausted he was. The part of his mind that was still treating this like an offbeat dream suggested that perhaps going to sleep and waking up might do the trick. He hadn't tried that yet.

The rest of his mind was doubtful that would have any impact. Everything about this felt too mundane, too real, to be a dream.

He walked down the hall and pushed the bedroom door open.

Mel was in the bed. Lit by the small lamp on the bedside table, she looked very fetching with the sheets pulled up to her shoulders.

"Took you long enough. Not nice to make Mel wait."

Evan swallowed hard. "I was thinking of making something to eat."

"Really, Mr. Can-Opener Gourmet? What were you going to make?"

Evan had no answer to that, of course. It had been the first thing to pop into his head and sounded lame even as the words left his mouth. He shook his head instead of answering.

"I really need to get some sleep. I've got to work tomorrow."

"No, you don't," she said with a sly smile. "You already told me you were off."

"Ah." Evan hadn't considered that she might know more about his immediate schedule than he did, but of course it was possible.

Mel patted the bed beside her. "Come on, big fella. Let's see what you've got." She let the sheet fall away.

Evan felt like an animal with its leg in a trap. It was just that in this case, the trap was beautiful and beckoning.

He took a deep breath and gave in to the inevitable.

Chapter Five

Evan fell into a sleep that was so deep, it was nearly a coma. When he finally opened his eyes, he was not terribly surprised to see he was in the same reality. He didn't move and listened carefully, trying to hear if Mel was still there.

The only sound was birds singing outside the bedroom window. He sat up and saw that the bed sheets were thrown back on the other side.

"Mel?" His voice was sleep-clogged and hoarse. He cleared his throat and again said, "Mel?"

There was no answer, but as she had shown last night, she sometimes liked to hide and not answer. He glanced at the numbers on the small clock radio beside the bed. He blinked, thinking that the time had to be wrong. The red digital numbers read *11:33*.

"No way," Evan mumbled. "There's no way I would sleep until 11:30." He stretched and had to admit that he did feel rested and clear-headed. He was thankful for that, since he had no real plan about what to do with this new situation he found himself in.

He trudged into the kitchen and found a note. It was in Mel's flowing, rounded writing, which was still familiar to him after so long.

Had to go home and change before my shift. See you tonight?

There was no signature, but she had kissed the paper and her lipstick remained.

See you tonight? Evan knew he was in deep with Mel, and he wasn't sure how to extricate himself. Slowly distancing himself, then breaking it off hadn't worked. He knew he needed a new plan.

A growling in his stomach reminded him that he hadn't eaten anything since he had woken up in this life. He opened the refrigerator and saw that what Mel had called him—*Mr. Can-Opener Gourmet*—was accurate. He had hoped to at least find some eggs he could scramble, but the fridge was basically bare beyond a few condiments and a cucumber that had definitely seen better days.

He normally started his day by drinking a pot of coffee—a necessity in a job that often required you to work around the clock. Today, he felt rested enough from his ten or eleven hours of sleep that he didn't feel like he needed it. He did need something to eat, though.

He opened several cupboards, finding pots, pans, bowls, and plates. Eventually, he hit on the one cupboard that had some food in it. Even there, it wasn't much, but there were two cans of pork and beans, some minestrone soup, and a can of pickled beets. None of that sounded great to him, but he grabbed the soup and looked for the microwave.

But of course, the microwave wasn't there, because very few homes had them in 1973, and certainly not struggling young doctors who had yet to earn a good paycheck. He knew he could heat the soup up on the stove, but that seemed too much of an effort.

Instead, he dug the can opener out of the silverware drawer—there were only three knives, forks, and spoons in the little plastic holder—and opened the can of pork and beans. He stood over the sink and ate, scraping the sides of the can, trying to get every last bit. It felt like the more he ate, the hungrier he got.

He tossed the can in the garbage can beside the counter and noticed the wall phone. There was a long, looped cord hanging from the handset, and Evan remembered that was so he could take the phone into the living room.

Forget about cell phones. When did we get cordless phones? I've got a lot of adjusting to do.

Seeing the phone had an impact on him.

1973. Mother is alive. She'll be expecting to hear from me. Or maybe she heard from me yesterday and doesn't expect to hear my voice for another week. This is all so damned complicated.

Evan's relationship with his mother was complicated, to say the least. His parents had divorced when he was young and he'd barely had any contact with his father since then. It had been he and his mom against the world, as she reminded him often. To Evan, it had seemed more like her against him than the two of them as a united front.

They hadn't lacked for things. His father had at least partially made up for his absence by agreeing to a very fair divorce settlement and sending a healthy child support payment on the first of every month. That had lasted through Evan's first four years of college, but had stopped when he went on to medical school.

Even so, his mother had taken what she had gotten in the divorce and had started a small florist shop just off of Main Street in Middle Falls. She proved to be an excellent entrepreneur and that little shop had taken care of her until the end of her life.

He picked the phone up and saw the little push buttons on the handset. He closed his eyes and was not surprised that he managed to summon up his childhood phone number. He punched the numbers in and listened to the distant, tinny ringing.

On the fourth ring, he heard his mother's voice. "This is Camille, can I help you?"

That was so like his mother answering the home phone as though she was at the flower shop, with important things happening, when she was likely just sitting at the table doing the *New York Times'* crossword puzzle. In ink, of course.

"Hello, Mother, it's Evan." Without conscious thought, he had fallen into the more precise, formal way that she always spoke.

"Oh, Evan, dear. Is everything all right?"

Is everything all right? That is a question I'm not prepared to answer at the moment.

"Everything's fine, Mother. Why?"

"Well, I just heard from you two days ago. I didn't expect to hear from you again until next week."

Evan nearly lied and said, "Well, I have some news to share with you," but he managed to catch himself. He knew he would have had to come up with some news and that he was no good at spontaneous lies. He didn't think she would be pleased to hear how he had spent the night before. So, he said, "That's right, I did call you just a couple of days ago. Working these twenty-four-hour shifts, I completely lose track of time."

"I understand. Mothers worry, though. You'll be through with these horrible shifts soon enough. I remember when your father went through the same thing. I had to work double shifts too, just to help us make ends meet. We barely saw each other."

"It's a miracle I was ever conceived."

"Don't be crude, Evan. No one likes that."

"Sorry, Mother." He wondered when the last time was that he had seen her in this life. She lived right there in Middle Falls, but he had only gone home on rare occasions after college. They got along better that way and it didn't force Evan to dredge up bad memories.

"Well, if you don't have any news..."

Evan recognized his hint to get off the phone. "I'll call you next week, Mother."

Another person might have felt emotional at having the opportunity to talk to their mother, who in their memory had been dead for many years. Evan was rarely emotional, though, and that was especially true when it came to his mother. The memories he did have of her were not what nostalgia was made of. Whatever contact he'd had with her in his adult years had been exclusively out of a sense of obligation.

He clicked a button and put the phone to his ear. He heard a steady dial tone. He dialed another number from memory and waited until a woman's voice answered.

"This is Dr. Sanderson. Can you connect me with someone who can tell me when I'm scheduled next?"

Evan winced a little. He should have known the name of the person in charge of scheduling and not had to call them *someone*, but it was the best he could do.

A moment later, a woman's voice came on the line. "Hello, Doctor. This is Mary. Lose your schedule?"

"Yes, I did."

"I'll put a new one in your locker. You're not scheduled to come in until tomorrow at 8:00 a.m."

"Thank you, Mary. You're a lifesaver."

"So everyone tells me," Mary said.

Evan hung up and looked around the quiet apartment. The unmoving reality had begun to work its magic on him. What he had recently thought of as his real life was fading. He decided he would spend at least a few minutes before he went to sleep every night reviewing that life and its trappings. If he suddenly woke up in that world again, he didn't want to feel lost.

For now, though, his to-do list felt overwhelming. There were the practical concerns, like the fact that there was no food in the house. That would be easy to remedy. There were the pressing but not immediate problems, like how to get away from Mel. Most importantly, Evan knew he had to find a way to properly take advantage of this unique opportunity he had been offered.

He needed to contemplate and decide if he wanted to follow a similar life path—finish his residency, become a board-certified surgeon, marry Becky—or if he wanted to branch out and try a few different things. The thought of taking the road less traveled gave him an excited feeling in his stomach. His previous life had been so meticulously planned out, and not always by him, that the idea that he could do things differently was enticing. Not to mention the fact that he knew what would be coming much of the time.

He put those larger decisions off for the moment and decided to focus on the easier part of the list while he was still adjusting. He fished his wallet out of his back pocket and looked inside. There wasn't much there. A five-dollar bill and two singles, a picture of him and his mother, and his driver's license.

He tapped his fingers on the counter. He knew he was relatively poor much of the time he had been a resident, but he was sure he had more than seven dollars to his name. He wondered if he would have to go to the Middle Falls Bank and ask for his balance. He frowned, certain there was a better solution.

He opened a small drawer at the far end of the kitchen and found what he had hoped for. Something deep in his subconscious memory had reminded him where he had kept the checkbook. He opened it on the counter and saw that whoever had been living this life before him had the same meticulous habits. Every entry for the previous year and a half was jotted down in his neat handwriting.

Doctors were notorious for having bad handwriting, but his mother had worked closely with him on that since he was very young. She told him that he would break the cycle of unreadable prescriptions.

Evan's eye went straight to the bottom line of the check register. It showed he had a balance of two thousand, three hundred and twelve dollars. He breathed a little sigh of relief. He wasn't rich, but since he saw entries for his rent and utilities already written down, he knew he wasn't completely broke.

He scooped his keys off the counter, locked the door, and hustled down the steps to the parking lot.

Evan felt something that was unusual for him. He felt lighthearted. In his first life, everything had gone essentially to plan, but he had found little joy in it. He had kept himself in great condition, but he had been in his late seventies when he went on the cruise with Becky. No matter how carefully you look after yourself, there is no comparison between that age and the sweet elixir of being young again. The little aches and pains that had inevitably gathered in his lower back, knees, and ankles, were gone.

It wasn't just the physical aspect, either. Looking forward, he began to feel hopeful. As he had aged, his life's path had become more and more solidified. At this moment, he began to feel the possibility of change.

For the first time since he had woken up in this life, he began to hope that he *wouldn't* be transported back to his first life.

It was another warm spring day in Middle Falls and he cranked the window down in the Galaxie as soon as he started it up. He turned the radio on and KMFR was playing *Yesterday Once More* by the Carpenters.

Evan never paid any attention to the lyrics of songs on the radio and completely missed the connection to his own life.

Chapter Six

Evan pulled into the parking lot of Artie's. It was early afternoon, and most of the lunch crowd had come and gone, so there were plenty of spots to choose from.

It had been decades since he had eaten at Artie's, but it was one of his pleasant memories of Middle Falls. He had been in second grade when Artie's had opened as a small shack, and in fourth grade when the Artie's that still existed today opened.

He pushed the red button on the speaker and ordered a burger basket and a Diet Coke.

There was a hesitation on the other end of the speaker. Finally, the woman's voice said, "A burger basket and a *what?*"

"A Diet Coke," Evan answered, thinking that the speaker must have crackled and his words lost.

"We've got Coke, root beer, and 7-Up to drink. Would you like one of those?"

Evan closed his eyes and shook his head slightly. "Sorry, yes. Can I just get a Coke, please?"

While he waited for his order, he tried to remember when Diet Coke had appeared on the scene. It had been so long ago in his first life that he had forgotten it wasn't always on the menu everywhere. He tapped his fingers on the steering wheel and contemplated whether that was one of the things he could exploit. He realized at once that it wouldn't be easy.

He couldn't just fly to Atlanta, Georgia, stroll into Coca-Cola headquarters, burst into the CEO's office and say, "Two words: *Diet*

Coke." Beyond that, he didn't have any idea how to formulate the sweet-tasting, zero-calorie drink, so he was essentially useless.

Knowing that it was coming and that it would eventually be huge, wasn't that much help to him. He thought of the other technological improvements that were coming over the next few decades. The VCR, the compact disc, the cell phone, personal computers. All were huge moneymakers that disrupted the market. But he was not an engineer. He could no more have explained the science behind a VCR than he could have said how the Apollo rockets had reached the moon.

Knowing a device was going to become popular was kind of useless, as far as inventing something.

Of course, that wasn't the only way to profit off knowing what was coming. He could always invest in companies that were going to be on the cutting edge of developing those new technologies. He also knew who many of the major players were, like Bill Gates and Microsoft, Steve Win or Steve Pasternak and Buddha, or Jeff Bezos and Amazon.

That was all grist for the mill for the future, though. None of those breakthroughs would happen for years, so he needed to focus more on the here and now, when he only had a couple of thousand dollars to his name.

It was Mel who brought his food out to him. He had managed to completely forget that she was working today. This kind of slip was not unusual for Evan. When he had a big challenge that he was thinking over, he tended to lose track of the smaller details of life.

Mel smiled fetchingly as she brought the tray out. "Couldn't wait until tonight to see me, huh? Can't say as I blame you. I am pretty awesome."

Evan tried to summon up a laugh and smile, but it came out more like a groan and a grimace. "Yep, you can never get too much Mel."

Mel dimpled, batted her eyes, and put the tray on the window. "I heard what you said to Terri, about a Diet Coke? You are too funny. I never know what you're going to say next."

"Half the time, I don't know what's going to come out of my mouth," Evan agreed. He regretted being there and having this conversation with Mel, but it was too late to do anything about it. He made a mental note to be more aware going forward and let it go.

"Two-thirty-five," Mel said, suddenly all business.

Evan did a quick inventory of his pockets. The two singles wouldn't do it. He would have to give her the five. He didn't want to give her a hundred percent tip, but it felt odd to ask for change back from a woman he had slept with only a few hours earlier.

Reluctantly, he said, "Just keep the rest of it."

Mel's response told him she had expected no less. She used the changemaker on her belt to count out the $2.65 and dropped it into her pocket. "See ya, handsome," Mel said, waggling her fingers. "Gotta run."

Evan returned the wave, then picked up his Coke, took a drink, and looked for a drink holder to put it into. There were no drink holders in his Galaxie, of course, so he tried setting it on the dash. That was too precarious, so he took another drink and set it back on the tray. The pork and beans he had eaten earlier had not come close to filling him up, so he dug into the burger and fries.

In his first life, he had been served fancy burgers at various functions and restaurants. Nothing ever came close to what Artie's served every day. He closed his eyes and enjoyed the small perfection of an Artie's burger basket.

When he was finished with the food, he drained the last of the Coke. Somehow, even that tasted better than what he could remember it tasting like in the twenty-first century.

Did everything taste better in the seventies, or am I just painting everything with a rosy glow?

A different carhop came out to deliver an order and saw that Evan's tray was empty. "Be right back, hon," she said, then hurried on with her delivery. A moment later, she returned and lifted the tray, "Or should that be *Doctor* hon?"

"Just Evan is fine, really."

The carhop favored him with a lovely smile, then hurried inside.

Evan turned on the engine, put it in gear, and got out of the parking lot before he had any more of an interaction with Mel. If he was planning to make a slow break of it with her, he was doing a terrible job, having sex with her the night before and then coming to where she worked the next day.

He pulled in right across the street from Artie's, in front of Smith and Sons Grocery. He went inside and grabbed one of the small shopping carts. He couldn't help but compare this experience to when he had stopped at Costco a few weeks before he had gone on the cruise. This little shopping cart would have fit inside the mammoth Costco cart with room to spare, not to mention the difference between the square footage of the stores.

Still, there were pleasures to be found in the little local store. People there seemed to know his name, or at least recognize his face. The young boy he had seen the day before was back again, this time stocking bananas. He asked, "Can I help you with anything?"

"No, I've got it, thanks," Evan said, pushing the cart quickly through the small fruit and veggie section. He didn't want to get too many things that might go bad. Working the kind of hours he did, he knew most of it would spoil before he had a chance to eat it.

He did grab a dozen eggs, a block of cheddar cheese, some bread, lunch meat, and a few more cans of soup. On the way to the checkout counter, he went down the cereal aisle, but passed up the sugary breakfasts. He knew that was a terrible way to start a long day of patching people up in the ER. He did pick up a box of Cream of

Wheat, though. That box looked almost identical to the one he had last bought.

"Nice to know that some things don't change much," he mumbled to himself.

"Everything changes, boyo, don't fool yourself." It was an old man dressed in overalls and a gray-striped work shirt. He dropped that bit of wisdom, then pushed on down the aisle, leaving Evan in his wake.

Evan paid for his groceries, got his checkbook out, and asked, "Can I write this for ten dollars over?"

The woman behind the register didn't even bother to look at him. "No problem. I know who you are, Dr. Sanderson. We know where to find you if you kite a check on us."

That made Evan glance up suddenly, but he couldn't tell if the woman was joking with him or not. If she was, she did a magnificent job of keeping a straight face.

He took the ten-dollar bill, picked up the paper bag with his groceries, and strolled out to the Galaxie.

He sat in the idling car, wondering if he had any more errands he needed to accomplish in this first day back in 1973. He decided that he wanted to actually cook a meal that night, but realized that what he had just bought wouldn't do the trick for that.

He ran back inside, quickly grabbed a few more groceries, added a six-pack of Rainier beer and went to the checkout counter again.

The woman behind the counter took his measure and said, "Typically, it's easier if you get everything in one trip. Planning on making a few more runs through the store?"

Evan didn't answer her sarcasm, but wrote another check, picked up the second bag, and headed for his apartment.

He found a great spot right next to the stairs and carried both bags up. He still needed to count the number of apartments he passed before he got to his own, so he was paying attention to that and almost tripped over a man sitting in a metal folding chair in front of the unit next to his.

"Oh, sorry," Evan said, stopping just short of the man. He looked at him to see if he recognized him, since they had obviously been neighbors once upon a time. The man was young—early twenties—and had long black hair that curled around his ears and over his collar.

"No problem, man. No harm, no foul."

Evan looked closer and saw that the man had a cooler sitting next to him and a beer in his hand.

What kind of a guy just sits in front of their place drinking beer on a weekday afternoon?

The man tipped his beer in a salute to Evan, then nodded to the cooler. "Want a beer?"

Evan held one of the bags a little higher. "Got a six-pack in here."

"Good enough," the man said, tipping the chair back so that the front legs lifted off the ground. "I'm Jimmy. Grab a chair and bring one of those beers back out with you if you want. We can watch the world pass by."

Evan squinted a little at the young man. Since he had introduced himself, he had obviously never met him before in this life. Evan would never have invited someone he had just met to sit and drink a beer, but he reminded himself that there are all kinds of people.

"Thanks," Evan said, putting a smile on his face. "No chairs like that in my place."

"It's *all* I've got," Jimmy said with a shrug. "You go put your groceries away and bring a beer back out. I'll get you a chair."

Sitting and drinking a beer with this stranger was low on Evan's priority list, but he couldn't figure out how to turn down the friendly offer. "Sure. I'll come back out."

Evan inserted the key into his lock, and Jimmy said, "Hey, we're neighbors. I didn't catch your name."

This was the moment when Evan typically answered *Dr.* Sanderson, but he didn't feel like it this time. Instead, he said, "Evan."

"Cool," Jimmy said, then looked back out over the parking lot as if there was something interesting to see out there.

Evan set the grocery bags on the counter and put everything away. When he was done, his refrigerator wasn't exactly bulging, but at least there was *some* food in there. He folded the paper bags and slipped them into the space between the fridge and the counter, joining a number of identical bags.

He stood and dithered, trying to think of a way not to have to go back out and drink a beer with his new neighbor. He looked around the apartment, hoping some other important job would leap to his mind, giving him an excuse not to go. There was nothing.

With a sigh, Evan unhooked a Rainier from the plastic ring and poked his head out the door. He was hoping against hope that maybe Jimmy had gone inside, forgetting all about him. Instead, he saw that Jimmy had placed his first dead soldier on the railing and was working on a second. A second folding chair sat next to him.

Evan walked out and showed his own beer, either as a rite of passage or a ticket for entry. He sat down and popped the tab on the Rainier, took a swig and let out an involuntary, *Aaah*. It was almost a natural law that the first taste of beer be followed by a guttural appreciation.

Jimmy had seemed friendly when he almost stumbled upon him. That didn't change, as his expression was half-smiling, still staring at the parking lot. He didn't talk a lot, though, and that was fine with Evan.

They drank most of their beer in silence before Evan said, "What do you do?"

In answer, Jimmy pointed to a green and brown truck parked in the gravel next to the apartment parking lot. It was a container truck with the words *Bronson Septic* and the motto *We're #1 in the #2 Business!* written down the side.

"Don't blame me for the pun. It's my uncle's sense of humor." He glanced at Evan out of the corner of his eye. "It is kinda funny, though."

That observation made Evan laugh a little.

"Your uncle, huh? You gonna be the boss someday?"

"That's the plan. A septic business is something that often passes down from one family member to another. It's hard to get someone excited about being up to your elbows in poop all day. Kids dream about being baseball players or astronauts, but no one dreams of coming home smelling like a septic tank every day. It's easier to rope people in that are already in the family." He took a swig of his beer, then said, "What do you do, man?"

"I'm a doctor."

Jimmy let the front feet of his chair come to rest. "What are you doing living in here, man? I'd figure a doctor would be in the snooty part of town. You divorced or something?"

That was a lot of personal questions, but Evan answered. "Doctors don't make a lot when they're serving their residency. They work us like rented mules and pay us crap wages. So here I am."

"Well, you've got something to look forward to then, I guess. Good for you." Jimmy tipped his can toward Evan, who tapped it with his own.

Before long, there were seven empty cans of beer lined up on the railing in front of them. The sun was dropping low in the sky, and Evan realized they had been sitting there for several hours. He watched as Mel pulled in. Now that he saw her in it, he remembered that she had always driven the yellow VW Bug. Somehow, it fit her perfectly.

She got out and Evan saw that she was once again wearing short shorts and a top that showed her flat stomach to good effect.

Beside him, Jimmy let out a long, low whistle of admiration. Evan grinned to himself but didn't say anything.

A minute later, Mel walked toward them, adding a little extra swing and sway to her walk. Stopping in front of Evan, she leaned over and kissed him deeply, then stood up and said, "Who's your good-looking friend?"

Jimmy offered his hand. "Jimmy Bronson. Very pleased to meet you and at this moment, reconsidering my life choices and wishing I had studied a little harder in school."

That puzzled Mel, who looked to Evan for an explanation. He just shook his head, stood up, and said, "Well, if I'm going to make dinner, I better get started."

"What can are we opening tonight?" Mel asked.

"I'm going to make you eat those words," Evan said. "Not to mention my spaghetti."

Evan had been a terrible cook when he was young, but over the years, he had added a few specialty dishes that he could make competently. When the standard was the ability to open a can, he knew he could do better.

Jimmy stood up and grabbed the two folding chairs, setting them inside his apartment. He grabbed the cooler and did the same, then said, "I'll get these." He picked up the empty cans.

"You guys have a good night."

"Good talking to you, Jimmy," Evan said, and he was surprised to find that he actually meant it. They had mostly sat in silence, but that had worked fine.

"You making spaghetti?" Mel asked.

"And garlic bread," Evan confirmed.

She looked at Jimmy and said, "Why don't you come over, too?"

"Oh, I don't want to intrude. You guys have a good night."

Evan suddenly found that he liked the idea of having Jimmy over for dinner. Having a third person present might make it easier to keep things on the straight and narrow with Mel.

"That's a good idea. Give me about half an hour, then come on over. Or, grab your cooler and come over now. That works too."

Jimmy looked from Evan to Mel and back, trying to discern the sincerity of the invitation. Finally, he said, "Yeah, okay, that's cool. I emptied a few septic tanks this morning, though, so I'll go take a shower first."

"Clean enough to sit by me and drink beers, but not clean enough to have dinner with a beautiful girl, huh?"

"You know it, brother," Jimmy agreed with no shred of embarrassment. "Dudes don't care what other dudes smell like, but I don't want to ruin everyone's dinner." With a grin, he disappeared inside his apartment.

"That was nice of you," Evan said to Mel, meaning it.

"He's cute. I've always got girlfriends that I can set up with a good-looking guy."

"Even a good-looking guy that pumps out other people's effluence?"

"Effluence?"

"Yeah, you know, their feces. Their poop."

"Oh, right. I think a lot of girls care less about that sort of thing than you might think. Not everyone is trying to snag a rich doctor."

"Just you?"

Mel balled up a fist and hit Evan in the arm, managing to give him a charley horse. She always seemed to know how to hit him where it hurt most.

"Is that what you think? That I'm after you cuz you're going to be rich?" Anger flared in her eyes, and Evan realized that he had relaxed his defenses a little and poked the bear.

He held up his hands in surrender and said, "Just kidding, Mel. I know you love me for my culinary skills. Speaking of which..." He went to the fridge and pulled out the hamburger he had bought. He crumbled it up into a frying pan and turned the burner on medium.

"I've never seen you cook before, not really," Mel said, her momentary flash of anger forgotten. "Have you been hiding this from me?"

Evan shrugged, then chopped half an onion and tossed it in with the hamburger. Next, he sliced some garlic razor-thin and added that, too, stirring it into the meat cooking on the stove.

Mel inhaled deeply and said, "I wasn't even hungry, but that smells so good!"

"Wish I had a food processor, this part would be easier," Evan said.

"A what?"

"A Cuisinart, or something like that."

Mel shook her head. "Sure, and you can put your Diet Coke in it, right?" She squinted at him as if she was trying to figure out what game he was playing.

"Ah, I think I read something about one coming out pretty soon," Evan said, trying to cover another mistake. He pulled out a large saucepan and opened cans of tomatoes and tomato sauce. After he poured that all together, he found a potato masher in his utensil drawer. "Crude, but it will do." He smashed the whole tomatoes until they were broken up, then added oregano, salt, and pepper to the pan and turned the burner on.

"It'll take a few minutes for that to cook together. Really, it would be better if I let the sauce simmer for a few hours, but I didn't think to start it."

"You were too busy with your new friend."

"I guess so, yeah."

They didn't have fresh-baked loaves of French bread at Smith and Sons, so he made do with regular sliced bread. Again, not ideal, but he had to work with what he had. He smeared the butter he had put out to soften when he got home on the bread and sprinkled garlic on it.

Watching him, Mel said, "I feel like I'm watching you be a doctor. You're just good at things. Competent."

That stopped Evan for a moment. She was right. He *was* naturally competent at most things. "Thanks," he said, slightly embarrassed.

There was a knock at the apartment door. Mel answered it, and Jimmy stepped inside.

"Man, you're a doctor *and* a chef? No wonder your girlfriend is the best-looking woman in Middle Falls."

"Ah, you men say the nicest things when you're hungry, or...whatever."

That made Jimmy grin and he looked away, almost shy.

"You didn't really need to bring your cooler with you," Evan said.

"You make the grub; I bring the beer. It's only fair."

"And I'd say I'd set the table, but there's no table to set. I will get the plates and silverware out, though."

While Mel did that, Evan put a large pot of water on to boil. The hamburger was cooked, so he mixed that in with the sauce, which was beginning to bubble. He turned the oven on to 400 degrees, slid the garlic bread in, then kept stirring the sauce.

Fifteen minutes later, everything was done. Evan thought the spaghetti wasn't as good as he could have made it if he had more time, but it wasn't bad for a rush job. They all heaped their plates with spaghetti and garlic bread and headed toward the living room.

Mel went to the closet and retrieved three TV trays. She opened them and set them in front of the couch and chair. "Just like fine dining," she said with a smile.

That whole day, from meeting Jimmy to cooking for the three of them, had not happened in any way in Evan's first life. That gave him hope that he could build a new and different future.

Chapter Seven

Evan felt like he had stepped back onto a treadmill for the next few weeks and months.

From time to time, he made mistakes in the ER, but it was nothing that caused a real problem. He might ask for something by a brand name that didn't exist yet, or initially recommend a prescription drug that wasn't available in 1973, but he soon learned to avoid that.

What he couldn't avoid was the incredible hours he was required to put in and the exhaustion that went hand in hand with that.

His body was young, but it still had its limits. Where he was really lacking was in the willingness to subject himself to eighteen- and twenty-four-hour shifts.

By the time the calendar turned to June, he was contemplating something that would have been unthinkable in his first life. He thought about dropping out of his residency.

He knew there would be hell to pay for doing that, not least from his mother. After she had groomed and trained him from the time he was small to be a doctor, pushing him through college and medical school, she would find it completely unacceptable to have him give up on that.

Evan knew that if he did drop out, he would be permanently burning a bridge with his mother. For all he knew, the senior Dr. Sanderson might even put in a rare appearance to berate him for being so stupid.

Still, the thought—the temptation—lingered.

He had the actual template of how long it would be before he made a decent living as a doctor. He was twenty-seven, and knew that he wouldn't begin to make really good money until he was in his early thirties. In his first life, when that was just another goal he had set for himself, that was not a problem. He had lowered his shoulder and pushed. He made it.

Now, starting over at the beginning of that hill, he no longer thought he had it in him.

Another aspect was that he had already lived a good and full life as a doctor and surgeon. He knew what that was like. It was a good life, but even with his successes, he hadn't found it all that fulfilling. The trappings were nice, but the more he thought about where he was mentally and emotionally on the cruise with Becky, the more he realized it was a kind of hollow life. He had been focused, but had he really been happy?

Since he honestly had no idea what happiness was, or even what it looked like, he had to admit that the answer was *no*, he wasn't truly happy.

The final piece of the puzzle was that he knew so many things that were coming. At least, he *thought* he did. He had been reading the newspaper, trying to compare the news of the day to the way things had happened in his previous life. His challenge was that during this time in his first life, he had been wrapped in the bubble of his residency and really hadn't been aware of much of what was going on around him, so it was hard to be sure.

His working theory was that although he could change things in his immediate orbit, like becoming friends with Jimmy, he didn't seem to have influence on larger scale events. He couldn't remember exactly when Richard Nixon had resigned, but there were stories about Watergate in the newspaper daily and the congressional hearings had already started. Evan felt confident that this world was heading toward the same result as it had in his previous life.

Too bad, he thought. *I always liked Nixon. Thought he was a good man.*

Holding onto the idea that the world would develop more or less in the same way it had in his first life, Evan was interested in finding a way to become much, much richer than he had been. He wanted to go from being *very comfortable* to being wealthy. Not just to be a millionaire, but perhaps a billionaire. That idea appealed to him, and he knew he would never get that kind of wealth as a surgeon.

It is fair to wonder what it is that drove Evan. The simplest explanation is that as a twig is bent, so grows the tree. When a child is set upon a particular path, it is difficult for even the adult to see another way.

In a story as old as time, he knew he would need to have money to make money, even if he did know what was coming.

The safest route, both from an emotional and a financial standpoint, was to just keep on doing what he was doing. He estimated that he would have enough money put away by 1978 or 1979 to put some of his fledgling plans into motion.

That also meant several more years of grinding out the shifts and living in less than luxury through the remaining years of his residency. That wasn't impossible, but it wasn't appealing.

The real question that he faced was, if he didn't just stick it out at the hospital, what else could he do that would put him in a position to make some of his plans come to fruition? That was a sticking point. Even with a college degree, there weren't many places where he could just jump in and make good money. In fact, he couldn't think of a single one.

If he'd had some financial backing, he supposed that he could try just opening his own small practice, but he didn't have that, and small, single-doctor practices weren't a road to riches, either.

For the moment, he just kept slugging away at the endless shifts at Middle Falls General and waited for something else to occur to him.

He also began to feel the tension in his relationship with Mel. In some ways, he felt like they were doing a little better this time around. He was sure that personal relationship milestones, like what had happened with her in his first life, were more fluid than larger, historic events. That meant that he didn't see the oncoming date when things had gone sideways as set in stone, but even so, it made him nervous.

He'd had months to think about how to deal with Mel and still hadn't come up with much of a plan. At the moment, his only idea was not to worry too much about pulling away from her and to definitely not break it off with her on the same day as he had in his first life.

One afternoon when he was not at the hospital, he drove out to Middle Falls Falls. Mel was working at Artie's, Jimmy—who had become a closer friend than he'd ever had in his first life—was off pumping septic tanks. That gave him the chance to be alone and contemplate all these questions.

He tried to focus on the matters at hand, but he realized that he had perhaps made a bad choice of location for deep thoughts. This was where he had chosen to end his first reset life. At the time, he hadn't thought of that act as committing suicide. It was more of an extension of the experiment he had been committed to when he had first woken up here.

He had been a little out of his head at the time and hadn't thought—at least consciously—that it was an echo of the earlier disaster with Mel.

In his first life, Evan had been focused on very little other than surviving his residency and moving on to what he wanted to do next. That hadn't left much of his attention for something like a serious girlfriend. Nonetheless, that was exactly what he had found himself with when Mel had moved into his life.

For much of their time together in that first go round, Evan was fine with the way things were. Mel was a beautiful girl, vivacious and fun to be with. It was only when she started taking the next steps toward a more meaningful relationship that he realized that wasn't what he wanted. He began to panic, to feel trapped.

When he considered the possibility of a real relationship with her, he knew that Mel wasn't what he wanted in a wife. She was a little too frivolous and carefree to really be thought of as wife material. He didn't want to admit it to himself, but he was also something of an education snob. The fact that Mel only had a high school diploma and a few credits at Middle Falls Community College bothered him. He envisioned a future where he would be hosting parties for important and elite people. He wasn't sure she would fit well in that world.

He was incapable of admitting to himself in that first life that he considered her good enough for a fling but not enough for something more.

For many people, there would have been other considerations when thinking of starting a marriage. Love, perhaps, or true compatibility. Evan just wasn't wired that way. He looked at things from a practical standpoint and didn't give much thought to those harder to define aspects.

Evan got out of his car and walked to the viewing area where he could see the falls tumbling down into the pool below. He thought about how he had started his campaign of pulling away during that first life. It had seemed the most appropriate—even the kindest—way to let Mel down at that time.

He had never been completely present in the relationship anyway, so some time passed before Mel noticed. Evan had a habit of staring slightly over the shoulder of the person he was talking to. He didn't think it was rude not to make eye contact, he was simply concentrating on what they were saying. Or, on something else completely unrelated. To him, that was the beauty of it.

Eventually, when Evan started making excuses why they couldn't get together or why they didn't go places together anymore, it became clear what was happening.

Mel went with it for a time, but when she realized that it was only getting worse, she called him on it.

Evan was not much fun to argue with. When faced with confrontation, he generally just withdrew into himself even more than normal. The louder she got, the quieter he became. That might have made for an end to the argument, but Mel was perturbed.

As Glenn Close would say in *Fatal Attraction* a decade or so later, she was not going to be ignored. She was, however, willing to bide her time a little. Instead of escalating the argument, she had asked Evan to have a picnic with her out at the falls on the fourth of July.

The Middle Falls City Council had allocated a few thousand dollars for a firework display and everyone agreed that the falls was the best place to set them off. There was going to be a big crowd, with a live band during the afternoon and booths set up to sell food.

Unfortunately, Evan had been the proud possessor of the best possible built-in excuse for not attending. The fourth of July was among the busiest days of the year for the emergency room at Middle Falls General. It was all hands on deck, which definitely included the youngest doctors on staff.

He begged off the picnic on the holiday, but couldn't come up with a good excuse for the following day, so he had agreed to meet her there.

Evan turned away from the falls and looked at the grassy area where Mel had everything set up in that first life.

She had laid out a red gingham tablecloth on the grass. She wasn't a great cook, but she had stopped at Artie's and brought some burgers and fries with her, along with glass bottles of Coke.

It was hard to say which was prettier—the setup or the young woman who sat on the grass with her long bare legs curled up beneath her.

Evan had been both working up to and dreading this very moment for months. He had believed it was better to do it fast and get it over with than to drag it out. He waved at Mel as he got out of the car. He saw that there was another couple also there enjoying the lovely summer day. He thought that was good, hoping that having other people around would convince Mel not to make a scene.

Evan was a highly intelligent man, but not very bright when it came to reading people and predicting how they would react.

He knelt down in the grass beside the tablecloth and got straight to it.

"Mel, we shouldn't see each other anymore." He had rehearsed that line over and over in his head and thought that was what was best. Simple, straightforward, with no room for misinterpretation.

Mel's wide, welcoming smile froze. Her eyes took on a dangerous glint.

"You don't get to do that, Evan."

That stumped Evan for a moment. *Is that true?* he wondered. *Do I not get to say that we're not going to see each other?* He wasn't always on solid footing in these situations, but this time, after due consideration, he felt like he was in the right.

"I believe I do." In Evan's mind, he was saying *I considered what you're saying, and I don't agree.*

What Mel heard in the coldness of the words was, *Go to hell, Mel.*

Evan had pictured this scene in his mind on the way there and had thought at that moment she might say something like *Oooh!*, then stand up and storm away in her cute little VW Bug.

That was not what she did.

She looked down at the plates of Artie's food that she had laid out, grabbed one of the hamburgers, squished it up and threw it at Evan. Mel had once been a pitcher on the Middle Falls softball team, and at that moment, it showed. The burger splatted dead center on Evan's face. It dropped onto the nice gingham tablecloth but a splotch of ketchup dripped off his nose.

She didn't stop there.

She picked up everything within reach and threw it at Evan. If she'd had a butcher knife, his life might have been in danger, because she only saw red at that moment. Instead, the deadliest thing she could lay her hands on was the cute little wicker picnic basket. By the time she got to it, Evan had backed up a few feet and was able to bat the basket away.

Mel's lovely complexion had gone red and blotchy. Tears ran down her face. She was speaking, but it was hard to pick out any actual sentences. Instead, her words came across as a shorthand for fury, a woman done wrong.

When she was reduced to grabbing handfuls of grass and throwing it, she stopped the attack. Her chin fell to her chest for long moments.

Evan was as frozen as a doe in the headlights of an onrushing Camaro. This situation had not evolved the way he thought it would at all, and he had no idea how to steer it back to safer ground.

Mel jumped up, looked around wildly, then ran to the fence line that kept people away from the edge. She jumped it easily—Mel was a good athlete and the fence was only three feet tall.

The young couple who had been holding hands and canoodling looked at her, shocked. The girl let out a small scream, and the boy said, "She's gonna jump!"

Evan looked at them as if realizing for the first time that was a possibility. He hurried to the fence and, in what he thought was a reasonable voice, said, "Come on, Mel. Let me help you over."

She turned to him; fire still alight in her eyes. "Go to hell, *Doctor Sanderson.*" The way she said it made it feel like the title was a curse. "I can climb over on my own."

She never did, though.

That was the moment when her foot slipped and, surprise replacing fury on her face, she pinwheeled her arms. She tried to catch her balance and reach for Evan at the same time.

He jumped forward and managed to just brush her fingertips but could not find a hold.

She fell backward and disappeared over the side.

Evan yelled "No!" and leaped the fence himself. Mel was floating face down in the water a hundred feet below.

The young man who had yelled that she was going to jump hurried over to help Evan. "We've got to get down there."

Evan nodded numbly, then began to climb down. He was not a rock climber, but in moments of high stress, his mind quieted. He was able to pick out something that resembled a path to the water.

He made it most of the way down to her when his foot slipped. He grabbed at the root of a small tree to steady himself, but it pulled loose from the dirt. When he realized that a fall was inevitable, he gave into it and pushed off, hoping that he wouldn't hit more rocks on the way down.

He nearly made it. He landed feet first on a large boulder that jutted just above the pool of water. He screamed as he felt the lateral malleolus bone in his left ankle break. A moment later, he was on his back in the pool of water, Mel's dead body floating beside him. The current from the falls caused her to bob and bump into his shoulder.

Above, the boy shouted down, "My girl has gone to call the police. We'll get someone here as fast as we can!"

It took twenty minutes for the police and fire truck to arrive at the falls. With the excruciating pain in his leg and Mel's corpse bumping up against him, it felt like years to Evan.

In the end, the firemen lowered a rescue ladder down. That allowed an EMT to reach Evan, but there was no way to get him back up. For a time, there were four of them—two EMTs, Evan, and Mel's body—bobbing in the water at the bottom of the falls.

Finally, the police reached the caretaker of the city park, who showed them a mostly hidden path down to the water. Only then were they able to carry Evan on a stretcher back up to the parking area.

Evan had been glad that there were people there when he had first arrived, hoping it would cause Mel not to make a scene. He had been completely wrong about that, but in the end, it was helpful having them there. They were witnesses to what went down and saved Evan from falling under suspicion for murder.

As it was, Evan took an unexpected trip to the ER, where he irritated the nurses and doctors who took care of him by critiquing their work as they labored over him. He spent the next six weeks on crutches, hobbling around and doing his rounds.

Most people would have been emotionally devastated to have their girlfriend die in front of them.

Evan went over the whole thing from start to finish a few times, tried to pick out what lessons could be learned at each stage, then forgot about it.

And now, here he was again, back at that same spot, once again reviewing those lessons. This time, Mel was still alive. More than anything he wanted to avoid a crisis situation in this life.

He began to think that the best thing for him to do was just to pick up and leave everything—the unwanted residency, the unwanted girlfriend—behind.

That would have been a cowardly decision, but he was saved from making it the very next day.

Chapter Eight

Evan's day at the falls had not brought him the clarity he had hoped for. He was still sure he didn't want to stay as a resident at Middle Falls General. He was still sure he wanted to get out of his relationship with Mel. He still had no idea how to accomplish either of those things.

He thought that perhaps the mistake he had made in his first life was that he had tried to force the issue with Mel. In this life, though he didn't make any conscious effort to pull away from her, it seemed to be happening naturally.

When he had first dropped back into this life in April, they had a healthy sex life. It was a surprise to Evan when, in June, he realized they hadn't been together for nearly a month. It was easy to put that down to his crazy shifts at work, or how exhausted he was when he got home, but whatever the reason, it wasn't happening anymore, and Evan wasn't going to encourage it.

Mel still came over to visit on many nights when Evan wasn't working. He had gotten in the habit of making dinner and on most nights, invited Jimmy over to join them. It used to be that Mel stayed over almost automatically, but the last few weeks, she had kissed him lightly on the cheek and said, "Gotta get up early tomorrow," before breezing out the door.

Each time that happened, Evan thrilled a little inside, thinking that perhaps this lifetime, she was the one who was leaving him. If that was the case, he wouldn't stand in her way, and he certainly wouldn't threaten to jump off any cliffs.

One Tuesday evening toward the end of June, he was on the back patio of his apartment. He'd set up a small grill there and had three hamburger patties cooking. He'd made a potato salad that afternoon and thought they could all three sit on the balcony and watch the river far below while they ate.

He had just put the potato salad on the table and pulled the plates out of the cupboard when Mel and Jimmy walked in together.

"Almost done," Evan said. "You guys like mustard and ketchup on your burgers, right?"

Mel and Jimmy cast a sidelong glance at each other, then said, "Yes," together.

"You two are in harmony tonight," Evan said, as clueless about social cues as ever.

"Listen, Evan," Jimmy said, running his hand through his long curly hair. "There's something we need to talk to you about."

The *we* need to talk to you was a bigger clue yet, but not enough for Evan.

"Oh? Good. Dinner conversation is good, right? Let me grab the patties from the back, then we can sit down and talk."

Another longer look between Jimmy and Mel. Jimmy finally shrugged and said, "Sure, buddy. That sounds good."

It was a quiet dinner. Normally, when they got together, it was the gregarious Jimmy who started the conversational ball rolling and Mel who jumped in with an amusing observation or to act out a funny thought. On this night, the two of them matched Evan silence for silence.

Evan finished his burger first. His burgers were different from Artie's—the buns he found at the store were never as good—but they were still tasty. He wiped his mouth with a paper towel, then dug into the potato salad. He frowned a little. "Should have put more pickle in it."

Only then did he glance at Mel and Jimmy, whose plates were still full, their food untouched.

"What's wrong? Is there something wrong with your burger? I thought mine tasted fine."

A look of enduring pity crossed Mel's face. "Evan, we need to talk."

"I know," Evan said, nodding. "Jimmy said that. I just thought we should eat the food while it's hot."

Mel reached out and laid her hand on Jimmy's knee. She arched her eyebrows and leaned forward a little, as if to say, *Get it?*, but that wasn't enough to clue Evan into what was happening. It would have been obvious to almost anyone else, but not Evan. He just scooped up a little more potato salad and chewed, waiting to hear what she was going to say.

Mel sighed, then glanced at Jimmy. He nodded his head as if to say, *Go ahead.*

"Evan, I haven't been able to figure out how to tell you this, but Jimmy and I are together now."

The light dawned in Evan's eyes. He tilted his head back and his mouth formed an "O" as if to say, *Oh, I should have known that, shouldn't I?* Then he frowned and set his plate down on the floor.

Mel and Jimmy both tensed, unsure what was coming next.

Evan looked out over the view of the river, then turned to face them both. "Sorry. If I was better at this sort of thing, I'd have probably picked up on this."

Mel stood and put an arm around him. "*You* don't have anything to be sorry about. We're the ones who feel bad."

"Do you? Oh. Sure, I get that. Leaving me and choosing to be with my friend instead. Yeah, that's a little awkward, isn't it?" He made a shooing gesture with his right hand. "Don't worry about it."

This was not the reaction either Mel or Jimmy had expected. Jimmy laughed a little nervously. Mel stepped back and reached for Jimmy's hand.

"You don't mind?" Mel asked. There was mostly surprise in her voice, but perhaps the smallest hint of underlying tension, too. It was obvious that she had expected Evan to put up at least a little fuss. A cross look or a couple of curse words at a minimum. Instead, she got this. Nothing, essentially.

The two newly announced lovers couldn't see what was happening inside Evan's head. If they had, Jimmy would have felt completely relaxed, and Mel might have been even more unhappy.

The only thing that Evan felt was relief. He had somehow managed to accomplish one of his two primary goals without doing a thing. Mel was no longer his problem.

"I hope we can still be friends," Evan said, because that was the only thought in his head.

"Of course we can, buddy," Jimmy said. "We were worried that you were going to freak out when we told you and not want to talk to us anymore."

Evan shook his head as if that surprised him. "I don't see what good that would accomplish. I like you guys."

"We like you too," Jimmy said. "We're relieved that we can still be friends."

And so they were.

Things weren't the same, of course. There were many nights that Mel only went to Jimmy's apartment, going in and out without Evan ever noticing. Still, Evan managed to catch one or the other of them on the walkway outside the apartments and invite them for dinner about once a week.

At first, those dinners were somewhat quiet because Jimmy and Mel still felt a little guilty about how their relationship had started, whether Evan held it against them or not. After a few nights, though, that feeling passed—after all, they *had* come clean—and the get-togethers returned to being enjoyable for everyone.

Evan still thought about quitting his job at the hospital—giving up his medical career altogether. Part of the problem was that the residency was designed to give him real life training to do the job in the future. He'd already had the training. He'd done the job. Even though it was now in his past, he didn't feel the need to repeat it.

Two things stopped him from doing it. The reaction he knew would come from his mother, and the fact that there was nothing better on the immediate horizon.

Camille had bragged about his becoming a doctor so loudly and for so long to anyone who would listen that he knew the impact giving it up would have on her. She would probably close the flower shop for a week in mourning, not to mention the possibility that she would stop speaking to Evan.

That didn't bother him much, but he didn't want a big blow-up argument. Unsurprisingly, after what had happened with Mel, he had been a little gun-shy about those.

So, for the rest of that summer, and into the fall, he continued on with his shifts.

He never looked to replace Mel in his life. He felt that he had dodged that bullet once and had no interest in reloading the gun and putting it to his temple a second time.

Although he kept a vigilant eye open for an opportunity to do something else career-wise, opportunities were limited in a town the size of Middle Falls.

When October rolled around, he made a bold decision. He decided to give notice that he was leaving the hospital, even though he didn't have a new plan in place.

To the outside world, the decision was insanity. The idea of leaving a good job that would inevitably lead to financial success in pursuit of nothing was unfathomable.

Dr. Chin, the senior doctor on staff at Middle Falls General counseled him on several occasions. "Never seek a permanent solution to a temporary pain," he said on one occasion. "You've got so much invested already. Why quit when you're so close to the finish line?" on another.

All those words of wisdom fell on deaf ears, though. Evan knew why he was doing it, even if he didn't know what he was doing next. In November, he gave notice at the River Crest Apartments as well. He may not have known what was on the horizon, but he was sure he wouldn't be doing it in Middle Falls.

He said goodbye to Mel and Jimmy—who seemed happier and more intertwined every time he saw them—by cooking a full Thanksgiving dinner.

He had packed up much of the apartment by that point, so he cooked in his unit and they ate together in Jimmy's. Mel had been at work on Jimmy and he had upgraded his folding card table and metal chairs into an actual dining room table and chairs.

The three of them carried turkey, stuffing, mashed potatoes and gravy, green bean casserole, and pumpkin pies from one apartment to the other.

When they sat down to dig in, Mel shook her head. "I don't get it, Evan. When I first met you, you couldn't make macaroni and cheese out of the box without burning it. Then all of a sudden you turned into a real cook. How is that possible?"

The difference of a lifetime's experience, Evan thought. Instead of that, he said, "I was throwing you off the scent."

That may have made sense somewhere in Evan's brain, but to Mel and Jimmy, it was just another of the weird things he said from time to time.

That dinner was the last of the social commitments he had in Middle Falls. When he quit the hospital, his mother had reacted as he had predicted. He chose to tell her over the phone. She actually screamed in shock, then began to rail at him, using curses, invectives, and threats, all while wondering if he had lost his mind.

Evan hung up the phone. When it rang again immediately, he picked it up and hung it up again. It was a battle of wills for several minutes to see which would give up sooner—Camille's dialing finger or Evan's willingness to pick up and immediately hang up. It was an eventual draw, with Evan deciding to unplug the phone.

The day after Thanksgiving, Jimmy borrowed his uncle's pickup and helped Evan move his furniture and boxes into a storage unit at the edge of Middle Falls.

Evan spent his final night in Middle Falls sleeping in a sleeping bag in an apartment that was bare other than the two suitcases he was going to take north with him.

He had never been spontaneous in any way in his previous life, but he was rectifying that with this big move. It was so unplanned that he wasn't even sure where he was heading. He would probably spend a night or two in Portland, then move on to Seattle. Those were big enough cities that he thought he might find an opportunity there.

He had closed out his bank account and had twenty-nine one-hundred-dollar bills in an envelope hidden under the driver's seat of the Galaxie. He had the rest of his bankroll, which wasn't much, in the front pocket of his jeans laid out on the floor beside him.

There were no overhead lights in the bedroom, and he hadn't thought to leave even a small lamp out, so when it got dark late in the afternoon, it was dark in the room, too. He could have got in the Galaxie and driven to Artie's or gone to a movie at the Pickwick, but that felt wrong to him. He wanted to get started on the next phase of his life and didn't want to prolong this chapter.

By 6:30, he was in his sleeping bag, sound asleep.

Chapter Nine

Having gone to sleep so early, Evan woke up in total darkness. He tried to see what time it was on the watch he'd laid on the floor beside him, but couldn't make it out. He decided it didn't matter. He had finished everything he needed in Middle Falls, and was free to leave.

He took a shower, then packed up his toiletries and stuffed that small bag into his bigger duffel bag.

Meticulous to the end, he walked through the apartment one last time, searching for things that might be left behind. He didn't find anything, and so he left his keys on the kitchen counter, opened the door, and stepped outside and into the next phase of his life.

It wasn't yet 5:00 a.m., and it was still full dark, but he felt rested, energized, and ready to go. He slung the duffel bag over his shoulder and jogged lightly down the concrete stairs. He tossed it in the trunk next to the suitcase that had his clothes, then, shivering in the cold November morning, he got behind the wheel and started the Galaxie.

He wasn't sure how he was going to make his money yet, but he did know one thing. At his first opportunity, he was going to trade this car in for a better one. The heater eventually blew enough warm air on the windshield to defrost it. He turned the headlights on and illuminated the River Crest building.

"With any luck, I'll never see you again," he said to himself and turned out of the parking lot. He drove through the deserted Middle Falls streets. The only vehicle he saw was a Middle Falls police officer sitting with his prowler idling in front of the Do-Si-Do.

Evan tipped him a small salute, but when he looked at the cop more closely, he saw that though the engine of the prowler was idling, the cop himself had leaned back in his seat and was fast asleep.

Two minutes later, Evan passed the city limits sign and headed toward I-5.

When he had made his escape plan, this idea to jump, hoping a net would appear, had seemed brave and adventurous. Now, turning onto I-5 North and heading toward Portland, it just felt a little foolhardy.

He wished he had *some* sort of a plan, so he made one on the spot.

He had lived in Seattle with Becky for twenty-five years, so he knew that area and was comfortable there. That was where he would likely end up, if only because he knew the geography of the area. Before he committed to that, though, he decided to spend at least a night or two in Portland.

He left so early that he approached the southern limit of the city just as the sun was coming up. In another place and time, he would have undoubtedly Googled the best places to stay, the best restaurants, and what any can't-miss attractions there were.

In 1973, he approached the city knowing nothing.

In many cities, Interstate 5 skirted the edge of the downtown area, but not so in Portland. Evan let his mind wander and before he knew it, he had missed a turn, or taken a turn he wasn't supposed to, and found himself on the surface streets of downtown Portland.

As cities go, Portland was smallish. In 1973, it had less than a million people living there. If you counted the surrounding suburbs, it easily topped that, but it wasn't a city on par with a real city like Chicago or Los Angeles.

Evan didn't worry too much about losing the way north. The point of being in Portland today was to drive around the city, get the lay of the land, and see what he could see.

The first thing that drew his attention was a small eatery with a flashing neon sign that read *Harve's Diner*.

Evan found a spot in the small parking lot, went inside and slipped into a comfortable booth. He instantly liked everything about the place. There was no obnoxious music playing to lift the spirits of the customers. The smell of coffee was strong and the waitress who approached him looked like she wouldn't take any guff off of anyone.

That was fine with Evan—he had no intention of handing out any guff.

She didn't ask if he wanted coffee, she just flipped over the thick ceramic mug in front of him and poured steaming coffee inside.

"Know what you want, hon?"

"Can I get two eggs over easy and some toast?"

The waitress, whose name tag read *Billy Jo*, jotted a quick note on her order pad with the stub of a pencil. "That'll be right up."

She turned toward the opening to the kitchen with unlikely grace, slipped the page onto the carousel and hollered, "Flop two, then shingle with a shimmy."

When Billy Jo brought the eggs and toast to Evan a few minutes later, he said, "Is there a good place to stay here in the area?"

She took him in before she answered. He was wearing a non-descript gray shirt, Levis, and had come in wearing a jacket that was probably too light for the cold weather. He didn't look wealthy, but it was obvious he wasn't a near-homeless person just looking for shelter.

"Corporate or mom and pop?"

Evan considered, then said, "Mom and pop, I think."

She tore another page of her order pad off and wrote *Restful Inn, 2033 Jackson*, then laid it on the table. "Go two blocks up, turn right, it's just a block down on the left. Come see me at the counter when you're ready to settle up."

From the moment he walked in until he used the second piece of toast to sop up the last of the egg yolk, he had never seen a menu. He pulled a couple of singles out of his pocket and tucked them under his plate. Evan was lacking in many of the social graces, but he never forgot to tip at least twenty percent.

He paid the bill, which wasn't much more than the tip he left behind, then got back in the Galaxie and followed her directions. Evan smiled when he saw the Restful Inn. It was well-named. Rather than being ostentatious, it looked as comfortable as an old pair of slippers. It was a single-story brick building with a welcoming office, and he saw that you accessed each room from outside.

The room was eleven dollars for the night. Somewhat surprisingly, they let him check in even though it was barely nine in the morning. The room was clean, with a full-sized bed, a dresser and nightstand, and a small television. Everything he needed to stay a night or two while he looked around the city.

He had left Middle Falls so early that morning that he had plenty of time to explore the Rose City. He didn't really want to hit the tourist spots, museums, and the like. More than anything, he just wanted to drive to different areas of the city, park and walk the neighborhoods to see if anything fit what he was looking for.

Eventually, Portland would be recognized for its slogan of *Keep Portland Weird*, which it had borrowed from Austin, Texas. In the twenty-first century, it would be lampooned by the series *Portlandia*, which made fun of the city's lovable hipsters.

In 1973, though, it was more of a generic West Coast city. Powell's books, which eventually became world famous, had just launched a year or two earlier. The Portland Trail Blazers had played their inaugural season three years earlier and were the region's only major sports franchise.

Before it became famous for its hipster vibe, Portland was more of a blue-collar city. Evan didn't mind that at all.

He spent the day walking through the tall buildings of downtown, then moving out a little and checking out the parks, rivers, and bridges.

It was a nice town, and the people were friendly. He felt like a stranger, though. There was nothing familiar or homey. He was sure he could build that connection over time, but he couldn't think of a reason to do that when he already had that less than two hundred miles to the north in Seattle.

He had stopped in Portland to see if anything really grabbed him, but nothing did.

He backtracked to the Restful Inn, parked outside his room and walked back to Harve's diner. Once he found something that worked, Evan was unlikely to experiment.

He had meatloaf and mashed potatoes that were delicious and so plentiful, he couldn't finish the plate. He left another nice tip and walked back to his room.

Portland had been a pleasant stop on the trip, but it didn't feel like home.

He flipped on the television in his room just in time to hear the familiar voices of Caroll O'Connor and Jean Stapleton singing the theme song to *All in the Family*. He sat on the edge of the bed with a smile on his face. When the show had been on during his first life, he had either been in medical school or in his residency, so he had rarely had time to catch any of the episodes.

Thirty minutes later, he was still sitting on the edge of the bed when *M*A*S*H* came on. He stretched out and gave in to the wonderful CBS Saturday night lineup with *The Mary Tyler Moore Show* and *The Bob Newhart Show*. That was more television than he had watched at any other point in either one of his lives, but that was part of the charm of his new life. He could do whatever he wanted to whenever he wanted to do it. At least he could until he ran out of money. He thought of the almost three thousand dollars hidden under the seat of the Galaxie and wondered how long that would last.

He knew the answer was *not very long* unless he got a job and started to earn something to add to it, but that was exactly what he intended to do.

At 10:00, he was tempted to continue watching *The Carol Burnett Show*, but he had started his day at oh-dark-thirty, and he was just too sleepy.

He lay down on his bed and soon drifted off to sleep. One of his last conscious thoughts was something a realtor had said to him in his previous life. He and Becky had been looking for a home in Seattle for what felt like years, though it was only months. When they had rejected yet another home as unsuitable, the realtor smiled and said, "Often, scratching a possibility off the list is almost as good as finding the one." She had been right. They had found *the one* just a week later.

Evan was hoping that the same would be true in finding his city to settle in, and that Seattle would be the one.

He slept in a little the next morning. He asked the nice woman at the front desk of the Restful Inn for directions back to I-5 and decided to forego a third meal at Harve's. Instead, he was on the freeway and headed north by 10:00.

The traffic on I-5 between Portland and Seattle was often busy and even a little hectic. But on a Sunday morning, the driving was easy, though Evan did have to keep his eye open for standing water as the Galaxie tended to hydroplane a bit.

He passed signs for areas that were completely unfamiliar to him, even though he had lived in Seattle for decades: Mossyrock, Morton, Onalaska. Several times, he got a nice view of Mount St. Helens, still lovely and looking like a perfect scoop of ice cream. It wouldn't blow its top for another seven years.

He passed through the twin cities of Centralia and Chehalis, but they looked more like wide spots in the road than actual cities.

When he got to Tacoma, things finally started to look more familiar. The rain let up and a sudden memory hit him. He rolled his window down a few inches and sure enough, there it was. The terrible smell that had been known as *The Tacoma Aroma*. In the coming years, the smelting plants and other polluters would be shut down and young people would have no idea why that nickname had stuck.

Just north of Tacoma was the city of Fife. It was early afternoon and he had begun to regret having skipped breakfast. He pulled off the interstate and followed signs to something called the Poodle Dog. This place was like Harve's Diner on steroids. The sign out front proclaimed simply, *Good Food*.

And it was. Evan thought he might be getting in the habit of eating too many heavy meals and promised himself that he would eat more salads in the coming days and fewer calorie-packed giant-sized servings. He decided to start that the next day, though, and ordered pork chops and a baked potato—the Sunday Special at the Poodle Dog.

When he was finally able to push away the plate, he got back on I-5 north.

Just a few miles past a mall that had a sign that read *Southcenter*, he came around a curve and there was the city of Seattle. This had always been Evan's favorite view of the city. It was like it had just popped up out of the ground fully formed.

It looked different than he remembered, of course. Dozens of skyscrapers hadn't been built yet. Smith Tower, the Seafirst Building, and of course the Space Needle were easily visible, though. The sun came out and the city glistened like the jewel it would eventually be nicknamed for—the Emerald City.

He had wondered if it would still engender a feeling of familiarity when he saw it, since it was a different city than it had been when he had last seen it. He needn't have worried.

He hadn't arrived at the city proper yet, but he felt like he was home.

Chapter Ten

Before he chose where to put down his roots, Evan decided to spend some time driving around the city. Without even thinking about it, he drove to the Magnolia district, which was where he had lived for many years with Becky.

He drove to the exact spot where they lived, but found only an empty lot. That made sense since their home had been built in the late nineties, but it was odd seeing grass, bushes and trees where their house should have been.

Seattle became an expensive place to live—and Magnolia was one of the more expensive areas—but that hadn't happened yet in the early seventies. With only a few thousand dollars to his name and wanting to save money for his future plans, though, Evan knew he would be looking for a less-expensive option than finding a rental in Magnolia.

He considered the possibility that he might even have to move to one of the more suburban areas, like Mountlake Terrace, or Kirkland, which were on the other side of the bridges that crossed Lake Washington.

At the same time, he felt drawn to the downtown area. He couldn't have said why, exactly, except that he thought that would be the more vibrant area and would be ripe with opportunity to use his foreknowledge to his own benefit.

He turned the Galaxie toward downtown and found it a very different place than what he had last seen.

Homelessness was a big issue in Seattle and many major cities in 2023. There were tent cities and encampments scattered through the city. There were homeless people in Seattle in 1973, as well, but not in the same numbers and there were no visible places where they gathered, with the possible exception of Pioneer Square, where there were often people sleeping on the park benches.

Evan drove down First Avenue, past the Pike Place Market and found a place to park a few blocks away without much difficulty.

Pike Place didn't seem quite as touristy as it would eventually become. Instead, it was filled with people who came to actually do their fruit and vegetable shopping for the week. Evan bought a bag of Granny Smith apples and carried them back to his car. He didn't know how long he was going to be staying in a hotel, but he knew that if he left the apples in the cool temperatures of the car, they would stay good for quite some time.

It didn't take long for Evan to decide that he liked this version of Seattle more than the one he had last seen. The downtown area didn't seem as congested, many of the taller buildings hadn't been built yet, so it felt like more sunlight reached the sidewalks. People were dressed nicely, with most of the women wearing dresses and many of the men in suits or sports coats.

He had no particular place in mind to spend that first night, but he drove to what he had known as the International District, which was called Chinatown at that point in time. He looked for a hotel that might be inexpensive there, but didn't find anything, so he moved a few blocks north and parked near Pioneer Square.

This was among the oldest parts of Seattle and looked much like it had when he had lived there. He noticed a large bus idling right along the square. It was empty, with its door open. Evan tried to think about what a bus would be doing in that particular spot but couldn't come up with anything.

He took one of his apples out of the bag and sat on a bench, eating it and watching what was happening.

One by one, the homeless people who had been scattered around went to the bus, accepted a brown bag, then boarded. Evan saw a man walking in that direction and said, "Excuse me, can I ask what's going on?"

The man, who had a weathered face, rheumy eyes, and a scraggly beard, nodded in the direction of a well-dressed man standing by the bus door. "They're giving a sack lunch and offering us ten bucks to get on the bus."

"Do you know where it's going?"

"Nope," the man said with a shrug, "but wherever it is, I'll have more food than I have right now and ten bucks in my pocket."

"Can't argue with that," Evan said.

The other man gave Evan a wink of agreement, then shuffled forward to accept his bag.

The rush to board soon passed, but the bus wasn't full and it continued to idle in place. Evan finished his apple, tossed the core in a garbage can and approached the man standing at the door.

The well-dressed man smiled at Evan and said, "Good afternoon, sir."

"Afternoon. Where is the bus heading?"

"We're going to Portland."

A sudden realization hit Evan. They were luring the poor and hungry onto the bus and shipping them off to their neighbor to the south.

It was obvious from the way that Evan was dressed that he was not in need of that offer, but a new couple of people dressed in rags lined up behind him.

"Excuse me, sir," the man at the door said, then nodded at the couple. He reached behind him and handed each of them a brown bag, and they got on the bus.

Evan walked away, shaking his head. He guessed that this was not a city-government-approved operation but was perhaps something organized by the people who owned businesses in the area to keep the surroundings more aesthetically pleasing. He sat back on the bench and watched. He supposed there was nothing illegal about the idea. They weren't kidnapping anyone, and a homeless person would not be any worse off in Portland than they would be in Seattle. For all he knew, there was a similar operation in Portland, shipping people down to Sacramento.

If I found myself homeless, Evan thought, *I would head to Southern California. It would be much nicer to be without a roof over your head in San Diego than it would be to suffer through a Pacific Northwest winter.* He didn't stop to think how he would accomplish getting from Seattle to San Diego if he had no money. It was unlikely that people would stop to pick up a hitchhiker dressed in rags who looked like they hadn't bathed in some time.

Not much later, every seat in the bus was filled, the last of the brown bags were handed out, and the well-dressed man got on the bus and it pulled away.

Evan looked around and saw that the square, which had been filled with the homeless when he had arrived was now crawling with people dressed in their Sunday best, out for a walk.

Nature abhors a vacuum.

Evan turned up the collar on his jacket and realized that if he was going to be outside in the coming days, he would need to buy a heavier coat. As soon as the sun went down, it got cold quickly.

Darkness had snuck up on him, and he needed to get serious about finding a room for the night. He decided to drive north to the University District. He knew there were places to stay there that wouldn't cost too much. He walked back toward the Galaxie and reached in his jacket pocket for his keys. He didn't notice that the three young men who had been hanging around, leaning against a building as he passed, fell into line behind him.

Evan reached out with the key, but that same moment, the three men surrounded him.

"I'll take your keys," the man standing to his left said. His voice was neither gruff nor loud. It was, however, confident.

Evan froze. He had never been confronted with the potential for actual violence in any of his lives and had no idea what to do. "Wh-what?" was all he managed to say.

"Your keys," the man repeated. "Now." To emphasize his point, he showed Evan a knife with a long blade. The other two men moved close—so close, he could feel them pushing against him.

"It's not a very nice car," Evan said. He had never been good in an emergency and being on his third life had obviously not changed that.

The time for conversation was apparently over. The man to his right swung his fist into Evan's hand that was holding the keys. They flew up into the air, and the man with the knife caught them neatly. "Go on now," the man said, gesturing with the knife.

To his horror, Evan realized that everything he owned was inside that vehicle. His clothes, yes, but most importantly, his small nest egg he needed to start his new life was hidden under the seat.

"Wait," Evan said, suddenly desperate to stop what was happening but unable to come up with any plan that would get him out of this situation.

The man with the knife nodded to the man on Evan's left. That man swung something that looked like a sock, but it had something inside it. It caught Evan just behind his left ear, and the next thing he knew, he had fallen to one knee, then pitched face-first beside the front tire, scraping his cheek against the pavement.

"Good shot," the man with the knife said, then opened the driver's door and jumped in. He leaned across the front seat of the Galaxie and unlocked the passenger door. The other two men hurried around and hopped in, one in front and one in back.

Evan never completely lost consciousness, but he had a difficult time making his body work the way he wanted to. He had seen an explosion of light when he had gotten clipped, but that had faded down to an encroaching darkness.

The man behind the wheel started the Galaxie, put it in gear, and floored it. The car jumped forward, with the back tire missing Evan's head by inches.

Seconds later, Evan managed to work his way up to a kneeling position and watched helplessly as the Galaxie's taillights disappeared around a corner heading north.

A couple walking along the sidewalk saw the last of the action and hurried to Evan's side. "You all right, fella?" The man grabbed Evan's elbow and tried to help him up. He managed to get to his feet, but felt woozy, stumbled a couple of steps and sat on the curb next to where the car had been parked.

"These kids," the woman said shrilly. "They think they can just take whatever they want. No sense of decency."

The man, who was dressed in slacks, a white shirt and a warm coat, knelt in front of Evan. "Can we help you? Give you a ride home, or to the police station?"

"I don't have a home," Evan said without thinking.

"Oh," the man said, then moved back a bit. He stood, dusted the grunge off his knees, and said, "Well, I'm sure sorry this happened to you." He and the woman hurried away, heads together.

Evan gingerly probed the lump that was forming behind his left ear, doing some quick triage on the wound. There was no blood, but he knew he was probably concussed.

He was also alone in what suddenly felt like a foreign land, with no money, no transportation, and no idea of what to do next.

Chapter Eleven

The harsh reality of the situation settled in as Evan sat on the cold concrete.

He did an inventory of his remaining assets. He reached in his pocket and pulled out the cash he had there. It wasn't much. Thirty-two dollars and some change. He had the clothes on his back and nothing else. They hadn't bothered to take his wallet, but that didn't do him much good anyway. He had no credit cards, just his driver's license.

That was the moment that a typical Seattle drizzle settled in. It wasn't what any self-respecting weather front would call *rain*, it was just those cold, tiny drops that managed to hit any piece of exposed skin.

Evan looked up at the sky as if to ask, *Now this?* He regretted doing so instantly. The lump behind his ear sent a sharp stab of pain into his brain.

He knew that whatever he did, he couldn't just sit on the curb. He had to do something. He stood up, swayed a little, but found his balance.

What's the first thing? Evan thought. *Report the car as stolen to the police? Probably.*

He looked around Pioneer Square. The combination of drizzle and darkness had more or less emptied the area. The small shops around the square were dark, closed for the evening. He searched his mind, trying to remember where the local police department was. He finally decided that it wasn't that he couldn't remember, it was more likely that he had never known. He'd never had reason to interact with the Seattle Police Department until that moment.

He saw a man huddled under the arch of a doorway, smoking a cigarette. He walked toward him, but gingerly. Each step reminded him that he wasn't functioning at anything close to full capacity.

"Excuse me," Evan said to the man, who had been staring off into the middle distance. "Can you tell me where the police station is?"

The man was in no hurry to answer. It was possible he was in no hurry to do anything. He took a long drag on his cigarette, taking Evan in. He flicked some ashes onto the ground, then said, "Turn right at the corner, then left on Fifth."

"Thank you," Evan said. At that moment, he wished he could have switched places with the man. He was obviously homeless, with his belongings scattered around his feet in plastic bags, but he was *settled* in that fact. He had a routine. It might not have been pleasant, but he didn't have to ask himself what was next at each step of the way.

Evan, on the other hand, who had been in quite a lovely position until a few minutes earlier, now had no idea what was coming. He turned the collar up on his jacket, wishing he had bought a heavier coat while he still had some money. He followed the man's directions and within a few minutes, he had arrived at the downtown precinct of the Seattle Police Department.

He waited for the light at the corner to change so he could cross the street. He didn't think it was wise to jaywalk right in front of the station.

The precinct was one of the few places in the downtown area that wasn't closed on a Sunday night. Overhead lights cast a warm, yellow glow over the entrance.

Evan knew that in another twenty or thirty years, the entrance into any metropolitan police station would look very different. There would be guards posted at the doors, there would be bulletproof barriers and metal detectors to pass through to even get in the door.

In 1973, there was none of that. Evan pushed through the heavy door and saw a bored older man in uniform sitting behind a counter. The officer didn't bother to look in Evan's direction until he stood directly in front of the long, polished counter.

"Can I help you?" The man's voice was laconic, his eyes sleepy.

"I've been assaulted and carjacked."

"Car-what?" the man asked.

"Carjacked," Evan repeated before realizing that maybe that phrase wasn't in vogue in the seventies. "Sorry." He took a deep breath and started again. "Three men attacked me and stole my car."

The man behind the counter looked at Evan for two beats. The Sunday paper was spread out in front of him, and it was obvious he had been hoping for a long, crime-free evening to read the funny pages. Now, Evan had obliterated that hope. He sighed, folded over the section of the paper that had Li'l Abner at the top, reached into a drawer, and pulled out a form.

"All right," the man said, obviously bored with the whole process before it even started. "Start at the beginning. Where were you when this happened?"

Thirty minutes later, Evan walked out of the station feeling even less hopeful than he had been when he had arrived. The man behind the counter had asked where he could be reached, and of course, Evan did not have an adequate answer. He considered giving the officer Jimmy's phone number in Middle Falls, but he knew that would lead to another call he didn't want to make and really couldn't afford. Long distance was expensive in the seventies, and his funds were extremely limited.

Instead, he had promised to return as soon as he had a phone number, and that had been that. His expectations were low in terms of the police solving the crime. He didn't expect them to send an all-points bulletin or even a *be on the lookout for*, but he hoped that if the car turned up wrecked on the side of the road somewhere, he would find out about it.

He harbored a tiny sliver of hope that perhaps the men would just drive the car somewhere and dump it when it ran out of gas without doing a thorough search. If he could get his car back—even if it was dented or didn't run—but recovered his missing cash, his plans would be back on track. Seattle had a good Metro bus system, and he knew he could get wherever he needed to go using that.

All of that seemed like a distant pipe dream as he stepped back into the misting rain of a Seattle Sunday night. He was sure that he had enough money in his pocket to rent a room for the night at one of the flophouses downtown, but he couldn't justify that expenditure. If he blew his small remaining nest egg in twenty-four hours, where would he be the next day?

He started walking in a zigzag pattern through downtown, looking for any business that might still be open. There were a few, but they were mostly elegant restaurants, where a dinner would be prohibitively expensive. What he wanted was a place where he could spend a couple of dollars, get some food, and be able to sit inside where it was safe and warm for a few hours.

He thought that in a city the size of Seattle, that would be easy, but he was wrong. There were coffee shops aplenty, but all of them were shuttered, waiting for another work week to fill them up with businesspeople, secretaries, and students.

Evan walked until he was tired, then found a doorway of his own where he could sit out of the rain for a time.

It didn't escape him how he had been casually observing the plight of the homeless just a few hours earlier and in a single twist of fate, he had somehow joined them. He sat on the cold tile, pulled his legs up to his chest for warmth, and considered his options.

He could call someone and ask for help, but who?

He had given notice at Middle Falls General, but he had also completely cut ties with them. He had casual friendships with Neil Cartwright or Ann Weaver, but not the kind that included emergency phone calls and requests for money.

He had left on good terms with both Jimmy and Mel, but he couldn't picture himself calling them, either.

That left only his mother. He had burned that bridge a few weeks earlier and hadn't even told her he was leaving town. Still, he knew parenthood was one of the ties that bind. He was sure that if he called her and said he was in Seattle and in desperate straits, she would either drive straight to him or at a minimum send him some money.

The interest on some loans was simply too high, though, and that was true of the crow he would have had to eat with Camille. He pictured the conversation he would be forced to have with her and shuddered.

If outside help wasn't coming, he would need to rescue himself. No matter how he thought about it, though, he couldn't picture what that looked like. He was intelligent, had a medical degree and had served a year and a half of his residency. He'd never had any other kind of job, so he didn't really bring that much to the party.

Evan knew that he could try to restart his residency, although it would be somewhere other than Middle Falls. They had already brought in another bright young doctor to replace him. Even if he decided to go down that road, though, it would be a long, involved process and wouldn't help him out of his immediate need for shelter and a job.

He followed these thoughts round and round in his mind for more than an hour. The cold seeped up from the tile and into his spine. He stood, stamped his feet, and decided he had better keep moving.

He started walking aimlessly, turning left and right with no particular destination in mind. It was just past 2:00 a.m. when he saw something he had just about given up on. There was a brightly lit sign that read, A *Fine Restaurant* with a picture of a dog inside a small doghouse.

Based on the exterior, Evan wasn't sure about the *A Fine Restaurant* part, but it looked like an oasis to him because it was open and didn't look expensive. He walked through the double door into a small area where many people had obviously stamped the rain off their shoes and boots.

A waitress who looked like she had been working at the same place for sixty or seventy years pushed by him. "Find a seat and take a load off."

Evan did just that, gratefully. The place was surprisingly crowded for a restaurant in the middle of the night. The interior was on the dark side, and there was a lingering smell of fried food and coffee. It had been a long time since he had eaten lunch in Fife and the one apple he had eaten since was a nearly forgotten memory.

The same waitress walked by and dropped a menu off without a word. Evan looked at the top of it, which read, *All Roads Lead to The Doghouse.* Evan thought that he couldn't argue with that.

His waitress, who wore a name tag that read *Doris*, came back with a coffee pot. "See what you want?"

Evan was in no mood to hurry through this small island of warmth and calm he had found. "Just coffee to start with, please." He turned his cup over and Doris poured it full, then went on her way.

Evan put his face over the cup and let the steam warm him. He took a long drink, set the cup down and smiled. For the first time since he had been whacked on the head, he felt like he knew where he was going to be for at least the next hour or so.

When Doris came back to warm up his coffee, Evan asked if he could get a chiliburger that late at night.

"Yep," Doris said, then moved on to a table filled with what looked like a bunch of twenty-something revelers who had come in after a party of some sort. Evan couldn't help but smile when he saw how they straightened up and said, *Ma'am* to Doris when she stopped by their table. It was easy to see who was in charge at the Doghouse.

The chiliburger was delicious and finished warming whatever corners of Evan that the coffee hadn't reached. He continued to sit and drink coffee for several hours after his plates had been cleared away.

Finally, Doris approached and said, "You can stay here as long as you want, but I'm going off shift now." She laid a ticket down on the table and waited.

"Of course," Evan said. He pulled his small reserve of notes out and placed a five-dollar bill on the table.

Two minutes later, Doris was back with his change. She started to turn away, then stopped and looked back at him.

"Just get into town?"

"Kind of," Evan said. "I've had a very bad day."

Doris nodded. Evan supposed that she saw people having all kinds of days, working overnight at a place like the Doghouse. She pulled a matchbook out. The outer cover showed the same dog inside the same doghouse as the sign outside. She opened the cover, wrote something on the inside, then dropped it on the table.

"If you need a little help, go to that address. Ask for Marge."

Evan looked down at the matchbook, then tried to make eye contact with Doris. He couldn't quite do it, but he nodded his thanks. He felt a lump in his throat. The people who had stopped when he had been robbed had evaporated, the police weren't interested in helping him, but Doris from the Doghouse took an interest in his well-being.

He looked outside and saw that the sky was turning pink. He had made it through his first night in Seattle.

Chapter Twelve

Before he left the Doghouse, Evan went into the old-fashioned men's room and washed his face, then ran wet hands through his hair. Not a shower, but it was the best he was going to do.

He walked on stiff legs out of the Doghouse and onto the sidewalk. It was Monday morning and the city had come to life. The skies overhead were full of ominous dark clouds, but at the moment, there was no rain falling. Evan hadn't slept in twenty-four hours and felt muzzy-headed and in desperate need of a nap he knew probably wasn't coming.

He wondered if there were any temporary employment places in Seattle in the early seventies. He wasn't afraid of manual labor. He had worked at construction sites in the summers during his college years. Most importantly, he thought that most of those places paid at the end of each workday. If he could manage to earn a few dollars every day, he thought he might be able to afford a cheap room to sleep and shower in every second or third night.

He found a payphone, but someone had clipped the metal cord that held the phonebook, so he walked until he spotted another one. This time, the phonebook was still attached. He searched through the Yellow Pages, hoping to find temporary employment agencies, but the pickings were slim. He dialed the number for one of the few listed in the downtown area, but the receptionist said they only hired out office temps. She didn't come right out and say so, but Evan got the idea that these were not jobs for a man.

He abandoned that idea as untenable for the moment and stepped out onto the sidewalk. Downtown Seattle was busy but not chaotic. The vast majority of men wore suits and ties, the women—young, for the most part—dressed nicely in dresses or skirts. Everyone seemed to have a mission. Everyone was going *somewhere* and seemed to be in a bit of a hurry to get there.

Only Evan stood and gawked, having no particular place to go.

When Doris had given him the matchbook with the address on it, he had thought it would be something he investigated as a last resort. Now, he found that all of his resorts had been used up and he was down to his last one.

He pulled the matchbook out of his pocket and walked toward the address. He didn't have all Seattle laid out in a map in his mind yet, but he thought it was probably near Pioneer Square. Something kept pulling him in that direction.

He arrived at the address a little past 9:00 a.m. It was an old brick building surrounded by other buildings that all looked like they were built in the early days of the city. There was nothing special about it. There was a sign in front that read simply, *The Mission*.

Do-gooders, Evan thought. *I guess that's what I need right now.*

He stood outside and watched the building for a few minutes. It wasn't that he was suspicious that there were nefarious people about. He just had to work up his nerve to enter.

Rain started to fall, and this time, there were actual rain drops. That encouraged Evan to go inside.

The interior of the Mission matched the exterior. That is, it was old, with weathered floors, tall ceilings, and the smell that often comes with many people being crammed into a small space overnight.

At the moment, though, the big room he stepped into was mostly empty. There was one man sitting on a bed in a corner of the room, talking to himself. Another man swept the aisle between beds. The beds themselves had been stripped down to the mattresses.

At the back of the room, there was an old sign that read, *Our mission is to help those who need help the most.*

Evan waited near the door for several minutes, ready to leave if need be. No one seemed to take any notice of him. Finally the man with the broom approached and pointed at Evan's feet.

"Oh, sorry," Evan said, and moved aside so the man could sweep where he stood. The man didn't respond. "Can you tell me if Marge is here?"

The man swept on for a moment and Evan began to think that he might be both deaf and mute. Finally, he hooked a thumb toward a door at the back of the room.

"Thank you," Evan said and realized that his feet were probably dirty from walking outside. He didn't want to dirty up the aisle where the man had just swept, so he stepped to the entryway, wiped his feet several times on the rug, then headed for the room.

He passed by the man who was talking to himself, then knocked on the door.

"Yes?"

When he opened the door, Evan saw that this was a small office. There was an old wooden desk with two straight-back chairs on one side and a rolling chair on the other. The walls were bare except for a framed painting of Jesus in the Garden of Gethsemane, a holy glow around his head.

A woman sat in the rolling chair. She had steel-gray hair that was arranged stiffly. Evan's first thought was that a strong wind could blow into the room and her hair wouldn't ruffle a bit. His heart sank when he saw the woman's expression. It was pinched and not friendly at all.

"Doris from the Doghouse said I should look you up."

The woman nodded. "I can always count on Doris to send me new customers."

Evan balked at the word *customers*, and Marge noticed. "Don't worry. Everything at the Mission is free, at least as far as money is concerned."

That didn't really set Evan's mind at ease.

Marge's face settled into a more pleasant expression. "We are a Christian organization. That means that while you are here as our guest, you will adhere to our rules and standards. No drinking, no cursing, no trying to sneak a woman in."

Evan relaxed a little. He didn't like to drink, his mother had beaten most curse words out of him as a child, and he couldn't imagine trying to bring a woman into this situation. He was just hoping to find a bed for a night or two while he got his feet under him.

"Are you a Christian?"

"I'm not anything," Evan answered honestly.

"That's fine. You don't have to be Christian to stay here. Jesus told us to invite everyone to our table and that is what we do here. As long as you don't mock those who have faith, we will welcome you here if we have room."

"Do you often run out of spots?"

"Every night," Marge said, and her expression turned mournful once again. "Even more so on these cold and rainy nights. We operate on a first-come, first-served basis, but you can help yourself by helping us."

"How's that?"

"There are a lot of chores that need to be done here. Laundry, sweeping, keeping the bathrooms clean. If you spend an hour or two doing chores, I'll put your name on the list and we will save a bed for you until six o'clock."

"That's very fair, thank you. I would be glad to help out."

"Good. You can go and find Mike and he'll direct you. He'll be the one with the broom." Marge turned her attention back to an open account book in front of her.

"One more question, if I can?"

There was the tiniest flash of irritation in Marge's eyes, but it passed quickly. "Of course."

"Is there an employment agency that handles day workers in the area?"

Marge pulled a pad from the middle desk drawer and wrote an address down in tight, neat handwriting. "You'll be too late for today. They hand out all jobs by eight o'clock each morning. Still, you should go and check in with them and tell them what you're capable of, any special skills, that sort of thing."

"Do you think they might need a good ear, nose, and throat surgeon?"

Evan had intended that as a joke, but Marge simply said, "They're more likely to need someone with a strong back who doesn't mind hard work."

Evan took that as his cue to leave. He found the man with the broom—Mike, he remembered—and asked him if there was anything that needed to be done.

Mike nodded absently and indicated that Evan should follow him. He led him to a large bathroom that had three shower stalls and half a dozen toilets. After pointing at a bucket and mop in one corner, he left, still without saying a word.

"From a cushy job handling nasal surgeries to becoming a second-year resident and then swabbing out toilets," Evan said quietly. "Follow me for more life coaching tips."

Evan set about his task, thinking only of having a warm place to lie down and sleep that night and the possibility of having a shower in the morning. Being stranded and homeless in a strange city had a way of helping set your priorities straight.

When he finished, he dumped the gray water down a drain in the corner and stood with his hands on his hips, proud of what he had done. He didn't know if he should get Mike to inspect his work or not, but decided that was unnecessary.

He went back into the main room and saw that someone—Mike, he guessed—had put clean sheets and blankets on all the beds. After getting no sleep the night before, those freshly made beds were like a magnet, pulling him toward a nap. He resisted, though. He still had miles to go before he slept.

There was no one in the room and Evan looked up at the big old clock on the wall by the door. It was 1:30. He was trying to get the rhythm of life here in the Mission. He had a hunch it might be his home for a time.

He wanted to stop at one of the small restaurants in the area and get a hot meal, but the money in his pockets felt lighter all the time. Instead, he went to a small convenience store a block away and bought a can of Pepsi, a meat stick, and a bag of chips. Not a healthy meal, certainly, but easy on his budget. Evan had no idea what the minimum wage was in Washington in 1973, but he assumed he would find out soon. He couldn't imagine that any work he found initially would pay more than that.

He walked to the address Marge had given him. It was a small, dusty storefront with a hand-painted sign over the door that read *Labor, Inc.* It didn't look like there was anything going on there. In fact, Evan thought it might be closed. He approached the door anyway and saw it was just a small office with a few desks scattered around. He tried the door, and it opened.

From the back, a woman's voice said, "No more jobs today. Come back tomorrow."

"Hello?" Evan said. "Marge from the Mission said it might be good for me to come by this afternoon so I'd be ready to work tomorrow."

A short, round woman poked her head out from behind a divider in the back. "Okay, take a seat. I'll be right there."

Evan looked at the three desks and chose to sit at the one that had a phone sitting on it. The other two were covered with a layer of dust marred only by a few butt prints.

A few minutes later, the woman walked toward Evan and sat down across from him. She handed him a clipboard and without looking at him, said, "Fill this out. If you don't have an address or phone number, just write *Mission*, and I'll know how to get ahold of you."

There wasn't much else for Evan to fill in. He wrote his name, social security number, and where it asked for special skills, he wrote "A strong back and a willingness to work hard."

The woman accepted the clipboard back and said, "Thank you, Mr....Sanderson. Any day that you want to work, make sure you are here in front of the building by 6:30. We start handing jobs out at 6:45. We provide gloves and transportation to the job and back." She looked at Evan for the first time. "Are those the only clothes you have?"

Evan nodded.

"You'll need something heavier. Most of our jobs are out in the weather and it gets cold this time of year. We'll pay you at the end of each workday, though, so you'll be able to get some warmer clothes."

"Thank you," Evan said, rising. "I'll be here by 6:30."

The woman, whose name Evan did not know, nodded and seemed to have forgotten about him by the time he got to the door.

From there, Evan walked back to the police station. He was bone-tired and his feet hurt, but he wanted to check to see if his car had been recovered before he went back to the Mission.

There was a different police officer at the desk when he went in this time, but he was able to locate the case file. Unsurprisingly, nothing had turned up. Evan left the address and phone number at the Mission as his contact information. He didn't tell the officer he was staying there, but he could tell by the man's expression that he recognized it.

"We'll call Marge if we get anything in on your car."

When Evan stepped out into the chilly late afternoon, he felt oddly optimistic.

It had been less than twenty-four hours since disaster had struck, but Evan felt that a plan was falling into place. He was starting from the lowest possible rung of the ladder, but he didn't feel as lost as he had the night before.

He returned to the Mission to find that it was already getting crowded. Men hung around in small groups, talking and drinking coffee out of Styrofoam cups. Evan felt like a complete outsider, which he was.

Mike spotted him and waved him over. "You did a good job on the bathrooms. Thank you. Most people half-ass it and call it good."

Evan was a little surprised that Mike spoke to him and wondered why he had been so silent that morning. He tried to hide that and said, "It was no problem."

"I showed Marge what a good job you did. She put you on the list for tonight. I'll show you where it is." Mike led Evan toward the back of the room and pointed to a bed that was three spots away from the back wall. "These are the best beds because they're farthest from the door. It gets a little colder up in the front."

Evan sat on the bed, which sagged a little. "If I leave for a while, will someone take it?"

Mike shook his head. "Not tonight. It's been assigned to you."

"I think I'll go find something to eat then."

Mike hesitated. It was obvious that he didn't like to speak much, and Evan got the idea that he kept his own counsel most of the time. Finally, he said, "There's no kitchen here, so no hot meals, but there's an aid society that drops off bagged meals for us every day. Sandwiches, chips, a pickle most days."

Evan considered both the dwindling cash in his pocket and how good a bowl of hot soup might be in one of the local cafés. His thriftiness won out in the end. "That would be great, if there are any left."

Mike nodded, went into a room at the back, and returned with a brown bag. He handed it to Evan and said, "Drinking fountain is outside, or you can drink from the sink in the bathroom." He grinned; the first real expression Evan had ever seen on his face. "I hear they're pretty clean tonight."

Evan recognized that Mike had made a joke and returned the smile.

Mike wandered away and Evan sat on his bed. *His* bed, at least for one night. He opened the brown bag and found a tuna sandwich, an apple, and, as promised, a pickle.

It was all delicious.

Evan was hesitant to remove his shoes. He didn't have a locker or anything, and he wasn't sure whether petty theft would be rampant inside the Mission. At the same time, it didn't feel right to put his shoes on the clean blanket.

He looked around and waited until he saw what someone else did. A man three beds over took his old boots off and slipped them under the bed. That gave Evan the confidence to do the same.

At the front of the room, Mike stood up and said, "I'll be doing the reading tonight."

The room had been abuzz with conversation, but everyone quieted down immediately.

Mike said the reading was from Romans, Chapter Twelve. He spoke softly and even though the room was quiet, his voice barely carried to Evan at the back. He caught a few words here and there about feeding your enemy and how God instructed everyone to care for the hungry.

Evan wondered if that verse was the same every night. He thought it would be a popular topic there in the Mission. He girded himself to hear more readings and perhaps some testimony, but after just a few minutes, Mike closed the book and the buzz of conversation started up again.

The lights were still on overhead and it was obvious that most people were not ready to turn in, but Evan felt so tired that he couldn't sit up anymore. He laid his head down on the small pillow and pulled the green blanket up to his shoulders.

He fell immediately into a hard sleep.

Chapter Thirteen

Evan was so exhausted and sleep-deprived that he expected to sleep straight through the night, but he had not experienced sleeping in a homeless shelter.

People got up and wandered around in the middle of the night. The back of the room might have been warmer, but it was also closer to the bathroom, so he heard every flush of the toilet or urinal. Many of the homeless were suffering from different mental health issues, so even at 3:00 a.m., there was a small cacophony of voices and sobs mixed in with loud snores.

Evan was so tired that he slept through the first four or five hours, but after that, he drifted in and out.

At 5:00, he felt rested enough that he threw the covers off and padded into the bathroom.

Evan was a modest person. During his first life, if anyone had asked him if he would get completely naked in a place where forty or fifty strange men were nearby, he would have laughed. It had been two days since his last shower at the Restful Inn in Portland, though, and he needed the feel of hot water to unknot the muscles in his neck and back.

He stripped naked, intending to try to get in and out of the shower quickly, before anyone else came in. He hoped that by showering so early, he would be alone.

That was a pipe dream. As soon as he stepped into the shower stall, two other men wandered in. They seemed to be friends and held a conversation about where they were going to look for breakfast as they turned on the showers on either side of Evan.

Minutes later, two other men came in and seemed content to wait for one of the showers to open up. Evan did his best to ignore everyone. He soaped himself up with the small, rough bar of soap that was on offer, then used the soap to wash his hair. When he stepped out, he found that the towel, although clean, wasn't very big. He felt self-conscious about standing naked and drying himself off with a towel that didn't come close to covering him.

No one else paid any attention to him. Naked men in a shower room were not an unusual or interesting sight.

Evan got dressed and hurried back to his bed, where his shoes were. He was surprised to see that even though it wasn't even 5:30 yet, most everyone was awake. Someone had put the coffee pot on and several people stood in line, waiting for it to be ready.

Evan slipped his shoes on, grabbed his jacket, and went looking for Mike. He found him by the front door, broom already in hand.

"I'm hoping to find some temporary work today, and I have to be there soon to get in line. I'd like to do some chores for a bed tonight, though. Will there be something for me to do when I get back?"

Mike looked at him, considering. "I'll save something for you. I'll put you on the list for tonight."

"Thank you, Mike," Evan said, then hurried out the door. He still hadn't figured out what role Mike played at the Mission—counselor, fellow homeless, janitor—but he seemed to be in charge when Marge wasn't around. It was windy and wet outside—par for the course in Seattle in November. He pulled his collar up against the rain, ducked his head and quick-stepped it toward Labor Inc.

The woman had said to be there at 6:30 and it wasn't even 6:00 yet, but there was already a small line of men waiting outside. For the most part, the men seemed to be about Evan's age—late twenties—though there were a few who looked younger and one man who appeared to be in his fifties.

Evan stuck his hand in his jacket pockets and got in line. He was curious and would have liked to ask some questions of the men who were already there. He was sure they were veterans of this process and would know the answers. Evan was no good at striking up conversations, though, so he just waited and listened.

The men around him seemed to mostly know each other, and talked quietly about things like whether the Seattle Supersonics were going to be any good that year, or whether it was going to snow that week.

A few minutes after 6:00, the same woman Evan had talked to the day before bustled around the corner, umbrella overhead. She saw the line of men waiting and said, "Sorry I'm late, sorry!"

The men all smiled and joked with her. "The three things we can count on," one young man said, "are death, taxes, and Brenda being late on the days it rains." There was no sting in his words, and it was apparent that everyone there except Evan knew Brenda.

She took it good-naturedly, unlocked the door and everyone pushed inside, glad to be where it was dry, if not necessarily warmer.

There were seven men ahead of Evan in line and another five who had lined up behind him.

"Let me turn the heat on, then I'll get us going," Brenda said, hurrying to the back. A moment later, a whoosh of warm air came from overhead.

She hurried back to her desk and looked up at the man at the front of the line. "Clayton, number one as usual. Farm, warehouse, or the old fire station?"

"On a day like this, I'll gladly take the warm, dry warehouse."

Brenda made a note of it, then looked up at the next man in line. She continued on through the line until Evan was up. "Warehouse help is full. Farm or firehouse?"

Evan had no idea what either of those jobs might entail. He couldn't fathom working on a farm when he was in the downtown area. He was sure that would entail a bus or van ride to the north or south. He wanted to get back to the Mission in time to put his time in and get a shower, so he said, "Firehouse," then stepped out of line. He was sure he would be told what to do next.

As it turned out, *firehouse* simply meant helping to haul away the remnants of an old firehouse that was being torn down in the south part of the city. He and five other men ended up grouped together. They were put in a van and drove through traffic for twenty minutes.

A man dressed in work clothes and a hard hat who was obviously in charge of the project met them at the van. He looked the men over, then divided them into teams. He handed Evan and the older man a sixteen-pound sledgehammer and took them to an area where a large concrete slab had been half torn up. He gave Evan a pair of work gloves and said, "Got your gloves, Pedro?"

Pedro—the older man—didn't answer, but just took a worn pair of gloves out of his coat pocket.

"One of you break up, the other one hauls. Got it?"

Evan realized that he was going to spend the next eight hours doing a job that could be summed up in a single sentence. He looked at Pedro, who he figured was at least twenty-five years older, and said, "I'll break up if you want." He thought that would be the harder job and wanted to give the older man a break.

"We'll switch out," the older man said. "That sledge gets heavy after a while."

At first, swinging the hammer felt almost effortless. There was something satisfying about slamming the heavy head down onto the concrete and watching it break up.

Pedro was right, though. In about half an hour, the muscles in Evan's back and neck tightened and the sledgehammer felt heavier and heavier.

Pedro noticed and said, "Let's switch." The older man was much more efficient with the way he swung the hammer. He didn't lift it in such a tall arc, and Evan realized he had been doing it wrong and wasting energy.

He lifted broken pieces of concrete into the heavy-duty wheelbarrow and hauled them to a dump truck on a ramp, feeling confident he could do this job correctly, at least.

He and Pedro switched jobs every thirty minutes or so. The two things required different muscles and let them rest one muscle group while wearing out another. It made a twenty-four-hour shift at Middle Falls General Hospital seem like a vacation day.

It was a cold day, but as hard as they worked, Evan didn't feel it at all. In fact, he unzipped his light coat in mid-morning and left it that way.

He had noticed that the other men all had either a lunchbox or brown sack with them. He hadn't thought to stop at a store and buy something for lunch, so while the others were eating, he found a comfortable spot out of the rain, leaned back, and closed his eyes.

He had almost drifted off when he felt something nudge his leg. He opened his eyes and saw that Pedro was sitting next to him, holding out a banana. Evan nodded, said, "Thank you," and gratefully peeled it. It had been too long since he had consumed his brown bag dinner the night before. He had resigned himself to being hungry until they got back downtown and had entertained himself with thoughts of buying a big dinner then.

The older man sat next to Evan without a word. He poured something hot from his Thermos into its red plastic top, then offered it to Evan as well.

He thought it was probably coffee and was glad to have it. Instead, it turned out to be minestrone soup. It was still warm and was so good that Evan almost cried. He gulped it down, handed the cup back, and said, "That's so kind of you. Thank you."

The man shrugged, poured some more soup into the cup, and sipped at it. "No big deal. I've been there."

Evan didn't have to wonder about where *there* was. It was where he was sitting. Broke, hungry, and alone.

"I'm Evan." He stuck his hand out.

"Pedro," the older man said, shaking the offered hand. His hand was different from Evan's. Hardened and calloused from doing this kind of labor for many years, while Evan had the more delicate hands of a surgeon. If Pedro noticed, he didn't say anything.

The day eventually passed and Evan survived without his back giving out, though he thought that might happen a time or two. At 4:45, the blue van with *Labor Inc* written down the side pulled up, and he climbed gratefully on board.

The driver fought their way through heavy traffic on the way home. Evan didn't care. He leaned his head against the cold window, closed his eyes, and listened to the slow slap of the windshield wipers, the grumbling engine, and commercials playing on the radio station. He soon drifted off.

When they pulled into the Labor Inc. parking lot, Brenda was there with an envelope for each of them.

Evan walked like an old man, half bent over and shuffling along. He accepted the envelope and said, "See you in the morning." He waited until he was a block away to open his pay envelope and look inside. There was a slip of paper detailing what his day's labors had netted him. Eight hours at $1.60 per hour—$12.80. Once the various taxes were taken out, he was left with two five-dollar bills a quarter, and a dime.

Evan started to laugh a little helplessly. He had almost killed himself for ten bucks. He reached into his front pocket and pulled out his roll of bills, realizing that he had added more than a third to his wealth.

He was torn between wanting to get a hot meal and getting back to the Mission to put his time in. He decided that if he gave in to his stomach first, he might very well end up sleeping in a doorway somewhere. He walked the few blocks back to the Mission. It was dark by the time he got there and when he went inside, his heart sank. The place was packed with men trying to get out of the cold.

He found Mike, who took him into another section of the building he hadn't seen before. It was a large laundry room, with three commercial washers and three big dryers. There was a pile of white towels on a big flat table.

"Fold those like this," Mike said, demonstrating how the towels should look. "Then carry them into the shower room and put them away."

"Sure," Evan said. He tried to keep the exhaustion out of his voice. "Then what?"

"That's enough for tonight," Mike said and hurried away.

Evan looked at the small mountain of towels and was sure Mike had taken it easy on him for some reason. This was a much easier task than cleaning the bathroom had been. He set to work and in half an hour was finished folding. He found a yellow laundry cart, stacked the towels in them, pushed them into the shower room and put them away.

Mike saw him come into the main sleeping area and led him to the bed he had used the night before. "This is yours again."

"Thank you, Mike. A bed has never looked so good."

Evan glanced at the clock on the wall. 7:45.

As Mike was turning to leave, Evan stopped him. "Do you think I've got time to run out and get a hot meal?"

"We lock the doors at nine o'clock sharp. If you're back before then, you're good."

Evan wanted to lie down on the bed and not get up until the next morning, but he knew he needed more nutrition than he'd had that day. He forced himself to go back outside and found a little café that was just getting ready to close. The waitress gave him the fisheye when he walked in. No one ever liked a customer appearing five minutes before closing.

"I'll be fast, I promise," Evan said. There was a chalkboard with the special of the day written on it. It was a toasted cheese sandwich, a bowl of tomato soup and coffee for $1.29. "Can I still get the special?"

The waitress nodded and walked to the back of the restaurant.

She reappeared shortly with the soup and sandwich. The bread was still warm from the grill and the cheese dripped down the side. The tomato soup smelled heavenly.

Evan dug in. He had eaten at the best restaurants on the West Coast in his first life, but he had never tasted anything as delicious as this simple dinner. As promised, he ate quickly, laid two singles on the table, and hurried back out.

His back and feet ached, but he felt warmed from the inside out and for the first time that day, he felt full.

He got back to the Mission just a few minutes before another man did the night's Bible reading. The words didn't reach Evan, though.

He was in his own world. It had been a brutally hard day, but he stretched out on the bed, thinking how good that dinner had been.

Chapter Fourteen

Evan didn't sleep any better the second night than he had the first. The constant rise and fall of noise of the Mission was still strange to his ears, so it didn't matter how exhausted he was, his sleep was fitful.

His plan for the next day was simple. Get up early, show up at Labor Inc., and take whatever job they had for the day. Earning ten bucks a day, he wasn't going to get ahead fast, but by staying at the Mission for a bit, he thought he could slowly build his bankroll up to a point where he could actually start what he had set out to do.

That was his plan. As Mike Tyson would say at a future date, *Everybody's got a plan until they get punched in the mouth.*

Evan's punch came as soon as he attempted to roll out of bed a little after 5:00 a.m. He managed to get his feet on the floor, but when he tried to stand up to go to the bathroom, his lower back screamed in protest. He winced and tried to move to find a comfortable position. There was no comfortable position.

His legs felt like lead, his head ached, and every muscle group he had used the day before reminded him of the sins he had visited on them. He took a few staggering steps toward the bathroom, looking like he was in his eighties or nineties instead of his twenties.

I need a shower, he thought. *That will set me right.*

The morning before, he had been a little anxious about getting naked in a room full of strangers. This morning, he was just focused on his struggle to get his underwear off without sending a wave of pain through his body.

One man was already in the shower. Evan took the stall at the other end and cranked the hot water on high. He stepped into the spray with a sigh. Dropping his chin to his chest, he let the water stream over his neck and back. For the first time that day, he was able to stand up nearly straight.

He washed himself quickly as more men had come in behind him and were waiting their turn. He considered joining the back of the line and getting another shot at the blessedly hot water but knew he didn't have time for that. He put his dirty underwear back on without stopping to think about how many days he had worn the exact same clothes. Once he was dressed, he hobbled back out to his bed, sat down, and reached for his shoes.

A stab of agony from his lower back actually made him cry out a little. He gritted his teeth and looked around, hoping no one had noticed. There were a lot of downsides to living in a homeless shelter, but one of the advantages was that no one paid much attention to you. You could have a small breakdown and go unnoticed if you wanted to.

He flopped sideways on the bed and curled his legs up under him, waiting for the throbbing pain to pass. When it finally did, he sat up gingerly and reached for his shoes much more carefully. He managed to get them on, but it was a battle.

When he thought of getting to the firehouse and lifting that heavy sledge or pushing that wheelbarrow up and down the ramp, he knew there was no way he could do it. He didn't want to show up and be unable to work, or worse, do subpar work. He knew he was going to have to take the day off from Labor Inc.

Once he decided that, he felt a little weight off his shoulders. It was like not studying for a test at school, then finding out it was cancelled at the last minute.

Knowing that he didn't have to hurry out the door let Evan relax. He resolved to spend the day doing some of the other things that were on his to-do list instead.

He stretched back out on the bed and did his best to relax his muscles. The noise of early morning at the Mission washed over him. He closed his eyes and when he opened them again, it was 8:45.

Any day that starts with a nap can't be all bad. Still, he knew he couldn't laze the day away. He had things to do and people to see. He needed to take an inventory of how much money he had but didn't think it was wise to flash even a tiny bankroll around. He went into the bathroom, sat in a stall, and pulled his money out.

It didn't take long to count it. Including his change, he had twenty-eight dollars and seventy-two cents. He had been cut loose on the streets of Seattle for three days and he was only down about five bucks from where he had started.

Evan walked into the main room intent on finding Mike and telling him that he would be around more today and that he was happy to help with chores. He walked on stiff legs to the coffee pot and poured himself a cup, then spotted Mike by the entrance, holding his nearly omnipresent broom.

"I'm not going to Labor Inc. today, so I'll be free to help around here. Just tell me what to do."

Mike looked at him and said, "Can't say I'm surprised. I saw you try to put your shoes on a few minutes ago."

Evan realized he hadn't gone quite as unnoticed as he had thought.

"This place won't really empty out until about noon or one. Come back then, and I'll have some jobs for you."

"Thank you, Mike." Evan really looked at him, suddenly curious. He appeared to be in his mid-sixties, with a fringe of white hair and a pair of glasses that didn't quite sit right on his face. Evan was sure that he was probably homeless, too, but he didn't have the same wild eyes or weathered face that many of the men who stayed at the Mission did. Instead, he was always calm and in control. Evan thought he would like to get his story if he got the chance.

"Can you tell me where I can find a second-hand clothing store?"

"St. Vinnie's is over on 4th and Union. They'll have something for you."

Evan wasn't sure what St. Vinnie's was, but he knew where 4th and Union was.

Bolstered by the nap and the coffee, he stepped out onto the sidewalk. A breeze rustled the last of the leaves that had fallen, but it wasn't raining.

Seattle is a city built on a hill and when you travel east or west downtown, you're probably going to be climbing or descending. Normally, that wasn't a big deal—most of the hills weren't that steep—but with the way Evan's legs felt, every step up was painful.

By the time he got to 4th and turned toward Union, he felt the need to lean against the side of a building and rest for a minute.

I guess this work will get me in shape. I would have said I was already in shape when I woke up here, but there's a big difference between walking thousands of steps up and down a hospital corridor and what I had to do yesterday.

When he caught his breath and his inflamed leg muscles settled down, he looked up and saw a sign ahead for St. Vincent de Paul.

As soon as Evan stepped into the thrift store, he knew he was in the right place. Right at the front of the store, there was a decent couch for $5.00, and a table lamp for $1.50. He didn't need furniture, but he knew this place would be in his budget.

Toward the back of the store, there were long racks of clothing, mostly sorted into sizes. Evan spent an hour going through the racks, looking for things that would fit him. None of the clothes were stylish, but that was the last thing Evan was worried about. He wanted warm, practical clothes. He set a budget of $5.00 for this. Not much, but he reminded himself that he would have to work half a day to replace that money in his bankroll.

He found a faded pair of jeans that were still in good shape, two heavy flannel shirts that were a little big, but would do fine, and a bag of white socks that looked new. When he had his small pile of clothes, he knew he needed something to carry them in. He didn't want to be the homeless person carrying his possessions in a plastic bag. He found a backpack that had once had the University of Washington logo on it. The logo was half gone now, but the rest of the bag itself was fine.

The backpack put him fifty cents over budget, but he decided to splurge. There was no underwear for sale, so he would have to look elsewhere for that.

He went to the front counter and the clerk told him that the whole store was ten percent off that day, which brought him in right at his budget.

He smiled ruefully to himself as he realized that the fifty cents he had saved made him happy. There had been a time when he spent lavishly and without consideration.

He slung the pack over his arm and headed back out. He wasn't far from the downtown police station, so he turned in that direction. The officer he had spoken to had said they would call the Mission if they found any information about his car, but he didn't think the case of the missing Galaxie would be high on anyone's priority list. He didn't want to think about the car being recovered and sitting in some tow lot with all his money in it while he broke concrete for $1.60 an hour.

When he got to the station, there was a short line of people in front of him. His stomach grumbled and he decided to get something to eat when he was done with the police.

THE AMBITIOUS LIVES OF EVAN SANDERSON

As he stood, he did small stretches, trying to loosen up his calves, thighs, and lower back. No one paid him any attention. Slightly unusual behavior was unremarkable in the downtown precinct.

After twenty minutes, he stood in front of an officer he hadn't seen before. He had memorized the case number he had been issued, so when he got to the front of the line, he said, "Good morning, I am here to see if there's any news on case number PW402178451."

Apparently, someone rattling off their actual case number was more than slightly unusual, because the man behind the desk turned his head to the side and said, "Hey, Frankie, come here."

When a second man—Frankie, apparently—came over, the first officer said, "Do it again."

"What's that?" Evan asked, slightly flummoxed.

"What you told me before?"

Still unclear on what was happening, Evan said, "I wanted to check and see if there's any news on case number PW402178451."

"Whaddya think of that?" the first officer asked as though Evan was a chicken playing tic-tac-toe.

Frankie was less impressed. He shrugged and wandered away toward a coffee pot.

"Okay," the first officer said. He grabbed a stubby pencil and said, "One more time."

Evan reported the case number for the third time. This time, the desk officer wrote it down. "Gimme a sec."

He left the desk and was gone long enough that a new line began to form behind Evan.

Finally, he came back and said, "You're in luck, Mr. Sanderson. We have your vehicle."

Chapter Fifteen

This stroke of luck made Evan turn his head and say, "Pardon?" His life had felt like it had spun out of control since the three men surrounded him. Now, he might get back on track in one sweet gift from the gods.

"We've got your vehicle. It's being held on our lot out on Pacific Highway."

A lot of things had changed in Seattle in this new world, but Pacific Highway, sometimes shortened to *Pac Highway,* and in stretches called *Aurora Avenue,* or *Old 99,* was the same. Evan knew where it was, but also knew that it was a long stretch of road, and that his vehicle could be close, or many miles away.

"Do you have the address of the lot?"

The officer didn't answer, but instead wrote an address down on a notepad. He tore it off and handed it to Evan. "They're open from nine to five every day."

Evan really wanted to ask *Is there almost three thousand dollars under the seat?* But he knew that was a bad move. He could find out soon enough.

"Thank you very much," Evan said, stuffing the note into his front pocket. He hurried out of the police station feeling lighter than he had in some time. The small backpack bounced against him as he walked and he wondered if maybe he wouldn't need those clothes after all. If all went well, he might have his suitcase back by that night and he could stay in a proper hotel.

The thought of having a real hotel room brought him up short. He had told Mike that he would be back that afternoon to help with chores. But if he got his car, his money, and his clothes, he wouldn't need to stay there that night. He was torn between going back to the Mission and spending some time working, or heading straight out to the impound lot where his car was.

He was too impatient. He needed to check under the seat of his car as soon as possible. That being the case, the next step was figuring out how to get to where his car was. He could hire a cab to take him, but he thought the address was quite a few miles away, and if his money wasn't still there, the fare would be more than he could afford to spend.

He decided to just start walking. Even if it was seven or eight miles, he thought he could get there before it closed. The idea that he could be back on track was overwhelming and he didn't want to wait. He started walking south and eventually made his way over to Pacific Highway.

In another decade, this road would be the hunting ground of the Green River Killer. In 1973, it felt a little sleazy and rundown, with pawn shops, cheap motels, and convenience stores lining both sides of the road and prostitutes gathering at several corners. They ignored Evan as he hurried by. Their potential johns had vehicles of their own.

As he walked, Evan stuck his thumb out, hoping to catch a ride. Traffic was heavy, but no one seemed to be in the mood to pick up a hitchhiker. After he put several miles under his boots, he realized he hadn't eaten all day and stopped at a 7-Eleven. He grabbed a large coffee, a couple of Baby Ruth candy bars, and a package of Ding Dongs. He figured that the carbohydrates would give him energy and the caffeine in the coffee would keep him awake.

Evan checked his watch as he walked. He also checked the addresses on the buildings, trying to estimate how far he still had to go.

He soon realized he was in a race against time. The addresses weren't following fast enough to keep up with the minute hand on his watch. Evan realized that there was a real chance that he could arrive at the lot after it closed. He wasn't at all sure what he would do then, so he picked up his pace.

He missed his deadline by fifteen minutes. By the time he arrived at the lot, darkness had fallen, but there were a dozen poles with strong lights illuminating the parking lot. He hurried to the entrance and found a rolling gate with a chain and padlock on it.

He briefly considered trying to scale the fence. He was consumed with the idea that he might be within a few feet of his money. One glance at the nine-foot fence and the barbed wire on top convinced him that was a bad idea.

He had been so focused on getting to the lot on time, he hadn't paid any attention to what the area looked like.

It was bleak. He had left most of the businesses behind a mile or so before and this was a more industrial, rural area. No stores, no cheap motels, just factories and lots with heavy equipment stored behind imposing walls and fences.

Evan berated himself for being a fool. If he had simply done the right thing and stayed at the Mission one more day, he could have gotten a decent meal and a night's sleep, then started out in the morning. Instead, he was in a bad area after dark with nothing but a bag full of clothes.

In the way it happens so often, that was the moment it began to rain. It was light at first, but the clouds had been dark and ominous all day. Evan knew it could start to pour on him at any moment.

He didn't want to abandon the place without at least *seeing* the Galaxie, though. He walked along the fence line, scanning the vehicles. He finally spotted it clear at the back. It was surrounded by other vehicles, so he couldn't see its condition, but at least it was there.

The rain increased and he knew he had to find some sort of shelter. He saw a bridge that crossed a small river or stream perhaps a hundred yards away. His legs were like lead—he hadn't recovered much from his work the day before—but he hurried as quickly as he could.

When he reached the bridge, he ducked under, which at least got him out of the rain. Much of the area under the bridge was grassy and slick, but at the very top, against the concrete underpinnings, there was a graveled area.

He climbed, slipping and sliding as he went. He finally reached the top, put his back against the concrete, and sighed.

He ran a litany of things he wished he had done differently through his head while he caught his breath. He wished he had just had a little patience and waited a day. Barring that, he wished that he had just taken the leap of faith and hired a taxi. Failing that, he wished, at a minimum, that he had at least bought some extra food at the 7-Eleven. A bag of chips or a candy bar would have really hit the spot right at that moment, and he might have considered committing a felony for a microwaved cup of soup.

Then he remembered that 7-Elevens didn't have microwaves yet.

He stewed in his own regrets, but it was not enough to keep him warm. He pulled his wool cap down over his ears and huddled in his own misery for a bit, then decided to be at least a little more proactive.

He pulled one of the flannel shirts out of the backpack and put it on over his other shirt, then put his jacket back on. He took two pairs of the white socks out of the plastic bag and put two layers on each hand to stop them from freezing. There wasn't much else he could do, so he leaned back and listened to the near-constant droning of tires going across the bridge overhead.

It was a torturously long night. He tried to sleep, but the cold had gotten into his bones and even when he stood up and stomped around, he couldn't get his circulation going. He amused himself by counting the cars overhead for a few hours, but nodded off briefly and lost track.

When the first light of dawn came, Evan was as miserable as he had ever been. He hobbled out from under the bridge and looked back at the car lot, still locked up tight. He glanced at his watch and saw that it was just a few minutes past 6:00 and that he likely had almost three hours left before he could get access to his car.

He spent part of that time fantasizing about how this could play out. He dreamed that he would find his money still under the seat, and that the Galaxie would be in good shape. He even conjured up the idea that there was half a tank of gas left in the old girl. It was a dream; he could create anything he wanted.

A few minutes before 9:00, an old pickup truck rolled up to the gate. A heavy-set man in overalls eased out of the truck, opened the padlock, and swung the gate open wide. He climbed back into his truck and pulled through to a small shack just inside the fence.

Evan was hot on his heels. As the man was unlocking the door to the shack, Evan hurried up from behind, saying, "I'm here to check on my car."

The man in the overalls jumped in surprise, then whirled around to face Evan, his eyes wide. "Where did you come from? I didn't hear a car."

"I walked," Evan explained patiently. "Because my car is in here."

The man seemed to recover his equilibrium and said, "Which vehicle is yours, and do you have some ID?"

Evan fished in his back pocket for his wallet, then produced his Oregon Driver's License. "It's a silver Ford Galaxie. I can see it right over there." He pointed to the spot where he had seen it the night before.

The man nodded and took Evan's license. "That one came in the night before last."

"What kind of shape is it in?"

The man's grin made Evan's stomach sink. He could tell that whatever came next wasn't going to be good.

"Well, it's still got four wheels. They drove it pretty hard and put it away wet, I'd say."

"Can I see it?"

"Sure. I'll need the impound fee first." He opened the door of the shack, stepped inside, and ruffled through some paperwork on his desk. "Not too bad. $42.50."

"What?" Evan almost shouted, his voice strangled. "Someone *stole* my car. I didn't choose to have it put here."

It was obvious that the lot attendant had heard this complaint before. He nodded sympathetically, but said, "It's just the way the system works. The people who took it aren't here to pay the fee."

Evan was reeling. He was near bottom physically after spending the night freezing under the bridge and now he was being told that he would have to pay more money than he had in the world just to *see* his car.

"I don't have it. I don't have that much."

The man dropped the invoice back onto a pile on the desk. "Well, you can come back and get it another day. Most of that money is for the tow, though. There will be another $3.50 every day it sits here. Eventually, they'll just scrap the car to pay the bill."

Evan rubbed a hand over his face, trying to find a solution, but none was forthcoming. "Is there any way I can just go look at it?"

The man looked around as though his boss might be hiding somewhere on the lot and fire him on the spot for breaking the rules. "Not supposed to let anyone see their vehicle 'til they've paid their fees." He grinned again, a little slyly at this point. "If you've got a fiver on you, I'll let you go take a look at it."

Evan shook his head. He'd worked four hours breaking concrete to earn five dollars. He didn't want just to give it to this man. At the same time, he couldn't think of what else to do. He turned his back so the man wouldn't see how much money he had, then pulled a five-dollar bill out of his small bankroll. He handed it to the man reluctantly.

"Go on over," the attendant said with a magnanimous wave. He sat down, seemingly having forgotten about Evan immediately.

Evan hurried over to the Galaxie. He had forgotten to ask for keys but didn't want to go back to the man and get held up for another five bucks. He said a small prayer that the doors were open.

He needn't have worried. Two of the windows—the driver's side front and passenger's side back—were broken out. The Galaxie looked like it had been used in a demolition derby. The small crease that had been in the side now was a huge dent that ran from front fender to back bumper. The passenger door was smashed in, and the hood had been knocked askew and was held down with a piece of rope. Even the trunk had flown open.

The Galaxie had ceased to exist as a practical mode of transportation.

Evan closed his eyes and came to grips with it.

If the money is there, that won't matter that much. I can still make things work.

He went to the back first and saw that the trunk was empty. That wasn't great—all his clothes and any other possessions had been there—but it wasn't as critical as the money that was under the seat.

He hustled around to the driver's side door and saw that it was locked. It wasn't much of a deterrent, as he could just reach in and unlock it.

The door opened with a squeal and Evan dropped to one knee on the wet, muddy ground. He reached a hand under the seat.

His fingers touched the envelope.

He pulled it out triumphantly.

That victory lasted only a moment.

The envelope was empty.

Chapter Sixteen

Evan's head drooped down and he rested his cheek against the upholstery of the Galaxie.

Everything felt very heavy to him at that moment, and he didn't think he had the strength to pick up and go on. And so, he just knelt there, feeling the wet from the grass soaking into his leg.

Twice in his existence, he had winked out in one place and opened his eyes in another.

He wished fervently that this would be the third time. "Smite me, Almighty Smiter," Evan mumbled. That request didn't work. He stayed stubbornly in that place.

After sixty long seconds of feeling sorry for himself and the cruel blow that had been dealt him, he stood up and brushed a bit of mud off his pants leg.

He had left the small bit of security and friendliness that he had found behind in hopes of finding his lost money. He had gambled and lost, but the game was not over.

He trudged back to the shack, already thinking of the long walk back to Seattle, the Mission, and worrying that he had given up another day's work at Labor, Inc. The ten bucks that he could clear there each day wasn't much, but it would keep food in his stomach and allow him to sock away at least a few dollars.

The man in the shack stepped out as Evan approached.

"Pretty rough, eh?"

"Yes." Evan looked the man in the eye and said, "Look, I don't have the money to get it out of impound, so I'm just going to leave it here. I guess you guys will do what you want to with it."

A shrewd expression came over the lot attendant's face. "Listen, I can maybe help you out with that a little. If you want, I can give you something for it if you'll sign a bill of sale over to me."

Evan narrowed his eyes, suspicious now. "What will you do with it?"

"I've got a friend who runs a junkyard. We can scrap it for parts. The engine and interior are still in good shape."

Evan nodded, thinking. His options seemed obvious. Walk away with nothing, or turn a negative into at least a small positive.

"How much?"

"Forty bucks."

A laughable amount of money, really, compared to what he had lost.

It would also more than double the amount of money Evan had to his name. It would give him a few options. If he wanted, he could take a cab to the Greyhound station downtown, then buy a ticket back to Middle Falls. He could apologize to his mother and he knew she would take him in.

He closed his eyes and pictured himself back in his childhood bedroom in his mother's cozy house. There would be food on the table and for the small price of his self-respect, he could start over again.

It was an enticing prospect.

"I'll take it."

The man stepped inside and produced a bill of sale, already filled out.

"Pretty good system you've got here, taking advantage of people who are in trouble."

The man didn't seem offended at the accusation. "I ain't holding a gun to your head. Don't sign it if you don't want, and be on your way, forty bucks poorer. I can let it sit here for a couple of months and maybe get it cheaper at auction. Just trying to help you out."

Evan reached for the paper and pen, held the paperwork against his leg and signed it, handing it back.

"Pleasure doing business with you," the man said. He handed Evan a twenty and two ten-dollar bills.

Evan stuffed the money in his pocket and walked back to the highway. He turned north and with his pack on his back, trudged toward the city.

It took him more than an hour of steady walking to get back to the first convenience store. He paid for a large coffee and poured five packets of sugar into it. He wandered around the store, picked up enough food so that he knew he could put some of it in his pack. That was according to plan.

During his hungry night under the bridge, he had vowed that he would always try to have at least *some* food with him at all times.

Outside the convenience store, he tore open a pack of Twinkies and stuffed one into his mouth. He swallowed it almost without chewing, then bit into the second one. As he stood there, drinking his coffee, eating his junk food, he tried to come up with a new plan.

He had already changed his mind about going back to Middle Falls and throwing himself on the questionable mercy of his mother's good graces. He decided that the misery of living on the street was preferable to the soul-killing apology he would have to give her.

Beyond that, he couldn't think of anything much beyond going back to the Mission tonight, then going to work at whatever hard labor was available the next day. He inhaled a bag of Fritos, finished his coffee, and threw his trash away, then set out on the long walk back to downtown.

He walked for the rest of the morning and into the afternoon. At one point, he noticed that the sole of his shoe had come loose and flapped with each step he took. That was another hit to his bankroll, because he knew he couldn't work outside without decent shoes or boots.

Evan had walked or worked more in these three days than he ever had in his life. That showed when his left hamstring tightened up just as he got back toward the industrial area at the south end of downtown. He limped the rest of the way, doing his best not to slow down much.

He was hungry again by the time he got to the Pioneer Square area, but he walked right past the café where he had gotten the delicious toasted cheese sandwich. It had taken him most of the day to get back. Darkness was falling, which meant the Mission would be filling up.

He was stiff from two days walking and no sleep, but he willed himself to hurry along the sidewalk, moving from side to side, trying to weave through the late afternoon pedestrians.

It was fully dark by the time he reached the Mission, but in early December in Seattle, that happened before 5:00. He knew he was cutting it close, but he desperately hoped that there would still be a bed for him.

He pushed open the door and felt the comforting blast of warm air wash over him. The odd mix of smells—old wood, freshly laundered sheets, and the body odor of so many people—had already become familiar and welcome to him.

He looked around, hoping to find Mike. He saw him at the back of the big room, talking to two other men who were still wearing their heavy coats and wool caps. Evan double-stepped it to them, but didn't interrupt their conversation, which went on for some time. He shifted from foot to foot until he became impossible to ignore.

Finally, Mike said, "What do you want, Evan?"

"I'm hoping for a bed."

"I was hoping that you would come back yesterday and do the work you had promised to do. I held a bed for you, which I'm not supposed to do. I thought I could trust you. Instead, I got in trouble with Marge. She's a stickler for the rules."

Evan considered his situation. An apology was obviously necessary, but how about an explanation? He tried to line that up in his mind, but the whole misadventure, from hearing his car had been recovered to this moment, seemed like too much to explain.

"I'm really sorry, Mike."

Mike didn't say anything, but just stared back at him. He was an even-tempered man, but it was obvious that Evan standing him up had made him angry.

Evan swallowed hard and said, "So, do you have any beds for the night?"

"Nope. Just gave the last two to Charlie and Bill here. There's no room at the inn tonight. We're closing the doors soon, so I'm going to have to ask you to leave." Mike didn't wait for that to happen, but turned his back and picked up the conversation he'd been having with the two other men.

Evan's heart sank at the thought of another night in the freezing cold. At the same time, he knew he had no one but himself to blame. If he had come to the Mission like he had promised, he wouldn't be on the outs and things would have turned out the same with the Galaxie and his money anyway.

Evan's shoulders slumped, but he turned and walked out of the warmth and into the blustery night.

He was more exhausted than he'd ever been. He knew if he could just find a place out of the wind and rain, he'd be able to fall asleep.

He walked until he found a likely doorway that wasn't already occupied. He moved into the farthest, darkest corner and sat down. He didn't know if he should be worried about getting mugged again or not, so he put his pack on his chest with his arms through the loops. When he pulled his knees up, that made a pillow of sorts. Enough of a pillow for him to almost immediately drift off.

That blessed sleep lasted about an hour until he woke up because of a sharp pain in his legs. He opened his eyes and saw a homeless man and woman standing over him, kicking him. Their clothes were rags, they were both missing most of their teeth, and their eyes were rheumy.

Even so, they managed to occupy the moral high ground.

"Get out of here!" the woman shouted, spittle flying from her mouth and hitting Evan in the face. If that hadn't been enough to get Evan moving, another swift kick from her silent partner did the trick. The problem was that both his legs were asleep. When he tried to stand, he just toppled over to one side. That exposed his backside, which earned him another kick.

"Stop!" Evan said, trying to maintain some dignity. "I'm leaving, I'm leaving."

The kicking and spittle-flying mercifully stopped as the couple backed up enough to give Evan a chance to pull himself to his feet. He limped out of the shelter of the doorway and into the full blast of a Seattle windstorm.

"Oh, come on!" It was a plea to the heavens that he was sure would go unanswered. He saw the light of a small café across the street and hastened toward it. The inside was well lit and nearly empty. Evan hurried to a table and sat down.

A waitress in a green uniform came over with a coffee pot and filled the cup to the brim. "If you want something to eat, you'll have to hurry. We close in twenty minutes."

Even glanced at the clock on the wall. It was 7:40. He couldn't be sure what time he had taken shelter in the doorway, but he knew he hadn't gotten much rest.

"No problem. Do you have any pie left?"

"Got a slice of apple with your name on it."

"I'll take that."

The waitress winked at him. "Ice cream is a dime extra, but I'll throw it in for nothing if you can be done by closing time."

"You can count on it."

The waitress hurried back with the pie, a perfect scoop of vanilla ice cream sitting on top.

"Is there an inexpensive place to stay anywhere close to here?"

"Clean or inexpensive. Take your pick, but you can only choose one."

"My budget says *cheap*."

"The Arroyo is nearby. It'll set you back about five bucks. I'd check for bugs in the bedding before I crawled in if I was you, though."

Evan shuddered. For the briefest of moments, an image of the Egyptian cotton sheets that Becky had always kept on their bed flashed through his mind. He forced it away and said, "That's perfect. Thank you."

Even sharing a bed with crawly things was better than getting kicked in the ribs by a homeless person whose domain he had accidentally invaded. He knew he could always sleep in the bathtub, assuming the room had its own bath.

He ate the pie, which was delicious, paid the bill, and was out the door five minutes before closing time. He followed the directions the waitress had given to the Arroyo. It lived up to the image he had in mind for it. The lobby was dark and dank, with a clerk behind a plexiglass window. The Seattle police station might not have needed extra protection in 1973, but the Arroyo did.

A fat man sat behind the plexiglass, listening to a local news-talk radio station.

Evan considered bolting, but knew that he had to get some sleep or he was going to fall over. "How much for a room?"

"Four bucks for the night. Fifty cents extra if you want towels and access to the showers."

Evan laid a five-dollar bill on the counter. "I'll take the deluxe room, thanks."

The man looked at him, checking to see if he was being sarcastic or not. He must have decided he didn't care, because he slipped a small white towel, a packaged bar of soap, and a room key through the small opening in the plexiglass.

There was a room number on the key—316. Evan knew that meant that his room was on the third floor. He looked around for an elevator hopefully, but there was none. He figured he might have just about enough strength to reach the third floor before he collapsed.

He made it to his room and found that, like many things, the Arroyo's reputation was overblown. The room wasn't much. A twin bed, a small nightstand, and a room so small he could almost reach out his hands and touch both walls, but the sheets were clean and the floor was swept.

He dropped his pack on the bed and went down the hall to check out the shower facilities. Those weren't as clean as the ones at the Mission, but aside from the risk of athlete's foot, Evan didn't think he would catch anything. He emptied his bladder, then hurried back to his room.

He lay down on the bed and took a moment to enjoy the fact that the room was warm, there was no wind, and he wasn't being rained on. Best of all, there was a low percent chance that he would be woken up by being kicked.

Evan had no alarm clock, but he used a mental trick he had instilled in himself as a small child. Even as exhausted as he was, he made himself repeat, *I'll wake up at 5:00 a.m.* over and over in his mind. It had never let him down yet.

Interlude
Universal Life Center

The Watcher named Max bent over his pyxis, deep in concentration. Over his shoulder, another Watcher peered into the pyxis.

"Oh hello, Charles," Max said. "I didn't hear you there."

"My apologies. I was just walking by and glanced down at the life you are watching. This is a tricky one, isn't it?"

"It is," Max agreed. "Not his present circumstances, so much as everything else. He's so single-minded, so focused on a single goal, he never takes the time to look inside himself. I'm afraid he may need several lifetimes to become aware."

"That's interesting," Charles said. "May I?"

"Of course," Max said, handing his pyxis to Charles. In the world of the Universal Life Center, Max was a solid middle-class citizen, liked by everyone, loved by most. Charles, on the other hand, was special, and everyone knew it. He was special in that he saw and knew things that no other Watcher did, and he did his best to use those special skills to help others.

Charles took the pyxis and tipped it one way and then the other. He frowned, then gave it a hearty counterclockwise spin. He watched a few scenes unfold, then said, "Oh yes, there it is. That's what is causing this." He shook it slightly and it reverted back to the scene Max had been observing. A young man in his late twenties was walking down a city street.

"What can we do to help him, do you think?" Max asked. "His focus is so keen on a single achievement that he can't see anything else."

Charles tilted the angle so that the scene moved backward. Now the young man was sitting at a desk across from a woman with stiff hair piled on top of her hair. "Oh! Look who it is."

Max leaned closer and smiled. "It's Margenta." His words were soft and kind. "She seems to be doing well in this life."

"You are not assigned to watch her?"

"No," Max said, shaking his head. "I don't know who is watching her."

"No matter," Charles said, bring the pyxis once again to the original scene of the young man walking down the street. He looked up above the image and began to write swirling equations, then wipe them away and try again. "I think there's only one thing for it, then."

"What do you think?" Max asked.

"He is so intent on his goal that he will not understand how empty it is until he has achieved it. Let's give him a small leg up."

Ahead of the young man walked a well-dressed man carrying an attaché. Charles tapped on the pyxis and a strong wind came up, scattering the man's papers everywhere.

"There," Charles said. "I think that's all the help he will need."

Chapter Seventeen

Like it always did, Evan's mental wakeup routine worked like a charm.

Right at 5 a.m., he woke up, ran down to pee, then jumped into the hot shower. That alone felt like it was worth the money he had spent on the room. He dressed in some of his new clothes and finally was able to change everything but his underwear. His goal for the day—aside from working a full shift—was to find a few new pairs of underwear.

When he returned to his room, he looked around with a sense of instant nostalgia. As mean as it was, it was the nicest place he'd had since he had left Portland. He had managed to sleep straight through the night, since there weren't any conversations, snores, or cries from the rest of the homeless.

Evan managed to work for Labor Inc. for five of the next seven days. They didn't seem to hold it against him that he had taken a few days off. This was one of the few benefits of working for them.

Over that week, he worked a variety of jobs and was pleased to find that not all of them were as backbreaking as what he had done on the first day. That week, he worked in a warehouse, stacked wood for an older couple, and even worked in an office hauling boxes from one spot to another. On most of the days, he found himself paired with Pedro, and that was a plus. Having thrown the beginning of his friendship with Mike away, Pedro was the closest thing he had to a friend.

No matter what work he did, the pay was the same. At the end of the day, his pay envelope held ten dollars and change. Every day that it cost him less than that to live, he felt he was gaining on things.

Pedro wasn't someone who needed to talk a lot, but when they sat together eating lunch, he shared a little of his life. He'd had a wife and daughter, but had lost both when he drank too much. Now he was clean, but had lost complete track of them. He worked to live, hoping that he would find them again someday, never thinking that his daughter was now grown and his wife had possibly remarried. It was the slim hope of finding them that kept him going.

When Evan thought about his long-term plan to become wealthy, though, that seemed a distant dream at best, but like Pedro, it kept him going.

He managed to get back in at the Mission, even though Mike showed no interest in doing special favors for him anymore. The first chance he got, he knocked on Marge's door and apologized for what he had done and explained that Mike had only been doing him a kindness that day. He started to explain what had happened and why he hadn't shown up, but Marge held up a hand to stop him.

"You don't need to waste your time explaining. It's in the past. We have rules here for a reason. Dealing with what we do and with the budget we have, we need rules, or we'll descend into chaos. Mike knows that now, and it is forgotten. Those rules will apply to you, just the same as they do to everyone we help. That's all you need to worry about."

Evan knew that was the end of the conversation, so he nodded and left her office. He found Mike and apologized again, then said, "Marge is such a hard case. Is that just her personality?"

Mike looked at Evan as if he was trying to decide how much, if anything, to say. "It's not my place to say. We wouldn't have the Mission without her. You and I would be fighting with someone else to find a place to sleep. Instead, we're here. It ain't much, but it's better than sleeping out there, where everybody seems to hate you just for being alive."

Properly put in his place again, Evan just agreed that was true.

Mike half-turned to leave, then reconsidered. "If you knew the whole story, you wouldn't think she was a hard case. You'd understand. She's had a tougher life than any of us." He nodded to himself, confirming the truth of that statement, but walked away without saying what that tough life had entailed.

Evan knew that he was never going to get where he wanted to be by working dead-end jobs for ten bucks a day, but losing everything on his first day in Seattle had put him on a different path.

He knew he could have found a way to catch on to the lower rung of the medical community. He did have his medical degree, after all, and with a few phone calls or letters, he could have proven that. That would have been enough to at least get him on as an aide at one of the local hospitals or clinics.

He didn't want to do that any more than he had wanted to stay in Middle Falls and finish his residency.

Was that job easier than the manual labor he was currently doing? Of course. For his own reasons, it simply wasn't something he wanted to do. He knew there was something better, he just didn't know what it was yet.

He caught his first real break several weeks later. It was the week before Christmas. Seattle was in the grips of a minor storm, which meant that there were a few inches of snow on the ground, and the temperatures were near freezing.

Evan decided to make his weekly splurge. He went back to the Arroyo and put his money down for a room that included a shower. He had bought a used copy of Heinlein's *The Door into Summer* off a rack at a drugstore and was planning on spending the day lying on his bed, reading and watching the occasional snowfall.

The book turned out to be a fast read, and he blitzed through it in just a few hours. There was no TV in the room, and he wasn't willing to spend the money to go see a movie, so he decided to bundle up and go back to the drugstore for another book to read.

He had bought a used heavier coat and gloves. He put them on and walked down the stairs to ground level, then turned right toward the drugstore.

He had only walked half a block when a gust of wind stirred up. Ahead of him, a well-dressed man lost his grip on a sheaf of papers and they scattered around the sidewalk.

Evan hurried ahead and scrambled around, chasing the papers. When he was done, he had a stack of them and turned toward the man, handing them over.

"A little worse for wear, but not too bad," Evan said, brushing a few snowflakes off the paper.

The man, who was tall and slim, was wearing a suit and overcoat, his gray hair perfectly combed even in the wind. "Hey, thanks, friend." He reached in his pocket and pulled out a wad of bills. He peeled off a couple of singles and held them out.

Evan held his hand up and shook his head. "Don't worry about it. What kind of a person would I be if I didn't help or took money for doing so?"

The answer seemed to surprise the man. He turned his head slightly and took Evan in.

Evan wasn't dressed sharply like the man, but he was dressed warmly and didn't look homeless either. He had mastered the art of looking okay even while living mostly on the street.

"Say, do you have slacks and a white shirt?"

"Sure," Evan said. He didn't, but he knew he could get them, and something about the question raised his hopes.

The man put the papers into a valise, then plucked a business card out of his pocket and tapped it against his other hand, as if deciding on something. "Do you have a job?"

"Yes, but I'm always hoping to find a better one."

"That's the right answer, isn't it?" The man looked closer at Evan. "You're older than I usually hire, but you've got the right look." He handed the card over. "I'm William Gatling. I'm the General Manager of the Renaissance."

"The restaurant?" Evan's eyebrows shot up. It was one of the nicest in Seattle. "What kind of a job are you talking about?"

"Parking cars," William said with a smile. "I know it doesn't sound like much, but my valets make more than a lot of my other employees. I have a Renaissance jacket if you have the slacks and a white shirt. Are you interested?"

It didn't take Evan any time at all to answer. The thought of parking cars every day was much preferable to the physical labor he had been doing.

"Yes. When can I start?"

William smiled again. "Good attitude. Why don't you come in tomorrow around two and we'll fill out your paperwork. You can start tomorrow night if you want. The address is on the card."

"No need," Evan said without thinking. "I've eaten there many times."

That was true, as far as it went, but that had been in another lifetime. It had been one of the places he and Becky had celebrated birthdays and promotions.

William nodded, narrowing his eyes. It was obvious that he thought he would have recognized the young man standing in front of him if that was true. Evan made a mental note to be more careful. He got the idea that this man was not a fool.

"Thank you for the opportunity. I'll be there."

William waved, then walked away.

Evan couldn't wipe the grin off his face. He forgot about buying a book and started walking. Buying a decent pair of slacks and two white dress shirts would put a bit of a dent in his bankroll, but he was sure it would be worth it.

He turned toward St. Vincent De Paul, hoping to find what he needed used. He found a decent pair of dark slacks there that were just a bit too big around the waist, but he knew he could cinch his belt a little tighter. There were no white dress shirts in his size that didn't come with rips or yellow stains around the collar, though.

He paid for the slacks, which were only a dollar, then turned north toward the Pike Place Market, where Penney's was. When he had lived in Seattle, he had done most of his shopping at Nordstrom or the Bon Marché, but he knew that Penney's and Sears were more in his budget at the moment.

He felt slightly out of place walking around the well-lit store. Everyone shopping there looked comfortably middle class, which Evan knew was several notches above where he was at that moment. He went to the men's department and looked first on the closeout rack.

No luck there. Evan's size in such a popular shirt type would likely never filter its way down to be on clearance.

He swallowed hard and moved to the regularly priced goods. He was amused to find some wild choices in what he thought of as such a staid and conventional retailer. Wide collars and bold colors seemed to be the order of the day.

"Can I help you, sir?"

Evan turned to see a matronly woman with half-glasses perched on the end of her nose. He lifted up the sleeve of a brightly colored shirt helplessly and said, "I'm just looking for several white shirts. Business wear."

"Of course, sir. This is our young man's fashion section. You're looking for our men's section. Come with me." She led him to a wall at the back of the department. She looked at him appraisingly, then plucked out two shirts wrapped in clear plastic. "These will fit you. If for any reason they don't, just bring them back with your receipt."

Evan glanced at the price tag and swallowed hard. They were $4.99 each. These two shirts would set him back a full day's wage at Labor Inc.

"That's perfect. Thank you."

Evan paid for the shirts, then slipped the plain St. Vinnie's paper bag inside the J.C. Penney bag. He walked half a dozen blocks in the falling snow until he saw the Renaissance. It was one of the few things that looked unchanged from when he had last seen it in his first life.

The Renaissance was high concept, as well as high class. The front of the restaurant looked like a lovely castle, with a false front showing soaring turrets that rose up into the sky. Evan had no interest in going inside. He knew that a nice dinner there would set him back a week's wages. But if he *had* gone in, he was sure he would have found thick carpeting, a dimly lit dining area where the movers and shakers of Seattle could dine with some privacy, and knock-off versions of famous artworks. His favorite had always been a painting of a wandering troubadour who looked a lot like Jimi Hendrix, and whose lute was played left-handed. If you looked closely, all the paintings had little jokes worked into them.

To the right of the building, there was a short driveway and a lighted sign that read *Renaissance Valet*.

Evan watched a sports car pull up and an older man and a young woman got out. The man tossed the keys to a young man who hustled up, then walked arm in arm into the restaurant with his date. Or secretary. Or whoever she was.

The young man—who was indeed wearing dark slacks, a white shirt, and a deep burgundy jacket—jumped behind the wheel and roared off into the alley. Evan glanced at his watch. Five minutes later, the young man returned at a jog and hung the keys on a board.

That told Evan that the cars were parked at least a block or so away, but not terribly far. He walked back to the Arroyo, once again timing himself. It took him twenty minutes to walk from the Renaissance to where he was staying.

He unpacked the shirts from their packaging and frowned at the deep-set wrinkles. He pulled the pins and cardboard out and flapped them, but the wrinkles remained. He didn't have an iron, but there was always what his college roommate had called *the bachelor's iron*.

He hurried down the hall to the shower, turned it on as hot as it would go, then hung the shirts just outside the stall. His twenty-first century sensibilities balked at wasting water like that, but he was determined to make a good first impression.

That task accomplished, he realized that, as so often happened, he hadn't eaten anything that day. He went back to the diner a few blocks away and ordered a club sandwich and fries.

All in all, it had been an expensive day, paying for a night at the Arroyo, buying the new clothes, and now having a full meal instead of grabbing something from a small store.

Even so, walking back to his room, Evan felt lighter than he had in quite some time. If he could get away from killing himself every day doing manual labor and earn more money, he would be back on the path to what he wanted to accomplish.

Chapter Eighteen

Evan was at the Renaissance at 1:45 the next day. William hadn't told him where to go, so he just walked into the main entrance. An elegant woman with silver hair piled on top of her head stood behind a tall, narrow desk.

"Just one today?"

"Oh, I'm not here to eat. I met William yesterday and he hired me to be a valet." Evan hesitated. "At least, I think he did." Another hesitation. "I'm almost sure he did."

The woman smiled and said, "If you're here and know his name, I'm sure he did." She pointed to a door at the back of the lobby. "Go through that door, then down the hall to the second door on the left. Linda will process your paperwork and get your jacket."

The door opened behind Evan and a whoosh of cold air came in. He knew that would be actual customers, so he hurried to the door, down the hall and knocked on the door with the sign that read *Personnel*.

"Come in."

Evan pushed his head in and said, "William said you would help me with my paperwork. I'm supposed to be a valet."

Linda was perhaps a few years older than Evan, with long dark hair and cat eye glasses. She shook her head in mock frustration. "I swear, he never tells me anything. I might as well be a mushroom back here."

"Kept in the dark and fed a bunch of..." Evan stopped, realizing where that sentence was taking him. "Baloney?" he finished lamely.

"Yeah," Linda said with a laugh. "Baloney." She stood up and walked to a file cabinet, pulled out several sheets of paper, and handed them to Evan. "We're supposed to have an application on file for everyone we hire, so fill that out, then your tax information." She looked at Evan and said, "You're older than most of the valets we hire."

"That's what William said. Do you think that's going to be a problem?"

"Not if you can keep up. Those young guys out there hustle."

"Last week I was breaking up concrete and hauling it in a wheelbarrow. I'm ready to transition to parking cars and running back and forth."

"Sounds like a good career choice." She pointed to a small desk in the corner of the office. "You can sit there and fill out the paperwork."

Fifteen minutes later, Evan found himself back in the hallway, the Renaissance's newest valet. Linda had given him a burgundy jacket like he had seen the day before, which felt a bit like a uniform.

He went to the door at the far end of the hall and stepped out into the alley at the back of the restaurant. He walked around the corner and saw two young men standing next to a heater, rubbing their hands together to keep warm.

They turned and saw Evan. One of the men smiled and waved him over, while the other scowled. The friendly man held his hand up and said, "Nick. Valet extraordinaire."

Evan waved back and said, "Evan. Nice to meet you." He looked at the other man, who was still scowling at him. Nick punched the second man in the shoulder and said, "Don't worry about Vince. He's not the friendliest guy, but when the chips are down, he'll be nowhere in sight."

Vince shared his dirty look with Nick. "We don't need anyone else. We keep rotating this fresh meat in over and over. They take a share of our tips for a few days, then they disappear." He looked more closely at Evan and said, "And now they're hiring old men, to boot." He made a disgusted sound, then turned and walked away while lighting a cigarette.

"Seriously," Nick said quietly. "Don't worry about him. He's like that with everyone."

"No problem. Can you tell me how we're supposed to do things?"

"Couldn't be any easier. When someone pulls up, you give them a card from here. Tear off the bottom and attach it to the keys they give you. Drive their car over to our garage, then hustle back here. When they come out, reverse the process. If they see you hustling, they like that and it means better tips. That's why we always take off running."

A blue Ford sedan pulled into the space. Vince, who had been all dark clouds and rain, suddenly turned sunny. "Good afternoon, sir. Just you this afternoon?"

"I'm meeting someone. Can you keep this somewhere close? We won't be here all day."

"Yes, sir. I'll park it right at the front."

As soon as the man had gone into the restaurant, Vince's expression clouded over again. He slid behind the wheel of the car, tuned the radio to KJR AM, and pulled away.

"Next car, watch what I do, then ride with me to the garage. That's about all there is to it. This is a job that requires fast feet, but not much in the way of thinking."

"Sounds perfect to me. How many of us are there?"

"There are four others that aren't here right now, so you'll be the seventh. Someone is on duty any time the restaurant is open. It gets a little busy about lunchtime, but we really get cranking around six or seven. We have to stay until the last vehicle is claimed, which is usually around eleven or a little after. On holidays, it's all hands on deck, and we're constantly running. We're closed on Christmas, but these next few weeks we'll be slammed with office Christmas parties and the like."

"Sounds like I got here at a good time." Evan was curious about how much they earned in a shift, but he felt like he would find out soon enough.

A minute later, another car pulled in. Nick stepped forward, handed the man a card, and gave him a quick salute. Once the man was in the restaurant, Nick nodded his head toward the passenger seat and said, "Hop in."

"Do we salute all the customers?"

"No," Nick said with a grin. "We call him *The Colonel*, but I have no idea what his rank was. He's former military, though. You'll get to know the regulars soon enough. The Colonel comes in for lunch at least twice a week. We think he might be sweet on Marla, the maître 'd." Nick pulled smoothly away, turned down the alley, then right. They drove down another block then turned down into a basement parking area. There were large signs on both sides of the entrance that read, *Renaissance Valet Parking Only! Violators will be towed at their expense.*

"This is our home away from home."

Evan looked around and saw that there were plenty of spots to park. "So when someone asks to have their vehicle parked at the front, where do we put it?"

"Wherever we want. They'll never know. A lot of guys just like to throw their weight around and we let 'em. It's good for our tips. We get paid minimum wage, but make most of our money hand to hand." They slid into a spot and climbed out. "If you walk back, it takes about seven minutes. If we hustle, we can make it in half that. Keep up with me."

Nick took off up the ramp at a run. Not a full out sprint, but a nice steady pace. Evan took off after him and was a little out of breath by the time they turned the corner again.

"How old are you?" Evan asked.

"Twenty-one. You?"

"Twenty-seven. Never thought that was old until now."

"Don't worry, you'll get your breath soon enough," Nick said.

Both Vince and Nick were slim and looked like they could run all day.

There were no cars for a few minutes, then Vince took the next one. When he was gone, Nick said, "We're supposed to take turns parking. Sometimes Vince likes to jump the line on new guys, though. Just a heads-up."

Evan nodded and wondered to himself what he would do if the young kid *did* try to do that to him. He supposed he would just let him get away with it. It probably wasn't worth the hassle.

Things were slow for the next few hours. The lunch rush was done, and since the Renaissance didn't have a standalone bar, there weren't a lot of late-afternoon customers.

Inside, the line cooks prepped, the floors were vacuumed, silver polished, windows washed, and anticipation built.

Outside, Evan, Nick, and Vince neatened up their already neat area and mostly tried to keep warm. Typically, there would have only been two of them on shift through the afternoon, but Linda, who made all the schedules, hadn't known Evan was going to be there.

Shortly after five, cars began to arrive regularly. There was never much of a rush to park the cars. They didn't get tipped then. Things got a little more competitive when diners came out to collect their cars.

As Nick said, he and Vince knew the regulars. That meant they knew who was likely to slip them a five spot, who might give them a couple of quarters, and who might stiff them altogether.

By 6:30, things were flying. The early dinner crowd was leaving, the first office Christmas party was arriving, and Joey, a fourth valet had arrived.

There was plenty of business to keep them all busy, but as the evening progressed, Evan noticed that Vince did exactly as Nick had said he would. He would take his turn, then do everything in his power to jump back to the head of the line, especially when Evan was in front.

That irritated Evan, but he did his best to stay calm and let things work out on their own.

Vince returned with a Cadillac and pocketed a three-dollar tip, then got to the back of the line. Evan was next up when a well-dressed couple came out the double doors and headed toward them.

"You got lucky, man," Nick said. "That's Mr. Everson. He's our best tipper. He gave me a twenty a few weeks ago!"

In a flash, Vince moved past Evan, intent on collecting the big tip.

Evan was not much of a fighter. He had never taken any self-defense lessons or studied any of the martial arts. He had graduated from medical school, though, and that had included extensive studies of anatomy. He knew exactly where the peroneal nerve was, for instance.

As Vince tried to whiz past him, Evan slashed his knee out, hitting that nerve dead on.

Vince's momentum carried him forward a few feet, but that leg had become useless and he pitched forward, completely out of control. He was so surprised that he didn't reach out to catch his fall and slammed face-first into the blacktop. He hit his nose first, opening a long, bloody gash, then bounced and hit his mouth, chipping his front tooth.

That was much more damage than Evan had intended to inflict, but he was a student of medicine and anatomy, not the finer points of physics and a body in motion.

Behind him, Nick said, "Whoa!"

Mr. Everson and his wife stood back, unsure of what was happening.

Evan turned to Nick and said, "You handle them. I'll help Vince."

Everything had happened so quickly that Nick wasn't at all sure what had gone down, but he knew that the most important thing was to take care of the customer. He hurried past Evan, who was kneeling beside the fallen Vince.

Nick took the ticket from Mr. Everson and headed off for the car at a dead run.

Evan rolled Vince over and inspected the damage.

His nose was almost certainly broken, he had a chipped tooth, and road rash that started at his forehead and ran to his chin. It looked horrible, and Vince's face was likely to look like something from a horror movie for quite some time, but it was nothing too serious.

Vince sat up, saying, "What the hell happened?" His voice sounded extra nasal.

"Come on, man, let's get you out of the way." Evan reached under Vince's arms and helped him over to the valet station, where he was at least slightly hidden from view. He leaned him up against the wall and said, "Tip your head back a little."

Just then, Joey ran back from parking a car, looked down and said, "Holy shit!" under his breath. "What happened?"

"Vince tripped. Do we have a first aid kit? I've got some training."

"Inside. I'll go get it." He took off like a shot.

There was nothing else Evan could do for Vince at the moment, so he stood, put his hands in his pockets and tried to whistle in a way that said, "Nothing to see here, folks."

A minute later, Nick pulled up with the Everson's car. He helped Mrs. Everson in, then hurried over to Vince just as Joey came back with a first aid kit.

Vince was starting to focus on the world again, but still wasn't operating at a hundred percent.

Evan accepted the first aid kit, laid it on the pavement and flipped it open. He nodded as he took an inventory of what was inside. It was a basic kit but had what he needed.

"Vince, listen." Evan's voice was calm and in control—a voice he had used for decades of being a doctor. "You've got a broken nose. It would be better to fix it sooner rather than later. I won't touch it if you don't want me to, though. I'm sure somebody can run you up to Harborview and get it fixed, if you'd like."

"We don't get insurance," Nick muttered in Evan's ear.

There was fear in Vince's eyes as he looked from Evan to Nick and back again. He swallowed hard and said, "Go ahead."

Evan nodded and with the steady hands of a surgeon, he reached out, placed his hands on either side of Vince's nose and made one quick adjustment.

There was a definite popping sound that made both Joey and Nick wince and turn away.

"Mother pussbucket!" Vince screamed. "What the hell?"

Evan moved back a bit, looking at his handiwork. The nose had been angled to the left, but now it was relatively straight again. He unrolled some gauze and stuffed some up into each nostril. "It'll be better if you breathe out of your mouth for a little while."

Evan removed the antiseptic spray from the kit, found a clean gauze pad, and sprayed it. "This is going to hurt a little, but I've got to clean you up or it's going to get infected."

"Is it going to hurt worse than whatever you just did to my nose?"

Evan considered that. "No, probably not."

"Go ahead."

Evan expertly cleaned the wound, causing Vince as little pain as he could. "It's going to be tough to bandage that without wrapping up your entire face. How are you getting home?"

"The bus."

"Good. You shouldn't be driving right now. You might have a concussion. When you get home, don't go directly to sleep. If you start to feel nauseous or dizzy, you should go into the ER whether you've got insurance or not. Tomorrow, you'll need to go to the store, get some antiseptic and keep it clean until it begins to scab over. That'll take a couple of days. You should probably take it easy until then."

Two cars pulled up in quick succession, and Joey and Nick ran to help them. That was the moment that William Gatling came out through the doors. He had obviously heard that something had happened in the valet area.

"What's going on here?"

"Just a trip and fall," Evan said. "I've got a little medical training, and he's fixed up for the moment."

William looked into Vince's eyes. "Do you think you need to go see a doctor?"

"No, sir," Vince answered.

William looked at Evan. "When Joey or Nick gets back, have them bring my car around." He looked down at Vince and said, "I'll give you a ride home. I don't want you scaring the other bus riders."

Evan was impressed again at the man's kindness and the fact that he knew his employees well enough to know how they got home.

"Come inside and tell the maître d' when the car gets here."

Yes, sir," Evan answered.

When Joey and Nick returned, Evan passed on the message about Mr. Gatling's car, and Joey ran to retrieve it.

Nick reached into his pocket and pulled out a wad of bills. He counted off five singles and handed them to Evan.

"What's that for?"

"Mr. Everson tipped me ten bucks. I'll split it with you."

"Cool," Evan said. "And thanks."

Being one valet short, Evan, Nick, and Joey ran themselves ragged between then and closing time.

By the end of the night, Evan was exhausted, but happy. He didn't know what the future held between him and Vince, whether there would be more trouble or not. What he did know was that when his shift was over, he had thirty-five dollars in his pocket. He thought that when he got the hang of things, he'd probably make forty bucks a night or so.

That night, he was so happy and felt so rich that he spent forty cents to ride the Metro bus back to Pioneer Square.

He didn't even go by the Mission. He knew it would be full, and that was fine. He went back to the Arroyo and paid for two nights in advance.

Evan felt like he was on his way.

Chapter Nineteen

It was incredibly busy at the Renaissance between Evan's first day and New Year's Eve.

There were two and sometimes three different Christmas parties held at the restaurant each night, while still trying to fit in the regular customers.

Evan soon learned the system and his muscles adjusted to a lot of running and no lifting.

Vince was out for more than a week after his fall. Even when he did come back, William told him to do his best to stay out of the line of sight of customers so he wouldn't scare them. That obviously cut into his tips and increased everyone else's.

After a few days of that, Evan pitched the other valets on the idea of each of them taking ten percent of their tips each night and giving it to Vince. It was only four or five dollars from each of them, but added up to enough to keep Vince afloat.

No one ever asked Evan if he had tripped or knocked Vince down on purpose. It all happened so fast that not even Vince himself remembered what had happened. Once he came back to work, his attitude had changed. He was more wary and cautious about things—especially around Evan.

Evan had stopped staying at the Mission and had begun paying for a room at the Arroyo by the month, which saved him a buck a day.

The day before Christmas, Evan wasn't scheduled to work until three in the afternoon. He sat on the twin bed in his room and carefully counted his money. Where once he thought he would be down to zero, he now had over three hundred dollars to his name. It was a far cry from the money he'd had when he had first rolled into town, but he had a new gift now—the gift of perspective.

When he had arrived in Seattle, he had accepted that he had money, that he had always had money, and that he would always have money. That first night in the city had rearranged his perspective. Somehow that three hundred dollars made him feel much more snug and secure than the three thousand had.

That morning, he hopped on the bus to Pike Place Market and bought huge bags of apples, pears, and oranges. He found a stall that sold homemade candies and bought five pounds of them. He even picked up one of the fresh flower bouquets that were always on sale at the market. He was heavily burdened when he got back on the Metro bus and headed for the Mission.

He knew he wasn't in a position to repay the debt that he owed, but he wanted to do something. He felt a bit like Santa when he walked in with his bags of fruit, candies, and flowers. He looked around for Mike but didn't see him. He went to the back of the big room and, straining under the weight of the bags, knocked on the office door. He pushed in without waiting.

Marge was sitting at her desk.

"Ho, ho, ho," Evan said, but the greeting trailed off when he saw her pinched face and red-rimmed eyes. "Everything okay here at the Mission?"

When Marge met his eyes, she shook her head and fresh tears ran down her cheek. "Mike's dead."

Whatever Christmas cheer Evan had evaporated. He sat down hard on the chair opposite Marge.

"What happened?"

"We're not sure. He got hit by one of the Metro buses yesterday. We don't know if he stepped in front of it, or if he was pushed, or just fell off the curb."

Evan set the bags on the ground, forgotten.

He did something he would have thought he was incapable of. He stood up and walked around the desk and reached out to Marge. It was like hugging a board, but he didn't let go. Finally, she patted his arm and said, "But life goes on, doesn't it? Have you brought us something?"

He reached down and picked up the flowers. "These were for you."

"Are they not for me anymore?"

"They still are, they just don't feel like much now." He looked at the other bags on the floor and said, "This is just something for everyone here. Some fruit and candies."

"I'll hand them out tomorrow for Christmas. I know it will mean a lot to everyone." She paused, then said, "I'm glad to see you doing so well."

So well. Evan was a car runner for a restaurant and lived in one of the worst hotels in Seattle. But still, he knew Marge was right. By comparison with where he had been just a few weeks before, he was living a successful life.

THINGS SLOWED DOWN at the Renaissance in January. There were too many valets for the number of cars that came through on every shift and Evan was sure he could see the handwriting on the wall. He figured it would be *last in, first out*, and he had been the last in.

It didn't happen that way. Joey's girlfriend moved out of state to take a job and he decided to follow her, then another valet named Otto got accepted into a culinary arts school in San Francisco. Thanks to the money he had made being a valet at the Renaissance, he was able to afford it.

That meant that Evan could live in the lifestyle that he had become accustomed to—a room at the Arroyo, regular meals, and riding the bus to and from work—and still manage to sock money away.

As 1973 had crossed over to 1974, he felt the pressure to increase his bankroll in order to meet the goal he had set for himself, which would come due in just two years. He did the math and realized that if he continued to work at the Renaissance for those years, he would almost certainly not have enough money to accomplish what he wanted.

He didn't really have an alternate plan, though, so six days a week, he showed up at the restaurant, kept his nose down, and worked hard.

Evan and Nick became friends, though there was quite a difference in their lifestyles. Nick still lived at home and poured most of the money he made into fixing up his 1972 Chevy Nova or taking his girlfriend on dates.

In the spring of that year, Nick arrived at work flushed with excitement. "I called and put my notice in this morning," he announced to Evan.

"Why in the world would you do that?"

"Got something bigger on the line. My uncle in Alaska is first mate on a crabber that sails out of a town called Seward. He says I can make a year's salary in just a few months. I think if I work through the season there, I might be able to afford to buy a house when I get back."

That dream seemed so distant to Evan that it caught him off guard. He was still happy to be able to afford a room at the Arroyo.

"Congratulations, man," Evan said. "Sounds like you've got a plan."

"You know that means you'll probably end up as the head valet, then."

"How much more does that pay?"

"Ten cents an hour."

"What will I do with all that extra cash?" Evan wondered.

Nick's prediction came true. A few days later, Linda asked Evan to come into her office and offered him the opportunity to be the head valet. There wasn't really much responsibility that went with the role, essentially just making sure the Renaissance's standards were upheld and finding a replacement if someone called in sick.

Evan accepted and walked back to the valet area, where he was greeted by the other valets on duty, down on one knee, heads bowed.

"You guys are hilarious," Evan said.

His run at the top of the valet food chain at the Renaissance was short-lived. After just a few days, Nick showed up for one of his last shifts, grinning broadly. He hurried to Evan and said, "Knock, knock."

"Okay, I'll play along. Who's there?"

"Opportunity."

"Opportunity who?"

"The opportunity to come with me and work on a crab boat in Alaska, that's who!"

Evan blanched. That was something he had not anticipated. He immediately thought of what he was hoping to accomplish and how much money Nick had said they could make in a single season in Alaska. He might be able to accomplish his goal after all.

"I'm in."

"Of course you're in! You'd be crazy not to be in!"

"How sure are you about this? I don't want to quit my job and then be out on the street."

"As sure as I can be. My uncle thought they only needed one more deckhand, but somebody who works for him got a chance to be first mate for someone else and he jumped at the chance. The spot is yours if you want it. I told him what a great guy you are."

In his first life, Evan had followed a single path from school to career, never able to consider anything else. In the here and now, he enjoyed his job at the Renaissance and felt like he was fairly compensated. He knew that if he was going to meet his ambitious financial goals, though, he was going to have to make a switch.

"I'll give Linda my notice right now. When do we leave?"

Nick grinned. "Uncle Bill said he'd send me a ticket for a flight that leaves next week. When I told him about you, he said you'd have to buy your own ticket, but he can pick us both up at the airport."

Buying a ticket to Alaska would take a good-sized chunk of Evan's bankroll, but he didn't hesitate. He marched into Linda's office and told her that he was quitting and could only give her a week's notice.

She leaned back in her chair and looked at him. "We give you a raise and you quit, huh? That's a new one."

"Got a chance to catch on with a fishing boat in Alaska."

"That's a lot of money, but it can be dangerous."

"I'm not afraid to die." Having done it twice already, that was true.

"You don't have to be in a hurry to do it, though," Linda said. "But we often find out that someone has quit when they just don't show up anymore, so a week is fine. Good luck, Evan. It's been nice having you here and I've only ever heard good things about you. If the fishing thing doesn't work out for you, you're welcome back here."

"Tell William I appreciate the opportunity, please. It's helped me a lot."

It wasn't as easy to buy an airplane ticket in 1973 as it was in the twenty-first century. He considered trying to call the airline directly to make a reservation, but with no credit card, he wasn't sure how that would work.

Instead, the next day he went to a travel agent and gave them the flight number that Nick had provided. Booking that close to departure cost him a little more, but for under two hundred dollars, he had his ticket.

The next few days flew by. On the day before he left, he stopped by the Mission again. Marge was once again behind her desk and the thought occurred to him that she might never leave that spot.

"Just want to let you know that I'm leaving town. I got a chance to go up north and work on a fishing boat."

"I've heard that's dangerous. But then, sometimes just crossing the street can be dangerous, can't it? Thank you for letting me know. Usually people just disappear and I never know what happened to them. If I think of you, I'll picture you on the deck of a ship, being tossed to and fro by large waves."

"I'm feeling a little seasick just thinking about it."

Evan wasn't sure what he would need for his new life as a fisherman, but he went to St. Vinnie's one last time. He bought a duffel bag and some heavy work clothes. He packed everything he had to his name in the duffel and spent one last night at the Arroyo.

In the morning, Nick and his parents picked Evan up in front of the hotel and drove him to Sea-Tac Airport.

His new life was waiting.

Chapter Twenty

Evan had been to Alaska exactly one time in his first life, and that was when Becky dragged him along on the Alaskan cruise. Beyond getting off the ship for lunch or dinner, he had never actually set foot in the state.

He didn't have much of an idea what to expect, then, when their plane touched down at the airport in Anchorage, nicknamed *the crossroads of the world*. In giving up a good steady job and opting for a potential bigger payoff, Evan had jumped off the deep end of the pier, not knowing if a net would appear to catch him or not.

On the flight out of Sea-Tac, Evan let Nick have the window seat. It was Nick's first time on an airplane, while he had flown dozens of times going on vacation with Becky or being flown in to speak at medical conventions. He found himself leaning across Nick and looking through the window as they flew over the towering mountain peaks. He soon figured out that the version of Alaska he had seen on the cruise had little to do with the reality of the state.

When they got off the plane, Nick pointed ahead at a short, bald man dressed in jeans and an old work coat. If there was a family resemblance between Nick and his uncle, Evan couldn't see it.

"Hey, boy!" Bill said when he greeted them. "You've sprouted up." He looked at Evan and shook his hand. "Bill Tripton."

"Evan Sanderson. Thank you for giving me the opportunity."

Bill squinted a little at him and Evan saw that though he was probably only in his mid-forties, his face was weathered.

"Son, I'm not giving you anything. You'll either earn it, or you'll find yourself back on dry land so fast your head will spin."

Evan grinned. "That's the way I like it."

"Then we're going to do all right."

They grabbed their luggage and headed out of the airport. There was bright sunshine and the temperature was in the upper fifties—about what it had been back in Seattle.

"Warmer than I thought it would be," Nick said.

"No igloos, either" Bill said with a wink. "Come on, I'm parked this way."

Ten minutes later, they were moving through the modest traffic of a small city, which is what Anchorage was in 1973. It had a population that had barely reached fifty thousand. Even so, one out of every six people who lived in Alaska called Anchorage home.

They made one stop at a large grocery store. When they pulled into the parking lot, Bill said, "We go out and set the pots tomorrow. We'll be gone for a couple of weeks on this first trip, so I've got to pick up the grub."

The grub seemed to mostly be huge packages of meat. Bill dropped twenty pounds of hamburger into the cart, then big packages of pork chops, roasts, and whole chickens.

He winked at Nick and said, "We won't let you starve, at least."

Bill seemed to shop indiscriminately. He never referred to a shopping list, but just pushed up and down each aisle, grabbing dozens of cans of soup, large quantities of lunch meat, boxes of cereal and loaves of bread. When he was done with his assault on the store, their cart was piled high.

Evan goggled at some of the prices he saw. A loaf of bread was only 29 cents in Seattle, but was 69 cents here. Everything he saw was likewise inflated. He understood why people worked hard for a few months, then took their earnings to what Alaskans called *the outside* to spend it. He was glad that he would be staying onboard the ship. He was certain that he wouldn't be able to afford to pay the cost of rent if the price of groceries was any indication.

They threw the groceries in the back of Bill's old pickup and left the city behind. Nick sat in the middle of the bench seat, which left Evan with the window. When they left the city, they passed Turnagain Arm, a section of Cook Inlet. The blue water sparkled in the sunlight of an early June afternoon and Evan thought he had never seen a more beautiful place.

They passed through small towns named Moose Pass, Bear Creek, and Crown Point before arriving in Seward. If Anchorage was a small city, Seward barely deserved to be called a town. The *Welcome to Seward* sign said it had a population of 1,596 hearty souls.

They turned off the highway before they got to the town itself and dropped down to the harbor. Bill parked the truck in a large gravel lot. Evan jumped out, slung his duffel over his shoulder, and staggered a little under the weight of three grocery bags.

"Don't kill yourself, boyo," Bill said. "Leave some of those here, no one will bother them. We're going to have to make two trips anyway."

Evan nodded and gratefully put some of the groceries back in the truck, then he and Nick chased after Bill, who was hurrying toward the harbor.

Two overpowering smells immediately assaulted their noses. First was the smell of all the different seafood that was unloaded at the harbor and transferred to the canning and processing facilities. Following immediately after that potpourri of fish and crab was the nearly overwhelming smell of creosote, which had been slapped on seemingly every piece of wood in the harbor.

Evan wasn't sure that he would ever get used to that combination, but did his best to put it out of his mind. He hadn't given any thought as to what the boat they were going to be living on might look like. Now, he looked ahead at the ships both large and small that were tied up to the docks.

There were a number of large vessels that looked modern and clean. Bill did not go toward any of them. Instead, he walked straight to an old boat that looked like it had known better days, and that those days were long ago.

It was more than a hundred feet long and had been painted black at one time, though now it was more rusty than black. To Evan's eye, he thought it was a small miracle that it was afloat. Out of the corner of his eye, Evan saw that Nick might be thinking the same thing.

Bill turned, saw their expressions and looked first at the large, modern vessels, then his own boat.

"This old girl will still be bringing crabs in long after those things have sunk to the bottom, don't you worry."

There was a name scrawled across the front of the bow—*The Diver I*. Such a name indicated that there might be a *Diver II* somewhere as well, but Evan didn't want to ask.

"Isn't *Diver* kind of a bad name," Nick asked, "for something that is supposed to float on top of the water?"

"Kids," Bill muttered, then jumped easily across the open space between the dock and the deck of *The Diver I*.

Evan and Nick stood at the edge of the dock, unsure of what to do.

"What, are you wanting me to roll out the red carpet for ya?" Bill asked.

"I thought there might be a gangplank or something to get across," Nick said hopefully.

"Oh, Jesus, Joseph, and Mary," Bill said. He jumped nimbly from the ship to the dock, turned and jumped back. "If an old man can do that, surely you young pups can handle it. Just throw your duffels over, then toss me the groceries and jump."

Evan nodded, tossed his bag onto the deck, then leaned across the open space and handed his groceries to Bill. For the briefest of moments, he wondered if he was about to wake up back in Middle Falls General again, then jumped.

He made it easily.

Bill shook his head and wandered away muttering about kids today.

Nick stood on the dock, still a little uncertain.

"It's really no big deal," Evan said. "Toss me your bag."

Nick did, then handed his bag of groceries across. Just as he was working up his courage to jump, Bill came back and said, "Of course we did lose Charlie last year trying to come aboard. Missed the whole shootin' match, hit his head on the way down, and drowned before we could fish him out."

Nick's courage evaporated, and he stood rooted to the dock.

"Then again, Charlie was in his eighties and he was drunk as a skunk." Bill laughed and turned away again.

Nick glared at his uncle, then gathered his courage once more and made the jump, landing easily.

Bill reappeared once again. "Come on, I'll show you to your bunks. You'll be in together."

Even tied up in the harbor, *The Diver I* shifted and swayed slightly under their feet. Bill was sure-footed as he walked. Evan and Nick were slightly less so.

Bill led them down a level and into a room that was just big enough for two narrow bunks and a small space for them to walk between. There was no closet and no room for one. Bill pointed to a shelf with a lip on it above each bunk. "You can put your stuff up there, but for now, just toss your duffels on the bed. We've got a lot to do before we shove off in the morning."

As soon as they dropped their bags on their bunks, they hustled out and picked up the rest of the groceries. They carried them into the kitchen—this time making the long step from dock to boat without the drama—and met Burdon. That wasn't his real name, but as soon as he introduced himself, he said he was a big fan of Eric Burdon and the Animals, so he had adopted it.

Burdon was a jack-of-all-trades on *The Diver I*. Part mechanic, part cook, part Alaska lore expert. If you wanted to know anything about the state, its history, or its inhabitants, you could ask Burdon. If he didn't know the answer, he could make up something on the spot that sounded reasonable. At that moment, he was serving in his capacity as a cook and was complaining loudly about what Bill had bought for the trip.

"Oh my stars and garters," Burdon said. "He never thinks about what things might go together, or what I need to make a recipe. What am I supposed to do with all this?"

Bill came up to the kitchen from below and said, "Oh my God, Burdon! Are you still complaining? If you don't like what I bought, go into town and buy it yourself." He turned to Evan and in a lower voice, said, "He's only happy when he's complaining, so he's happy all the time. Come on, I've got a job for you two."

The way he said it made Evan think it was probably not a glamorous or fun job, but after the wide variety of things he had done for Labor, Inc., he figured he could handle it.

Bill took them to the main deck via a set of metal stairs that were so narrow and steep they might have been more properly defined as a ladder.

There were hundreds of crab pots stacked on the deck. These were not the small pots that tourists used to catch a few crabs at the beach. They were huge, five feet across at the bottom, then narrowing a bit at the top.

Off to one side, there was a big plastic tub with a lid on it. Beside that were dozens and dozens of small containers.

"It's a simple job," Bill said. He pulled the lid off the tub. Evan and Nick peered over the edge, then gagged slightly. The tub was filled with great mounds of fish which, by the smell, were well past their pull date. Some were whole or nearly so, while others were torn to pieces.

Bill grinned at his newest deckhands, then put his head over the tub and took a deep breath, inhaling the odor of the semi-rotting fish. "That's the smell of money, boys. You'll come to love it."

"We will?" Nick asked, looking a little green.

"Here's all you've got to do," Bill said. He plucked one of the small containers up, opened the lid, then reached his bare hand into the pile of fish parts. He scooped up a handful, stuffed it into the container, then shut the lid. There was a thread of rope that ran through the top of the container with a hook on the end. He wiped his greasy, fishy hand against his work coat, leaving a long stain of scales and guts.

"Load all these containers up so we'll be ready to drop them with the pots tomorrow." He stretched and looked at the sun, which was still fairly high in the sky. "When you're done, come into the kitchen and we'll throw together something for you."

Evan looked at the mountain of small containers and nodded.

"Oh, if you're one of those delicate types that needs to wear gloves to handle the chum, there are some over there." Bill nodded toward a few pairs of blue rubber gloves hanging on a nail.

Nick and Evan watched Bill drop down to a lower compartment.

"I'm definitely one of those delicate types," Nick said, heading for the gloves. "He didn't say if there were clothespins for our noses, did he?"

"Breathe through your mouth if you can," Evan advised and accepted the offered rubber gloves. He slipped them on and reached into the tub of chum. The bits of fish were slippery even wearing the gloves. He grabbed a glob and stuffed it into the tub, then closed the lid and set it on the deck behind him. "One down, only a few hundred to go."

His medical and surgical training hadn't been too much help to him in this life, but that experience served him well here. He was accustomed to sights and smells that a non-doctor would find revolting, while he was not bothered.

He reached in and grabbed a second scoop and filled another container. He glanced at Nick, who was still working up his nerve.

"Put your mind somewhere else if you need to. Think about your girlfriend and the last time you were together, or scoring the winning touchdown in high school or whatever."

"I wasn't a football player, but yeah, I can think of Annie. She smells a lot better than this stuff."

They went to work until the containers were all filled with chum. When they put the last one on the deck, Evan straightened his back and groaned.

"I'm not sure what's wrong with me. I feel like I'm about to pass out, but it can't be that late." He looked at the sun, which was still up, but hung lower on the horizon.

"It's 10:30," Bill said from behind them. "The longest day of the year is just a few days away. It won't get really dark at all, then." He looked the filled containers over and said, "Good job, boyos. Come on in and get something to eat."

They climbed up the steep stairs to the kitchen and sat down at the table in the small dining room. There was a half-inch lip around the table that would keep food from sliding off when the seas got rough.

Burdon brought in bowls of soup and sandwiches on a tray. Until that moment, Evan hadn't thought he was hungry, but seeing the food, his stomach tightened.

They demolished the food in record time.

Bill had sat across the table drinking a cup of coffee while they ate. "You boys better head to bed. We'll be pushing off around 6:00, as soon as the others get here."

Evan nodded and they walked like zombies to their small room. He kicked his shoes off but didn't bother to undress before he fell across the bed, exhausted.

Chapter Twenty-One

Evan woke up to a rumbling vibration below him. He realized that the ship's engines must be right below their bunks.

He went down the hall and used the bathroom—which Bill had told him was called *the head*—then hurried up onto the deck. There was a flurry of activity there.

Two men Evan didn't know stood on the dock holding onto the ropes that had kept *The Diver I* moored. Two others stood on the deck below, ready to receive the ropes. Evan glanced up at the wheelhouse and saw that Bill was there.

One of the men on the deck saw Evan and waved. All of the new men were young. Other than Bill and Burdon, it looked like Evan was the oldest person aboard.

"Can I help?" Evan asked. He had no experience of any kind with the operation of a boat. To that point, the sum total of his experience was how to fill a container with chum.

"Nothing that needs to be done yet," the young man answered. "I'm Doug. That's Jesse."

"Evan. I'm new, so just tell me if I'm in the way or if there's something I need to be doing."

"You're fine. We'll let you know if there's something you need to do. You should go up to the wheelhouse and watch Bill take us out of the harbor. It's worth seeing."

Evan wasn't sure exactly how to get to where Bill was. He went through the kitchen, where Burdon poured him a cup of coffee. "If you want anything in it, there's milk in the fridge and sugar over there."

"Thanks. I take it black."

"Do you now?" Burdon answered with a grin. "More power to ya."

Evan took a sip and nearly choked. "Is that coffee?"

'It's better than that. It's *ship's* coffee."

Evan was almost afraid to ask, but did anyway. "What is ship's coffee?"

Burdon pointed to a battered old coffee pot that sat on the stovetop. "We're not too fancy. We just pour the grounds into the pot, then add water and boil it up. When it gets too weak, we add more coffee. When the grounds pile up too high, we throw the whole mess out and start over again. If you weren't a man before you drank that coffee, you will be after."

"I can't disagree," Evan said, though part of his twenty-first century brain balked at the distinction. "I think maybe I'll have a bit of sugar after all."

"Thought you might," Burdon said with a wink.

Evan put two heaping teaspoons of sugar into the deep black of the coffee, tasted it, and still winced. He added one more.

"How do I get up to the wheelhouse?"

"Through there, turn left, then up the stairs."

Evan followed the directions and stuck his head into the small room where Bill stood at the wheel. His legs were wide apart and he looked for all the world like the image of an old whaler, heading out to sea.

"Mind if I come in?"

"Come on, we're just heading out. I see you met Doug and Jesse. They're good kids."

"They're so young."

"They are, but they've been out on the water since they were kids. They'll show you the ropes. Where's my nephew?"

"I think he's still asleep."

Bill shook his head. "Sleeping his life away." He leaned forward and looked up into the clear blue sky. "Gonna be a great day. If you want, you can go out the door and there's a ladder that'll take you up on top of the wheelhouse. That's where you get the best view."

Evan set his coffee cup down and did just that. He stood on the highest point of the ship as Bill maneuvered *The Diver I* through the harbor. They ran alongside the breakwater for a few hundred yards, then headed for the gap in the harbor walls that led to the open sea.

They passed a pier where a bald eagle stood with half a fish in its mouth, the other half at its feet. It looked at Evan with unblinking eyes, and he understood what it was like to look into the gaze of a true alpha predator. They moved out into Resurrection Bay, which was surrounded by snow-capped mountains.

Evan watched the incredible scenery for a long time, then felt a little guilty for not pulling his weight. He climbed down the ladder, and as he did, he glanced over the side and saw that two otters were racing alongside the boat. They dove, twirled, and swam on their backs, easily keeping up with the pace of *The Diver I*.

Evan stuck his head back into the wheelhouse and asked, "How fast are we going?"

Bill glanced at a gauge and answered, "About three and a half knots." He glanced at Evan and could tell by his expression that the measurement meant nothing to him. "That's about four miles per hour. I can get the old girl up to five knots if I push her, but there's no sense in being in a hurry. The important thing is, she'll get us there."

There wasn't much for the crew to do while they headed to the location where they would drop the pots, so everyone relaxed.

"Don't worry," Burdon said, "there'll be plenty of work to go around soon enough. Take it easy while you can."

Evan spent the rest of the day out on the deck, breathing in the incredible air, feeling the sun on his face and watching the water. At one point, a pod of dolphins raced alongside the ship jumping, doing tricks, and playing with them. He shook his head. He had thought he had built an enviable life as a surgeon. This day showed him a small bit of what he had missed. He promised himself that even if he met his lofty goals, he would never forget again.

Late that afternoon, Bill finally killed the engine, and the vibration and noise, which had become part of the experience of being onboard, quieted. He dropped down from the wheelhouse and said, "We're here, boyos. Let's grab something to eat, then we'll go to work."

"It ain't my first rodeo," Burdon said. "I've got stew on the stove, ready to eat."

Evan met the other two deckhands, Tim and Anthony, and they all sat around the dining room table while Burdon set a huge pot of stew in the middle. A stack of bread and a slab of butter sat alongside.

Everyone served themselves and as soon as the spoons hit the stew, the compliments came.

"You've outdone yourself, Burdon," and "This is the best goddamned stew I've ever tasted," and "This is the best, Burdon."

Evan tasted the stew and thought it was good, but that the praise might be a little over the top. He looked around the table quizzically.

Bill leaned toward him confidentially. "It's one of the rules we have on the ship. Burdon starts out as the cook on every trip. But if anyone complains about the food, *they* become the cook until someone else is foolish enough to say something."

"They've got it figured out now, damn them," Burdon said. "They don't have to be so obvious about it, though."

All the other deckhands looked at each other and grinned.

"It really is good," Nick said.

"Now *that's* the spirit of things, boyo," Bill said.

There were no leftovers. Everyone seemed to know that they wouldn't be eating again for a while and filled their bellies.

"I'll take care of the dishes and leave the real work to you all," Burdon said.

Everyone stood up and walked out on the deck where the pots were stacked in row after row. Jesse walked to one of the stacks and gracefully lifted the top pot off. He turned toward Nick and Evan and said, "They're big and a little awkward, but once you get the feel of them, they're no trouble. They're not very heavy." He jutted his chin toward the containers of chum they had filled the day before. "Bring me one of those."

Evan hustled over, picked one up and handed it to Jesse. He reached through a small door and hung the hook to the top of the pot, then let it dangle from the rope.

"There, one down." He set the loaded pot on the deck and Tim attached it to a long rope that wound around a hydraulic spool. "Now we've just got to do another hundred or so of those."

Everyone was kept busy over the next four hours, baiting the pots, then using the hydraulics to drop them over the side. The last thing to go over the side was an orange buoy that marked the spot where they had made the drop.

Evan looked around the vast body of the Pacific and said, "Will we just stay here? It seems like a buoy would be easy to lose."

"No, we'll move on in just a minute," Jess replied. "This just looks like endless water to you, but to Cap'n Bill, it's like his backyard. He'll know exactly where they are. As expensive as those pots are, he won't risk losing them."

When they finished, it was nearly eleven at night, and it had finally started to get a little dark with the sun dipping toward the horizon.

The main deck had been cleared of half its pots, but there were still another hundred or so to be dropped.

Evan stretched, exhausted again, but happy. He had survived the first day's work with no major mishaps. "What do we do with the rest of those?"

Jesse clapped him on the back and said, "Don't be in such a hurry." Then he grinned and added, "Bill will take us to another spot tomorrow, and we'll do the same thing all over again."

Nick pointed at the bait boxes that were left over. "What about those? Aren't they going to rot? Should we put them somewhere?"

"Nope," Jesse said. "We *want* them to rot. The more they stink, the more they attract the crabs. They crawl in looking for dinner, then can't get out."

Evan elected to skip whatever Burdon had served up for dinner. He was dead on his feet. This time, he at least managed to crawl out of his clothes, which were stiff with salt water and chum, before crawling into the sleeping bag on his bunk.

He woke up to complete quiet. He slipped on some clean clothes and went outside. It was a little like the experience of falling asleep as a kid. You fell asleep in the backseat or on the couch, but when you woke up the next morning, you were tucked into your bed. For Evan, he had gone to sleep with no land in sight. Now they were anchored off a small piece of land, *The Diver I* rocking gently back and forth with the waves.

He went down to the kitchen and poured himself a bowl of cereal, then sat down to eat. He had the room to himself until Burdon came in and peered inside the coffee pot. He added a heaping tablespoon of coffee to it, then turned on the burner. "It'll be quiet around here for a while. We ran pretty late last night to get here. When Bill gets up, we'll head out to the second drop spot. It's not too far. Maybe an hour or two."

"What then? Go back and pick up the first string?"

Burdon shook his head. "No, Bill likes to give the pots a few days to trap as many crabs as he can. We should be back here by dinner, then we'll just lay up for a few days and relax. We'll need it. Those days when we pull the pots, we sometimes work fourteen-hour shifts, and we'll have two lines to pull up."

There wasn't much for Evan to do for the next few hours and he began to learn the rhythm of life aboard a small crabbing boat. There were long periods of intense physical activity where you couldn't take the time to stop and go to the bathroom. That was normally followed by hours or even days of inactivity. Having nothing to do and plenty of time to do it in an area like they were in was definitely a reward, not a punishment.

Evan still wasn't sure how much he would get paid at the end of this adventure, only that he would be paid a full deckhand's share. During the quiet times, he would think about what it would mean to him to get not just back on his feet again but to be able to reach his goals.

Evan had spent much of his time in his first life keeping up on the latest surgical techniques, of course, but his hobby had been reading about businesses in journals, books, and online. He had been especially interested in big successes and failures. One of the stories that had fascinated him was the story of Harrison Bettis, who had founded the Buddha Computer Company with the men who would later be known as *the two Steves* – Steve Win and Steve Pasternak.

Harrison had made what some considered the biggest business blunder of all time when he had elected to leave the company in the earliest days and had sold his ten percent share in Buddha for a thousand dollars. Buddha became the first company to be valued at a trillion dollars, making the shares that he sold worth a hundred billion dollars.

Evan believed that if he could position himself in the proper place at the proper time, he could buy the shares that Mr. Bettis didn't value all that highly. If he was able to do that, he knew he would be set forever.

That wasn't enough, though. Evan had ambitions well beyond that. He knew critical turning points in many industries. As a nobody, he wouldn't be in a position to implement change. But, if he was one of the richest men in the world, people would listen to him.

His ambition wasn't to be rich. It was to be the richest person who had ever lived.

Chapter Twenty-Two

They dropped the second string of pots the next day, then went back to the same small island they had stayed at the night before. After they cast anchor, Bill announced that they would stay there for two days before returning to reclaim the pots.

On the first day, the toilet in the head quit working. Burdon, the jack-of-all-trades and master of none looked at it and pronounced that it was down until they got back to port.

Evan and Nick, the two *cheechakos*, or greenhorns, looked at each other.

Nick spoke up first. "Then where do we go to the bathroom?"

Burdon nodded, sympathetic. "We all gotta go, right? Come on, I'll show you."

Evan assumed there was some sort of backup plan for an emergency like this, and there was, of a sort.

Burton led them through the narrow passageway that ran alongside the port side of *The Diver I*. Eventually, they came to a spot where the metal railing had an opening of perhaps two and a half feet.

"There ya go," Burdon said, pride evident in his voice. "The whole great Pacific is your toilet now. Just whizz right off the side of the boat."

Evan nodded, then, dreading the answer, said, "What if you need to poop?"

"Ah, right," Burdon answered. "Good question." He demonstrated by miming dropping his pants, then gripping the railings on either side of the opening and pushing his tush out over empty air. "That's all there is to it. And before you ask the next obvious question..." He fished in an oversized pocket of his overalls and came out with a half-roll of toilet paper and stuck it on an eightpenny nail that was driven into the wall opposite the opening. "There's your TP. All the comforts of home."

Evan closed his eyes and imagined doing that maneuver in the middle of a storm, when the waves were tossing the ship to and fro. He grimaced, but said, "Thanks, Burdon. That'll be great."

Burdon gave them a wink and a smile before walking away, chuckling.

"*Thanks, Burdon. That'll be great,*" Nick said in a mocking tone. "Are you freaking crazy? I'm not hanging my butt over there. One slip and I'm in the drink."

Evan rarely made jokes, but he said, "Here's the plan then. We'll use the buddy system. Whenever you need to take a crap, come and get me and I'll watch, so I can yell 'Man overboard!' when you fall in."

Nick seemed to consider that, then said, "I don't want anyone watching me take a dump."

"Gotta pick your poison," Evan said. He walked away, chuckling, much like Burdon had.

There wasn't much to do around the boat for the next forty-eight hours, so everyone was at loose ends.

There were a lot of naps. A poker game started in the dining room, but Evan knew his limitations, which included knowing how to play poker. He sat out the game, which went on deep into the night.

He kicked himself for not bringing something to read on the trip, and so asked around to see if anyone else had brought something they weren't reading at the moment. He struck out until he got to Bill, who lit up and said, "Come with me."

Evan followed him to the captain's quarters, which really weren't any grander than any of the other rooms, except Bill didn't have to share with anyone. He did have a small closet, though. He opened the door and dug around at the bottom before emerging with a pile of magazines.

He handed them proudly to Evan with a slightly lascivious wink. "There ya go. That'll keep your mind occupied."

Evan flipped through the magazines. They were all of a certain type, with lurid covers and titles like *True Crime Detective*, *Startling Detective Adventures*, and *Popular Detective*. Most of the covers featured scantily clad women in dangerous situations. Being tied to a chair seemed to be a popular thing in these magazines. They all blared the titles to articles like *The Gutter Waits for Girls Like Me*, or *I'll Drown You in My Dreams*, and *A Dirge for the Painted Blonde*.

This stack of magazines couldn't have been further removed from Evan's interests, but he knew that the nearest library or bookstore was many miles away. He accepted the magazines and hoped that maybe he could find something worth reading in them. He also made a mental note to buy a stack of paperbacks when they docked back in Seward.

When the poker game broke up, someone dug an old, beat-up backgammon game out of a cupboard. That was more Evan's speed. The others weren't even sure what the rules were, while Evan had played in backgammon tournaments from time to time. He knew he could have hustled them—playing dumb, then enticing them into making bad bets—but he didn't have the heart. Instead, he gave free lessons until everyone who wanted to learn was at least competent and knew how to play properly.

In the end, the two days passed quickly and Evan found that he was enjoying the camaraderie of being stuck in such close quarters with a group of men he didn't know. In his first life, he had dozens of acquaintances, but no real friends. These men fell into the same broad bucket, but he found that he felt more comfortable with them than he had with his fellow doctors.

Early on the third morning, Bill fired up *The Diver I's* engines and they motored slowly toward the first place where they had dropped their line.

Just like Burdon had predicted, Bill navigated directly back to where the orange buoy bobbed. To Evan, the ocean was just great, rolling gray waves. To Bill, it seemed to be as clearly marked as if there had been roads and street signs.

They arrived at the buoy late in the morning, and again, Burdon fed them all until they were stuffed. Everyone knew this was where they would really do the work they had signed on for.

As they sat around the table eating the meat and potatoes Burdon had cooked, Evan sensed a certain electric anticipation. There was no way to know what kind of a catch they were about to harvest. If Bill had picked correctly and found a spot where the crabs were plentiful, they would fill their tanks. If he missed—if he was off by even a few hundred yards—then their time and effort might have been wasted.

Bill took Nick and Evan aside and said, "On this first line, don't worry about anything but sorting and tossing." He nodded toward an old plastic diagram that had been there so long it looked like a museum piece. Pointing to an illustration, he said, "Flip them over. If their underside looks like that, they're female and they go back in." He tapped the other drawing and said, "These are the males and off they go into the holding tank. Got it?"

"Do they pinch?" Nick asked.

"Of course they pinch. They're crabs. Just pick them up from behind and you'll be fine, Nancy." He shook his head and said, "I can't be sure you've got my blood running through your veins."

Nick looked crestfallen, and Bill looked regretful. "Sorry, boyo. I didn't need to say that. We'll look out for you. Just take your time.

Once they're on the deck, they're ours and we can take our time sorting them."

Nick nodded, but Evan could see that he was still stinging from the rebuke.

Evan jumped in and said, "What kind of crab are we going to bring up? Kings?"

"Kings," Bill said, almost spitting the words out. "Not now, not here. Wrong season. We're after Tanner crabs."

"Huh," Evan said. "Never heard of 'em."

"Well, they've never heard of you either," Bill said. "You probably have, though. Ever seen snow crab?"

"Sure."

"Chances are good that any snow crabs you've ever eaten were Tanner crabs. We might get a king crab or two that wanders into one of the pots, but that's not what we're after. They'll just go into the dinner pot tomorrow, freshest crab you've ever had. Swimming this morning, in our stomachs tonight." Bill turned to walk away, then said, "Most important thing is, don't wander too close to where we're pulling the pots up. If a wave hits, the boat will tip and you'll go right over the side. If that happens, we'll do our best to pull you up, but if you get tangled in the rope and pots, they'll drag you under." He looked from Nick to Evan. "You'll be fine. Get your gloves on, then if you get a pinch, you won't even feel it."

Evan hurried over to where the rubber gloves were hanging that they had used to fill the chum traps. He handed a pair to Nick and pounded him on the back. "We'll do good. Think about all the nice places you'll be able to take Annie when you get home."

Nick nodded. "I'm gonna take her back to the Renaissance and let someone else park my damned car."

Burdon was in the wheelhouse, and he maneuvered *The Diver I* until it was right alongside the buoy, then Jesse reached over and hooked the rope attached to it with a long pole. He dragged it close and attached the soaking rope to a hook connected to the hydraulic puller.

Bill was the hydraulic operator and he pushed a lever forward and the buoy lifted out of the water and landed on the deck. Doug and Tim grabbed it and wrestled it to the side. Just a few seconds later, the first pot came up.

Everyone seemed to be holding their breath until it was lifted high enough for everyone to see that it was teeming with crabs. Anthony and Jesse worked like a team and dragged the pot, heavy now, onto the deck. Together, they lifted it up and Jesse released a catch that scattered everything in the pot at their feet.

Anthony lifted the now empty pot up and balanced it on his thigh. He duck-walked it to another part of the deck and dropped it out of the way.

Just a few seconds later, another pot appeared and Doug and Tim grabbed it and went through the same motions.

"What are ya waitin' for, numbskulls?" Bill yelled at Evan and Nick. They had been standing transfixed at the ballet being performed in front of them. That jolted them into action, and they ran forward, leaned down, and each picked up a crab. They turned them over and noticed the pattern. Nick threw his overboard, while Evan tossed his into the open holding tank.

Jesse threw his hand up and said, "Hold up!"

Bill pulled the lever back and the hydraulic quit pulling.

Jesse ran over to where Evan and Nick were sorting the crabs one by one. "It ain't rocket science, boys. Pretty soon you'll be able to tell the females from the males just by looking at their eyelashes."

Nick and Evan both looked at the crab in their hands and confirmed that they didn't actually have eyelashes.

Jesse reached down and scooped up three crabs in each bare hand, flipped them over and sorted them so fast it seemed he didn't even look at them. Two went overboard, four went into the hold.

"Try doing two at a time. You'll get the hang of it." He looked at Bill, made a twirling motion with his hand, and the hydraulic roared into life again.

The rest of the day went by in a blur. Everyone on deck was in constant motion, grabbing pots, emptying them, stacking them, and on to the next.

Evan and Nick got better at grabbing and sorting the crabs as the day wore on.

The four young men who were doing most of the actual work seemed to never tire. They didn't take one break during all the long hours of hard labor, but when they pulled the last pot onto the deck, everyone took a well-deserved rest.

Evan and Nick cleaned up the last of the crabs and threw them overboard or into the holding tank.

They had indeed caught several king crabs that day. The Tanner crabs were tiny in comparison, weighing somewhere between one and two pounds. The king crabs were so big that Jesse was able to hold one of its legs in each hand and even spreading his arms as wide as possible, it wasn't stretched to full length. Those were delivered to Burdon in the kitchen.

Evan stood and worked the kinks out of his neck and back. He looked at Jesse and said, "Now I see what everyone was talking about. That was a good day's work."

"You're crazy man. That was just the appetizer. We'll go in and grab some food while Bill gets us to where we dropped the second line, then we'll pull that one."

Evan didn't mind hard work, but the idea that he was only half done for the day caused his shoulders to sag.

"Come on, old man," Jesse said, "some food will fix us right up, and then we'll be back at it."

What Evan found was that, although the food was good, when he stood up to go back on deck after eating, his muscles had tightened up and he walked a little like an old man. He looked around at the others and saw that they didn't seem to be feeling the effects of their day's labor the same way.

At a little after 9:00 that night, Bill sighted the second buoy and pulled alongside it. He hustled down from the wheelhouse and said, "Let's go, boyos, our fortune awaits."

They worked through the night pulling up the second string. It finally got mostly dark around 2:00 a.m., and Bill flipped a switch and bright overhead lights lit the deck.

They worked on.

At 3:30, it started to get light again.

When they finished with the second string of pots, both their holding tanks were full, the pots were restacked on the deck, and the crew was dead on their feet.

Everyone but Bill and Burdon sacked out in their bunks. The two older men sat together in the wheelhouse, drinking ship's coffee and watching the changing sea as they navigated back to Seward.

They pulled back into the harbor that afternoon, loaded with crab. Bill made arrangements to offload their catch the next day, and Tim, Anthony, Doug, and Jesse, who all had places to stay in Seward, hopped off the boat and headed home.

Bill took a good look at Evan and Nick, who were a little rough around the edges. He led them to the dock and pointed to a large metal building.

"That's the fisherman's lounge. It's not much, but they've got washers and dryers and hot showers. If you fish on a boat from the harbor, it's free. If anybody hassles you, just tell them you're with *The Diver*."

They gathered their dirty clothes—essentially all of them—into their duffels and headed toward the building.

Bill was right. It wasn't much, but there was a big room with a few sofas, chairs, and a television. Off to the side was a laundry room and showers.

"Looks good to me," Evan said. "You grab the first shower; I'll start my laundry." He threw his clothes in and sat down on one of the couches in the lounge. He turned the TV on but couldn't focus on what was playing.

Five minutes later, he was out cold.

Evan had survived his first crabbing trip.

Chapter Twenty-Three

Evan didn't get rich as a crabber, but he did do well, especially compared to what he could have earned elsewhere.

That very first trip netted him almost four thousand dollars. When he got his check, he realized that he had completely recouped his lost nest egg and then some.

He and Nick made five more ten-day trips out into the Pacific with Cap'n Bill before the Tanner crab season ended. When it was over, Nick flew home. He was a very young man with a life back in Seattle, a girlfriend he mooned over endlessly, and a thick wad of bills in his pocket. Evan knew that if he had been in the same place, he would have been on the first plane home as well. He was honestly proud of his friend for sticking it out as long as he did.

When they returned from their last trip out, everyone except Evan, Bill and Burdon left the ship as soon as they got their last check. It was quiet on *The Diver I* after that. Evan stuck around, but knew that he needed to come up with the next phase of his plan.

On the third day after they got back, Bill returned from a trip into town and said, "I ran into an old friend."

Evan correctly interpreted that as meaning that he had tossed down a few beers with another one of the grizzled old fishermen that gathered there.

"He told me about a job opportunity if you're interested."

"I am, and I should be, since I've just been hanging around here, eating Burdon's food and living rent-free."

Bill waved that concern away. "You can hang out here on the ship as long as you want. You can stay until seining season starts, and I can even connect you with someone who salmon fishes. Then you can make some real money."

"When is that?"

"September."

"I appreciate that Bill, I really do. But it's just the end of July. I can't hang around here and mooch off you for that long. What's the job?"

The truth was, Evan had been considering going back to either Seattle or Middle Falls. He thought he probably had enough money to accomplish what he wanted if he budgeted carefully and got another job there. He was always open to increasing his bankroll, though.

"You've heard of the pipeline?"

Evan had heard of it, of course. Everyone knew about the Trans-Alaska Pipeline. He just hadn't thought about it in a long time.

"Sure. Are they building it now?" In his first life, he had never paid any attention to when the pipeline was built.

"They started this spring. Gonna take years, though. They pay good wages. Not quite as good as having a good crabbing season, maybe, but the work is a lot easier, and there's not a lot of chances to spend it, depending on where you catch on."

That combination of good wages and a lack of places to spend it sounded good to Evan. He figured that the more remote you were, the better money you were paid.

"How would I go about it?"

Bill reached in his shirt pocket and pulled out a bar napkin with a phone number scrawled on it. "Call this number and tell them Barry Silverson recommended you. That'll at least get you an interview."

Evan accepted the napkin and put it in his pocket. "Thank you, Bill." He stood up from the table.

"Leaving already then?"

"No time like the present."

There was no payphone at the harbor, so Evan walked into Seward proper. It was a nice little town, with one main drag that led down to the water where all the businesses were located. The side streets were filled with apartments, houses, and smaller businesses. There was a service station at the edge of town that had a payphone. Evan went inside and bought a pack of Juicy Fruit gum and asked for a couple of dollars in quarters.

He stacked them on the metal shelf under the phone and dialed the number.

Three minutes later, he stepped out of the phone booth, feeling a little dazed. An hour before, he had been sitting on *The Diver I*, drinking ship's coffee—which he had finally grown accustomed to—and now he had an interview in Valdez as soon as he could get there.

He walked back to the ferry dock and bought a ticket to Valdez that left very early the next day. It was a little expensive, but he was feeling flush and the ferry would get him there in only five hours. The bus stopped at every wide spot in the road and would take much longer.

Evan had learned one lesson well from his misadventures in Seattle. With his very first crabbing check, he had opened a bank account and kept his money safely deposited there. He always kept some cash with him, but never so much that it would really hurt him if he lost it.

Ferry ticket in hand, he walked back to *The Diver I* and packed up his things, which didn't take long. He picked up the stack of men's detective magazines and took them back to Bill.

He shook his hand and said, "I really appreciate you giving me a shot, Bill."

"You caught on pretty fast, boyo. If you get tired of working on that pipeline, come back next year and I'll hire you again."

Evan spent the rest of the day doing laundry at the fisherman's lounge, then waiting for time to pass so he could catch the ferry.

Burdon took pity on him and challenged him to a series of cribbage games that lasted for hours.

Evan left in the middle of the night while Bill and Burdon were asleep. Goodbyes were not his forte.

The ferry left at 5:00 a.m. sharp, but he was able to board half an hour earlier.

They only made one stop between Seward and Valdez and that was at the tiny town of Whittier.

The layover wasn't long enough for Evan to explore the town, so he stayed on the ferry and waited to leave for Valdez. The ride across Prince William Sound was stunning, but the truth was, Evan had become used to the amazing beauty that Alaska had everywhere. He sat in one of the comfortable chairs inside and soon fell asleep. He woke up a few hours later as the ferry's horn announced their arrival at Valdez.

Evan walked into the warm late-summer air, once again a complete stranger in a strange land. If the previous year had taught him anything, though, it was how to adapt to new and strange circumstances.

He went to the headquarters of the Alyeska Pipeline Service Company, which ran the whole shebang. It was a big, ugly, two-story building on the edge of town. Inside, the place was buzzing, with hundreds of people milling around talking, looking for the right place to be, or just working.

Evan spotted a woman with a clipboard. He always gravitated toward people carrying clipboards because they tended to know where the bodies were buried.

She was short, dressed in regular office attire, and was standing like an island of calm in the chaos.

"Hello," Evan said, trying to pitch his voice to carry over the buzz of humanity around him. "I spoke to Mr. Galbreath yesterday. He told me to get here as soon as I can for an interview."

The woman looked around and said, "He seems to have told a *lot* of people to come in for an interview. What's your name?"

"Evan Sanderson."

She referred to her clipboard, flipping through page after page of names. On the fourth page, she found Evan. "He's on the second floor, room 216. Go and wait there. If he doesn't get to you today, come back first thing in the morning and you'll get in."

"Thank you," Evan said and hurried toward the staircase. He found room 216 and opened the door to find a dozen men already sitting there ahead of him. There was an empty chair in the far corner, so he walked toward it.

The man next to him leaned over and said, "Better take a number or they'll never get to you." He nodded to a ticket dispenser like you might find at a butcher's.

"Thanks," Evan said, hustling over to grab a ticket. He sat back down and said, "Does it move fast?"

"Sometimes. Sometimes not. Haven't been here long enough to figure it out, really."

Evan nodded his thanks and settled in to wait. There hadn't been any place to leave his duffel bag, so he took the paperback he was reading out of it and slid the bag under the chair.

"You here to apply for anything special?" the man next to him asked. "I hear they're looking for longshoremen, mechanics, and truck drivers."

Evan grinned ruefully and said, "I'm not qualified to do any of those things."

"Me neither," the man said. "I came all the way from Ohio, though, so I hope they've got something for me."

"Ohio? Really?"

"It's tough out there. Nixon's Phase 2 didn't do any more for me than his Phase 1 did, and that was exactly nothing. They finally got him yesterday, though."

"They what? Pardon?"

"They got him. Didn't you hear? He resigned yesterday. Ford's president now. Not that it'll make any difference. Doesn't really matter who's sitting in that chair, the little guy tends to get screwed."

"I guess I've been out of the loop. I've been living on a crabber in Seward. No TV, not even any radio."

"You're probably better off for it," the man said.

To Evan, Nixon's resignation had been an event so far in his past that he hadn't thought about it for years. It did show him one thing, though—that no matter how he changed his own personal circumstances, the big events of the rest of the world seemed to be unchanged.

Evan sat in the same chair for hours, watching the clock on the wall and wondering when Mr. Galbreath would stop seeing people for the day. He decided that if he didn't get in today, he would show up a few hours before the building opened and get in line.

He needn't have worried, though. At 5:45, his number was called over the loudspeaker, and he pushed through into the inner office.

A small, balding man sat behind a very large desk that was piled with so many folders they looked like they might topple over on him.

"Come in, come in, close the door behind you."

"Mr. Galbreath?"

"Yes, though there are times I wish I was someone else. Sit down." Galbreath picked up a file folder from his left and opened it in front of him. "Name?"

"Evan Sanderson. I spoke to you yesterday."

"If my life depended on remembering who I spoke to an hour ago, I'd be a dead man. I assume that if you're sitting in front of me, you're supposed to be." He looked at Evan for the first time. He seemed to notice that Evan had his duffel bag with him. "Looks like you're ready to go. Good. Any special skills?"

Well, I'm a board-certified surgeon, Evan thought.

"I'm not sure, honestly."

"Can you operate heavy equipment, or are you a cook, or a mechanic used to working on large engines?"

"No," Evan admitted.

"Laborer," Galbreath said.

"I'm good at organizing things, if that helps."

"Maybe. I'm going to put you at our supply house at Milepost 217."

"So I've got a job? Great, and thank you."

"Son, I'm hiring anybody that walks through that door and can fog a mirror. Since you're upright, I assume that means you can do that."

"Yes, sir. Can I ask where Milepost 217 is?"

Galbreath looked at him like he might be dense. "It's at Milepost 217. That's it. That's all there is. There's a warehouse where we store parts needed for the pipeline, a garage, and a dorm for the men who work there. No women. Is that a problem?"

"No, sir. How do I get there?"

Galbreath scribbled on a sheet of paper, then picked up a heavy stamp and slammed it down on the paper. "Take this to room 121." He glanced at the clock on the wall. "They'll still be there, or they better be." He folded the file shut and handed it to Evan. "Take this down there and they'll process you. They'll find you a place to sleep tonight and ship you out tomorrow."

As so often happened in Evan's new life, things happened so fast his head was spinning.

He took the folder, slung his duffel over his shoulder and went in search of room 121.

An hour later, he had filled out the needed paperwork and was given a voucher for a room and a meal at a local hotel.

He was scheduled to catch a bus to Milepost 217 at 8:00 a.m. the next morning.

Chapter Twenty-Four

By late the next day, Evan learned that Milepost 217 was almost exactly as exciting as the name implied.

The distance between Prudhoe Bay and Valdez, the alpha and omega of the pipeline, was approximately 800 miles. To be more efficient, Alyeska installed supply depots at various points along that distance.

Milepost 217 was, logically, two-hundred-and-seventeen miles along that path. That meant that in terms of being near to civilization, they simply were not. It was an outpost that was completely self-contained. The men who worked there also slept and ate entirely within the compound simply because there was nowhere else to go.

If someone desired, they could put in for a leave every six months and take two weeks to go somewhere that had movie theaters, stores, and, not to put too fine a point on it, women. Almost everyone took that chance, because while they were there, it was an unending series of what the workers called *seven-twelves*. That is, working twelve-hour shifts, seven days a week.

It was an ideal setup for Evan, who did not ever feel the need to leave the compound. Aside from his burning ambition to accomplish major things in this life eventually, there wasn't much else he needed. After being homeless and working hard labor for $1.60 an hour, living at Milepost 217 and earning $12.00 an hour seemed like a dream job.

He started as a warehouse grunt, but as he had told Mr. Galbreath, he did have a knack for organization. He saw patterns and inefficiencies where others simply saw chaos. Initially, he just worked as he was told, moving and loading whatever was necessary.

In his off time, he designed and sketched out better ways to do those same things. It took him some time to find someone who was willing to listen to him—management is rarely known for listening to grunts—but when he did, the systems were implemented and even taken to other supply depots up and down the length of the pipeline.

Evan was moved into a supervisory role, which allowed him to think more and move boxes less, which suited him fine. It also meant a nice bump in pay, up to $18.00 an hour. Working twelve hours a day, he was earning good money and socking it all away as there was virtually nothing for him to spend it on. Even with taxes taken out, he was still able to save almost five thousand dollars a month.

Milepost 217 was far enough south that it didn't see the unending darkness that covered the northernmost parts of the pipeline for much of the winter. Even so, it only got a few hours of light every day. The compound was surrounded by snow in late November that was still there when the spring thaw finally came.

When May of 1975 arrived, Evan had a decision to make—whether to continue on with Alyeska, or give his notice and return to Seward to go crabbing with Bill.

He enjoyed his time working at the warehouse. It was essentially like playing a real-life game of Tetris every day. But there was an element of unrelenting sameness to it, too. Once he had the systems in place, they more or less ran themselves and much of the challenge had gone out of the job.

In mid-May, he gave his two weeks' notice to Alyeska and called Bill to tell him he was on his way. On the first day of June, he hitched a ride on a truck going south to Valdez, then caught the ferry and reversed the route he had taken nine months earlier.

As soon as he stepped off the ferry in Seward, he knew he had made the right choice. At the compound at Milepost 217, he had felt completely enclosed. In Seward, walking along Resurrection Bay to the harbor, with Mt. Marathon to his right, he felt his world expand again.

When he arrived at *The Diver I*, Evan was happy to see not only Bill and Burdon, but also Nick, another year older, and at least slightly wiser. He told Evan that when he got back to Seattle, he had learned that Annie was seeing someone else. After a summer spent dreaming of her and how they would spend his crabbing money, it broke his heart.

"But not for too long," Nick said with a laugh. He pulled his wallet out and showed off a picture of a beautiful brunette. "That's Cindy," he said, with no further explanation necessary.

Tim and Anthony didn't come back for this season, though Doug and Jesse did. The two who were missing were replaced by two young workers who were almost as green as Evan and Nick had been the year before.

Nick took great pleasure in leading them to the chum container, dipping his bare hand into the stinking fish, and filling a container. When he was done, he wiped his hand on his coat and said, "If you're a little more delicate, there are rubber gloves over there you can use."

Some things never change, but they do go around in circles.

If fate was cruel, some terrible accident might have befallen Evan that summer on *The Diver I* as he prepared to launch his grand plan.

The arm that lifted the pots might have had metal fatigue and collapsed with him tangled in the ropes and taken him under.

A small wound could have become infected and septic and killed him before they reached land.

A rogue wave might have hit the boat at the most inconvenient time, washing him overboard into the freezing Pacific.

None of those things happened.

They made half a dozen successful trips out and back, further padding Evan's bank account to a point that he was confident he could manage what he wanted to do.

After the last trip at the end of July, Evan and Nick walked into Seward to grab something to eat at the Alaska Shop, which was a combination drugstore, tourist trap, and café. Evan picked up a few more books to read, they had a good lunch, and were walking back to the ship when, for no good reason, they took a different route home and Nick once again fell in love.

Not with a girl, but with a car.

It wasn't beautiful, but it *was* a 1967 Chevrolet Chevelle Super-Sport. It had a layer of dirt and leaves on it that spoke to the fact that it hadn't been driven in some time. There was some body damage on the rear quarter panel and the windshield had a spiderweb of cracks running across it.

Evan watched Nick as he circled it like a hunter after his prey. He wasn't the only one who noticed. A woman who appeared to be in her mid-forties, dressed in a floral housecoat, came out on the porch and said, "Ain't she a beauty?"

Evan looked at her like she must be either crazy or talking about something else altogether.

Nick just nodded, a dreamy expression on his face. "I don't suppose it's for sale?"

Evan's head snapped around, unable to believe that those words had left his friend's lips.

"Well, nah," the woman said. "It ain't. It belongs to my husband, really, but the title *is* in my name." She paused long enough for Nick to set the hook in himself a little deeper. "Of course, he ran off a month ago and I ain't seen him since…" She let the words hang there in the air, tantalizing Nick.

"I'll give you five hundred dollars for it."

"Oh, I couldn't take that. No sir. This is a classic. L34 396 in it. You know what that means."

Nick nodded and mumbled, "350 horsepower." Then he shook his head as though he wasn't sure what he had been thinking to offer so little for so much. "Does it run?"

"Like a dream," the woman answered. "You wanna hear it?"

Evan laughed. He knew his friend was a goner.

"If I could, yes, I sure would."

The woman disappeared back into the house for a minute, then came out with a few keys on a keyring. She walked around to the driver's side and opened the door, which squealed like a stuck pig. "Just needs a little WD40," she said primly. She scooted into the seat, inserted the key, and a deep, resonant rumble came from the engine.

"That's it then, isn't it?" Evan said to Nick. "You're a dead man."

"I'll give you a thousand."

The woman sighed, turned the engine off and quiet returned to the street. "I'd take two."

Evan couldn't help himself. He actually guffawed.

The woman shot him a glance that told him to stay out of her game.

Nick was in love, but he wasn't stupid. "I'll go fifteen."

"Cash?"

"Cash in my pocket right now."

"I'll go get a pen."

Ten minutes later, they were lurching down the street in Nick's brand-new possession. The windshield was so dirty and cracked that Evan worried about Nick's ability to see the road. The interior was as nasty as the exterior, but Nick only saw beauty. He looked at Evan and said, "I've got my Nova all fixed up now. I needed something to work on this winter."

"Nick, we're in Seward. You live in Seattle. What are you thinking?"

"I'm thinking I'm going to drive this bad boy over the AlCan Highway."

Evan shook his head and closed his eyes. The Alaska-Canadian Highway had been built during World War II to enable military vehicles to drive from the mainland to Alaska. Eventually, the AlCan would be worked on and most of the road would be paved. In 1973, there were still hundreds of miles of gravel roads and potholes big enough that a Winnebago could fall in and never be seen again.

Still beaming, Nick glanced at Evan and said, "If you'll chip in for gas, you can come with me. It'll be cheaper than a plane ticket."

Evan thought about what kind of gas mileage the Chevelle got and doubted that was true, but he wasn't in a huge hurry to get home, and he didn't want Nick driving it alone.

"*If* we take it into a good mechanic, replace that windshield, and give it a good going-over so we don't end up stranded in the middle of nowhere, I'll bite."

"Yes!" Nick said, pounding on the steering wheel. "Road trip!"

"Road trip," Evan agreed, though somewhat less enthusiastically.

Before they returned to the boat, they swung by a garage. When they pulled in, a man in greasy overalls came out wiping his hands on a rag. "That's Vern's SS. What are you doin' with it?"

"It *was* Vern's SS. Now it's mine. His wife just sold it to me."

The mechanic whistled and shook his head. "When Vern gets back, he's gonna be *pissed*. What'd you pay her for it?"

"Fifteen hundred."

The man whistled again and said, "Well, at that price, he might not be *completely* pissed."

"We want to drive it down to the mainland. Can you give it a good going over for me? Replace any frayed belts, change the oil, maybe drop a new windshield in for me?"

The man rubbed his chin as if wondering how he could fit the car in with all his other responsibilities.

Evan looked in the bay of the garage and saw nothing but dust bunnies and oil stains. He guessed that Nick was about to make a second person's day a lot brighter.

"Leave it here with me for a few days and I can do that for you. I'll have to get a windshield in from Anchorage."

"Sure thing. We'd like to take off on Saturday if we could."

Evan looked the man over and said, "Just remember, Nick here has the bill of sale. If this Vern happens to come back between now and when you're done, this vehicle doesn't belong to him anymore."

The mechanic held his hands up defensively. "Don't worry about it, buddy. Vern never has two nickels to rub together. That's why it looks the way it does. Besides, I think he took off with Penny from the Stagger Inn. I don't expect to see him for a few months."

Evan nodded, happy that they had an understanding.

They walked back to *The Diver I*. Nick had stars in his eyes and could already see what the Chevelle would look like when he was done with it.

They killed three more days onboard the boat, waiting for the car to be ready. Nick couldn't help himself, though, and walked into town to check on the progress every day.

On the fourth day, Evan went with him—the car was ready to go.

It didn't look much different to Evan's eye, but it did have a new windshield and when Nick started it, it did sound a little smoother.

"It'll get you wherever you're going now," the mechanic said.

Evan wasn't as confident, but he knew he was too far in to back out now. Nick drove them back to the boat, noticing every little difference in the car. Evan felt a little sorry for Cindy, Nick's girlfriend in Seattle. He had a hunch she might be playing second fiddle to this hunk of Detroit steel.

They parked the Chevelle in the harbor parking lot and hurried to the boat. Nick wanted to show off his new vehicle to Bill and Burdon.

They found them in the kitchen.

"Someone was here looking for you while you were gone," Burdon said to Evan.

That didn't seem too unusual. Evan had made a few friends in Alaska, and they all knew this was where to find him. There was something about Burdon's expression that made Evan think there was something else going on.

"Did they give you their name?"

"Yeah," Burdon said and produced a business card. The fact that whoever it was had left a business card told Evan he didn't know who it was. Burdon handed him the card, which read *Alvin Timmons, Private Detective.*

"Listen," Bill said, "we don't care why someone's looking for you. A lot of people come to Alaska to get away from something, and it's none of our business. But we didn't like the way this guy looked. You can stay here as long as you want, but if I had this guy looking for me, I'd probably be moving on."

Nick looked at Evan, a little worry showing in his eyes. "We were gonna take off pretty soon anyway. Maybe we should leave now."

"I'm not running from anything," Evan said honestly. "I don't have any idea why someone would be looking for me. But, yeah, if he gave you guys a bad vibe, I guess I'd just as soon not run into him."

That made Nick and Evan's leave taking a little more abrupt than they had planned.

"I'll be back here next year, same time, same place," Nick said.

"We'll be here," Bill answered. "We'll never get away from *The Diver.*" He looked at Evan, perhaps expecting him to confirm that he would be coming back, too.

Evan just smiled and shook both of the older men's hands.

He knew he wouldn't be coming back.

Chapter Twenty-Five

Evan and Nick left that afternoon, headed first for Tok, then ready to make the thirteen-hundred-mile journey across the Al-Can.

They had only been in the car a few minutes before Nick glanced at Evan. "I'm your friend, right?"

Evan knew where this line of inquiry was going, but he went along. "Of course."

"You can tell me. Are you some kind of desperado on the run from the law? Or perhaps you're a man who seduces innocent married women then has to leave town when the husband catches on?"

That made Evan laugh. "I'm definitely not a desperado, or a bank robber, or a seducer of housewives. I'm telling you the truth. I don't have any idea why this guy is looking for me. I sleep good at night. No guilty conscience here."

Nick tapped his fingers on the steering wheel. "That's exactly what you would say if you *were* a bank robber on the lam, isn't it?"

"Probably so," Evan agreed.

They were both feeling pretty flush, so instead of sleeping in the Chevelle, they decided to get motel rooms wherever they were available. They spent their last night in Alaska in the small town of Tok, then crossed over into Canada the next morning, heading for home.

At a later time, they would have needed passports to cross into and out of Canada, but in 1975, all they needed was their Oregon driver's licenses.

Evan knew that if Nick hadn't made his impetuous purchase, he would have taken a plane and been in Seattle already. Since he had no real idea what he wanted to do once he got there and still felt like he had some time to kill before he jumped into the next phase of his plan, he didn't mind taking the slow route home.

Once they crossed over to the Yukon, the scenery was still beautiful, though in Evan's opinion, not nearly as staggering as what Alaska offered. There were long flat stretches of road with not much to look at.

But then came the wildlife. Over that first full day driving through the Yukon, they saw bison and caribou by the hundreds, foxes, bears, and porcupines. Evan wished he had thought to have bought at least a little Instamatic camera to take pictures, but he hadn't. Instead, he did his best to just live in the moment and capture each animal in his mind's eye.

The road was every bit as bad as Evan had feared. They only averaged thirty or forty miles an hour and spent their time dodging potholes. By the end of the second day, they both felt like they might need a chiropractic adjustment and to have their fillings reset when they got back to civilization.

They had a blowout on the second day, which wasn't critical. They had made sure they had a good spare in the trunk and were able to make it to the next place that passed for a town to get a new tire.

There were long stretches when they wouldn't see another vehicle for an hour or more at a time and Evan had a fear that if they broke down, they'd have to wait forever to be rescued. It didn't happen, though. The mechanic in Seward had done a good job and they made it from Tok to the border crossing in five days, and in more or less one piece.

When the Seattle skyline came into view, Nick turned and said, "What an adventure!" He drove for another mile and said, "Hey, you never told me where you're going next. Where should I drop you off?"

"I never said, because I'm not really sure."

"You could come and stay with me, but I'm going to be at my parents' house until I get a place of my own. You could sleep on their couch, though."

"As tempting as that is, why don't you just drop me off at the Greyhound station."

"Sure thing, brother."

Half an hour later, Evan was outside the bus depot, bag in hand, feeling a little dazed. He hadn't decided where he was going until the issue was forced, but he walked inside and bought a ticket to Middle Falls.

He went over his plans for what was next on the ride to town and felt like he had things arranged in his mind by the time the bus passed Artie's and pulled into the Middle Falls bus depot.

There was no one to greet him, of course, and that was fine with him. The only person he could think of that might have shown up would have been his mother, and he thought she would not have been happy to see him.

His first stop was the downtown branch of the First Bank of Middle Falls. He had closed his account when he had left on his grand adventure but wanted to put his bankroll somewhere safe.

He approached the counter and said, "I'd like to open an account."

"Of course, sir," the young man behind the counter said. He wore a gold name tag embossed with the name, *Bobby Parsale*. "Will that be with cash?"

"I've got a cashier's check." He laid the check on the counter and pushed it toward him.

Bobby's eyes fell on the amount of the check, which was more than ninety-six thousand dollars, and said, "Do you want to deposit the entire amount?"

"I think so."

"Very good," Bobby said. "The cash won't be available in your account until the check proves valid. That will take two to three days."

Evan had a hundred and fifty dollars in cash in his pocket. "That's fine. I'll stop back in and check in a few days. I'd like to buy a car, but I'll wait until the account settles."

"I'll put a rush on it for you. Stop back and check with us tomorrow or the next day. We're open from ten to three, Monday through Friday."

Evan took his receipt and wandered out into the late-summer sunshine. He really was at loose ends. He knew he would need to grab a room for the night at the Falls Inn, so he turned in that direction.

He threw his duffel bag over his shoulder and stopped at Smith and Sons Grocery. He needed a new razor and a few other toiletries. The selection at Smith's was limited, but he knew they would have the basics.

He turned down the aisle and saw a woman with a baby in one hand and a shopping basket in the other. She set the basket on the ground, picked a can of something up and put it in the basket.

Evan realized who it was.

"Mel?"

She looked up in surprise, still cradling the baby in her left arm. If Evan had been surprised to see her, she seemed completely shocked to see him. "Evan? We thought you were gone for good!"

"Looks like you've been busy!" Evan looked down at the curly-headed blonde girl in the crook of her arm, then noticed the baby bump.

"We got married just a couple of months after you left," Mel said. "Then this little missy came along." She smiled down at the little girl and said, "This is Allie."

"She's beautiful," Evan said automatically. He looked closer at Allie and realized it was true. She was her mother made over, except Mel didn't have drool on her chin, of course.

"Where've you been? We've wondered and talked about you, but never heard a word."

"I've been keeping a low profile," Evan said, then realized there was no real reason for him to do that. "I worked in Seattle for a while, then I went to Alaska. Did some fishing and worked on the pipeline."

"That sounds exotic."

"Well, no, not really. Everything worked out well, though."

"Are you back to stay now? Going to work at the hospital again?"

That seemed so far away from anything Evan had considered that he blurted out, "God, no!" He recovered a little and said, "I'm just here for a little while. I'm going to be moving to California. There's a business opportunity down there I'm going to pursue."

"We always knew you'd make it big."

"How's Jimmy?"

A wide smile lit Mel's face. "He's Jimmy. A ten-year-old in a man's body. His uncle retired a few months ago and he's buying the business out. *We're number one in the number two business* and all that, you know. When I'm not busy running after Allie, I do the books for the company. We're doing fine."

"Well, I won't keep you," Evan said. "Sure good seeing you, though."

A sudden thought seemed to hit Mel. "You should come for dinner tonight. I know Jimmy would love to see you."

Evan couldn't think of a single good reason to turn down the offer, so he said, "Sure. You guys still at the same apartment?"

"Oh, gosh, no. We're buying a house over on Primrose. You remember where that is?"

"No, not really."

"It's not far from the hospital. Turn left on Cardinal, then right on Primrose. We're at 111 Primrose Lane. Dinner will be around six. That gives Jimmy a chance to get home and wash the stink off."

"I'll see you there."

Evan walked away, picked up his razor and other things, and left the store in a slight daze. He got a room at the Falls Inn and sat on the bed, staring out into the parking lot.

He remembered the Mel he had known in his first life. Crazy, crazy Mel. That image he had in his head didn't match up at all to the young housewife he had just been talking to. Her hair wasn't perfectly done, she didn't have any makeup on, and she had bags under her eyes.

And she looked happy. Really happy.

Maybe it was me, not her, Evan thought. *Maybe it was just me that made her so crazy.*

He rolled that thought around in his mind for a while, looking for the truth of the idea. He couldn't decide how much validity it had, so he let it go.

He was hungry and considered going to Artie's for a burger basket, but when he looked at his watch, he saw that it was already five o'clock and knew that Artie's would have to wait. He opted instead for a shower.

He followed the directions Mel had given him and soon found 111 Primrose. It was a little cottage, but it was cute, with flower beds out front and a neatly mowed lawn. Jimmy's septic truck was parked alongside the house.

Evan could hear a baby—Allie, no doubt—screaming loudly when he walked up to the front door. The living room window was open, and white curtains ruffled in the breeze. It was a perfect picture of a young couple's domesticity in the mid-seventies.

Evan knocked, and Mel's voice yelled, "Come in!"

He felt a little strange just walking in, but he did. Mel was in the kitchen, baby once again on her hip with a Binky in her mouth, which had momentarily stopped the screaming.

Just then, Jimmy emerged from the back of the house. His hair was wet, obviously just out of the shower. A small cloud of shampoo and soap scent preceded him into the living room.

"I almost couldn't believe it when Mel said she ran into you." He turned his head to the kitchen, "Did you get Evan a beer?"

Mel cocked her head at Jimmy. "Do I look like I have time to play bartender?"

"Right, right." Jimmy looked at Evan and made an *oops* expression, then went into the kitchen, opened the fridge, and got three beers out. He put one on the counter for Mel, handed another to Evan, and cracked the third open.

Evan wanted to ask if Mel was really drinking while she was pregnant, but he couldn't remember exactly when that became standard advice. He decided that one beer wasn't going to hurt the baby and kept his mouth shut.

Over dinner, the conversation revolved mostly around Evan. He told them the whole story, from how he had gotten knocked on the head and lost everything, to how he had made it to Alaska and now home.

"That's absolutely incredible," Mel said. "What a story. You should write a book."

"I'm not much of a writer," Evan demurred. "And honestly, what you guys are doing here is what's incredible. When I saw you last, you had just gotten together. Now look at you. You've got a family. A house. A business."

Mel reached out and laid her hand on Jimmy's. "We had just gotten together, but I think we already knew, didn't we?"

"When you know, you know, right?" Jimmy confirmed, then belched.

"Gross," Mel chided him. In her highchair next to Mel, Allie laughed at her dad, who stuck his tongue out at her.

Several hours and several beers later, Evan finally left the house.

He wasn't sure what to think. Mel wasn't crazy, she was obviously not a gold digger, and maybe she had been with him just because she liked him, not because he was a doctor. He felt his whole perspective on things shift a little.

In his head, he tried to picture himself living in that little house with Mel and a baby. He and Becky had never had kids, so he had no idea if he would have been a good dad or not. He had enjoyed Allie's antics, but at the same time, it was kind of a relief to shut the door behind him and enjoy the quiet.

He decided that quiet domesticity probably wasn't for him, certainly not yet.

He turned his mind toward what was next. That made him smile.

He was eager to get started.

Chapter Twenty-Six

Nearly two years had passed since Evan had left Middle Falls to seek his fortune. He had been busy during much of that time, but when he was holed up in the Arroyo, or during downtimes on *The Diver I*, or after working on the pipeline, he'd had plenty of time to plan.

That plan started with the kind of car he bought to take to California. He had enough money in the bank that he could have bought any new domestic vehicle without thinking too much about it. From this point on, though, it felt like every decision he made was important.

To that end, he bought an olive green 1974 Chevrolet Caprice. It wasn't flashy, wasn't the newest model, but it represented the image he wanted to project.

Evan knew that he could have stayed in Middle Falls until the new year. He didn't really have much to do in California for another six months.

Being this close to his mother made him a little nervous, though. Middle Falls was a small town—running into Mel on the first day proved that. His mother mostly stayed home or at her flower shop, but every time he went out, Evan knew that someone would likely see him and hurry to the shop with the juicy gossip.

He couldn't have said why he returned to Middle Falls in the first place. It might have made more sense for him to stay in Seattle until it was time to go south. He had just felt an inexplicable pull, but now that he was here, he was anxious to leave.

He regretted depositing all his money in the First Bank of Middle Falls. He hadn't wanted to carry the cashier's check around with him, but this little bank was not part of some larger network. He would need to find a bank that was part of a regional or national chain so access to his money would follow him wherever he went.

He felt silly closing his account so soon after opening it, so he elected to withdraw a few thousand dollars in cash and got another cashier's check for twenty-five thousand dollars that he could deposit in a more suitable bank when he got to California.

Just four days after he had arrived back in Middle Falls, he tossed his duffel bag into the spacious trunk of the Caprice—which he liked much more than he ever had the Galaxie—and drove to Interstate 5. This time he headed south.

It took him two days to arrive in Los Altos. He could have made it in one but saw no reason to push himself.

In 1975, Los Altos was a quiet suburban city with a population of a little over thirty thousand. The area was already known to be part of what was referred to as Silicon Valley, a nickname adopted because of the region's affiliation with the silicon transistor.

It did not yet resemble the high-tech hotbed that it would in another few years when major corporations were launched and a doghouse might sell for a million dollars if it had its own lot.

It would also be the birthplace of Buddha Computers in the spring of 1976.

Evan pulled into the parking lot of an inexpensive motel at the edge of the city. He paid for three nights and hoped that when those days were up, he would have found more permanent lodgings.

The first thing he did was grab the phonebook out of the drawer by the bed and look up Harrison Bettis. He had no interest in calling him, but he was very interested in knowing where he lived.

The next morning, he gassed up the Caprice at a Chevron station and bought a map of Santa Clara County. These were the moments when he longed for his iPhone, when he could have punched the address in and it would have given him turn by turn directions.

Instead, he looked up the street in the index, then squinted at the small print on the map. He located it eventually and drove straight there.

Mr. Bettis lived in a nice neighborhood, which wasn't surprising. Evan remembered that he had been a successful executive at a large gaming company when the two Steves had recruited him to be *the adult in the room* at Buddha computers.

That wasn't too far off, since both of the boy geniuses were under twenty-five years old and Bettis was in his mid-forties.

Evan stopped for coffee and found one of the little free newspapers that featured trivia and hyper-local news items, along with ads. He noticed an ad for *Silicon Valley Realty* and jotted down the address. Being a business, it was much easier to locate than the Bettis home.

He checked his hair in the rearview mirror of the Caprice, then went inside the real estate office. The woman at the front desk introduced him to Cal Williams, who she said was the agent on duty. Cal was young, dressed in a suit, and seemed very eager to help Evan.

"I've inherited some money," Evan lied. "And I'm thinking of relocating to this area."

"Wise decision," young Mr. Williams confirmed. "I only see prices going up here. I think we might get to the point where ordinary houses are selling for a hundred thousand dollars."

"That would be something," Evan agreed. "But before I buy, I want to live in the area for a time. Get a feel for it. So, I'm looking for a rental right now."

Williams looked a little disappointed—a rental commission wasn't close to what he might make on a sale, but he recovered quickly. "We've got some lovely rentals available right now."

"Actually, I drove through an area that I'm interested in this morning." Evan opened the map and spread it out between them. He pointed to the neighborhood where the Bettis house was located. "Do you have anything in this neighborhood?"

"Oh. I'm not sure. That's the Fairwood neighborhood. Let me look in our book and see what we have available."

As it turned out, they did have something available. It wasn't right next to where Mr. Bettis lived, but that would have been too much to hope for. It was on the same street, though and was just a few blocks down.

"Would you like to see it?"

"I'd like to rent it."

"But you haven't seen it yet."

"Do you have a picture of it?"

"No, not yet. It's a new listing."

"Tell me about it."

Reading from a card in front of him, Williams said, "It's a postwar cottage with two bedrooms, a full bathroom, and a fenced backyard. It comes partially furnished, and it's renting for three hundred dollars a month."

"I'd like to fill out an application for it. I'm staying in a motel here in town, but I'd like to be able to move in as soon as you can process the application."

That proved a little trickier than it might have been because Evan didn't have a previous landlord he could use as a reference and the only personal reference he could think of was Jimmy and Mel.

Money solves a lot of problems, though, and when Evan offered to pay three times the normal deposit on the property, any concerns evaporated, and he was approved.

He had rented the property sight unseen, but when he got the keys, he thought it was perfect. It was small, which fit him fine. He moved the totality of his belongings in—which still consisted of just his duffel bag.

He sat on the couch in the cheery living room and looked around, quite content with his new beginning.

He realized that since the day he had moved out of his apartment at River Crest almost two years earlier, he hadn't had a place to call his own. He had stayed at the Arroyo and been grateful just to be out of the elements. Then he spent months onboard *The Diver I* and had shared a room while he was working on the pipeline.

Evan being Evan, he couldn't help but do a little math. He had spent five dollars a day to stay at the Arroyo. For that, he had gotten an eight by ten room with a bathroom and a shower down the hall.

For approximately twice that, he was renting a cute, comfy cottage in a great neighborhood in one of America's up and coming cities.

The difference was, when he was working at Labor, Inc, that three hundred dollars a month would have taken every penny he earned, even if he broke his back laboring every day.

Starting the next day, Evan took long walks around the neighborhood. He varied the timing of his walks, but he always went by the Bettis house twice on each walk. Within a few weeks, he had a pretty good idea of Harrison Bettis's schedule. He left for work early each day, between 7:30 and 8:00 a.m. He got home from work consistently between 6:00 and 6:30. On weekends, he mostly stayed home. Evan had no idea if he was single, married, or had kids.

Once he had his schedule down, Evan would sit in his Caprice a block or two away from the Bettis house and follow him to work. He read a book for hours, waiting and watching to see where Harrison Bettis went for lunch.

He hit a goldmine when he followed him one Tuesday morning and saw that instead of going to work, he stopped at a small restaurant. Evan followed him inside, but didn't see him anywhere. As he ordered breakfast, Evan casually asked the waitress if there was a meeting of some sort held there.

"It's the Go-Getters Networking group. They're here every Tuesday. They meet in our banquet room."

Two weeks later, the Go-Getters Networking group had a new go-getter, Evan Sanderson.

When asked to introduce himself, he said that he had inherited some money and was looking for a place to invest.

"I've heard good things about this group," Evan said, smiling.

By Christmas, he had struck up enough of a friendship with Harrison Bettis that it didn't feel odd to invite him for lunch.

In January, they took advantage of a nice break in the weather to play a few rounds of golf.

By February, Harrison invited Evan to his house for dinner. Harrison did the cooking himself, as Evan had discovered that he was not married. Their conversations were always casual, about what was happening in the local business scene and where they saw it going over the next decade, the local arts scene, and travel.

Evan told Harrison about working in Alaska. Harrison told Evan about a new venture he was starting.

Evan was predictably interested in that venture. He didn't pry or ask too many questions, but he did make it clear that he was open to hearing about its progress.

Harrison often spoke about a business he had launched five years earlier, which had failed and sent him into bankruptcy. It was an experience that stuck with him and something that colored his present decisions. To say he was risk-averse was an understatement.

Finally, after six months of friendship, he told Evan something about the inner workings of Buddha. He revealed that he had received a ten percent share in the company, but that he was concerned. The other founders had taken out a line of credit to build computers, but their first contract was with a company that was notorious for running behind on paying invoices.

Harrison was concerned that the company would accumulate debts, not have the cash to pay them, and the creditors would rightfully seek that money from the three partners. He saw shades of his previous business fiasco.

Evan held onto his nerve. That might have been a time to strike, to inquire if Harrison wanted to sell, but Evan gambled that it might still be too early.

A month later, when they were playing a round of golf, Harrison mentioned that the other partners had offered him eight hundred dollars for his shares of Buddha. Their logic was that if he was concerned about potential losses, he might be happier with a small amount of cash and no debt exposure.

"Are you thinking of taking it?" Evan asked, nearly holding his breath.

"I am. I know there's a lot of upside with this company, but there could be disaster too. I've seen too many of these startups flame out before they get anywhere."

"That's understandable, but eight hundred dollars seems like too little money."

Harrison shrugged. "The whole company is cash-poor right now, including both of them. I don't think they could come up with more."

"I can. I don't want to see you sell yourself short. I'd give you five thousand dollars for your shares."

"Oh, I couldn't let you do that. It's too risky, and that's too much money. We're friends. I can't take advantage of you."

Evan leaned in conspiratorially. He saw a foursome walking toward them and knew that he had to be quick. "I haven't told you how much I inherited."

"I would never ask," Harrison said.

"Half a million bucks," Evan lied. "I've got too much money sitting in the bank earning me almost nothing. I need to find some places that could take off. I think Buddha could."

Harrison nodded, addressed the ball, and sent a shot down the fairway. As they walked, he said, "I like it. I've got an attorney we could talk to."

"We can use your guy if you want, but I've had a guy lined up and on retainer since I got here. We can meet with him this week if you want."

Two days later, Evan and Harrison met in the offices of Mason, Tracker, and Tracker.

Two weeks later, the paperwork was done, and Evan was the proud holder of ten percent of what would one day be the world's richest company.

Chapter Twenty-Seven

What did Evan do after securing his financial future? Did he buy an island where he could build his own Bond-villain lair to plot the rest of his takeover of the world?

If not that, did he at least take a year-long vacation to some secluded beach where he sat by the rolling waves, drinking tropical concoctions with umbrellas in them?

Failing that, did he at least spend long days and nights contemplating how he would use his eventual wealth to bring his enemies, both real and imagined, to their knees?

Evan did none of those things.

The ten percent of Buddha that Evan owned would eventually make him wealthy beyond almost all imagining. In the spring of 1975, that wealth was only a far-distant dream. In fact, in those early days, his ownership position was more of a debit than a credit.

For one thing, Buddha had not gone public yet and would not do so for another five years. It wasn't as easy as going into a brokerage and buying up shares of a stock during an Initial Public Offering. Evan needed to be able to defend the deal he made with Harrison Bettis against the claims that the two Steves would launch against it.

That was why Evan had hired and paid the specific attorney he had and had only done so after doing much research over the previous years. That attorney—Gerald Tracker—specialized in just that sort of transaction and was one of the few people on the West Coast who could have devised and written a bulletproof contract that would stand up against challenges like the Steves launched.

The other downside to owning ten percent of the company was exactly what had caused Bettis to want to sell it—it made Evan partially responsible for any debts the company accrued.

In the end, the lawsuit from the two other founders of Buddha was handled the old-fashioned way, through negotiation.

Eventually, after Harrison provided an introduction and a ceasefire, Evan was able to convince them that where Bettis wanted no part of the company, Evan very much did. He also brought something with him that Bettis didn't have at the time—cash.

When you think of the eventual value of the company, the fact that Evan and his bankroll of less than a hundred thousand dollars was able to play a meaningful role in the birth of Buddha was ridiculous.

At a time when the company relied on a line of credit from a bank for only fifteen thousand dollars, Evan's willingness to put double that amount into the company's coffers was not to be scoffed at.

The Steves dropped their lawsuit, accepted Evan as a voting partner, and got on with the business of creating some of the world's best computers.

That left Evan to do essentially whatever he wanted. He wasn't involved in the company on a day-to-day basis. He was fascinated with the birth of such an iconic company, but he was not a computer guy. Beyond visiting the garage where the venture started and eventually dropping into the Buddha Campus from time to time, there wasn't much for him to do there.

Investing so much of his capital into Buddha also meant that although he would eventually be rich, that money wouldn't come for some time. In his first life, Evan remembered that Buddha had its IPO in December of 1980. Now that he had insinuated himself into the situation, though, he couldn't be sure that would happen in the same way or at the same time.

Large events that he had no personal involvement in carried on as they had in his first life. But other things, like Mel and Jimmy marrying and having a family, definitely changed.

So where was the formation and eventual public offering of Buddha on that scale? Evan didn't know and the only way to find out was to time travel the old fashioned way—one day at a time.

In the interim, he still had enough money put away to live, but he was aware that he would need to go back to work before his Buddha ship came in.

He spent the rest of 1975 in his small house in Los Altos. He continued his relationship with Harrison, which had turned into an actual friendship. Harrison continued to think that he had gotten the better end of the deal and often inquired whether Buddha had headed into choppy waters.

Evan spent the holidays of 1975 completely alone.

He didn't notice.

The first week of January 1976, Evan answered a knock at his front door. That wasn't too unusual. He didn't have a lot of friends, but there were always local girl scouts selling cookies or door-to-door salesmen trying to sell aluminum siding or something.

When Evan swung the door open, he found it was none of those things. Instead, it was a middle-aged man wearing a hat that had been out of style for decades.

"Evan Sanderson?"

"Who's asking?"

The man let his head drop to his chin as though he was about to cry. "You are the holy grail, son." He reached into his jacket pocket and produced a business card that read, *Alvin Timmons, Private Detective.*

"You're a hard man to find. You won't believe where I've been, trying to find you."

"I can guess. Seattle, Seward, and now Los Altos?"

"Those are just the places where I was close to finding you. I won't tell you about the false trails I followed."

"Good, because I don't really care. What can I do for you, Mr. Timmons?"

"Your mother would like you to call her."

Evan wasn't a big laugher. When he saw something funny or ironic, he might give a tight-lipped smile or perhaps even a small titter, but not a full-on laugh.

Except he did. Evan laughed so hard that he had to take two steps backward and hold onto the edge of the couch to keep himself upright.

Mr. Timmons did not join in.

"You know that's ridiculous, right? How much has she paid you?"

"Over the years? A substantial sum. I am not at liberty to reveal the amount. That's what took me so long to track you down, though. She kept running out of funds."

The idea that he was the cause of such an expense for his mother tickled him again. "Well, thank you, Mr. Timmons. You've delivered your message. You've fulfilled your contract. I hope it's worth what she spent on the whole thing."

"Can I ask you if you're going to call her?"

"You can. I will not."

"Son, your mother has gone to a lot of trouble to ask you to call her."

"She goes to a lot of trouble for a lot of things. One of those was making sure that I never had any interest in calling her again."

Timmons looked at him silently. Finally, he tipped his hat, said, "Good day, Mr. Sanderson," and stepped outside.

It was good to get that itch—wondering who had sicced the private detective on him—scratched. At the same time, his cozy little cottage didn't feel so cozy anymore. Timmons was likely reporting his whereabouts to his mother at that very moment.

He looked around the little house he had lived in for a year and a half. It had been a good place. Evan's plan was never to have anything that you couldn't leave behind at a moment's notice, though, and that included this little house.

Evan sent the realty his notice to vacate, along with a check for his final month's rent. He sold his Caprice to a used car lot first thing the next morning, then caught a cab to the bus depot and finally headed to San Francisco's airport.

He decided to do some traveling in the early part of America's bicentennial year.

He had wanted to take a year and go backpacking across Europe in between his college graduation and starting medical school. He had thought it would give him a good perspective on things. His mother thought it was ridiculous and forbade it.

Evan went to medical school.

That was then, this is now.

Evan had stopped cutting his hair a few months earlier, though he hadn't known why, exactly, at the time. He let it grow into a long ponytail and grew a beard. When he went first to New York and then on to Paris, he looked every bit like the grad student taking a gap year.

He still had enough money to stay in decent hotels and pay to go on tours, but he wanted to recreate the experience he had missed out on. So, he lived hand to mouth, stayed at hostels, and saw Europe up close and personal.

He spent four months bumming around the continent until the weather warmed up and he realized it was the middle of May. That made him think fondly of the times he had spent on *The Diver I*. He dashed off a postcard to Cap'n Bill and began the long trip from Amsterdam to Anchorage.

He arrived in Alaska on the last day of May and hopped a train for the ride to Seward.

When he got to the harbor, he had this terrible feeling that *The Diver I* would be gone. Sunk, perhaps, after all these years, or maybe just already out on an early season crabbing trip.

He was relieved to find it sitting in the same slip as it always did. He slung his same old duffel bag over his shoulder and made the easy jump from dock to boat.

"Bill, Burdon, where are you guys?"

It was Burdon who poked his head out of the galley. He took one look at Evan, shook his head and spat on the deck. "Holy hell, have you gone all Jesus freak on us now?"

Evan ran his hand through his long hair self-consciously. "No, but I came here straight away. I didn't want to miss the first trip of the year." He cocked an ear and listened. "Shouldn't we be getting ready to go out soon? Where's Bill?"

"Bill's dead," Burdon said matter-of-factly. "Had a heart attack in the bar and was dead before his head hit the sawdust. Exactly the way he would have wanted to go, too, the lucky bastard."

"Oh," was all Evan could manage. He hadn't exactly thought of Bill as a father figure, but he didn't have a lot of older men who had been an influence in his life, so it hit him.

"He left me this old bucket of bolts. I'm not sure if it was a gift or a curse." He looked at Evan out of the corner of his eye, almost shyly. "To tell the truth, I haven't done much to get us ready to go this year. I just haven't had it in me."

Evan absorbed that. If Bill's death had an impact on him, it must have been doubly hard on Burdon, who had been like a brother to him. He took a deep breath and said, "Well, there's nothing wrong with that. Why don't I go into town and get us a bottle. We can talk about it."

Burdon didn't say a word, but he did toss him a set of keys. "Bill's truck is parked where it always is. I could use a bit of a nip."

Evan bought enough booze for several nips and brought it all back to *The Diver I*. He might have missed any formal funeral that had been held for Bill, but he and Burdon gave him a proper two-man wake that night.

Evan was not normally much of a drinker, but sometime past midnight, deep in their cups, the two men decided they would carry on and take *The Diver I* out again. That it just wasn't proper for such a grand old lady not to be used.

"A ship is safe at harbor," Burdon said, "but that's not what ships are for."

Evan was almost sure that was a metaphor for something or other, but he'd had too many drinks and his brain was too fuzzy to puzzle it all out.

Before they both staggered off to their bunks, they had resolved to put a crew together, starting first thing in the morning.

First thing in the morning turned out to be a little after one o'clock in the afternoon, when Evan stumbled back into the galley and lit the fire under the ship's coffee. His mouth tasted like a litter box that needed to be changed.

He heard a stumbling sound behind him and a bleary-eyed Burdon wavered into the room. He sniffed delicately and said, "What are you trying to do, ruin a twenty-dollar drunk with a ten-cent cup of coffee?"

"Precisely," Evan said. "We've gotta be able to see straight if we're going to get out on the water."

It wasn't too hard, as it turned out. Evan called Nick, who had been moping in Seattle, sure that the season had been cancelled after Bill had died, at least for *The Diver I*. He promised to jump on a plane the next day.

"Not gonna drive that sweet little SuperSport up?"

A long silence, followed by, "I ended up wrecking that one so bad there was nothing left to fix. I was lucky to walk away from it."

That's the way it went with Nick and his true loves. They burned hot, but brief.

Burdon took care of the rest of the crew. He brought a mechanic on board to give the engines a once-over while Evan took Bill's old truck to Anchorage to pick up Nick.

Doug had caught on with another boat, but Jesse was quick to jump back on *The Diver I* and brought his little brother Greg and another friend named Walker. In a port town like Seward, it wasn't hard to find young people who were willing to jump on board a crabber.

The night before they pulled out of the harbor, Burdon told Evan he wanted him to be the first mate. That meant an extra quarter-share of the profits, but that was something that he wasn't worried about anymore.

"Thanks, Burdon. You should ask Nick, though. Bill was his uncle, so it would mean a lot to him."

Burdon did, Nick accepted, and when the season was over, he didn't go back to Seattle, but stayed in Seward and bought a little house. It had a garage, of course, because he found another muscle car—a '65 Mustang fastback this time—to work on over the winter.

When the season wrapped up, Evan's bankroll was healthy again. He didn't have any interest in going back to Europe, but Middle Falls wasn't calling his name, either. Now that he knew his mother was looking for him, he had no interest in being in such close proximity. He thought that he probably could have caught on with the pipeline again, but now that he didn't need the money anymore, that didn't appeal to him either.

He looked at how much cash he had, then estimated how long he would need to make that last until Buddha went public. He decided that if he was conservative with his spending, and if it went public around the same time as it had in his first life, he wouldn't need to work.

Evan Sanderson was, at his core, an ambitious person, though. Just sitting around reading books or watching television for a few years didn't appeal to him.

He decided to go back to school.

Chapter Twenty-Eight

Evan had not used his medical degree in this life, but he did still have it. With an undergraduate degree and his doctorate, it was easy for him to get into whatever college he wanted, within reason.

He couldn't have just waltzed into MIT or Stanford, but he knew he had his pick of any state college. He flew back to Seattle and looked at the University of Washington campus. He was planning on driving to see three or four other schools as well, but as soon as he walked onto the tree-lined campus of the UW, he felt at home.

It took a little doing for Evan to enroll, but he was very focused when he wanted to make something happen, and he was soon enrolled.

It was still inexpensive to live in the U-District in the late seventies. He spent the next four years living just off-campus and taking whatever classes he wanted. He didn't need any particular degree, so while he put an emphasis on business classes, he also studied Psychology, Social Sciences, and many of the world's great religions, hoping to find a clue to the strange life he was living.

That particular line of inquiry was for naught. Every religion seemed to have an idea about what happened after you died, but none of them had an explanation for waking up in your same life at an earlier date. He was sure that if this was happening to him, it was also happening to others, but he guessed that like him, they just weren't talking about it.

Evan didn't date during that time. He'd always had a relatively low sex drive and found that he preferred to continue on with his near-complete lack of intimacy than start a relationship that might turn out like the one with Mel.

The more he thought about what had happened with her in that first life, the more he decided that the difference in that Mel and the one in this life was him.

He did have a shock in his fourth year at the UW when he saw Becky sitting across from him at the Husky Union Building. He had the book *Lies, Damned Lies, and Statistics* open in front of him and was eating lunch when he happened to glance at the table next to him, and there she was.

He had put Becky so far out of his mind in this life—he had no intention of recreating their marriage—that he had completely forgotten that she had attended UW. He watched her with a certain sense of curiosity, but no instantly rekindled love of any kind.

In his first life, he had met Becky in the late eighties, so he had never seen this version of her. She was vivacious and lovely, laughing often as she and her friends sat together. She would never have recognized Evan, of course.

Nonetheless, he quickly finished his salad and left the HUB. He would never see her again in this life.

Evan made a few friends while he was going back to school. He was about a decade older than the average UW student, so everyone thought of him as the old man, which didn't bother him at all. He knew that in many ways, he was truly old enough to deserve that designation.

Evan didn't sign up for any classes in the first quarter of 1980. Instead, he packed up his duffel bag—the same one he had bought at St. Vinnie's years before—and threw it in the 1970 Ford Courier he had bought a few years earlier.

It had been reliable transportation, got good gas mileage for a pickup, and had made him very popular on weekends because college students were always moving. Once he had the Courier, he very rarely ever had to buy his own pizza or beer.

He took I-5 south through Washington, Oregon, and back to the Bay Area. Instead of settling back in Los Altos, though, he drove a few miles farther to Cupertino, where Buddha's first real office was located.

He was in an unusual position. Buddha was growing and it was becoming more and more obvious that the IPO would happen sooner, rather than later. That would make Evan a very rich man, a multiple millionaire many times over.

At that moment, though, he didn't have many assets to his name. A ten-year-old Ford Courier that was worth perhaps five hundred dollars, his duffel bag filled with clothes and toiletries, and less than five thousand dollars cash. The rest of his funds stayed safely in the bank.

The first thing he did was stop in at the Buddha offices. It was entirely different from the setup he had first seen in the garage of Steve Win's parents' home. It looked like an actual company, with employees, a warehouse, even a basketball hoop out back. The one thing that was unchanged was the Buddha logo, which Harrison Bettis himself had once designed and would soon be world famous.

When he stepped into the lobby, he was stopped by a receptionist, who told him that only employees were allowed past the lobby.

"How about owners?" Evan asked, a small grin on his face.

That was when Steve Pasternak, the jollier of the two Steves, happened to walk past. He stopped and blinked at Evan. They hadn't so much as heard from him in four years.

"The Ghost of Christmas Past," Steve said. He looked at the receptionist and said, "This guy's okay. He fleeced us out of ten percent of the company at the very beginning and now won't let go of it."

She gave Evan a quick once over—he still had his long hair and beard—as if to remember him if he showed up again. It wasn't good for job security to try to kick one of the owners to the curb.

Steve gave him a quick tour of the facility, then begged off, saying he had more work to do than was possible for any three humans. Before he showed Evan to the front door, he leaned in and whispered, "What do you see here?"

"I see a bunch of people working their asses off."

Steve nodded, then quietly said, "The IPO is scheduled and most people here are about to become millionaires." He turned away, then stepped back to Evan. "And they're just employees. You own ten friggin' percent of the whole thing. Best five thousand dollars anyone has ever spent, you lucky SOB." There was nothing harsh in his words. Steve knew he would soon be so rich he wouldn't be able to spend it all in ten lifetimes.

Evan was unsure how to react to that proclamation. He supposed he should look thrilled and surprised, but he couldn't quite manage it. To his mind, the die had been cast from the time he managed to persuade Harrison Bettis to sell.

"One last thing," Steve said as he walked away. "I saw Harrison the other day. You'd think he'd be pissed that he sold out." He shook his head. "He wasn't. He said he still thinks he made the right decision and that he's content with that. He'd rather be where he is now than the richest guy in the graveyard. Isn't that crazy?"

"Crazy," Evan agreed, and left the Buddha campus.

Evan found himself a small apartment in the poorer section of town. He knew he could have borrowed whatever money he needed against his stake in Buddha, but he was superstitious and didn't want to touch it. Instead, he decided to make his small remaining bankroll stretch until the IPO happened.

He considered finding a job. He had experience with hard labor and as a valet, after all. He made a monthly budget and figured that if he was frugal, the money he had would last. It wasn't that he didn't want to work, but he decided just to lie low and make some plans for the future. When the huge money came in, he wanted to be ready.

He didn't have to wait long. In September of 1980, Buddha Computer Company went public.

Evan Sanderson went from a net worth of four figures to eight figures overnight. That was just the beginning, of course. He recalled that in his first life, both of the Steves had divested themselves of most of their Buddha stock too early. Evan had no plans to make the same mistake.

He did sell enough of his shares to make himself slightly more liquid.

He didn't care where he lived, honestly, but to finish the rest of his plan, he needed to look respectable.

He used the influx of cash to buy a luxurious new construction house in Cupertino. It had seven thousand square feet, twelve bedrooms and sixteen bathrooms. Evan lived in about ten percent of that square footage. He did hire someone to keep the rest of it clean, though.

Evan put the second part of his plan into motion in the summer of 1981, after the dust had settled from the IPO.

Both of the Steves were media sensations and appeared on the cover of *Computing* magazine and *Business Week*, along with being interviewed—separately—by 60 Minutes. The separate interviews were necessitated by the fact that they no longer saw eye to eye about anything. They both worked at the Cupertino campus, but their offices were at opposite ends of the building and their paths rarely crossed. It was better for everyone that way.

Evan, meanwhile, flew completely under the radar. Everyone knew the Steves, no one knew him.

On a personal level, that was fine with him. Evan was ambitious—as much as anyone ever was—but he didn't find satisfaction in headlines or magazine covers. He danced to his own interior drummer, and he believed he would find happiness when his exterior situation matched that interior beat.

Still, to bring that picture into focus, he knew he needed to be known, at least in the proper circles.

To that end, he contacted Michael Trujillo, who had written a best-selling biography of the CEO of Ford Motors a few years earlier. Evan wasn't interested in anything so grandiose as a full-blown biography, but he did want people to know some of his story.

He pitched Trujillo on writing a lengthy article that covered his rise from homelessness on the streets of Seattle to how he earned his nest egg with the sweat of his brow in Alaska, to the prescient and savvy investment in Buddha that had made him rich. In exchange for writing the article, Evan promised to be completely forthcoming and honest.

For a business writer, that was irresistible fodder, so Trujillo flew to San Francisco. Evan himself picked him up at the airport in his jet-black 1981 Mercedes Benz 380 SL. The interview began as Evan drove them through the traffic back to Cupertino.

Trujillo probed and parried. Evan answered all questions honestly. Unless the reporter asked him if he was living the same life again, he had nothing to hide.

Instead of putting Trujillo up at a local hotel, Evan insisted on having him stay in one of the many empty bedrooms in his mansion.

They spent three days together. Trujillo always had his tape recorder running and he warned Evan that he would be fact checking everything he said.

The story was good enough—a true rags to riches tale—that Evan didn't need to embroider any of the details.

Trujillo sold the article to *Fortune Magazine* and it ran in the October 1981 issue.

Overall, Evan was pleased with the article, which was titled *The Horatio Alger Prototype is Alive and Well and Living in Cupertino.*

It met his goal, which was to start to build the idea that he was a business Nostradamus, able to see the future where others only saw today. That would help him accomplish the rest of what he wanted to do.

He was slightly taken aback by some of what Trujillo wrote, though.

The first paragraph of the article set the tone: *It is well established that the poor are crazy, while the rich are simply eccentric. Evan Sanderson, a millionaire many times over, though he is barely thirty, is eccentric.*

Evan thought of himself as the most down-to-earth, practical person there was, as far from *eccentric* as he could be.

The eccentricities that Trujillo found were the fact that though he lived in a large mansion, he only occupied a small portion of it. That even though he had a garage with luxury cars, Evan was most likely to drive around Cupertino in an old Courier pickup. That in the rapidly evolving Silicon Valley, Evan not only didn't have a computer, but he didn't even own a television.

Evan had thought those things were nothing out of the ordinary. Why would he dirty up more of his home than he needed to, or heat all those extra rooms? Why would he have a television when he would much rather read a good book? And his Courier? Well, he admitted that it simply reminded him of one of the happy times of his life as a student.

Soon enough, he shrugged the accusation of eccentricity off. Bemusedly, he said to himself, "Guess it's none of my business what other people think of me."

The same day the magazine hit the newsstands, his phone began to ring. Evan never answered it, instead letting it go into his answering machine, where he dutifully took down every message, then threw almost all of them away.

A few days later, his phone rang again. Evan stood bent over a notepad, ready to take down another name and phone number he would never use. Instead, it was a familiar voice.

"Evan, this is Mel. We've wanted to get in touch with you for months, but we didn't know how to reach you..."

Evan fumbled for the phone, cutting off the answering machine.

"Mel? It's good to hear from you. How are Jimmy and the kids?"

"We're good, Evan. We saw that you're doing really well for yourself. Congratulations."

Evan's stomach tightened, wondering if Mel would put the arm on him for some money. If she did, he would let her have whatever she asked for, but he truly hoped it was something else. In many ways, they were his two oldest friends, and he didn't want to be thought of as just a source of easy money.

The years had made Mel's voice a little deeper, and her tone was serious, as though she had something heavy to convey. She didn't delay in doing so.

"We've been trying to reach you because your mother is dead."

Chapter Twenty-Nine

Evan wasn't sure what to say. Instinctively, he knew this was one of those situations where social mores called for him to make a response, but the things that ran through his mind wouldn't work.

Ding-dong, the witch is dead was his first thought.

I don't care, was his second and most honest thought.

Some people who cut people out of their lives might regret that decision when that person dies.

For Evan, he had given himself the freedom to think that Camille was dead the moment he decided to quit being a doctor and left Middle Falls without telling her.

At the same time, this was a new data point. He'd had as little as possible to do with Camille, but things had obviously changed in her life. In his first life, she had died in the mid-nineties. Now, here she was dead and gone more than a decade earlier.

An idea clicked in his mind that he realized he should have understood earlier. It wasn't just his actions that would change things, it was also his complete *lack* of actions. In his first life, he had played the dutiful son, staying in contact, sending cards and making phone calls right up until the end. He had done that because he didn't know any way *not* to do that. This time, he had found the emotional wherewithal to break free.

"Evan, are you there?" Mel asked.

"Yes, I'm here."

"I'm sorry to tell you news like this over the phone. We just didn't know how to reach you when it happened."

Evan knew he should be asking at least a few questions. "When did it happen?"

"A few months ago. I'm sorry, I don't remember exactly. Jimmy and I both tried to figure out how to reach you, but we're not very good detectives. Until we saw the article, we had no clue."

"You two read *Fortune Magazine*?" Evan instantly realized that he should have kept the note of incredulity out of his voice, but it was too late by then.

If Mel noticed, she wasn't defensive about it. "What? Oh, no. We've got two kids in school, and Jimmy's expanding the business, which doesn't leave us time for anything. But there was a story about you in the *Middle Falls Gazette* today. You know, the whole *Local boy makes* good angle. I do manage to at least look at the headlines with my coffee in the morning. Now that I think about it, it did say something about some big writeup you got. It also said you're one of the richest people in the country."

"I guess that's right," Evan confirmed. Then, because Mel hadn't asked, he offered. "Do you guys need anything, Mel?"

"Us? No, we're doing fine. If you could give me an extra hour in every day, I could sure use that." She laughed a little, but it trailed off.

"How did it happen?"

"What?"

"Mom's death. How did it happen?"

There was a long stretch of silence on the other end of the line. Finally, Mel said, "I'm so sorry, Evan. She killed herself."

A sudden image jumped into his mind. "Did she jump off the falls?"

"What? Oh my God, no. What would make you ask that?" Another silence that Evan didn't step into. "It wasn't supposed to be made public, but you know how Middle Falls is. Everyone knew she hanged herself."

"That's an unusual suicide method for women," Evan said, his analytical mind taking over again. "Prescription medication is far and away more common."

"I can't be sure about this, but I heard from Mary, who heard it from her sister, who heard it from the medic who responded, that there was a note there addressed to you. I'm sure if you reach out to someone, they'll give it to you."

A shudder ran down Evan's spine. She had paid the ultimate price to once again deliver a message to him. For a minute, he pictured opening the envelope and finding that the entire message was, *Call your mother.* A small laugh escaped his lips.

"Oh, Evan, I'm so sorry to tell you like this. I wish I was there to give you a hug."

"Oh, I'm fine, Mel. I really do appreciate you reaching out and telling me. If you hadn't, I probably would have never known."

"Not coming home any time soon, then? I suppose you'll be jetting off to points unknown with beautiful women hanging on your arm."

"That's the image, isn't it? That's not for me. You know me and how I am."

"I do. We care about you, Evan. Please let us know if you're coming back home. You could probably buy and sell the whole town, but we'd still like to make you dinner. You can see how much the kids have grown."

"I'd like that, and I will," Evan said, and he meant it. Now that his mother was dead, he felt much more likely to go back to Middle Falls than he had been. "Say, do you know if someone has been appointed to handle her estate?"

"I do. Everyone knows everything about everyone. She hired a new attorney from here in town to handle things. It seems that she was very organized about everything."

"I have no doubt," Evan said drily. "She wouldn't be able to do it any other way. Do you know his name?"

"Thomas Weaver. He grew up around here. Do you know him?"

"No, that's not familiar. Thanks, Mel. I'll give him a call and see if there's anything I need to do to take care of things."

"Jimmy told me to be sure and tell you hi for him."

"Tell him the same for me." Evan nearly hung up, but before he did, he said, "You got a good one there, Mel."

"I know," she said softly. "Bye, Evan."

He called Information and asked for the number for the law office of Thomas Weaver. He dialed the number, and a man's voice answered. "Law Firm, Thomas Weaver speaking."

"Hello, Mr. Weaver. This is Evan Sanderson. I understand you're handling my mother's estate."

"Hello, Mr. Sanderson," Thomas's voice brightened. "I've been looking for you. My sincere condolences about your mother."

"We weren't in touch. An old friend reached out to me just now to let me know what had happened."

"Are you coming up to Middle Falls? If you are, we could meet instead of doing this over the phone."

"No, I'm very busy right now," Evan lied. "I won't be coming up."

"Of course. I read the article in the *Gazette*. Congratulations."

"Thank you."

"Your mother left everything to you. It's not an extensive estate, but she did own her house free and clear, and she had some other small assets."

"Would it be kosher for me to retain you to do some things for me?"

"That depends," Thomas said. "I couldn't do anything that would be a conflict of interest, but aside from that, I'd be happy to help."

Evan nodded from a thousand miles away. Any attorney who answers his own phone could probably use the business.

"I'd like you to form a non-profit foundation for me."

"Of course. That wouldn't be a conflict at all. What is the aim of this non-profit?"

This was a new plan, still forming in Evan's mind, and he hadn't gotten quite that far, yet. He thought back on his own darkest days. "I'd like it to assist the homeless."

"Of course. Wonderful." Thomas hesitated, then said, "There isn't a huge amount of homelessness here in Middle Falls, of course."

"I understand. This isn't just a Middle Falls non-profit. It will be more extensive."

"I see. Yes, I can certainly set that up for you. How would you like to fund it?"

"I'll send you a check today as seed money. Then, I'll add more to that over time. I'd like you to liquidate my mother's estate and put everything from that into the foundation as well."

"I see." The two words spoke volumes.

Evan could hear a pen scribbling notes on the other end of the line.

"Can you give me your address?"

Thomas did and Evan jotted it down. "I'll get a check off to you today."

"What would you like to call the foundation? Name it after your mother, perhaps?"

"God no!" Evan blurted out. "I don't care. Choose any name for it, but not that. Wait. No, I've got an idea." He had to search his memory to come up with the correct last name, but it eventually popped into his mind. "Call it the Marge Barrow Homeless Foundation."

"Marge Barrow. Got it. Who would you like to be on the board of this foundation? You, of course."

"I guess. Can you be on it?"

"If you wish."

"Place a call to the Mission in Seattle and ask for Marge Barrow. She should be on the board, too."

"The Mission, Seattle. That's a homeless shelter, isn't it?"

"It is. She'll know what to do with the money."

"One last thing, Mr. Sanderson..."

"Evan, please."

"All right. One last thing, Evan, your mother left a note for you in a sealed envelope. If you'll give me your address, I'll send it on to you."

Evan wanted to tell him not to bother but felt like he didn't want to involve this man in his family's dysfunction quite that much. He gave him the address.

When he hung up, he immediately wrote a check for a hundred thousand dollars, put it in an envelope and addressed it to Thomas Weaver.

A week later, the promised envelope containing his mother's last message arrived. Evan opened the envelope and felt nearly sick at the familiarity of his mother's handwriting.

He held it thoughtfully for a few seconds, then tossed it unopened into the trash and never thought of it again.

Chapter Thirty

There are a few truisms about money that applied to Evan Sanderson's third life.

It is difficult to make the jump from poor to rich.

It is easier to go from rich to *very* rich.

It is once again difficult to go from very rich to the *richest*.

Evan had weapons at his disposal that others did not. He had knowledge of what was going to happen years, even decades, before it did.

Even though he had that foreknowledge, that wasn't always enough.

Ironically, it was when he failed in his missions that he ended up succeeding.

One of his first forays into building his reputation was when he approached the Mars Company, manufacturers of Wrigley Gum and M&Ms, among many other products.

He remembered that Steven Spielberg had approached them about using M&Ms in his film *E.T. the Extra Terrestrial*. Mars had turned them down, Spielberg had instead turned to Reese's Pieces, and that brand had gotten a huge boost from the ensuing publicity. It was considered one of the bigger branding missteps in modern business history.

In early 1981, he wrangled an appointment with Mars and advised that they accept the product placement in the film when the opportunity arose.

The company thanked Evan for his input and showed him the door.

When the film came out and Reese's Pieces market share jumped, the Mars Company approached Evan and offered him a seat on their advisory board. He happily accepted.

His reputation was building.

Another of the giant foul-ups that he remembered was in the mid-eighties, when the Coca-Cola company got rid of the formula that had served them well for a hundred years and launched *New Coke* in its place.

Evan knew that the change would be a disaster for the company. As a nobody, he never could have gotten the ear of anyone at Coca-Cola. As a board member of Mars Company and the man who had turned five thousand dollars into a fortune, though, he was able to get a meeting. Not with the CEO, or someone on the board of directors, but at least with the president of the marketing division.

Evan flew to Atlanta in early 1984 and met with that man, Harley Stephenson. The first bump in the road was when Evan revealed that he knew Coke was planning on the change. That had not been announced to the public yet, and Stephenson immediately suspected industrial espionage in general and Evan in particular.

Evan hadn't anticipated that, but assured him that he was simply adept at reading the tea leaves and that he didn't want anything from the company. He wasn't holding the information hostage, or threatening to go public. He simply wanted to warn the company away from such a dangerous strategy.

Stephenson didn't immediately dismiss the warning. When someone with a fortune and a growing reputation like Evan flew across the country with a message, the least he could do was listen. He even mentioned it to the board.

Evan's advice was laughed out of Atlanta.

And that worked completely in Evan's favor. He didn't have any profit motive in warning them away, but he did have a motive to burnish his reputation once they didn't listen.

As soon as the news broke that New Coke was hitting stores, Evan went on a publicity blitz, telling newspaper, magazine, and television reporters what a disaster the move was going to be.

He was largely ignored initially, as the Coke publicity machine had geared up and there was a lot of positive word on the streets.

It didn't take long for the tide to turn, however. Consumers revolted and when they found they couldn't get the original formula, threatened to boycott Coke altogether.

Just seventy-seven days after New Coke was launched with great fanfare, the company pulled it from the market. Everything old was new again.

Coca-Cola got egg on their face.

Evan was seen as a business prophet.

From that moment on, his rise was inevitable and unstoppable.

He spoke to the Kodak company, who had designed the first digital camera in the seventies, but had essentially abandoned it because their film division was so profitable. Now, when Evan spoke, people listened. Kodak, instead of being left behind in the digital revolution, became a market leader.

For his invaluable advice, Evan was offered shares in the company, which became more valuable in the ensuing decades.

Of course, he knew what the big picture of the stock market looked like. He invested heavily in Microsoft on its IPO, then bought each dip and eventually rode it to many more billions of dollars.

He rode the dot-com bubble up, up, up, then sold just before the crash in the late nineties, making billions and billions more.

He fought to get a seat on the Blockbuster Video board so that when a young startup called Netflix came calling and was willing to be bought out, he was able to champion the idea.

In his first life, Blockbuster had passed on the opportunity, Netflix had exploded, and David felled Goliath.

In this life, thanks to Evan, Blockbuster acquired Netflix. When the era of DVDs and Blu-Rays passed, they were in a position to grow with their streaming giant.

Again, Evan was one of the prime beneficiaries of that growth.

He no longer had any need of publicity, but now couldn't stop it. *Inc. Magazine* featured him on its cover, staring into a crystal ball with the headline, *The Man Who Sees the Future.*

Evan met every goal he ever had in this life.

He was the richest man on the planet.

Even so, his day-to-day life barely changed. He had never wanted to actually *have* the money. There was nothing he wanted to buy, no experience he wanted to take advantage of. Becoming the richest man in the world was just another item on his life's to-do list. Once it was checked off, he essentially forgot about it as much as possible.

His immense fortune was a runaway train that no longer needed him at the controls. He turned his attention to trying to give it away, but couldn't come close to keeping up with how much he profited every day.

He gave millions of dollars to charity, but that never felt fulfilling. He always wondered how effective that money was, and whether it actually helped the people he intended.

He came up with a new idea and implemented it at once. He called the President of one of his companies and asked him to name the most trustworthy person who worked for them. The President assured Evan that he had no idea. He oversaw the making of money, nothing more. He knew nothing of the people who did the real work. He did, however, recommend the Vice President of personnel.

That Vice President was equally insulated from the day-to-day realities of the people who worked for the company. He did, however, recommend someone lower down the food chain.

Evan was not someone to give up easily, though he did realize exactly how isolated he was from all aspects of his various companies.

His life had become board meetings and reading memos, which slowly drained the life out of him.

Still, he didn't give up.

He fought through the layers of people, until he found a General Manager who actually had some contact with the people who did the actual work of the company.

Evan dialed him, hoping, hoping.

"Jasper," the man answered.

Evan wasn't quite sure if that meant the man's last name was Jasper or if that was his given name.

"Mr. Jasper?"

"Yes, as I said, this is Jasper."

"This is Evan Sanderson."

"Okay, all right, that's very funny. I don't have time for jokes. Who is this and what can I do for you?"

"This is Evan Sanderson. If you'd like to use video on this call, that should confirm it."

A moment later, the man's face, suddenly alarmed, appeared on Evan's phone. "Mr. Sanderson! I had no idea!"

"I understand. I seem to have lost complete contact with every aspect of my companies that actually do anything. Can you tell me, is there someone in the company who is sharp, yet trustworthy? I don't really want someone who is ambitious. I'm looking for someone who is service oriented."

Evan watched as the man ran through dozens, perhaps hundreds, of people in his mind. Finally, he settled on someone.

"I do have someone like that. His name is Murphy. Harold Murphy. We do strengths and psychological testing on all employees and he came back with the highest responsibility scores we've ever recorded."

"Very good. Can you have Mr. Murphy call me at this number?"

"Immediately."

Evan signed off the call and set his phone down. It wasn't immediate, but it was quick. Two minutes later, his phone rang again.

"Mr. Sanderson? This is Harold Murphy. Mr. Jasper instructed me to call."

"Mr. Murphy, I'd like you to give up the responsibilities you currently have and report directly to me now. Do you understand? I will call Jasper back and make the arrangements."

"Yes, sir."

"Where are you?"

That seemed to flummox young Mr. Murphy. "I'm in Indiana, sir. Where we all are."

Evan honestly did not know he owned a business in Indiana, but took him at his word. "I think you can start this project there, or wherever you want. I'm going to have a company car assigned to you, and give you an expense account of a million dollars a year."

"Sir?"

"That's just to cover your own expenses as you do the work I have for you."

"Yes, sir. What is that?"

"I want you to give away my money, but do it in places that it actually helps people. Not to charities and the like, but to people. People who are hurting. It can be the homeless, or single parents, or families that are suffering. I don't care who it is, I'd just like all this money to do some good for someone. I want you to drive around the country and find people who need help and give it to them. Understood?"

"No sir. I mean, yes sir, I understand, but I'm not sure how I will do that."

"That's all up to you, Murphy. You're a bright young man. I'll have Jasper give you the car and two cards. One will be for your personal expenses. The other will be money I'd like you to give away."

Obviously stunned by this sudden turn of events, Murphy said, "How much should I try to give away?"

"These sums of money get so huge, so fast that we almost can't comprehend them. I've been trying unsuccessfully to give money away for years, but I wake up every day with more of it. I'll put a billion dollars at your disposal. If you need more than that, contact me and I will make arrangements. I'd like you to write up a report once a month and tell me some of what you've done with the money. I don't care about the amounts, or a specific accounting. I'd just like to know that we are doing some good in this world. Understood?"

"Yes, sir."

Evan rang off, then called Jasper and made arrangements with him to carry out his instructions.

For the next few years, that monthly report from Harold Murphy was the highlight of Evan's life.

BECAUSE EVAN NEVER really *felt* wealthy, he didn't take the precautions that virtually all of his peers did.

He had a very basic security system. No bodyguards, no dogs. Even as the wealthiest man in the world—which he remained, no matter how much of his money he tried to give away—he had no security guards paroling the perimeter of his house.

That was his undoing when, in December of 2023, a mentally ill young man broke into his house.

Evan wasn't aware he had been broken into until he awoke to the man standing over him in his bedroom.

"What's this, then?" Evan asked, groggy.

The young man pointed a gun at Evan's head.

Evan thought back on his life. It had been fine. He had accomplished everything he had ever wanted, but he had never known any profound sense of happiness or satisfaction.

He took a deep breath and let it out. "Go ahead then."

Interlude Two
Universal Life Center

"Charles, do you have a moment?" Max asked.

"Yes," Charles answered, appearing over Max's shoulder instantly.

"I think this played out the way we planned. He achieved his goal."

"And found it wanting?"

"Of course. I'm not sure where to put him next. He's still got that early problem in his life, but I don't know if dropping him into it again will help him resolve it. He will be so young and helpless. I worry for him."

Once again, Charles took Max's pyxis and turned it this way and that, scrolling through several lifetimes worth of memories. "This may take more time. But if we don't help him face his fear, he will never overcome it."

"What do you think of this?" Max asked, spinning the pyxis back and pointing at a young family. His charge was only two years old, sitting on the floor, watching his parents fight. His head moved back and forth between them as if he was watching a tennis match.

"This is where his father leaves," Max observed. "He never comes back. Evan does not know him at all."

Charles peered at the pyxis more closely, focusing on the father. "He has much fear, as well."

"What can we do?"

Charles shook his head, thinking the problem over. He worked more equations in the air in front of him, then said, "There is no path to likely success here."

"But if we simply let him relive this trauma over and over, he will have a difficult time overcoming it."

"That's what my equations show, yes." Charles spun the pyxis so that the image jumped forward in time. The child, now a teenager, sat at a kitchen table, doing homework. "If we start him here, he might find his way, if he has the courage."

"That's it, then," Max agreed. "Let's see what we can do to help him get there."

Chapter Thirty-One

Evan Sanderson opened his eyes. He jumped as though he was expecting a bullet to enter his temple.

Instead, he felt a stinging pain across his back.

Behind him, a voice said, "Your mind is wandering again. Focus, Evan. Focus." It was a familiar voice, though one he hadn't heard in a very long time. Some voices stay in our heads no matter how we try to forget them.

He shook his head to try and clear it.

"Where am I?"

Another stinging blow on his back. "Don't be funny, Evan. Do you think I want to stand over you while you do your homework? Of course not. If you would just concentrate, I could be doing something else. Instead, I have to stand here, vigilant to your wandering mind."

The room around him came into better focus and Evan realized he *did* know where he was.

He had died twice before and both times had woken up in the break room at Middle Falls General Hospital. This was definitely not that.

This was worse.

This was the dining room in the house he grew up in.

This was hell, at least for Evan.

"Not here," Evan said, almost crying—not from the blows, but from the realization of what that meant. In his mother's house. Under her control. Unable to get away.

He realized that if he was sitting in this room, then he was young, though he couldn't have guessed just how young.

A moment before, he had been the wealthiest man in the world. He could have had anything.

Now he was small. Helpless. Defenseless.

Another blow lashed across his back. He didn't need to look to see what his mother was hitting him with. No matter how many lifetimes he lived, he would never forget the bamboo stick she used. He knew he would do whatever he needed to in order to make those blows stop.

He realized that a tear had leaked out of his eye. He reached up to wipe it away, but only got another strike across his back, harder this time.

"You can never show weakness. Is that what you are, Evan? Weak? Like your father? I won't allow it. You will be strong." Her voice was cold and distant, but there was menace in it. An unspoken promise of more pain if he didn't bend to her will.

He didn't turn to face her. He wasn't sure he could.

"It's not fair," he mumbled, then realized instantly the mistake that he had made.

"Fair?" Camille shrieked the word. She said it again, practically spitting the word out. "Fair. There is no fairness in this world. If you are weak and whining for fairness, the world will grind you under the heel of its boot. Now focus!"

Evan looked down at the notebook in front of him. There were equations written out. A thick textbook was propped up on the table in front of him.

He nodded and made a conscious effort not to sniffle the snot he felt in his nose. To not be *weak*. He focused on what was in front of him, waiting for another blow.

Before it came, he ran the finger of his left hand across the problem in the textbook.

For most people, being thrown from adulthood back to school age would have meant that the problem in front of him and the equation needed to solve it, would have been impossible.

Evan was not most people. He had focus. He had strength.

He realized with relief that the problem in front of him was not difficult. He took a deep breath, then began to work the problem. He wrote some figures on a piece of scratch paper, then wrote the correct formula in his notebook.

He didn't even bother to stop and say, "There. Done." He knew better. He went on to the next problem, then the next. He even took some small pleasure in ticking each of them off. He worked for a steady twenty minutes until he had finished every problem in the chapter.

The work came easily to him and allowed him to think of other things while he did it.

He wondered how old he was. To be more specific, *when* he had woken up. There were only a few clues. The problems weren't hard, so this was probably junior high school or maybe his freshman year in high school. That would make him thirteen or fourteen.

Grief almost overcame him, but he stuffed it down. He wondered what he could possibly do to improve his situation when he was so young. In all likelihood, he couldn't even drive legally yet. How could he get away from her?

He closed the textbook quietly, flinching slightly as he expected another stinging rebuke from the bamboo.

None came.

He finally allowed himself to look around the room, to make eye contact with his mother.

She wasn't there.

He had no idea when she had slipped away, but her instinct was as sharp as ever. She knew when he had locked into the process.

She came back into the room from the kitchen. "Let me see your work."

Evan blanched at the sight of her. She was young. He had thought of her as the iron-haired woman for so long that it was jarring to see her hair a soft brunette, her face unlined. There was nothing soft about Camille Sanderson. He recovered before she could comment on his recalcitrance and handed her his notebook, opened to the proper page.

She wore her reading glasses on a chain around her neck. Placing them on the end of her nose, she sat in the seat beside Evan. She smoothed the pages out and began to pore over them.

Evan had a very grown-up thought. *Does she really understand what she's looking at? She is an intelligent woman, but is she really able to look at my algebra homework and know if I'm doing it right? Or is she bluffing?*

Camille closed the notebook and handed it to Evan. "Very good. This is the kind of work you can do when you concentrate. Put your homework away now. It's dinner time."

Evan was grateful to get away from her penetrating gaze. He gathered up his books and took them to his room. The layout of the house was familiar to him. His room didn't give him much of a clue as to how old he was. He looked in the mirror over his dresser. It was shocking, of course, to see his more child-like face, but he was somewhat prepared for it.

That still didn't give him much help. Flashing on a sudden idea, he pulled his pants and underwear away from his groin and looked down.

That helped. He knew he was past puberty, at least. He looked around his room, which was plain and undecorated. There were no posters or artwork on the walls. No overflowing toy chest. Just a bed, nightstand, dresser, and a bookshelf filled with books.

He knelt in front of the books and ran his fingers along the spines. Two dozen Hardy Boys books, almost the same number of Jim Kjelgaard stories. He pulled a hardback copy of *Snow Dog* out and looked at the cover. There was something comforting about it, like finding an old friend in an unfamiliar and unfriendly place.

"Dinner!" Camille's voice came from down the hall like she was Mrs. Cleaver calling Wally and the Beav, with no indication that she had essentially been an SS guard a few minutes earlier.

Evan reluctantly left the comfort of his room and went back to the dining room. There were two place settings with plates already made. The plates were perfectly proportioned with a dry hamburger patty for protein, green beans and bread. None of it looked appetizing, but Evan remembered what happened if he didn't eat dinner.

He sat down opposite his mother and picked up his fork.

"Evan!" Camille said as though he had committed some terrible etiquette breach. He searched his mind, wondering what his faux pas had been.

"Vitamins first, always."

Evan nodded once. He had forgotten the vitamins. When he was very young, his mother had asked the pediatrician what vitamins would help his brain grow and function best. That was a question the doctor had never been asked before, but when Camille brought Evan in for his next appointment, he gave her a list. That list became her bible and she had made Evan consume them with breakfast and dinner from that point forward.

Once he left his mother's house, he never took any kind of supplement again.

Evan swallowed the handful of vitamins, then began to cut and chew his food mechanically. If there was any flavor in the meat, he couldn't taste it, but he chewed it until he could force it down with a drink of milk. He knew not to eat too fast, that would bring him another reprimand. Instead, without appearing to watch his mother, he timed it so that he finished his food just a few seconds before she did.

After the reminder to take his vitamins, they hadn't spoken another word through the meal.

When they finished, Camille dabbed at her mouth with her napkin and said, "It's getting late. I'll do the dishes and you can have an hour of free reading, then it's bedtime."

Evan glanced at the clock on the dining room wall. The hands showed it was 7:17. That meant that his mother expected him to be in bed, lights out, at a quarter after eight. He knew that would rankle him eventually, but for this night, he was happy to get away from her and be able to gather his thoughts.

He hurried into his bedroom and closed the door behind him. After grabbing any random book off the shelf, he sat down on his bed. He opened the book to a spot in the middle, then placed it across his lap, where he could grab it and appear to be reading if need be.

He tried to sort through his thoughts, but it was challenging. He had been living a perfectly fine life, with more money than he had ever needed, still in good health in his late seventies, and well quit of the woman who had terrorized his childhood.

Then, the break-in, his off the cuff answer to *go ahead then*, and he opened his eyes here.

The truth is, at some point, he had stopped thinking of the life he just left as his third one. After living in it for more than fifty years, it was just his life. He hadn't given much thought to what would be next as he aged.

If pressed, though, he would have felt some degree of certainty that when he died, he would open his eyes right back where he had the last two times.

Instead, this.

Evan berated himself. He knew well enough that two similar events do not guarantee a pattern.

He wondered what would happen if he did the same thing he had done in his second life. That is, run out to the falls and jump in. Would he wake up here again, or back in Middle Falls General, or some other spot altogether?

He didn't think he could do that. When he had jumped in his first reawakening, he hadn't thought of it as killing himself. He had been sure he had been in a dream and thought that was a way to shock himself back to his real life.

Now he knew that these lives were real, though they weren't entirely logical.

If he couldn't try that particular method to escape to a new life, what *could* he do?

He was, after all, a man, not a boy. He had well over a hundred years of life experience. He wouldn't be cowed by this small woman in the other room.

He knew that was all bluff and bravado. Whether he was a grown man in his mind or not, he was in a teenager's body. He hadn't quite figured that out for sure. In any case, he was physically too young to be able to stand up to the iron-fisted will of his mother. He had barely managed that as an adult.

The door opened silently before he had a chance to raise the book and pretend to be reading.

Camille's instincts were operating at one hundred percent. "What are you thinking about, Evan?"

Just thinking about how to get away from you, mother dear.

"Nothing. Just the book I'm reading."

She stepped across the room, cat-quick, and snatched the book out of his hands. She slipped it behind her back.

"Oh? Tell me about it. What were you thinking about specifically?"

Evan was glad he had at least glanced at the cover of the book and was doubly thankful for his outstanding memory. Maybe the vitamins he took all those years had helped.

"It's a book called *Fire Starter*. It's about two young people who get left behind by their tribes in the ancient past and have to figure out how to survive on their own. It led the main character, named Hawk, to invent a weapon that we would call an atlatl. I was just sitting here thinking that harsh circumstances can sometimes lead to great discoveries."

Camille narrowed her eyes. She had never read *Fire Starter*, but the picture on the cover did indeed look like the story he was telling.

"Good. Glad to see you are thinking about themes in the book instead of just reading to see what happens next. That is the sign of a weak mind." She put the book back into its spot on his bookshelf, then turned and offered her cheek to Evan.

If giving his mother a kiss wasn't the absolute last thing on Evan's wish list, it was pretty close. Nonetheless, he pursed his lips and put a dry kiss on her cheek.

"Goodnight, Evan."

Something occurred to him at that moment. His mother had never called him by anything but his given name. Never *son*, or *Ev*, or even *Hey, you!* Just one more strictly formal aspect of their relationship. It was more a business relationship than familial.

He didn't connect the dots and think about how he had replicated that with Becky in his first life.

Camille turned the light out and closed the door.

Evan quietly undressed and put his clothes in the hamper in the corner. He climbed between the sheets and stretched out, his hands behind his head. He fidgeted. That was uncomfortable. The bamboo stick had left light bruises there. He rolled over on his side, certain that he would never be able to go to sleep so early.

He let his mind wander over what possibilities existed for this life.

Just before he fell into a deep slumber, he came to a decision.

He would run away.

Chapter Thirty-Two

Evan was lost in a deep sleep, dreaming of other lives. Better lives. A sharp pain in his side brought him around. He opened his eyes to see Camille standing over him, one bony finger pushing into his ribs.

"Are you sick? I've been trying to wake you up for five minutes."

"I'm fine," Evan said groggily. "Just really deep asleep, I guess."

Camille looked daggers at him. Anything that was out of the ordinary turned her radar on high. She couldn't seem to think of any nefarious reason why Evan was so fast asleep. "I've laid your clothes out. There's oatmeal on the table for you. You've got twenty minutes until you leave the house. Don't be late. I've got to get into the shop. I have a big order of flowers coming in this morning. Big day next week."

Evan didn't ask why she needed a big order for the next week. He knew that meant that it was either the week before Valentine's Day or Mother's Day, the two biggest weeks of the year for her.

Evan quickly swung his legs off the bed and had gathered up his clothes and headed for the bathroom before Camille could leave the room. He urinated, then hurried to get dressed. He ran a comb through his short hair—not quite a crew cut, but not far off.

The clothes he got dressed in were definitely old-fashioned. Stiff blue jeans, a brownish button-down shirt and a T-shirt worn underneath. It made him miss the comfortable clothes and soft fabrics he had worn in his previous life.

He brushed his teeth quickly, then hurried to the dining room. He knew the clock was ticking and that he would have to leave soon.

He wanted to have more information before he did. He wasn't even sure if he should head to the high school or junior high. Both were on the same campus but at opposite ends.

He bolted his oatmeal so quickly that he knew if Camille was there, she would have been shocked and revolted. He grabbed the handful of vitamins and stuck them in his pocket, reminding himself to toss one here and there as he walked to school. There would be hell to pay if he forgot and she found them in his pocket, but he wasn't going to take them. He had decided to rebel in any way he could.

He downed his small glass of milk, then dashed into the kitchen, scrubbed his bowl and glass out and put them in the dishrack beside the sink.

He estimated that he still had seven or eight minutes to look around before he had to leave. There was no calendar hanging in the kitchen or anywhere else in the house, which surprised him. He stood briefly in the dining room, tapping his foot anxiously.

"It really shouldn't be this hard to figure out what year it is," he muttered to himself.

He looked for a copy of the *Middle Falls Gazette,* but there was none to be found.

He remembered that his books and notebook were still in his bedroom. When he retrieved them, the notebook fell open to his homework, and he saw that in his small, neat handwriting, he had written 02/10/59 under his name.

February of 1959, he thought. *I'm fourteen, then. Could be worse, I guess. Not so young that I have to wait forever just to be able to drive again. Still, why couldn't I have been dropped into 1962 or '63? Then I could easily take off and never look back.*

Knowing when it was also told him that he needed to walk to the high school instead of the junior high. He had been a freshman in early 1959.

He gathered up his algebra and history books and set his notebook on top of them. He unconsciously looked around for some sort of a backpack to put them in, but remembered that when he was in school, kids didn't yet use backpacks. They just carried their books in their arms.

He briefly wondered if he could start a new trend by putting his books in a backpack, but decided that for the moment, it was better to just fit in and not attract too much attention.

Another tiny flit of an idea flew through his brain. He set the books on the dining room table and flipped open his notebook. He looked inside the front cover, but it was blank. He flipped through the pages of homework, but that was all he found. When he turned to the inside back cover, though, he found a goldmine.

The Evan who had existed before this Evan had arrived had been very efficient. He had written not only his class schedule, but also his teachers for each class. Below that, in tiny print, he had written his locker number—118—and combination. There was something about those numbers—7, 29, 42—that jogged something else in his memory.

For the first time since he had opened his eyes in this life, he smiled. Nodding, he remembered that he hadn't wanted to lose his locker combination when he had first gotten it, so he had written it down. He hadn't wanted to risk it falling into the wrong hands, though, so he had written it backwards. He was sure his combination was really 42, 29, 7.

Under the heading *Second Semester*, he saw that previous Evan had written *English* as his first class, and *Jasper* as the teacher. He remembered that name, but not much else about that particular teacher.

Evan felt a little more confident as he closed and locked the front door behind him. He knew what time frame he had woken up in, where he needed to go, and even how to get into his locker. He felt like he could figure most other things out by context.

His confidence waned a little as he arrived at the high school. There were dozens, maybe hundreds of kids, and they were different from him. They looked essentially the same as Evan, but with a huge difference. They all belonged there. They had been there yesterday and the day before. He felt like an imposter.

Still, there was nothing for it but to plunge ahead. He had decided to run away as he was falling asleep the night before, but he wasn't ready to do that today. At his age, something like that would take planning.

He pushed into the noise and chaos of a high school fifteen minutes before the first class started.

The girls were all in skirts with nice tops; the boys mostly wore jeans and long-sleeve shirts. All of the boys had hair that was short enough to get them into the Army if they were suddenly drafted. Most of the girls had long hair pulled back in ponytails.

Everyone was gathered in small groups of three or four, talking and laughing.

Evan felt like Jane Goodall stepping into the midst of a troop of apes.

He prided himself on his memory, but that was as it applied to facts, to numbers, to techniques. He couldn't match up a single face with a name in his head.

He weaved through the crowd, keeping a friendly but neutral expression on his face, looking for locker 118. He found it and bent over, twirled the lock. He had been right—the combination in the notebook had been written backward. He was happy he had remembered that much, or he would have been in a bit of a panic.

He dropped his textbooks into the locker and looked for an English book. There wasn't one, but there was a copy of a book called *Great American Short Stories*. He grabbed that and saw that previous Evan had been kind enough to leave a bookmark at the beginning of Mark Twain's *The Million Pound Bank Note*. He closed his eyes for a moment, trying to recall the story. He knew he had read it, though it had been decades earlier. Something about two wealthy brothers who make a bet and use a poor man to settle it. Kind of a *Trading Places* for the nineteenth century. Evan wasn't sure he could comment intelligently on the themes presented in the book, but he figured he could bluff his way through if need be.

"Hey, genius." The voice came from just to his left and he looked up to find a familiar face. He smiled.

"Catherine!"

She fixed a hoity-toity expression to her face and said, "My, my, my. Aren't we formal today. Yes, 'tis I, Catherine of Clarke. A pleasure to make your acquaintance, Evan of Sanderson."

Evan remembered that teachers had called his friend Catherine, but when it was just the two of them talking, she had always been Cece, pronounced cee-cee.

Evan shook his head ruefully. "Sorry, Cece."

"It's all right, Sir Evan. Another rough night?" The sympathetic way she said it made Evan remember that Cece was the one person that he had told everything about his home life. The one person who knew what he dealt with every day.

They had been best friends since seventh grade, which was unusual in a small town in the fifties. Boys almost exclusively hung out with boys and girls with girls, until it was time to pair off for the various high school mating rituals.

Evan and Cece had been placed next to each other when both were making a short-lived attempt at playing the clarinet. Neither could play well at all, but by the end of the first semester, they had become friends.

That friendship lasted until early in their sophomore year, when Camille had decided that Cece was nothing but a distraction to

Evan. She forbade him to see her, to talk to her, and went so far as to contact his teachers to make sure that they weren't seated near each other and didn't talk during class.

Camille couldn't control what they did in the hallways, of course, but over time, the strain of trying to sneak around and pass notes just to communicate with each other became too much. There was never a moment where one or the other said, "This just isn't worth it," but eventually they stopped making the effort and the friendship died. No doubt, exactly as Camille had planned.

Losing his friendship with Cece was one of Evan's greatest regrets, and now here she was again. He thought it was likely that his mother would interfere with their friendship again, but for now, he had found an ally, or at least someone he could talk to.

"I would ask you if you finished the story for English, but I know better. *Of course* you finished it," Cece said.

"The Mark Twain one?"

Cece looked at him as if he was delusional. "Yes, the Mark Twain one. What other stories were we assigned this week? Wait. Don't answer that. If there's something else, I don't want to know."

"Did you like it?" Evan asked.

"Yeah, I really did. It says something about human nature, doesn't it? People don't even need to be wealthy; they just need to *look* wealthy."

Evan nodded, then said, "Have you ever noticed how much alike everyone in school looks?"

Cece glanced at the kids milling around them in the hall. "You mean like we're all just worker bees on the same assembly line?"

"That's a mixed metaphor if I've ever seen one."

Cece held her hand out in a formal way. "Catherine Clarke, master of the mangled metaphor. Pleased to meet you." The first bell rang and she said, "Come on, Jasper has no sense of humor about freshmen being late."

Evan followed Cece, while trying not to appear that he was following her. He had a pretty good recollection of where the classrooms were, but he wasn't confident he could walk straight to the English classroom without accidentally opening the door to the chem lab.

They found seats about halfway back and settled in. Evan looked around and had a hard time remembering anyone's name. He decided that he would just wait to see if someone spoke to him first and then act as though he knew who they were. He reminded himself that he didn't really need to say a person's name at the beginning of a conversation. In fact, it would be weird if he did.

Mr. Jasper talked about *The Million Pound Bank Note* for most of the class, then peppered the class with questions.

Evan thought he could have answered most of them as long as he didn't get too specific, but he was happy that he wasn't called on.

Just before the bell rang, Mr. Jasper assigned the next story in the book—*The World the Children Made*, by Ray Bradbury.

As they shuffled out of class, Cece said, "See you at lunch. I'm off to learn the best way to make deviled eggs and sew on a button so I can be a good worker bee for my someday husband."

Evan grinned. He had lost touch with Cece so completely that he had no idea what had happened to her after high school. He knew she was really intelligent, but he also knew that really intelligent women in the early sixties often had a challenging time getting ahead.

Evan remembered that his second period class was anthropology, in Room 218. He hurried back to his locker and grabbed the appropriate book, then hustled up the stairs and slid into a seat just a few seconds ahead of the bell.

This class was taught by Mr. Warner, and Evan had fond memories of him. It wasn't that he was the type of teacher that inspired students to be friends with him, because he wasn't, but he had just been an excellent teacher. Where many teachers were content with just assigning reading or problems, Mr. Warner lectured, then gave tests on those lectures.

That was more like the classes that Evan took in college and held his interest better.

The last period before lunch was P.E. Evan didn't mind that. He wasn't a naturally gifted athlete, but he wasn't clumsy and hopeless either. When it came to playing basketball, or dodgeball, or running endless laps, he was a solid middle-class citizen.

He enjoyed playing basketball during that period. Evan had done everything he could to keep himself healthy in his previous life, but there was nothing like trading a seventy-eight-year-old body for a fourteen-year-old one. He felt like he had wings on his feet as he ran up and down the court.

He and Cece had lunch together. The menu at the Middle Falls multipurpose room was very typical for the late fifties. A scoop of mashed potatoes with hamburger gravy, green beans, and a bread-and-butter sandwich.

The multipurpose room was crowded, but Evan and Cece sat directly across from each other and they spoke quietly. Also, no one paid any attention to what they were saying, so they felt like they could speak freely.

Evan leaned slightly across the table and said, "I think I'm going to run away."

Cece nodded, then said, "You've said that before."

That set Evan back. "I have?"

"Yeah, a few months ago, after another really bad night. Don't you remember?"

"I guess not." Evan was surprised, as he had no memory of ever even thinking of running away. He knew he had never tried to actually do it, so if he'd ever had any plans to do so, they had left his mind.

Just then, there was a scuffle behind Evan. He turned to see two bigger boys facing off with each other. A blond boy with terrible acne pushed the other boy and he fell halfway over the table. That boy, who was tall and a little gangly, jumped back up and took a big swing at the blond boy that missed by six inches.

"Fight, fight, fight!" a group of other boys began to chant.

The fight didn't last long. Two teachers ran into the scuffle and that was the end of that.

"Testosterone running amuck in Middle Falls High," Cece observed. She turned her attention back to Evan. "Have you made any plans? If you really do run away, I mean. What would you do? Where would you go?"

Evan stared at the remainder of his lunch. "That's just it. I don't know. I've got to make some plans."

Cece didn't do anything as useless as offer to help. They both knew that in 1959, no parents of a young girl were likely to offer to let a young boy come and live with them. And, even if they did, Evan knew that Camille would never allow it. The only way for him to get out from under her thumb was to disappear completely.

The rest of the school day passed easily enough. For an old man in a teenager's body, Evan acquitted himself just fine. For the most part, he stayed quiet and reserved. No one noticed anything different about him because that was likely the way he had always been.

When the last bell rang, he gathered up his homework and walked out into the cold February drizzle.

He decided to walk around behind the elementary school, since that allowed him to stay under cover for another few blocks. When he finally abandoned the protection of the walkway, he turned right toward home.

As he did, he saw a circle of boys. In the middle of the circle were the two antagonists Evan had seen arguing in the multipurpose room at lunch. He cut a path around the circle of boys. He didn't even remember the name of either of them and certainly didn't have a care who beat the snot out of the other.

He had just skirted past the boys when he heard a heavy blow land. His head turned automatically toward the sound, and he saw the blond boy with the acne go down in a heap.

"Come on, get up, Selden," the other boy taunted. "I've got more for you."

Another boy said, "Look at 'im. It's like he can't breathe."

That prompted Evan to move toward the boys, who were now acting skittish, as though they might bolt at any moment.

The fallen boy—Selden, apparently—was lying on his back. His eyes were wide and he was trying to gasp for air, but it was obvious he wasn't getting anything into his lungs.

Evan knelt next to the fallen boy. It was immediately apparent to him what the trouble was. Without looking up, he said, "Run to the office. Have them send for an ambulance."

No one moved, so Evan put an extra sharpness in his voice. "Now!"

Two boys turned and ran.

"I didn't hit him that hard," the gangly boy said. He took a few steps back as though he might flee.

"You crushed his windpipe," Evan said quietly. He stared closely at the boy, trying to see if he was getting any air at all into his lungs. He didn't think he was.

The boy was about to die.

Chapter Thirty-Three

A memory came into focus in Evan's mind.

This was the fight between Robert Selden and Frankie Garret. The fight that resulted in Robert's death and the ruination of Frankie's life.

It was a famous event in Middle Falls history, but Evan hadn't had reason to think about it for decades and it had slipped mostly into the dustbin of his memory until that moment.

He tried to focus on that distant memory. Frankie and Robert had some unknown beef with each other. Frankie had swung wildly, hit Robert square in the throat, and he had expired right there on the grass. Everyone had scattered, including Frankie, but with a dozen witnesses, it hadn't been long before the story got out. Frankie hadn't been prosecuted—his father was on the Middle Falls City Council and managed to pull some strings—but his life was effectively ruined. He was an alcoholic by the time he was twenty and killed himself in a car accident before he was twenty-three.

Fights weren't completely uncommon. They happened in every high school, even in Eisenhower's America. This one, through one horribly unfortunate punch, changed lives.

Evan was squarely on the horns of a dilemma.

He felt he could do something that might save Robert Selden, but what would that mean? Would there be a headline in the Middle Falls Gazette that read *Fourteen-Year-Old Does Miracle Surgery?*

How would he possibly explain that he knew what to do? What would Camille think?

Evan didn't know the answer to that last question, but he was sure that somehow, it would be bad.

A small voice in the back of Evan's mind said, *This is none of your business. It already happened, just like this. Just walk away.*

That would have been the easiest thing, by far.

Still, he couldn't walk away. It wasn't any physician's oath he had taken in a long-ago life. It was that he knew he couldn't walk away when he might be able to change what was happening.

It was that *might* that was the hardest part. Where would he be if he tried to help, but the Selden boy died anyway? Then there might be *three* lives ruined in one fell swoop.

He made the decision.

"Who's got a pocketknife?"

Immediately, the boy to his left reached in his pocket and handed a knife to him. Evan ran his finger along the blade, shaking his head.

"Okay, who's got a *sharp* pocketknife?"

Being a small town in the late fifties, four more boys reached out with their knives. Evan rejected another, then found one with a fine point and edge. "This will do."

"My dad says to always keep it clean and sharp," the boy said, though Evan didn't hear him.

He looked around and settled on a short boy with a crew cut. "Hand me your lighter."

"I don't smoke," the boy said, but the boy standing next to him put an elbow in his ribs.

"Come on, Victor. Everyone knows you smoke."

The other boys in the circle nodded.

Victor shrugged, reached deep into the pocket of his jeans, produced a Zippo and handed it to Evan. The other boys, instead of fleeing the scene, drew tighter around the fallen boy. There was a growing sense that they had a front row seat to something they would remember forever.

Evan flipped the lid of the Zippo opened and thumbed it to life. He held the blade of the knife in the flame, turning it this way and that until it glowed. He waved it in the air to cool it a bit, then grabbed a Bic pen out of his pocket. He pulled the cap off, then grabbed the tip of the pen with his teeth and pulled it out of the barrel.

He handed the lighter to the boy next to him and said, "Give me a flame." The boy did and Evan twirled the end of the pen in the flames enough to heat it, but not melt it. He pried out the blue piece of plastic at the top of the barrel and tossed it aside.

He was ready.

Evan had done thousands of surgeries in his life, but none were anything close to this. He looked down at the Selden boy, who was continuing to gasp for air with no effect. His face had gone from red to ashen.

Evan took a deep breath and knelt beside him. As calmly as his pumping adrenaline would allow him, he said, "I'm going to save your life. I need you to stay as still as possible, but this is going to hurt. There's nothing else for it though. It's the only way you're going to live. Understand?"

Robert nodded, then closed his eyes and rested his head against the grass. He did his best to stay still.

Evan took the knife and made two quick incisions in the boys throat. Blood pooled and seeped into the grass immediately. He took the barrel of the pen and inserted it into the hole he had just made. He pushed it far enough in that it connected with his trachea. Instantly, warm air rushed out of the pen. The boy gasped, but this time oxygen came back into his lungs.

Selden's eyes flew open wide at the miracle of oxygen reaching his blood.

"Don't move. I know it hurts, but we've got to keep you stable until the medics get here."

Evan kept his eyes on Robert's face. If he had looked at the boys standing around, he would have seen expressions that could only be called awe. It was almost as if Evan had casually flapped his arms and flown up into the sky.

"Is he going to be okay?" Frankie asked.

"I think so. He's getting air into his lungs right now. This is a horrible place to do an operation, but they'll be able to clean and sanitize the wound when they get him to the hospital."

The wait for the medics to arrive seemed to take forever, though it was actually about five minutes. As that time passed, Evan nodded slightly to himself as he held the pen in place. It was obvious why Robert had died in his first life—there was no way he could survive this long without oxygen.

Eventually a siren sounded from down the street. The boys who had been so fascinated by the proceedings a minute ago suddenly found themselves with a need to be somewhere else. By the time the ambulance pulled up, Evan and Robert were the only ones still there.

Two men dressed in white uniforms rushed forward to a sight so odd, it took them several seconds to put the picture together. "What in the hell happened here?" one of them asked.

Evan wished he could do something to deflect the spotlight from himself. What was he going to say, a doctor in a white coat ran in, did the surgery, then ran away? The truth of the situation would be told dozens of times by every boy who had been present.

"There was a fight. One boy hit another and crushed his windpipe."

The medic knelt beside Robert and stared at the neat incision and the barrel of the pen sticking out of his throat.

"Yeah, okay, but who did this?" His expression was incredulous. "Look at this, Gary, it's like something that you might have done in Korea."

Evan moved back to make room for Gary to examine his handiwork.

Gary let out a long, low whistle. He looked around as though there had to be more players involved in the scene. "Who did this?"

"I did," Evan admitted. "I used a flame to disinfect both the knife blade and the pen before I inserted it, but that was pretty makeshift. The wound will need to be treated with whatever you've got on hand, then a good run of antibiotics are probably in order."

Gary and the other medic looked at Evan with disbelief. "Aren't you a kid? Or are you some sort of midget doctor in disguise?"

"They prefer to be called *little people*. *Midget* is offensive to them. And I'm five feet tall, so I'm too tall to be a little person."

The men continued to stare at Evan in confusion.

Robert moved his eyes back and forth, following the conversation but finally attracted the attention of the two medics. They tore their eyes away from Evan and snapped back to the job at hand.

"Right, right," Gary said. "Go get the stretcher. This grass is too soft for the gurney."

The first medic ran for the ambulance and quickly returned with a canvas stretcher.

Evan looked toward the high school and saw a group of adults heading toward them. He knew there would be an eventual accounting for what had happened, but he wanted everyone's attention to be on Robert at the moment. He laid a hand on Robert's leg and said, "You're going to be okay now. Everything will be okay. They'll take care of you."

Evan picked his books and notebook up from the grass and walked away.

Behind him, he heard one of the medics say, "Hey, kid. What's your name?"

Evan just kept walking. He hurried down the sidewalk, then went several blocks out of his way so he didn't need to walk on the street that ran in front of the school.

Had he done anything wrong? No. Anything to be ashamed of? No.

Nonetheless, a feeling of great dread settled into him and would not leave. Standing and staring down at the dying boy, it seemed like an easy sacrifice. Now, with that boy on the way to the hospital, he felt like he had made a mistake.

He got home and found that the house was as dark and quiet as when he had left it that morning. He didn't even bother to turn the heat on, but went into his room and put on an extra sweater to keep warm, then sat down at the dining room table.

He worked feverishly on his homework. He tore through the algebra problems he had, took notes and wrote an outline for a term paper he had in anthropology, then dove in and read both *The Million Pound Bank Note* and *The World the Children Made*. The odd thing about the second story was that he almost instantly recognized that he had read it before, but under a different title. When he had read it, the story had been called *The Veldt,* and it had been part of a book called *The Illustrated Man* by Ray Bradbury. He assumed it had been published under this title earlier, then adapted for that book.

He was just finishing up the second story when he heard the door open. He froze as if he had been caught doing something wrong, though of course he had not.

Camille hurried in, unbuttoning her long coat and untying her rain bonnet, shaking the raindrops off of it.

Evan had opened his notebook to show his algebra homework and laid out the outline he had done for his term paper. Camille came straight to the dining room table. "I'm late because Mrs. Anderson wouldn't make up her mind on a bouquet. You've had plenty of time to work on your homework, so let's see what you've done."

She picked up the notebook with the algebra work just as she had the night before. She sat down and spent several minutes perusing it. If she didn't understand what she was looking at, she did a good job of hiding it.

"Good. Glad to see you are more focused tonight."

Evan's eyes involuntarily wandered to the bamboo stick in the corner, lurking there like an enforcer.

"What's this?" she asked, picking up his outline.

"I have a term paper due at the end of the year in anthropology. I got an early start on it."

Camille cocked her head in surprise. "Excellent." She picked it up and read it over. When she set it back on the table she said, "That's really very good. It doesn't look like something you copied directly out of the encyclopedia."

It shouldn't have looked like it was copied, since it was a simplified version of a paper Evan had written for a class at the University of Washington in his previous life.

Finally, Evan said, "Then I read a story that Mr. Jasper assigned for English."

"Tell me about it."

Evan recounted the story of the children who had a special room built for their entertainment and how, when their parents had tried to take it away from them, the children had arranged for their parents to be eaten by lions.

"What? Who would assign such garbage? I'm going to speak to the school board about this."

Evan had no doubt she would do so. The path between his house and the school board was well-worn. He had no doubt they winced when they saw her in the audience.

"Well, this is a major improvement over yesterday. You may go to your room and read until dinner."

Evan collected his homework together and carried his books into his room. He couldn't have said why, for sure, but he didn't shut the door all the way. He grabbed another book off the bookshelf and opened it in his lap. There was no way he could read. His stomach was churning, waiting for the inevitable shoe to drop.

He couldn't imagine what it would be. The police? A newspaper reporter come to write a story about the world's youngest surgeon? A Doogie Howser story three decades before anyone would know who Doogie Howser was.

A few minutes later, that crack in his door allowed him to hear a knock at the front door. He tensed, figuring that whatever was about to hit the fan had arrived. He put the book down on his bed and slipped quietly to his door so he could listen and prepare himself for whatever was next.

He heard voices. Quiet voices.

"What are you doing here?"

"We need to talk about our son."

Chapter Thirty-Four

Evan, hiding behind his bedroom door, searched his memory to try to dredge up whatever he could about Alton Sanderson. There wasn't much. Camille had destroyed the pictures that included him, or, if she otherwise liked the photo, wielded the scissors to cut him out. Evan could barely remember what his father looked like. He thought he might be tall, but that was very possibly because Evan had been less than three feet tall when he had seen him last.

Even opened the door a bit wider and put his ear to the crack.

"We agreed about this," Camille said quietly. "You get your floozie and I get our son. It's a more than fair trade, and I've kept up my end of it. Why aren't you?"

There was a pause, then his father said, "Something happened at the hospital today."

"I'm sure it did. I'm sure it does every day. But what does that have to do with Evan?"

Evan closed his eyes and tried to take deep breaths to calm himself. He could almost feel the excrement hitting the twirling blades.

"Evan apparently performed a surgery on a boy at Middle Falls today."

"What?" Camille's voice, which had been *sotto voce*, climbed in both volume and pitch. She recovered herself and said, "That's ridiculous. He's a boy, not a surgeon."

"I would have said it was ridiculous, too, but a boy was brought in with a somewhat crude but perfectly done tracheotomy today. I can tell you this, if he hadn't done what he did, that boy would be in the morgue tonight, not the hospital."

Camille rarely sounded unsure, but at that moment, she did. "None of this makes sense. Why would you say it was Evan."

"The boy can't speak but he was able to write a few words and he said Evan saved his life. The police investigated and spoke to some of the boys who were there. They all agreed that Evan had taken charge of the situation and saved the boy's life."

"I need to sit down."

Evan heard his mother's footsteps as she crossed the living room and sat on the divan. He momentarily closed the door nearly shut so he wouldn't be discovered eavesdropping.

"I want to talk to him."

"He won't even recognize you."

"The same is true for me, but this is serious."

Evan heard footsteps approaching. He hustled across the room, jumped onto his bed, and grabbed the book. In the half-second he had before the door swung open; he made an effort to look casual.

He needn't have bothered. Camille pushed the slightly ajar door open and stepped inside, closing it firmly behind her. "You shouldn't listen to other people's conversations." She fixed him with a strange look, as though she was perhaps seeing him for the first time. "Your father is here, though you already know that, don't you?"

Evan nodded. *Once busted, cooperate and throw yourself on the mercy of the court.*

"He wants to speak to you. First, tell me what happened today."

Evan felt like a bug under a microscope. There was no escape from her penetrating gaze.

"Some kids got in a fight. One of them got hurt pretty badly. I fixed it so he wouldn't die."

"Yes, I got that story. But *how* did you know how to do that?"

Evan considered his options.

Tell the truth. That wouldn't work.

Come up with a lie. That was not his strong suit, and never had been. He did his best.

"Some of dad's medical magazines were behind some other stuff in the garage. I read them because they were interesting and it showed how to do what this kid needed. I figured he was going to die if I didn't do anything, so I did my best. Isn't that what you would want me to do?"

For a poor liar, it was at least adequate. Perhaps enough to get him through the night.

"Don't sidetrack me with ethical considerations." She crossed her arms over her slender chest and tapped her fingers against her elbows. "All right, let's go speak to your father." She held up a finger in warning. "Be respectful."

Be respectful, Evan thought, *of the man you have bad mouthed all my life? Sure, Mother.*

Evan marched into the living room on leaden legs. He couldn't be sure if his mother had bought his story, but his father would surely know he hadn't left any such medical magazine behind.

His father was standing in the living room. Camille had not invited him to sit and he wouldn't take it upon himself to do it with no invitation.

Camille pushed Evan toward his father.

They took each other in.

Alton Sanderson was not as tall as Evan had envisioned and not really the boogieman he had been built up to be. He was perhaps five foot ten and was slender, with a receding hairline. Evan, who had lived to be nearly eighty with a full head of hair, was glad that gene had skipped him.

Alton looked at Camille. "May we sit?"

"Go ahead." It was permission, albeit grudgingly given. "He already knows you know what's going on."

Alton nodded. "That was an extraordinary thing you did today. If not for you, that Selden boy wouldn't have made it. I don't want you to get the idea that I'm mad at you, because I'm not. When they found out you were my son, though, the police wanted to know how you knew how to do it. They wondered if I was running some sort of a black-market medical school or something."

It was obvious that he wasn't serious about that, and Evan marveled that his father would ever make even a half-joke like that.

Alton glanced at Camille, then back at Evan. "I had to explain, of course, that I hadn't taught you anything, because I haven't seen you in years."

"Our life is none of their business," Camille said sternly. She touched Evan on the shoulder and he flinched away a bit, though she did not notice. "Go on, tell him what you told me."

Evan did, once again telling the complete fabrication that he had told his mother. As he did, he watched his father. He saw for the first time where he had gotten his brown eyes from. His mother's were hazel that tended toward green, but his father's were the same as his own. He thought that Alton narrowed his eyes a bit as he told his story, but if he knew it was complete nonsense, he didn't call Evan out.

When Evan's story was done, Alton nodded, then stood up and said, "Well, good then. That's quite a story." He reached out and laid a hand on Evan's knee. "I want you to know that however you learned how to do it, I couldn't have done a better job myself. You'll be a fine surgeon someday if that's the path you choose to follow."

Those unexpected words from a man Evan thought was monstrous had an impact. Evan's throat tightened, and he felt tears well in his eyes.

"*We've* got his future all planned out. Now, if that's all you needed, we'd like to get on with dinner."

In a different kind of story, Alton might have said, "To heck with cooking, Camille, let's go to Artie's."

This was not that type of story, and Alton just nodded and stood up. He snapped his fingers as if he had just remembered something. "Say, I've got your check for next month, if you'd like."

Camille was never one to turn down a check, so she said, "That's fine."

"My checkbook is out in the car. Evan, get your shoes on and come out with me, will you? So I don't have to come back in with it."

On the one hand, Camille didn't warm to the idea of Evan and his father leaving together. On the other, she liked the idea of not only having the check, but the fact that Alton would not need to return to the house. She nodded at Evan, who grabbed his shoes and slipped them on.

"Go ahead, tie them. We're not in such a hurry that we have to run around with untied shoes like a little hooligan."

Evan couldn't help himself. He glanced at his father, who was expressionless, yet managed to convey what he thought of Camille and her mannerisms. Evan looked down at his shoes so his mother wouldn't see his smile and make him pay for it later.

Alton didn't bother to say goodbye to Camille. It was obvious to everyone that his leaving would be welcome.

"Be right back," Evan said, and followed his father outside.

If someone had put a gun to his head, Evan wouldn't have been able to say what kind of car his father might drive. As it turned out, there was a sleek red and white 1959 Corvette parked in front of the house.

"Whoa," Evan said, authentically sounding exactly like the fourteen-year-old boy he was supposed to be.

"I wish I could take you for a ride in it, but..." Alton looked at the house and shrugged. "I'm really sorry about the way things have turned out here. I wish I knew you better."

"Honestly, until tonight, I never thought about you," Evan said and immediately regretted it when he saw the expression on Alton's face.

His father reached into the car and retrieved a checkbook, then scrawled some information across the front of it, fulfilling the old joke about doctors and their handwriting. He tore it off and handed it to Evan.

"Do you want to tell me how you really knew what to do?"

Evan squirmed a little, but couldn't come up with a lie that was any better than the one he had already told. He knew his father wouldn't be able to believe that, so he just shrugged and stayed quiet.

Alton leaned in close and said, "How many lives is this for you?"

Chapter Thirty-Five

Evan froze. His mind reeled.

What had his father just said?

There was no mistaking it, though.

How many lives is this for you? That means he knew. If he was asking the question, he was obviously going through the same thing. Ever since he had woken up in his second life, Evan had believed that he was the only one dealing with this strange life circumstance. He felt his entire perspective on the world shift in a matter of moments.

"Listen, son, I'm sorry, but we don't have much time. Camille is no doubt watching us through the window and she's done everything possible to keep us apart."

There were so many questions swirling through Evan's mind that he didn't know where to start. He picked a simple one.

"Why? Why is it so important to her to keep us apart?"

"When our marriage failed, she latched onto you. She had failed with me, but she was damned well going to succeed with you. She has isolated you from everyone and everything except her so she can mold you into what she wants."

"It just pushed me away."

"Of course. How could it not?"

Evan finally settled on one other question, knowing it was almost certainly his last chance to ask his father anything, at least for now. He chose the same question his father had just asked him.

"How many lives is this for you?"

"Five," Alton answered. "In my last life, I was able to fix this. I woke up early enough and wouldn't agree to being separated from you. But I keep waking up at different points in my life. Is that what's happening for you?"

"Yes. This is my fourth life, but the second one was really short."

"In my first do-over life, I woke up when I was young and just avoided Camille altogether. That wasn't the right decision either."

"So in that life, there just was no me?"

Alton nodded.

Evan's mind was spinning with the possibilities.

The door to the house opened and Camille said, "Evan! Come inside. Now!"

Alton nodded and said, "I'm sorry. I'll do something to help you if I can."

Evan looked longingly at his father. More than anything, he wanted to run around to the passenger side of the Corvette and say, "Let's go!" as they fishtailed down the street. He knew that was impossible.

Instead, he just nodded and mouthed, "Bye," and turned toward the house without a backward glance. Once inside, Camille said, "What were you two talking about?" The *you two* sounded like she was accusing Evan of being part of a conspiracy.

"He just told me I should listen to you, that you know what's best for me." This lie came easily to Evan.

"That's true, of course, but I'm surprised he was clear-headed enough to see it." She looked Evan over, seeking weakness of any kind, ready to pounce.

Evan kept his face an impassive blank.

"Go back to your room while I make dinner."

"We could always go to Artie's," Evan suggested hopefully.

"Artie's!" Camille spat. "We've got better than Artie's right here."

Evan had known it was a long shot, but he was interested to see the drive-in again in the fifties. He remembered as a kid that there was a tower out in front where they did radio broadcasts on the weekends.

Evan went to his room, happy to be alone to have some time to think about how his father had just rocked his world.

If there were two people going through the same thing in the same family, he wondered how many other people were dealing with it, too? How many others that he ran into every day were living their third, or tenth life?

Most critically, he wondered if there was anything he could do to get away from his mother and stay with his father. The two of them shared an experience that would make life so much better. They could compare notes, make plans, and relieve the feeling of secrecy that Evan had carried with him.

There was obviously a legal agreement in place about custody, but Evan wondered how ironclad that was. Since he was a teenager, could he go to the court himself and ask to spend time with his father?

These thoughts ran through his mind until Camille called, "Dinner," from the dining room. Evan abandoned what he wanted to think about and made sure his face was blank again before going out.

It appeared that Camille had been at least semi-serious when she had said she could make Artie's at home. At least, some of the same ingredients present in an Artie's burger basket were also there on his plate.

For the second night in a row, there was a flat patty of hamburger along with two slices of white bread. Camille hadn't attempted anything as exotic as french fries, but she had boiled some potatoes. She had even sliced a pickle and, in a final magnanimous gesture, put the ketchup bottle on the table.

"Isn't this nice?" she asked, spreading her napkin on her lap. "This way we can eat hamburgers and stay in the comfort of our own home."

"That's great, Mother. Thank you." He thought about saying, "This is a real treat," but that lie stuck in his throat and wouldn't come out.

He remembered the vitamins and knew that he wouldn't be able to get away with not taking them with Camille watching him, so he swallowed them with his milk.

"I know there isn't any Coca-Cola, but that is just bad for us. Sugar water and nothing more."

"Milk is great, Mom."

Evan opened the cap on the ketchup bottle and held it over his white bread, waiting for it to come out.

"You've got to tap it on the end," Camille said helpfully.

"Right." Evan hadn't used an actual glass ketchup bottle in many decades. He slapped his palm on the bottom of the glass bottle, and eventually, the ketchup dropped onto the bread. He smeared it around with his knife, then put the patty on and put some pickle slices on top. He took a big bite and found that, once again, the patty was completely tasteless. He wondered how she had managed not only to fail to season the meat but to cook any beef flavor out of it.

He smiled, gave Camille a thumbs-up and took another bite. All he wanted to do was finish his food—not too fast, not too slow—and get back to his room where he could think.

It was obvious that Camille was on her best behavior, too. When they finished their dinner, she cleared the dishes and said, "Why don't you get one of the encyclopedias out and we can read to each other from it."

Inside, Evan cringed and wanted to rebel. That sounded pretty close to the worst idea in the world. He had nearly forgotten about the endless evenings spent reading whole sections of the encyclopedia.

"That'd be great, Mom. Any letter in particular?"

Camille seemed to give it some thought, then said, "No, you've had a big day. You pick."

Evan went to the bookcase in the corner of the living room—the spot where a television might have sat if they'd had one—and ran his fingers along the spines of the *World Book Encyclopedia.* He pulled a volume at random and saw that he had chosen *R.*

They spent the next ninety minutes reading all about rabies, rabbits, and the rabbinical assembly.

Evan briefly considered smashing his face against the table until he broke his nose just for a change of pace, but he managed to resist.

When they finally finished, Camille said, "It's been a busy day. Brush your teeth and get ready for bed."

Evan decided that since she had been unable to solve the mystery of how her fourteen-year-old son had performed surgery, she had dropped it into the basket of *a busy day.* That was fine with him. The less it was brought up, the more he liked it.

Evan went into the bathroom, brushed his teeth and looked at his face in the mirror. Just a hint of acne on his forehead, but otherwise clear skin. He couldn't say he liked his haircut much, but it was 1959, four years before the moptops from Liverpool brought longer hair to the USA.

He glanced at the clock on the wall of his bedroom and wondered if his body would manage to adjust to going to bed so early. His mother had been right about one thing, though. It *had been* a busy day. He had a lot to think about and as he rolled over onto his side to contemplate everything, he drifted off.

When he opened his eyes again, it was still dark outside and the house was quiet. He tried to go back to sleep, but soon gave up on that. He slipped out of bed, picked out some clothes and headed to the bathroom.

He weighed flushing the toilet or not. It might very well wake up Camille, which would get him in trouble. However, not flushing a toilet full of pee away would almost certainly do the same.

He went ahead and flushed, then opened the door and waited to see if Camille would appear out of her bedroom. She did not.

Evan nodded to himself. He liked being the only one awake in the house. He gathered up his books and homework and went into the kitchen. He didn't find any cold cereal, but there was Quaker Oats oatmeal and Cream of Wheat.

He got the Cream of Wheat down, measured out the proper amount of water, and put it on the stove to boil. He added the cereal and timed it using the second hand on the kitchen clock. He had just removed it from the heat when he heard footsteps behind him.

"Evan! You'll burn the kitchen down. Who told you that you could use the stove?" Her hair was up in curlers and she wore an old housecoat that made her look less intimidating than she was when she was completely made up and ready to face the world.

This was another unanticipated problem. He wasn't even old enough to turn the stove on without adult supervision, at least in Camille's mind.

"No one. I just thought I was responsible enough to do it properly. The directions on the box are clear. I thought you'd like it that I took some initiative and helped you out. Would you like this bowl? I can make another one."

Camille definitely *didn't* like Evan taking some initiative, but she didn't say so. "No, that's fine. You have it. But make sure you ask me before you use the stove." She turned and went back to her bedroom, closing the door.

Evan grabbed the sugar bowl and sprinkled a teaspoon worth onto the cereal, then, in an act of quiet rebellion, added another. He knew his mother wouldn't approve, which made it all the sweeter.

It didn't take him long to finish, then he washed his bowl and pan and put them in the dish rack.

Camille emerged from the bedroom looking a lot more like she usually did.

"I think I might leave early for school today."

"You most certainly will not. What put such an idea in your head?"

"The library in the high school opens before the classrooms. I thought I could go there and work on my term paper."

"Glad to see you getting a jump on your paper, but that is exactly why we bought the encyclopedias. You can work on your paper here."

It was a good try, Evan thought, *but all for naught*.

He went back to the encyclopedias, which he was starting to dislike, and pulled two different volumes out. He opened one and worked a little, though he was mostly waiting for enough time to pass so that he could get on his way and be momentarily out of Camille's grasp.

As it always does, even when it crawls, time eventually did pass.

"Hurry now, don't be late," Camille chided him.

Evan shook his head slightly at the inanity of that remark, since he had wanted to leave half an hour earlier.

The gesture did not go unnoticed. "Don't be smart with me, young man. Nothing good ever comes from that."

"Yes, ma'am," Evan said, grabbed his coat and hustled outside, carrying his books.

The thermometer on the front porch read twenty-eight degrees. Evan pulled his collar up and turned toward the school.

Something had changed since he had arrived at school the day before.

That first day, he had been completely anonymous, able to walk through the halls like an invisible man. Today, when he walked in, everyone stared at him. People poked their friends in the ribs and surreptitiously nodded in Evan's direction as if to say, *There he is.*

Evan did his best to ignore the attention but couldn't help but notice that a pathway seemed to open in front of him as he walked. He went to his locker, avoiding everyone's eyes as much as he could. He decided to take both the collection of short stories and his anthropology textbook out of his locker so he wouldn't have to come all the way back before second period.

He sensed someone standing close beside him. He turned to see Cece.

"Listen, I know you want to be a doctor and all that, but isn't it a little early to start practicing on real live humans?" She paused a beat, then said, "Well, that's assuming that Robert Selden is a real live human. He's a teenager, so the jury might still be out on that one."

"You heard about it, huh?"

"*Heard* about it? It's all anyone is talking about. It's not every day that one of our own goes all Dr. Styner on us."

That stumped Evan. "Dr. Styner? Who's that?"

"Come on! Dr. Styner from *Medic*? Oh, wait, I forgot you live in one of those houses that still doesn't have a television."

"Nope, but we have encyclopedias! We spent an hour and a half—or maybe it was a century and a half—last night reading through the Rs."

"Poor kid. I'd say you should sneak out and come to my house. *Gunsmoke* and *Wagon Train* are on tonight. But if you got caught, I'd probably never see you again."

That caught Evan's attention. Cece had accidentally predicted the future, when Camille would indeed make sure that they didn't see each other. It was an odd friendship, since he had a vastly different perspective than she did as a late-fifties teenager, but it was really all he had and didn't want to lose it.

"Did you read the story?" Cece asked.

"Yeah, pretty good."

"I'd say so. Fed their parents to the lions. You should look into that."

"I saw my dad last night."

Cece nodded her head and said, "Ahh...did he come to see you for a consultation on your next surgery?"

"You're a laugh a minute, aren't you?"

"Sorry," Cece said as they walked toward English. "That's a big deal. How did it go?"

"He was different than I expected. He was different than Mother always said he would be."

"Color me shocked. Your mother is manipulating things to suit her own needs? Why I never!" When they were just about to step inside the English classroom, Cece touched his arm and said, "Seriously, though. How did you know how to do that? To save that kid's life?"

"Honestly, I don't know what to tell you," Evan said. He got a sudden flash of insight. The night before, he had wondered how many other people were going through the same thing that he was. He looked at Cece seriously and said, "How many lives is this for you?"

That stopped her cold. Finally, as if speaking to a child, she said, "One," very slowly, carefully enunciating the word. "How many lives have you lived?"

Evan laughed as though he had attempted a bad joke. "Yeah, one for me, too. Pretty sure one is all we get."

Chapter Thirty-Six

Evan was the celebrity du jour at Middle Falls High School for a time, but it soon passed. There was always something new on the horizon to replace whatever the latest curiosity was. Eventually, a previously unremarkable freshman did a keg stand out at the lake and Evan slipped off the radar.

There was a resurgence of curiosity when Robert Selden returned to school. He had a tube in his throat, but he could speak, at least a little. He got the same burst of attention that Evan had received. Perhaps even more. The kids of Middle Falls thought it was fascinating to have someone with a hole in their throat in their midst. They could relate more to that than what Evan had done.

The first time Evan saw Robert in the hall, he wasn't sure what to expect. He decided not to make a big deal of it and let him pass by. Robert noticed him, though, and made sure to give him a high sign and mouthed "Thanks" to him.

Life in Middle Falls in 1959 continued on.

Evan found that now that he knew *when* he was, he could handle things with Camille better. He supposed that part of his problem with her as a child had been that he had a natural intention to rebel in small but visible ways against the straitjacket she put on him.

Now, with an adult sensibility, he knew how to actually rebel while appearing not to.

He got in the habit of doing his homework at school or at the dining room table as soon as he got home. That eliminated any more scenes of Camille hovering over him, bamboo in hand.

He still rankled at how little freedom he had. The term *helicopter parent* was still decades away, but Camille was that and more.

In his first life, Evan hadn't any real freedom until he had gone away to college. It was a miracle that he hadn't gone crazy wild then, but his mother's brainwashing was still in effect. In some ways, he had realized, it had still been in effect when he died on the cruise to Alaska. Years of indoctrination, especially when done so young, were nearly impossible to shake off.

He was a successful surgeon, had his own business, was married to a beautiful woman, and owned an impressive house in a great neighborhood, but he never felt like his life was his own. He had felt detached from everything, right up until the end. Even after she died, the ghost of Camille had somehow hovered over him.

It wasn't until his third life, when he decided to pull up stakes and leave his residency, that he finally felt like he had shaken free.

More than anything, he wanted to have a chance to explore a relationship with his father. In that brief conversation with him, he had felt more connection than he'd ever felt with anyone else. Knowing that he lived just a few miles away, but that he couldn't see him was beyond frustrating.

He knew that he could have simply walked to the hospital, or to his father's home, but he also knew that there would be hell to pay for doing so. He wasn't prepared to do that until he felt like he didn't have any other choice.

One thing the connection with his father had done was convince him that he didn't want to run away. If he did that, he felt sure he might never see his father again.

After several months of dithering, Evan decided to write his father a letter. He looked his address up in the phone book and bummed a stamp off of Cece, who was all in favor of him trying to connect with Alton.

He didn't bother to write a lot. Longer and better conversations could be had later.

Instead, he just wrote, *There's got to be a way that we can connect. I'm willing to stand up to her if you are.* He signed it: *Your son, Evan (on life number four).*

He folded the single piece of paper into an envelope and dropped it in a mailbox on the way home from school that day.

He didn't expect to hear something back immediately, but as the days turned to weeks and then months, Evan thought that perhaps he had misjudged the situation. Perhaps his father was enjoying his bachelor life and didn't really want an old man in a fourteen-year-old's body living with him.

In mid-May of 1959, he was at home reading a copy of Steinbeck's *Of Mice and Men* when Camille stormed into the house. She threw the front door open so hard the glass trembled in its casing. She stomped across the entryway, threw a thick envelope down on the dining room table and screamed, "What do you know about this?"

Evan immediately clued in that this was his long-awaited answer to the letter he had sent. He couldn't imagine what else might make his mother so angry. Still, until he knew for certain, he wasn't going to show his cards.

He shook his head, pretending like he didn't notice that she was screaming. "I don't know anything. What is it?"

"He had me served. At my own place of business! Oh!" She balled her fists impotently. "I hate that man!"

"*Who* served you?" Evan asked innocently, now almost certain.

"Alton Sanderson." She wouldn't even label him as *your father* at that moment.

Evan felt a thrill run through him. This was exactly what he had been waiting for. "Is he trying to change the child support or alimony?" He asked it innocently, as though that might be the most logical thing.

"No," she said, her voice cold now. She turned suspiciously on Evan. "He is asking to amend our divorce decree to show joint custody. Now, what do you know about this? I *knew* you two were plotting things that night that he showed up here."

This was a point of decision for Evan. In his first life, he would not have had the strength to answer truthfully. He would have been barely more than a child. He reminded himself that was what Camille thought he was, but she was more than willing to bully him anyway.

He gathered his courage and said, "I sent him a letter and asked him to do it."

For a moment, Evan thought she might get so angry she would pass out or give herself an aneurism. Her face turned red, she sputtered, and she held both hands to her head as if to keep her brain in place. Then, as though the whole thing was too much for her, she slumped down in her chair.

Evan waited for the next phase of the eruption of Mount Camille, but it never came. She let her arm drop and her head loll dramatically.

"What have I done wrong?" She asked the question rhetorically, but Evan decided to answer. He let the façade of being a fourteen-year-old boy drop away and spoke to her honestly.

"You've tried to control too much. You've held on too tightly. I know you thought you were doing the right thing, but in the end, all you've done is push me away."

Camille turned and focused on Evan, narrowing her eyes at him. It was obvious that he had never spoken to her that way. He thought she might ramp up and work herself into a frenzy again, but she didn't.

Instead, she said, "I'm so tired," in a voice so soft he could barely hear it.

"Of course you are. How could you not be? You've been juggling ten thousand balls and killing yourself trying to keep them all in the air."

Camille didn't argue. She just nodded, agreeing to the truth of that.

"I know you were doing what you thought was right. You wanted to raise me to be the best version of myself that I could be. But you went too far."

For a brief moment, a light flared in her eyes, but it quickly faded.

"It's not right for a child to be so completely separated from their father. I get it. Things weren't good for you two. It was a bad marriage. I know he did bad things. But that doesn't mean I should lose out on him. He hasn't done anything to me."

Camille opened her mouth as if she was going to argue the point, but gave up before she could formulate the words.

Her reaction to him speaking up surprised Evan, but he was encouraged by it. He hadn't thought he would have a chance to have a real conversation with her, but here it was. He touched the envelope, but didn't open it.

"I don't think we need to do all this, though. And I don't want to leave you." This was the first lie Evan had spoken, but he felt it was necessary. He felt good about what was transpiring. Hopeful, even, that things could be settled peacefully. He decided that if he could spend some time with his father—every other weekend, even—he could survive the next few years with his mother.

His hope for peace dissolved in a blink.

Camille stood, straightened her clothes, and stepped to the corner where the bamboo stick was. With surprising speed, she grabbed it and turned on Evan, who was still sitting at the table. She swung the stick at him, strong and hard.

Evan was so surprised he almost didn't react. At the last possible moment, he raised his arm to block the blow, or it would have smashed into his face. As it was, he felt a sharp pain in his right arm. The medically trained part of his brain thought, *likely a broken radius*. He glanced down and saw that though there was almost instant swelling, at least the bone was still in the skin.

That was all he had time for, as Camille had lost her temper completely. She swung the stick at Evan, hitting him again and again, all the while saying, "You little *shit*. You shit! You shit! I won't have it!"

Evan was in a body that was fourteen, but he hadn't had his growth spurt yet. He was still several inches shorter than Camille and she outweighed him by twenty pounds. She also had the strength of momentary insanity as she rained down blows on his arms, his sides, his legs.

Each swing brought new levels of pain and Evan wasn't sure she would ever stop. He thought briefly that she might beat him to death. Immediately after, he thought that might not be so bad. Maybe he would wake up somewhere better.

Then self-preservation took over and he flung himself forward, butting her in the chest and stomach with his head. She stumbled and fell backward into the hutch, causing fine china to fall and shatter.

With no hesitation, Evan ran for the front door.

When she saw he was getting away, Camille roared at him, "Get back here!"

Evan opened the door with his one good arm and jumped off the front porch. That caused a huge wave of pain to emanate from his right arm, but fear propelled him onward. He ran to the sidewalk, turned left, and hobbled away. He didn't have a plan; he didn't have a destination. He just knew he needed to be away from her.

Camille recovered and ran after him, but she slipped on the top step of the porch and fell hard on her tailbone. Her scream of anger and pain reached Evan and encouraged him to run faster. He cradled his right arm in his left, which reduced his speed, but he was still able to put several blocks between him and his mother. He began to run in a random pattern through the neighborhood.

He glanced over his shoulder and couldn't see Camille behind him, but he knew she would be looking for him. He spotted a house that had high hedges running alongside it and headed for them. He crawled as far inside the hedges as he could and judged that he would be hard to spot from the street there.

It was freezing cold and it was starting to rain, but he decided he would rather catch pneumonia than go back to that house. He did triage on his wounds. His arm, which had absorbed the first blow, was the worst of it. He had caught a glancing hit just under his left eye that was bleeding, and he thought he would likely get a black eye in the next few days. Everything else just seemed to be bruises, though there were plenty of them.

He huddled, shivering for a long time, but didn't leave his hiding spot. Eventually Camille drove slowly down the street in her green Opel. She stopped and peered into each side yard, and Evan had a terrible fear that she would spot him hiding in the bushes. She rolled on past him without incident, though.

Evan cradled his arm, tried to forget about the pain, and was surprised to find himself sobbing. Being beaten, especially by your mother, is emotional, no matter how old you perceive yourself to be.

He felt like he had hidden in the bushes forever, but it had been less than an hour when it began to get dark. He saw the headlights of the people who lived in the house where he was hiding in the hedges. Again, he shrank back until the woman and her daughter went inside.

While he had sat there, he had formulated a plan. He crept out of the hedges and limped along the sidewalk. His body had stiffened while he sat in the wet and cold, and he was afraid that he might have misdiagnosed one of the blows to his leg. It was possible that was broken as well.

As bad as he felt physically, the more he thought about what had happened, the more optimistic he felt about his situation. He hadn't been able to plan an escape from his mother, but perhaps she had handed him one.

He kept a vigilant eye out as he walked and blended into more bushes or trees whenever he saw a car until he was sure it wasn't his mother.

Eventually, he arrived at Middle Falls General Hospital. He walked into the main entrance and up to the receptionist. He watched her face when he approached and knew that his appearance was perhaps worse than he had feared.

The woman behind the desk stood up and rushed to him. "We need to get you to the emergency room. Come, sit down over here, and I'll get someone to come get you."

"No," Evan said. "I just want to see my father. Dr. Sanderson."

Chapter Thirty-Seven

Evan looked around as he sat on the end of one of the emergency room beds. It was different than when he had worked there as a resident in 1973. Things were just as clean and antiseptic, but much simpler. He wondered if it was frustrating to his father to be practicing medicine in more primitive times.

He was still dressed in the same damp shirt and pants he had worn into the hospital, but he felt safe. His arm, leg, and various contusions ached, but that was a price he was willing to pay.

Just then, Dr. Alton Sanderson stepped through the door, his expression worried. When he saw that Evan was upright, he relaxed a little. A nurse dressed in all white followed him in.

Alton stopped in front of Evan. "Nurse, can we get a few warm blankets in here?" He didn't turn to watch as she hustled away. His attention was focused on Evan.

"Diagnosis?"

That made Evan grin. If anyone had heard the doctor ask the teenage patient that question, they would have thought him crazy.

"Pretty sure an X-ray will show a non-displaced fracture of the right radius. Caught a pretty direct blow on the fibula on my right leg. I thought it was likely just a bone bruise, but it's swelling and is probably worth an X-ray, too. Everything else is mostly superficial. Some contusions, and I'm having a tough time seeing out of my left eye, but that's just because of swelling. I don't think there's any damage to the eye itself."

Alton began his own examination, quietly making conversation as he did. "What field did you go into?"

"Ear, nose, and throat," Evan said, wondering at the oddness, the near impossibility of this conversation. "I owned my own shop up in Seattle."

Alton nodded as he probed gently at the left eye. "Good racket to get into. Always busy, but never overwhelmed."

The nurse came back holding an armful of green wool blankets.

"Let's get those wet clothes off and get you warmed up," Alton said.

If Evan had actually been fourteen, he would have been mortified to get undressed in front of this nurse, who was probably in her late twenties. In this situation, though, he just needed a little help with his wounded arm.

"We're going to need a full run of X-rays on that right arm and leg, and I'd like some taken of the upper right quadrant of his head to make sure the orbital socket isn't broken."

"Yes, doctor," the nurse said, then looked at Evan. "I'm going to get a wheelchair, then I'll take you down to X-ray."

"No need," Evan said, preparing to hop down off the table. "I can walk."

Alton put a gentle hand on his chest. "You might be *able* to walk, but until we know what's going on with your leg, you're wheelchair bound."

The nurse hurried out and as soon as she was gone, Evan said, "Doctors are the worst patients, aren't we?"

"If a little knowledge is a dangerous thing, what is a lot of knowledge?" Alton agreed. Brows knit in worry, he said, "Has she ever hit you before?"

"Yes," Evan said simply. "But nothing like this." He managed a grin through his dry lips. "She got served at work and that set her off. She came home boiling, then I told her that I had asked you to file the papers. She seemed to almost collapse for a minute, but I guess really she was just building up steam."

"What did she hit you with?"

"It's a damned inch-thick piece of bamboo."

"She just had that lying around the house when she needed it?"

Evan shook his head. "She uses it to help me focus when I'm doing homework."

"Son of a bitch," Alton muttered. Then, "*son of a bitch*," this time with more emphasis. He laid a hand on Evan's shoulder. "I never knew, son. I never knew what I was doing to you by leaving you there."

Evan shrugged. "No one did. The first time around, I didn't know how to tell anyone. I thought that if she was doing it, it must just be okay. Plus, I never would have told you, because she told me how awful you were every day. This time, I knew it wasn't normal, but I felt pretty helpless. Fourteen years old, no car or driver's license, no money. I was planning to run away until I saw you at the house. I knew if I did that, I'd never be able to spend any time with you, so I stayed."

Alton hung his head and was about to say more when the nurse returned with a wheelchair. He helped Evan down off the table and got him situated in the chair. "Bring me the X-rays as soon as they're developed."

An hour later, Evan was checked into a room of his own.

Alton walked in, smiling. "Pretty good diagnosis, Doctor."

"Thank you, Doctor," Evan answered.

"Your radius is broken, but we got lucky, it's just a hairline fracture. Your fibula isn't broken, just a deep contusion. No break around your eye, so you came through as good as could be expected. That blow to your face might have caused a concussion, though, so I'm ordering you held here for observation."

"Considering my options, that sounds pretty good. I'm not sure where else I would go."

"I know everything feels up in the air now, but don't worry, we'll get this taken care of. I think everything will be looking up for you. I can't promise what's going to happen next. I don't have as many legal rights in this situation as I would like, but I've got my lawyer working on it. For now, just relax. Are you hungry?"

"You know what? I am. Haven't eaten anything since lunch, and it was tuna casserole day at school, so I didn't eat much of that either. What's on the menu in the cafeteria?"

Alton made a face. "It's the hospital equivalent of tuna noodle casserole. How about if I get someone to run down to Artie's and grab you some dinner? Burger, fries and a chocolate shake sound all right?"

The mere thought of it almost brought tears to Evan's eyes. "I can't tell you how good that sounds."

An orderly pushed the door to the room open so hard it banged off the wall. "Dr. Sanderson! There's a disturbance in the lobby and they're asking for you."

The young man seemed flustered, but Alton was calm. "Right on schedule. I'll be back soon with some food." He left with the orderly and Evan was left alone to contemplate the events of the day. There were no televisions in the rooms at Middle Falls General in 1959, and he had left his copy of *Of Mice and Men* in the house when he ran out. The excitement of the day and the painkiller they had given him before putting the cast on his right arm worked their magic, though, and he drifted off.

He woke up to his father setting a white bag on the bedside table. He didn't need to ask what was in it, the aroma and grease stains on the bag told the story.

"Artie's delivery service," Alton said, reaching into the bag and pulling out fries, a burger, and a chocolate shake.

"Ohh..." Evan said, reaching for the fries. He stuffed several into his mouth and said, "What was the disturbance? Something with

Camille?" He had hesitated for a moment. Being with the one person on Earth who knew how old he was, it felt wrong to call her *Mother*.

"It had everything to do with her. She's so used to being in control of situations that when she isn't she doesn't know how to react. She is acting poorly."

"How did she know I was here?"

"When she couldn't find you, she called here and they confirmed you had been checked in. After that, she believed nothing could stop her from getting to you."

"But you did?"

Alton waved his hand around the quiet room. "She's not here, right? It wasn't me. I knew that she was likely to show up here and had placed a call to Sheriff Deakins and asked him to send a couple of deputies down."

Evan tried to feel bad for Camille, but when he closed his eyes, all he saw was her coming at him with the bamboo stick raised, a crazed expression on her face.

"Did they take her to jail?"

"No," Alton said, shaking his head. "She was practically frothing at the mouth when I wouldn't let her see you. I thought we might have to involuntarily commit her and haul her up to Portland for a mental health examination, but she seemed to realize that was imminent and managed to calm herself down. I did step in and mention to the deputies what she had done to you and they wrote her a citation to appear."

"I don't want her to go to jail. I just want to be away from her."

"Right. Having the citation creates a public record. It also gives us a bargaining chip. In the paperwork I had her served with today, I was just asking for shared custody and weekend visits. It's hard to predict what the courts will do, but I think we might be able to get full custody now, with her having supervised visitation. They're not going to want to risk the health of a minor."

A sudden connection popped into his head. In his first life, Mel had gone a little crazy and had died for it. In his second, when he was off the scene, she had been the picture of health and sanity. Now, in this life, his mother had blown up. He began to wonder if the connection was him.

"What are you thinking?" Alton asked.

Evan told him the story of Mel and what had happened in his first life, then how she had been in his second. "I'm starting to think it's me."

"People are going to respond the way they are going to respond. Don't blame yourself for what happened with your mother. She was like that before you ever arrived."

"Did she ever physically attack you?"

Alton looked out the window but nodded. "In the late forties, an abused husband didn't report it. He just got out of the marriage if he could."

He felt empathetic for his father, but also a little relief that he wasn't the carrier of crazy.

Alton took off his physician's white coat and draped it over the back of the chair. He loosened his tie and rolled up his sleeves.

"Getting comfortable?" Evan asked.

"I'm going to stay here with you tonight. It will give me a chance to see why the relatives of my patients complain about how uncomfortable these chairs are. You should get some rest."

Evan polished off the last of the burger and sucked on the straw in his shake until it rattled. "With Artie's in my stomach and a nap behind me, I don't feel very sleepy. Maybe we can just talk a little bit. There's a lot I don't know about you."

"And vice-versa," Alton said.

They talked deep into the night, sharing stories that very few people would be able to relate to. Eventually, the floor nurse came in and insisted that Evan get some rest. She gave him a pill in a paper cup and held up another with water and a straw. She looked suspiciously at the crumpled bag on the bedside table. "Who is bringing this food onto my unit?"

Alton smiled at her. "Someone broke in and left it. If it happens again, I'll grab them."

"You do that." She looked at Evan and said, "He's going to be out in just a few minutes now."

"Yes, ma'am," Alton said with a grin and settled back, trying to get comfortable in his chair. "People are right. This thing is damned uncomfortable. I've got to get some money in the budget for new chairs."

Things happened pretty quickly over the next few days and weeks, especially considering how slowly the wheels of justice usually move.

Evan checked out of the hospital the next day and moved in with his father. He thought that Alton might live in a big house, but it appeared that the Corvette was his one real luxury. The house he lived in was in a good neighborhood, but it was just a two-bedroom rambler with a den that he used for an office.

Alton contacted the school and gave them a shortened version of what happened and told them that his son was still under a doctor's care and wouldn't be back in school for some time. In reality, he didn't care if Evan ever went back. With as many years of schooling as he had, Alton thought that was enough.

He filed a temporary restraining order against Camille on behalf of both him and Evan. She showed up at the hearing to fight it, but Alton's attorney presented pictures of Evan's injuries and a letter from Evan himself stating that he was afraid she would attack him again.

The judge granted the restraining order for ninety days, to be revisited at that time.

If Alton thought that Camille would bend under pressure and give up her custody to avoid charges, he was mistaken. Over the next few months, she and her attorney fought every motion and counter-motion.

In the end, she had done it to herself. Partially based on Evan's testimony and request, the judge granted full custody to Alton.

Evan was free of his mother at last.

The day after the judge's decision, Camille Sanderson once again killed herself.

Chapter Thirty-Eight

When Evan Sanderson opened his eyes in February of 1959, he had felt trapped by circumstances.

By the summer of that year, everything had changed.

He thought he should probably feel bad about his mother committing suicide for the second time, but he couldn't quite manage it. She had been so distant and unreachable, so aloof, that even through three lifetimes, Evan never felt like he knew her. She certainly never felt like a nurturing, loving mother.

Until very recently, he had never felt like he knew his father, either. That was rapidly changing, though.

They sat together in the living room of Alton's small Middle Falls house and tried to plan out what their perfect life might look like.

One thing became quickly obvious. Neither of them had any clue how their unique life circumstances actually worked. Neither had received an instruction manual or even a few things jotted down on stone tablets. They were left wandering in the desert of their life, figuring it out bit by bit.

One thing they realized is that what they had in this life was special, simply because both of them were aware of the situation at the same time.

That being the case, they decided to truly optimize their time together in this life.

Evan explained his third life and how focused he had been on becoming rich. He told his father the whole story of how he had insinuated himself into the birth of Buddha Computers.

That story tickled Alton. He laughed, then said, "And when you got there—when you had more money than God—did that make for a wonderful life?"

That called for a bit of introspection on Evan's part, as he had never thought about it.

"It wasn't bad. I could buy anything I wanted, go anywhere I wanted."

"Was it fulfilling, though? Were you happy?"

Evan was silent a long time, then said, "I was happy in that life. But it wasn't when I was rich. I was happy when I was hanging out with friends and parking cars. I was happy on that bucket of bolts we called *The Diver I*. I was happy going to school at the University of Washington when my only goal was to learn something."

"What I'm hearing then—and correct me if I'm wrong—is that you were happy when you were working toward a goal, but once there, everything seemed a little hollow."

"Nothing to correct you on there. I had a goal, but once I reached it, yeah, it all felt a little empty."

"So maybe we need to come up with a different kind of goal."

Evan sat forward, intrigued. "I like goals. What are you thinking of?"

Alton steepled his fingers and leaned back. "Happiness. Adventure. Hard work. I'm thinking of making those things our goals. We have both lived our lives by the rules other people set. What the world expected. We went to school, got good educations, then went to work at good jobs. What did that get us? Not a lot, honestly. Not for me, and, it looks like, not for you. I think we ought to spend this life just living."

"Maybe we should do something to make some money first?" Evan asked.

"You did that once. You focused everything on making money. You made it, then what happened? Not much. That idea of needing security first is still playing by the rules of the world, or so it seems to me."

Evan stood up and began to pace. The idea was enticing. Exciting. "No rules."

"Well, some rules," Alton said. "Gravity still applies." He grinned, then said, "I think it will take a bit of time to get used to, but we can do it. We just need to apply our brains to the idea."

Evan stopped pacing in front of his father. He stuck his hand out and said, "Let's do it."

And so, do it they did.

Their first order of business was to write a list of their own rules that they would choose to follow. It was not a long list.

First, do no harm.
Second, help people where possible.
Finally, find meaning everywhere.

That first rule had once been part of the Hippocratic Oath. It had been dropped in more recent versions of the oath, but they once again adapted it as their own. To them, it meant they wanted to explore the world, to see what there was to see, but to do so in a way that did no harm to others.

They decided together that they had not done everything they could to help other people in their previous lives. They wanted to rectify that.

More than anything, they wanted to try to find their place in the world and why they were in it.

Evan wrote their rules down on a three-by-five card and showed them to Alton.

Alton looked at the list and said, "I think we're ready."

They had solidified their concept, but they weren't quite ready.

As much as they didn't want to be bound by the rules of the world, they also took their own first rule seriously. Alton interpreted that to mean that he couldn't just walk out of Middle Falls General without giving them proper notice. The board of the hospital accepted his notice, but because he was much more than a resident, they asked for six months to find a replacement. Alton agreed.

Meanwhile, Evan had no interest in going back to Middle Falls High, so he just dropped out. If Camille hadn't already killed herself, that might have pushed her over the edge.

Evan went to the Community College and sat for his GED. He then enrolled in the one class he really wanted to take—Photography. He had decided that he would be the official chronicler of this new life with his father. He would keep a journal and take thousands of pictures.

While Alton was finishing out his time at the hospital and Evan was studying photography, they listed the house for sale. It sold in November and was set to close in mid-January. By then, both Sandersons would be free of all obligations.

Financially, they were well set to begin their adventure. Alton had always been a good saver. By the time he sold the house and his Corvette, that translated into a nice little nest egg. That didn't include the fact that Evan was also Camille's sole beneficiary. He once again sold everything he inherited, but this time he tucked that money into a bank account.

There was only one person in Middle Falls that Evan cared to say goodbye to, and that was Cece. He hadn't seen her nearly as often since he had left school. Her parents were open-minded about her friendships with boys, but the fact that Evan had dropped out of school made him a little suspect.

Still, he cared about her and promised he would write from all ports of call.

January of 1960 began like every other January did in Middle Falls—rainy and windy.

That encouraged Alton and Evan to start their adventures in warmer climes. They winnowed their belongings down until each one only carried a single duffel bag. This was another aspect of Evan's third life that he remembered fondly. They climbed on a TWA flight in Portland, flew south to San Francisco, then caught a flight to Maui.

They had both been to the island in their previous lives, but it had only been for a week or ten-day vacations. This time, they were planning on staying longer. They stayed in a small motel for a few days but soon found a small house on the edge of Lahaina for rent.

It was also a bit rainy on Maui, but in a very different way. In Middle Falls, it tended to drizzle for hour after hour. The skies were always dark and foreboding, and it got dark so early.

In Maui, the rain tended to sweep in off the ocean, drench the countryside, then move on, leaving bright, beautiful skies.

They relaxed and fell into an easy routine for a few months. Their diet consisted of fresh fruit and vegetables, and they ate fewer heavy meals. The library in Lahaina was only a mile from their house, so the two of them walked there several times each week. They tended to do their reading in the two hammocks that were set up inside the covered back porch.

It was a good, lazy life and helped them unwind after the challenges they had faced the previous year.

In mid-March, they saw a *Help Wanted* sign on the bulletin board outside the library. A local farmer was looking for field hands for a pineapple harvest. That was something they had absolutely zero experience doing and so fit perfectly with their plan to try everything.

They wrote the number down and called the foreman, who hired them on the spot, with a caveat.

"I'll hire you, but if you don't work hard, I'll fire you before lunch. We don't waste good food on bad workers."

He took their address and promised to have a truck come and pick them up the next morning.

Picking pineapples was hard work. Both of their hands were soft from a lack of labor, and they got blisters through their gloves on the first day.

The foreman didn't fire them before lunch, or ever. He had his doubts when he saw how small Evan was, but small or not, he knew how to work.

Working in the fields, they came to think of the afternoon rain showers as a blessing, something to wash the sweat from their brows.

Standing in the fields, a blade in one hand and a gunnysack slung over their shoulders, they couldn't help but look at the sunlight on the hills, feel the warm breeze off the ocean and feel like they were in heaven.

The pineapple season only lasted a few months, and they were unemployed again. That did not bother them at all. They didn't need the money; they were only looking for the experience.

In the fall, they picked up another job helping to harvest sugar cane. Hard work, once again, but rewarding in its own way.

When they got home from that job, sweaty and tired, they often walked the few hundred yards down to a rocky beach and swam in the warm Pacific.

By the time spring of 1961 arrived, Evan had turned sixteen and finally had his growth spurt. He was now an inch taller than his dad but still had a bit more to grow.

They had enjoyed their year on Maui—loved it, in fact. They knew they could have stayed there happily for many more years. Decades, probably. They could have learned to surf, watch the tourists come and go, and lived the laid-back island life.

That wasn't exactly in the spirit of their adventure, though.

They bought a ticket back to the mainland, landing in Los Angeles, and decided to stay in the southern part of the country because it was still blustery in the Pacific Northwest.

Their time in Maui had not been expensive. Thanks to having two of them working in the fields, they returned with almost the same amount they had left with.

They decided that they would like to go south, through Mexico, Central America, then find their way into Brazil. Why? Because they had never been to any of those places. That was reason enough.

They bought a 1958 Ford F-100 with a camper on the back. It wasn't luxurious, but it beat sleeping out in the rain or with the scorpions.

They weren't in any hurry to get to their destination. Their life was about the journey, and they knew when they reached their eventual destination, they'd just have to come up with a new one.

They crossed over into Arizona and dropped south, intending to eventually go into Mexico.

Instead, just as they were pulling into Cobble Creek, Arizona, their truck broke down. They coasted to a stop on the side of a main road of what could charitably be called a town, but which was truly a blink-and-you'll-miss-it affair.

There was a small grocery store, a gas station, post office, a tiny hamburger stand, and beyond a few other dilapidated buildings and houses, not much else.

"All part of the adventure, right?" Evan said with a grin.

They walked to the gas station and found out that there was a single-bay garage attached. They spoke to the owner of the place, Manuel, and he agreed to look at their vehicle.

Alton and Evan pushed the truck to the station, and it didn't take long before the problem was diagnosed. The transmission was gone.

Alton asked, "Can you fix it?" but that was really the wrong question. The *right* question would have been "How long until you can fix it?"

Manuel promised them he could get a rebuilt transmission in, but that would take at least two or three days, then another day or two to repair it.

"I don't suppose there's a motel in Cobble Creek, is there?" Alton asked.

Manuel scrunched up his face as though the question might make him laugh. "No, no motel. Who would ever decide to stay in Cobble Creek?"

Alton couldn't argue with that.

"I've got a little place that's empty right now, though. I'll rent it to you for five bucks a day."

That price echoed in Evan's mind. The same price he had once paid at the Arroyo. He almost asked if there was a shower down the hall.

They took Manuel up on his offer and carried their duffels to their new temporary home. Manuel had not been overselling it when he had called it a little place. It was perhaps four or five hundred square feet. It did have a bedroom, a living room with a couch, what passed for a kitchen, and a bathroom so small only one person at a time could stand in it.

Manuel appeared at their door in the late afternoon and invited them to dinner with his family. Alton accepted at once. He knew they would have plenty of opportunity to sample the wares of the hamburger stand over the next few days.

Manuel introduced Alton and Evan to his wife Louise and their five children, all of whom appeared to be under seven. The kids moved and spoke so fast that it was impossible to put a name to them, but they reveled at the sense of family at that table.

Manuel spoke heavily accented English. At one point, there was a conversational crash and Alton asked Louise if she would translate a question into Spanish.

She looked surprised. "I don't speak Spanish."

Alton looked from one to the other.

"Manuel only speaks a little English. I speak no Spanish. It's why we're still married."

"And why we have five kids," Manuel said with a wink. "That's how we talk."

Chapter Thirty-Nine

As was often the case, especially in small towns, the time frame for repair of their truck didn't go according to schedule. It took a few extra days to get the transmission in, but when Manuel looked it over, he found it was defective. Back to the city it went.

When the replacement parts came in, there were some additional parts that were needed. Another delay.

If they had broken down in Phoenix or Flagstaff, these were issues that could have been dealt with in hours or at most a couple of days. In Cobble Creek, which wasn't the actual end of the earth but you could see it from there, it meant Evan and Alton were stuck for a month.

Manuel felt guilty for delaying their departure and so cut the rent on the little house down to three dollars a day. The small amount of money didn't really make any difference to them and in truth, they would have just as soon Manuel had it. They knew they would offend him if they turned his generosity down, though, so they accepted.

To say there wasn't a lot to do in Cobble Creek is an understatement. On their third day there, they asked Manuel if there was any work available.

He hesitated and said there was, but it wasn't usually the type of work gringos did.

"Exactly what we're looking for!" Alton had assured him.

The next day, they were back in the fields, doing the backbreaking work of an early lettuce harvest. They worked from early until late and earned hardly anything, but they felt glad to be useful again.

They were also able to work on their Spanish, which was very poor and made the other workers smile at their attempts.

On their third day in the fields, the blade of one of the workers slipped and cut a deep gash in his leg. It was in an unfortunate spot, and both Alton and Evan could immediately see that it was potentially life-threatening.

There was only a limited amount they could do in the field, but Evan removed his belt and tightened a tourniquet above the wound. Alton did a quick exam and said, "Not much we can do for you here." He looked at the field boss and said, "We've got to get him to a doctor. A hospital, or a clinic of some sort."

"We don't have one."

"Which?" Alton asked. "A clinic?" He knew that a hospital was too much to hope for.

"No. A doctor. The nearest doctor is a two-hour drive away over bad roads."

Evan and Alton exchanged a glance. They huddled together in a quick conference away from the wounded man.

"If we keep the pressure on, he should be able to make it," Alton whispered.

"I hate to use *should* when it comes to someone's life."

"What else can we do?"

Evan looked at the field boss and said, "You say you don't have a doctor. Do you have a clinic, though?"

"Yes. The doctor left a year ago and no one will come here. It's been empty since he left."

"Give us a ride to the clinic with this man. We can help him."

The foreman looked at the two strangers who had wandered into his field, unsure of whether or why to trust them.

The injured man had no such qualms. He reached his arms out to two of his friends and said, "Help me to the truck."

They half lifted, half carried him to the back of the foreman's truck and Evan and Alton jumped in beside him.

Reluctantly, the foreman threw another of the workers some keys and spoke to him in Spanish that was much too fast for Alton or Evan to understand.

Fifteen minutes later, they were back in Cobble Creek and the man pulled up in front of a rundown building with no sign identifying it. It looked more like a deserted office building than it did a medical clinic.

"This is it," the man said.

"Who has the keys?" Evan asked.

The man shrugged.

"Never mind," Evan said. He hopped down, ran around to a side window, and used his elbow to break a window. He crawled in, careful not to cut himself, and hurried to the front door.

He and his father mostly carried the man, whose dark complexion had gone pale.

They carried him through the dark interior. Evan flipped on the lights, but nothing happened.

He cursed quietly then took the man into one of the two small rooms with beds. They picked the one closest to the window so they could see.

There weren't a lot of supplies in the clinic. It looked like it had been broken into some time earlier and anything of real value had been stolen.

Alton found some disinfecting powder, a needle, and some catgut. He looked for anything that might numb the man's leg but couldn't find anything remotely close.

"Run down to the store and get whatever strong alcohol they've got. Tell them it's for the doctor's office."

Evan ran like he had wings on his feet.

Five minutes later he came back with a small brown bottle. "They didn't even ask me what it was for."

Alton took the bottle of whiskey out of the bag and said, "Drink this."

The man hesitated, so Alton said, "I'm going to have to do stitches with no anesthetic. The whiskey will at least dull the pain."

Hesitation gone; the man took a long swallow. Too long, as it turned out. He coughed and almost spat it all back up. He gathered himself, took a deep breath and another long draw.

Meanwhile, Evan cleaned the area around the wound and dusted it with disinfecting powder. If the man wondered why a teenage boy was working on him instead of the older man, he didn't say. He was busily trying to get as much whiskey in him as he could.

While Evan prepped the leg, Alton prepared to do the stitches. He turned to ask the man if he was ready. Their patient was flat on his back, staring at the ceiling, but perhaps not seeing it clearly. Alton took the bottle of whiskey from him before it fell to the floor.

The man was suddenly drunk, but not so much so that he didn't feel the stitches. He stiffened, but Evan lay across his chest and said, "Try to be still. I know it hurts, but it will save your life."

In his mind, Evan flashed back to saying something similar to Robert Selden just before he had done the tracheotomy. At the time, he thought he might be screwing his whole life up, but in the end, it had saved him.

Fifteen minutes later, Alton had done the fine work inside the leg and stitched up the wound. He stood and stretched his back. "As long as we can keep infection out of it, I think he will be fine."

Evan started opening cabinets, looking at what they had on hand. "Not much to work with here. We really should get him transferred to a hospital with real facilities."

"If he'll go, that will be the best thing." Alton paused, then said, "But how many migrant field workers have health insurance or can afford that kind of bill?"

"You're right. Probably none."

Just then, a woman's voice from the front of the building said, "Hola!"

"Maybe it's someone coming to pick him up," Evan said to Alton. "Hola," he said more loudly. It was one of the few Spanish words he was confident in. He poked his head out of the makeshift operating room and saw a dark-haired woman of perhaps thirty and a little boy who stood shyly behind her.

"Are you here to pick up..." Evan hesitated. He realized he didn't know their patient's name.

"No," the woman said. "Someone said that the clinic is open again. My boy fell and hurt his arm yesterday. I'm afraid it's broken, but I can't get him to a doctor."

The implication was obvious: Can you fix my son?

Evan opened his mouth to say that the clinic wasn't open. That there wasn't even power on. That they had no supplies. Then he glanced at the young boy, who was awkwardly cradling his left arm in his right, fighting back tears.

"Bring him back this way," Evan said, leading to the second exam room. On the way past his father, he said, "We have another patient."

They had no power, so obviously the ancient X-ray machine in the back wouldn't work. Evan lifted the boy up on the examination table, carefully avoiding hurting his arm. "How did he hurt himself?"

"Climbing a tree. He's always climbing everything. Last week I found him on the roof. I have no idea how he got up there." She brushed her son's hair off his forehead affectionately. "Can you help him?"

Evan did a quick examination, gently probing the arm, moving it slightly in one direction then another. "The clinic isn't really open."

"I know," the woman said softly. "I'm just hoping."

Evan nodded and made a decision. "I'll do my best for him." He raised his voice and said, "Dad?"

Alton appeared around the corner.

"What do you think?"

Alton repeated many of the actions that Evan had. "Probably a break in the ulna. Doesn't seem to be too bad. But we don't have any way to be sure."

"I don't think she's looking for certainty. I think she just needs help."

Alton nodded. "Let's cast it, if we can find the material."

They did have at least that on hand. They put a cast on the boy's arm and told his mother to come find them in a few weeks.

"Will you be here? In the clinic?"

"No," Alton said. "This is not ours. We're essentially trespassing right now. But we're staying in Manuel's house behind the grocery store. Come and find us."

The woman nodded, but said, "Do you know who owns this building?"

There was something about the way she said it that made Evan guess, "Manuel."

The woman nodded, helped her son down, and left.

Alton and Evan returned to check on their first patient, who was now stretched out asleep on the bed.

"We'll have to find someone to come get him, but we can let him rest for now," Alton said.

"Hello?" Another woman's voice from the outer office.

The two doctors—one still licensed in this life, the other only a teenage boy—soon realized that just because there was no clinic in Cobble Creek didn't mean that there was no need for one.

Throughout the rest of the morning and into the afternoon, a steady stream of people with ailments large and small showed up at the shuttered clinic.

Word spread fast in a town so small.

There were many things that Alton and Evan were unable to assist with. They could bandage up cuts, apply stitches where needed, and even put a cast on to immobilize an arm or leg, but that was the extent of it.

There were no prescriptions they could write, as Cobble Creek had no drug store and the clinic had long since been ransacked of anything it had.

Still, they did what they could for everyone that came in, even if it was only a possible diagnosis and advice on home remedies that could help.

When the sun set, they knew their day had to be finished. It was difficult enough working in the daylight with no electricity. Stumbling around in the utter darkness would be impossible.

Just as they had seen their last patient out the door and they were ready to return home, the lights suddenly came on.

"Too little, too late," Evan observed. "I wonder why someone had them turned on."

"Because you're here," Manuel said, coming through the door. He looked at them wonderingly. If not suspicion, something close to it was on his face. "Why is a doctor and his son coming to me, looking for work in the fields? It does not make sense."

Alton sighed. He knew there was no easy explanation that he could give that would make sense.

"You're right. I am a doctor." He almost added, "And so is my son," but that obviously wouldn't fly.

"Why are you here?"

"Haven't you ever wanted to just say, *to hell with it*, jump in a vehicle and drive into the sunset?"

"I have five kids. I think about it every day."

"Well, we did just that. If you want, you can call the hospital in Middle Falls, Oregon, and they'll tell you I was a physician there until last year. Then Evan and I decided that life's too short. We hit the road to see what's over the next hill."

"And that was Cobble Creek."

"Only accidentally," Alton said.

Manuel, who was also perhaps more than he had appeared to be when they had first met him, nodded. "I think you should stay. The town needs the clinic. It's been hard for people not to have a place to go."

With the overhead fluorescent lights showing just how dingy the place was, Evan said, "There's not much we can do here. Having the power on is nice, but there's not enough equipment or supplies for us to really help most people."

Manuel turned to Evan. "And what about you? Are you a doctor, too? Can I call a hospital in Oregon to check on you?"

"He's not a doctor, of course," Alton said quickly. "But he's been training with me since he was old enough to walk. He's got better instincts than most doctors I know."

Manuel nodded, taking the whole scene in. Finally, he said, "This place was okay when it was open. It was never going to compete with the hospital in the city, but it helped a lot of people. We could get it going again if we had a doctor. The people here can pay, just not very much. I would help."

"We were on our way south," Alton said. It was a pitiful excuse, and both Evan and Manuel knew it. "Maybe we could stay and help out for a while, though."

Evan put an arm around his dad. "I was hoping you'd say that."

Chapter Forty

Alton and Evan did stay in Cobble Creek for a while. The beautiful thing about the phrase *a while*, is that it can stretch to mean many different things.

For Alton and Evan, *a while* meant a very long time.

They had indeed been heading south when their transmission went out in the spring of 1961, but they never made it there.

They never made it to any of the more exotic locations they had talked about visiting.

And that was okay with both of them. They had set out on a search for meaning and they hadn't needed to travel nearly as far as they thought they would to find it.

They found it in the sagebrush, desert landscape, and mostly, through the people of Cobble Creek.

Manuel, who they eventually learned was the unofficial mayor of the town, was as good as his word. He did everything he could to get the clinic back up and running. With Alton signing on as the overseeing physician, they were able to reopen the small pharmacy and get the drugs they needed to at least treat basic illnesses.

They would never be able to treat serious illnesses, cancers, and the like, but they brought basic healthcare back to the area.

In fact, the population of Cobble Creek grew because the clinic was there. There were even some new construction homes built on the edge of town.

For the first few years, Evan and Alton continued to live in the tiny shack that belonged to Manuel. He didn't charge them any rent, but everyone knew that wasn't sufficient compensation for the Sandersons' work.

Two years into their time at the Cobble Creek Clinic, an old timer passed away without any known relatives. Alton and Evan had cared for him through the last two years of his life, and he willed his house to them.

It wasn't a mansion, but it almost was when compared to the tiny place where they had been staying.

Evan was every bit the doctor that Alton was, but in this life, he didn't have the credentials to show for it. That didn't bother the patients of Cobble Creek Clinic. They called Alton *Old* Doctor Sanderson and Evan *Young* Doctor Sanderson.

Alton worried about what would happen if he died suddenly and left Evan without credentials, so in 1969, when Evan was twenty-four, they sent away to a diploma mill in Costa Rica and Evan had his MD. It wasn't worth the very nice paper it was printed on, but they hoped that if the worst came to pass, he would at least have a chance of maintaining the clinic.

During their years in Cobble Creek, Evan stayed in touch with Cece. She graduated from high school in 1963, then from the University of Oregon with a degree in accounting in 1967. She got married the same year and divorced four years later. By then, she had a three-year-old son named Joshua and not much money.

Evan invited her down to Arizona and, with limited options and wanting to get away from staying with her parents again, she accepted.

Her friendship with Evan picked up as though they had seen each other a few days earlier, not almost fifteen years.

The house that Alton and Evan had inherited had three bedrooms and they insisted that Cece and Joshua stay with them as long as she wanted.

To an outsider, it might have looked like there was a romance between Evan and Cece, but as much as they loved each other, it was not in that way. The men of the house simply became Uncle Alton and Uncle Evan, and life went on.

The first time Cece got a look at the Cobble Creek Clinic's books, she nearly died of shock. Even saying that the clinic had a set of books was an overstatement. There *was* a ledger, but no one had bothered to make any notations in it for months. It wasn't unusual for the clinic to completely write off care for patients who had no money, or to take a chicken or a plate of tortillas as payment.

Cece rolled her sleeves up and went to work. It took her several months, but she soon devised a system that took their unusual accounting methods into account. More importantly, since the clinic had been limping along financially, supported mostly by Alton and Evan themselves, with the aid of Manuel, she helped them form a non-profit 501(c)3. That was a new program the government had rolled out a few years earlier, but something Cece was familiar and comfortable with.

That made them eligible for various grants and awards. They were able to finally replace the old X-ray machine, which only worked when it wanted to, among other things.

Joshua grew up in the clinic. He soon became an assistant to Evan and Alton, and by the time he was a teenager, he was able to help some patients on his own.

Cobble Creek only had a one-room school, but Joshua attended, got good grades and eventually got a scholarship to Arizona State University. Four years later, he graduated and stayed on to attend the University of Arizona Medical school.

By then, Alton and Evan knew that, beyond the occasional vacation, they were never leaving Cobble Creek. They hadn't seen the world like they set out to do, but they had put roots down and were important and beloved members of the community.

Alton met and fell in love with a woman from Cobble Creek named Theresa, and they got married in 1986. By then, it had been just he and Evan for twenty-seven years, but he slipped back into married life easily.

She made it easy. She became part of the extended family with Evan and Cece immediately. There had been a Theresa-sized hole in their lives for years, but they hadn't known it until she appeared.

Evan never married in this life. He never felt the need or desire. Alton, Theresa, Cece, and Joshua fulfilled his need for family.

When Joshua obtained his MD, he chose to serve his residency at Cobble Creek Clinic. There was plenty of work to keep three doctors busy, and this allowed them to have the occasional bit of time off.

With Joshua in place, it was possible that the clinic could have found another doctor or a physician's assistant and let Evan ride off into the sunset.

He never considered it.

In 1999, Alton was in his late seventies and was starting to slow down a little. He had begun to work half-days and take two or three days off each week. No one begrudged him that.

Evan's only concern was that Alton was becoming slightly frail. The time they had once spoken of and worried about—what would happen when one of them left this life—was approaching.

They consciously began to spend more time together and to plan for ways that they would hopefully be able to match up again in the next life.

One afternoon in June of '99, they went for a drive in the same old truck they had arrived in town with almost forty years earlier. They both had newer, nicer vehicles, but they had never sold the old Ford and took it up into the mountains above Cobble Creek.

They parked to eat some birria, a Mexican beef stew that Theresa had made them. They looked at the rough-hewn scenery that they had once thought they were only passing through.

"We never did make it to Brazil," Alton said with a smile.

"Or Costa Rica or Chile or any of the other places we talked about," Evan agreed.

"I don't mind a bit," Alton said. "We made the most out of this life, even if we did stay in one place."

"I think we made the most out of this life *because* we stayed in one place. Where would this little town be without doctors to care for them?" Evan shook his head, dispelling that thought. "This was the best thing we could have done with our lives."

"I wonder what we'll wake up to in the next life," Alton said. It was a question that was increasingly weighing on him.

"Whenever it is, we'll find each other. This life has been so sweet."

While they talked and reflected, an unexpected monsoon swept across the valley, bringing with it more water than the dry desert hardpan could handle.

"That looks bad," Alton said. They had seen many of these sudden summer desert squalls.

"Let's get in that old Ford. It's never failed us."

The Ford was parked at the top of a small rise. Evan could have scrambled up it easily, but Alton was much slower.

The water rose more quickly than they thought was possible. In moments, a blast of water came rushing down the arroyo.

Evan put Alton's arm around his shoulder. "Here, Dad. Let me carry you."

"I guess I've carried you long enough," Alton said, laughing in the face of disaster. They both knew it wasn't true.

Evan half-dragged, half-carried Alton up the slope. It was slow going, with the dry dirt crumbling under his feet and the water rising impossibly fast.

It was obvious that the water would reach them before they could reach the top. They stopped struggling.

"This is it," Alton said. His voice was calm and measured. "Leave me here and go on. You can get out of here."

"I don't have any interest in being here without you, Dad. We'll just let it come and open our eyes somewhere else. I love you, Dad. I'll do everything I can to find you."

"I love you, Evan. I'll look for you, too."

The water pulled the soil out from under their boots and they were swept along.

Afterword
Universal Life Center

Evan Sanderson opened his eyes.

He gasped for air.

"Dad?"

He looked around, unsure where he was. It was nowhere he could remember waking up before. He was in an all-white room. White floor, white benches, white walls, and white ceiling.

"Here, Evan," Alton said. "I'm here. We're still together."

"Where are we?" Evan asked.

"This is the Universal Life Center," a voice came from Evan's left. "I'm Max. I've been the Watcher for both of you through these lives."

Evan turned and saw that it was a sweet-faced man who had spoken. Beside him was a taller man with thinning hair, glasses, and watery blue eyes.

"Watcher?" Evan asked.

"Don't worry. You've made a big transition. This will all come back to you soon enough. It always takes a bit of time."

"Are we about to be sent somewhere else?" Alton asked. "Can we go together?"

"You can go wherever you want. You can stay here, you can jump back into your lives at any point, you can recycle and start over, anything."

"Is this heaven, then?" Alton wondered.

Max glanced at the man beside him and made a *comme ci, comme ça* gesture with his hand. "It is what it is. It is the place we all end up eventually." He smiled, and it was so lovely on his face that he could easily have been mistaken for an angel. "The good news is that you've already passed the entrance exam."

"Is that what these repeating lives have been, then?" Evan asked. "Some sort of a test?"

"Of a sort," the man beside Max answered. He nodded at them, then said, "I'm Charles. Some people learn what they need in a single lifetime and show up here, ready to go on to whatever is next. Many, in fact. Others have more complex things to learn and require more chances. The Machine makes sure that those that need more time, more lives, get them."

"I think that's kinder than the alternative," Evan said.

"Alternative?" Max asked, puzzled.

"I mean just starting people over as babies in new lives again and again, with no memory and no clue what they were doing wrong. At least I had a chance to figure things out."

"Yes. Just so," Max agreed. "You are welcome to stay here for as long as you like. Many of your true family are still finishing their current life. If you'd like, you can be here when they arrive."

Evan smiled. "I'd like that. Cece and Joshua?"

"Yes, of course."

"Theresa?" Alton asked.

"Yes. She will be along shortly."

Evan and Alton looked at each other and asked the same question at the same time.

"Camille?"

Charles answered this key question. "The three of you were in an interesting situation. It was complex. Too complex, really to be resolved in any one life. Camille is still working through things." He glanced at Evan and Alton. "I ran tens of thousands of simulations and formulated at least that many equations, seeking a way to untangle things. Max and I settled on this, but we both knew there was only the smallest of chances that you would find each other in your most recent life. You had both been struggling with a certain type of fear. It took great courage on both your parts to do so."

Evan looked at Alton. He felt like he was waking from a dream. Alton no longer seemed strictly like his father. The memories of other lives returned. They could both remember when they had been friends, brothers, sisters, or when their roles had been reversed.

Evan put his arm around Alton. "That is part of why I was so lost. I was separated from my true family. I was alone and lost." Evan nodded to himself at the truth of it.

"Just so," Max said. "But you found each other. The others will be along in due time. Now everything waits for you."

Coming Soon

The Topsy-Turvy Lives of Hattie Kildare

THE TOPSY-TURVY LIVES OF HATTIE KILDARE

A Middle Falls Time Travel Story

SHAWN INMON

Author's Note

Some books come easily to me. I wrote *The Tumultuous Lives of Karl Strong* in twenty-two days, for example. It seemed that every time I was about to run out of words in that book, another chunk dropped into my head.

The Ambitious Lives of Evan Sanderson didn't come to me quite as easily. It wasn't that it took me so long to write the book—I finished it in less than two months—but that I rarely saw what was going to happen more than a few pages ahead. That made for an interesting writing experience for me, and I hope it translates to a satisfying and unpredictable reading experience for you.

As I so often do, I started this book only knowing the name of my protagonist and the clue I had left myself in the title: ambitious.

Immediately, I saw that Evan already had what would be considered a successful life by most anyone's standards, but not really to his own. That was the jet fuel that propelled him through his initial second chance life.

In the Middle Falls Time Travel group on Facebook, we just had a discussion about how my protagonists try to enrich themselves.

Not all of them do, of course. Thomas Weaver, Scott McKenzie, Jack Rybicki, Effie Edenson and Karl Strong never made any real attempt to turn their foreknowledge into riches. In writing the first nineteen Middle Falls books, I've tried to show that there is no single path to finding the path onward.

But for those who do, the most common trick is to use their knowledge to play the stock market. That's an easy way to do it, though it does require some patience.

I think my favorite get-rich-quick scheme was Richard Bell's treasure hunt in Idaho.

A number of my protagonists made themselves wealthy, but Evan had a different goal. He wanted to be the richest of all, and he was willing to use every trick he had to get there.

Of course, if you've completed the book by now, you know that even though he met his ambitious goal, there was no true happiness at the end of that rainbow.

Evan's path to happiness included reconnecting with his father and finding a life of service. I think that's a pretty good way to go, too.

I'll admit that writing Alton Sanderson into the book was a bit of wish fulfillment for me. My own father died when I was five, so I never got to know him as anything but the larger than life icon who worked himself to death. By bringing Alton and Evan together and giving them a happy life, I think I was connecting the dots in my own wishful way.

Evan shared quite a few experiences with me. He lived in Seattle in 1973-74. I arrived in that beautiful city just a few years later, in 1978. Like me, Evan eventually attended the University of Washington.

The greatest similarity in our lives, though, is the time he spent on the crabber *The Diver I* in Alaska. That was the name of the vessel I sailed on as well in that same time frame. My memories of my first summer in Alaska working as a deckhand are so indelible that I never had to make anything up for Evan. The sights, smells, and the feeling of loading up the crab pots are forever stamped in my mind.

One of the things that you might have a hard time believing is true is the when Evan saw the bus loading with homeless people being shipped to Portland. If I had read that in a book, I would have thought that came from the author's imagination. In this case, it didn't. I witnessed the scene just as I relayed it in the book with my own eyes, albeit in 1982 instead of 1973 as it is shown in the book.

I know I took a chance in delaying the introduction of Evan's mother into the story. Her behavior and the way she raised Evan was a huge part of why he was the way that he was, but I wanted us to meet him and see him struggle with being a better human before we saw the why of it.

There aren't quite as many cameos from previous Middle Falls books as I sometimes manage to work in. Ann Weaver does pop up, though, as well as our old friend Thomas Weaver and a quick appearance from Margenta, known as Marge in this book, who was banished from the Universal Life Center in Karl Strong's book. I've gotten a few requests to write her full story, but I'm not ready to do that yet. For now, this quick glimpse at where she was will have to suffice.

Before I forget, I need to tell you what song I listened to as I wrote Evan's story. (If you're a new reader, I pick a single song and listen to it on endless repeat while I write each book.) This time around, it was the jazzy feel of Bachman Turner Overdrive's *Looking Out for Number One*. I'll always associate this song with Evan's adventures.

Up next will be *The Topsy-Turvy Lives of Hattie Kildare*. I've had Hattie's story in mind for quite a while now, and I'm looking forward to writing it. Hattie will have a few surprises in store for you!

Even though writing is a solitary business, publishing is not. I have a whole team of people who help me get each book into your hands, and I need to thank them all.

Linda Boulanger designed the cover, as she's done for so many of my books over the years. I don't know where I'd be without her.

Melissa Prideaux once again served as my editor, which entails so much more than just fixing my occasional grammatical errors. She helps me form and refine the story and I am grateful for how wonderful she is.

I write pretty fast, so I have a team of proofreaders who assist me in catching the final errors. Dan Hilton, Marta Rubin, Kim O'Hara and Steve Smith saved me from myself time and again.

More than anything, I want to thank you for doing the hard work of bringing my stories to life in your brain. You've given me my dream job, and I appreciate you.

Shawn Inmon
Tumwater WA
December 2023

Printed in Great Britain
by Amazon